THE
VANISHING
GIRL

Rob Birks

For Becca.

As long as stars are above us.

CHAPTER ONE

Isabella searched her eyes for any sign of the alien inside her. The mirror gave her nothing except a brow creased in familiar panic and lips bent with worry. She caught no one else glaring back through her own eyes.

What have you done this time? Isabella demanded with a thought. Although she got no response, she knew Paradise Moon was listening. The alien could hear just fine inside Isabella's head.

Quit hiding, ass hat. What did you make me do?

When Isabella had woken up in a toilet cubicle ten minutes ago, her last memory had been the bus from Reading town centre shuddering to a halt outside school. That had been this morning. Now, she was in the Year 11 girls' toilets and the school day was over. She glanced at her cheap plastic watch, hoping she had misread it. She hadn't. The alien trapped inside her had taken control of her body again, and she remembered nothing. She had lost another day.

Subtle flecks of purple blended with the chestnut in her eyes.

There you are, bitch.

Oh, come on! Relax!

Isabella grasped the edge of the sink to stop her hands from shaking.

Seriously, it wasn't that bad.

Paradise Moon sounded jolly. Not simply upbeat, but positively jolly. Hot fury prickled Isabella's cheeks.

What wasn't that bad? What did you make me do?

Jeez, I was only having a bit of fun.

"Tell me what you did!" Isabella shouted out loud.

A toilet flushed and the door of an apparently-not-empty-after-all cubicle ricocheted behind Isabella. A bottle blonde with perfect hair, perfect nails and a concerned expression passed behind her with a swirl of flowery perfume. She washed her hands with barely a sprinkle of water. "See you in detention, psycho." Flinging open the door, she swept into the corridor.

Once more, Isabella was alone. Only she wasn't. Isabella hadn't been alone since the day she was born.

This stress isn't good for you.

You think?! Why am I in detention?

You need to chill. Let's skip detention!

Closing her eyes to block out the world, Isabella clenched and unclenched her fists over and over until she didn't want to punch someone.

What's got into you? You're gonna get me killed.

When Isabella had been younger, the worst Paradise Moon had ever done after taking control of Isabella's body was to make her draw a fancy moustache on herself in permanent marker. Oh for those happy times. Last week, she had woken up behind the wheel of a stolen car, the inescapably acrid stink of burnt rubber creeping through a shattered moonlit window. Only after scraping the glass from her jeans, had she ditched the car and staggered home. Last night, a midnight breeze had sliced through her cotton pyjamas, waking her on a neighbour's rooftop. Another few steps, a careless slip…

I feel like you only want to focus on the negatives.

Just. Stop.

Full disclosure: I'm making no promises.

It's my body.

You're taking this very personally. Lighten up!

Lighten up?! Isabella opened her eyes. Even reality was kinder than the nightmares lurking in her head. In the mirror, she found only herself and a smear of dried gum on the glass. Any purple traces of Paradise Moon were gone from her eyes. For now. It took her a moment to doublecheck for tears and red rings around her eyes, then many more before her hands stopped shaking.

This deep into the afternoon, school was unnaturally quiet. Drifting down empty corridors, Isabella reluctantly arrived at the classroom where she usually served her detentions. She peeked inside.

"You're back," her teacher announced. This was disconcerting for Isabella, who possessed no memory of having left the classroom.

I hate you.

Ouch! Always so personal!

Miss Pilkington's porcelain face offered a kind smile from her desk, which strained under the mountains of exercise books piled high upon it. The teacher scribbled in a book, placed it neatly aside and selected another with weary inevitability.

Isabella spotted her schoolbag at the back of the classroom, where either another pupil or Paradise Moon had left it. Head bowed, she trudged down the central aisle, passing row after row of teenage faces smeared across graffitied desks. "Psycho," the bottle blonde whispered as Isabella passed her desk. "Psycho, psycho, psycho," everyone else whispered. Despite each smirking

3

face unleashing the same taunt, they were too quiet for the teacher to hear and too familiar for Isabella to care.

Miss Pilkington glanced up, her gentle features aiming for stern but missing by half a galaxy. "Lynch, if you don't take your boots off that desk right now, it will be detention tomorrow as well." Her voice was as delicate and fragile as tissue paper.

"Fine by me," muttered the boy beside Isabella's bag. As Isabella slid onto the bent plastic chair next to him, Lynch tipped back his chair and gazed at the ceiling. Despite his skull-emblazoned hoodie, skinny jeans and muddy boots propped up on the desk, enough uniform hung off him to suggest he probably was a student. A scowl of contempt lingered on his already stubbled face. "I will be anyway."

The teacher didn't challenge him. Instead, after a tired sigh, Miss Pilkington lifted her biro and returned to her marking with the expression of someone smelling a particularly malicious fart. Isabella wasn't surprised. Although she had never dared speak to Lynch in all their detentions together, school gossip was infested with rumours. Everyone knew he was in a gang. Everyone knew he dealt drugs in school. Everyone knew his mum was in prison. Some of it might even be true.

He sounds fun!

Great. He's definitely your type.

Hurriedly, she rummaged in her bag and pulled out her second-hand biology textbook. Pressing her fingers against her temple, she pretended to read and hoped Lynch wouldn't notice her.

"Awright," said Lynch, noticing her.

Busted.

Shut up.

Isabella's eyes found him over the rim of her textbook. The boy's lips spread into what he probably thought was a cheeky grin.

"This blows."

"Yep."

"I'm Lynch," he told her without a care.

Isabella smiled back with geeky awkwardness.

"You've got balls," he hissed, prompting Isabella to smile even more awkwardly. Lynch's expression shifted between a scowl and a grin. His face was not completely friendly, but it did promise life wouldn't be boring. "D'you really do it?"

Isabella stiffened, her empty memories itching at the back of her skull. "Maybe."

"Aww, you so did, didn't you? Everyone's talking about it."

Brushing her embarrassment behind a veil of dark hair, Isabella leaned closer. "What are they saying?"

"You know. Viagra in the water bottles during P.E. and a few more... batons in the relay than expected. Pretty funny stuff."

Isabella frowned. That explained her detention.

For the record, so worth it. You should have seen their faces! Not to mention their—

I really, really hate you.

"How come you're here?" Isabella asked Lynch, nudging the spotlight elsewhere.

Lynch shrugged. "Told the Head to screw herself, didn't I?" He said it so matter-of-factly that Isabella couldn't help but laugh. She couldn't imagine anyone caring so little about what other people thought. Was that even allowed? Lynch seemed to be enjoying her laughter. She certainly hoped he was.

Well, hello! I think someone's getting a crush!

5

Heat rose into her cheeks for the second time this afternoon. She prayed to every sleeveless queen of punk and long-fringed king of rock that the boy hadn't noticed. Hating herself almost as much as she welcomed this distraction from all her shit, she played the game. A calculated shrug, a bored roll of her eyes, no quick peek at the teacher because no one was supposed to care what a teacher thought anyway, and finally, taking great care to show absolutely no care whatsoever, another glance at Lynch. Her glance, which she'd practised too many times in the mirror, said everything and nothing.

Speaking as someone who can literally read your mind, I know what you're doing and I like it.

Usually, boys puffed out their chests after a glance like that. Or blushed. Or stammered. Or grinned like they'd just been pranked live on social media. But Lynch was so laid back it was almost impossible to spot his reaction. Isabella caught something in his face that might have been a smile. She couldn't help but smile back.

Abruptly, Isabella stopped smiling.

It began as nausea. Her skin tingled. Every nerve screamed. Her tongue tasted metal. Electricity. Blood. Sweat was seeping through her blouse. She was going to be sick. The air screamed, the world shook and everything broke.

Oh shit. They're here.

Who? What? Waitwhatthefu—

Near the front of the classroom, a bookshelf stopped behaving like a bookshelf. A bright portal of blue energy grew out of it, tearing textbooks and splintering wood. Wind bellowed. Blinding flashes exploded from the expanding portal, accompanied by wild, lashing tentacles of electricity. Chairs, desks and bookshelves tore apart. Shrapnel flew. The portal roared so loudly it shook Isabella's heart against her ribcage.

6

Breathless, she hit the carpet with everyone else, dragging her numb fear with her as debris crashed overhead. Whatever happened, whatever memories she lost next time Paradise Moon took control, she doubted she could ever forget this. Half a desk crashed through the window behind her.

The wind from the portal released one last gasp. Debris collapsed. The air crackled with dying sparks. Isabella almost breathed. Blocking out the portal's dazzling light with an outstretched hand, she stared through narrowed eyes now flecked with purple. The portal swirled and shone where the bookshelf had been.

We need to go. Now.

More than half the classroom was destroyed. Miss Pilkington's marking was a storm of snowflakes falling over the scattered splinters of her desk. Surrounded by bloody shrapnel, her teacher's body was stretched awkwardly across the carpet. Isabella stared at the ugly hole in Miss Pilkington's head.

I'm so sorry.

Lynch tugged on Isabella's arm, trying to drag her to the broken window behind them, but Isabella couldn't move. She couldn't look away. Blue light swirled around a skeleton as it stepped out of the portal with thunderous strides. If it had been caught in shadow, Isabella might have mistaken it for a deformed human. But the portal's brightness made the creature's metallic form inescapable. It reminded her of every sci-fi film she had ever watched—especially the bad ones. This metal creature was a machine. An android. A robot. A terminator. If it were possible to take only the most terrifying aspects of all those imagined terrors, Isabella was staring at the very real result.

What is that?

Bad news.

7

The metal creature jerked its head towards the bruised and bloodied students cowering on the carpet. Not daring to move, they stared back at the twin pinpricks of glowing crimson in the intruder's crooked skull. The metal creature marched through the wreckage.

Directly at Isabella.

I didn't think they'd find me. Not here! They don't know about Earth—it's in the middle of nowhere. No one's even heard of it.

"Come on!" Lynch shouted, although he was entirely frozen. Isabella wondered if perhaps he hadn't been shouting at her, but at himself.

Matching her actions to his words, Isabella grabbed his hoodie and pushed him through the shattered window. He had barely landed on the tarmac before his hand reached back for hers. Jagged glass bit Isabella's palms as she climbed after him onto the broken frame. She grasped his hand and dove through, not caring how hard the tarmac would hit her. Already she could feel warm daylight on her face.

Coldness wrapped around her waist as a metal arm plucked her from the air. Lynch shrieked and lost her hand. Instead of reaching back for her, he recoiled onto the tarmac. His face was a mess of terror. Kicking, spitting, screaming, she was hauled back inside through the classroom's window.

I'm sorry.

Isabella couldn't remember the alien inside her ever sounding so sincere. So scared. So... not herself.

I'm so sorry.

Tucking the girl under its arm, the metal creature spun on heavy heels. The classroom blurred behind Isabella as she was carried into the portal.

CHAPTER TWO

When Isabella finally remembered how to breathe, she was staring at a domed ceiling. Only a fistful of heartbeats had passed since the classroom. Her metal kidnapper hauled her from the portal's glow, her legs dangling behind it and her head bouncing in front. The domed chamber receded behind her as the creature broke into a booming sprint down a murky maze of cylindrical corridors.

So, this might partly be my fault.

When is anything ever not your fault?

Harsh, but not unfair.

Unable to hide the panic trembling inside her, Isabella smashed her fists against the metal creature's chest. After only a few blows, the cuts littering her palms screamed for her to stop. Reluctantly, she relented.

You seem upset.

Really? You spotted that?

This is a bit awkward.

No shit.

Like I said, I do feel slightly responsible and I'm happy to own that, but I don't think we need to overly dwell on blame here.

Isabella snatched another glimpse of the walls flying past her, but nothing made sense. It was too dark. Too alien. Too terrifying. Shadows swam and blurred as her aching lungs tightened in the grip of another panic attack.

Whoa, easy now.

I'm not… a bloody… horse.

Just breathe. Please?

Thread by thread, breath by breath, Isabella unravelled the terror knotted inside her.

Come on. One breath at a time.

Closing her eyes, Isabella found something that wasn't fear or rage and held onto it, listening to the alien inside her. Paradise Moon was all Isabella had.

One breath at a time. You can do this.

Isabella opened her eyes. Rusted pipes and a crackle of exposed wiring arced along the cylindrical corridor around her.

Tell me how we get out of here.

Well, let's just say we might need a little more bus fare than usual.

Where are we?

No idea, but it won't be any star system you've heard of. Hmm, maybe a rim world? This décor is so retro.

Before Isabella could light the fuse of her reply, her kidnapper hung a hard right through a circular doorway and stopped suddenly enough that Isabella half expected to hear the rattle of her internal organs being thrown against her insides. More gently than expected, her kidnapper sat her on a cold floor. It smelt of sewage. Immediately but ineffectually, Isabella pulled her jumper over her nose and peered over the top of her stretched collar. This small metal room was an air-raid shelter on steroids. Streaks of rust stained every wall amongst a detritus of disused pipes, motionless fans and corroded mesh grates. Her only escape lay behind the creature: a rusted oval door that hung open with a release wheel jutting from its centre. Red eyes followed her as she crawled backwards on her hands and bum into the far corner and hugged her knees tightly into her chest. The creature's silhouette inked out almost every hint of light leaking though the doorway.

What is it?

Them.

What?

Them. Not it.

You're lecturing me of all people on gender pronouns and you're doing it now?!

They're not gendered, but they are sentient. Well, technically speaking.

Technically speaking I hate you.

Outside the doorway, something big and heavy and metal stomped past.

You know each other, then?

Why do you think I was hiding on your quiet little planet?

Fine. Start talking.

Oh, it's not a terribly interesting story.

Then tell it quickly.

They're a Sau Daran. We... we created them. Spoiler alert: it didn't turn out how we hoped.

The what now and the hoo har?

Sau Darans. We created them.

We?

Yeah, y'know. Their gods.

Even though Isabella couldn't see the alien trapped inside her and had in fact never seen her, from the tone inside Isabella's head she could imagine Paradise Moon's embarrassed smile.

We'll address the issue of your holiness later, shit bag. What are our options?

No idea. Blind optimism?

An explosion thundered far off.

That sounded good.

Yeah. It's been a great day.

Isabella stole another glance at the creature and instantly regretted her decision. The red glow of their unblinking eyes was still terrifying. There were new reasons to be terrified too. Blood, perhaps Miss Pilkington's, was smeared over its metal feet. Isabella watched an unbidden memory of her teacher's ruined body loop through her mind in overdrive, every replay tearing through her heart with the delicacy of a chainsaw.

I really am sorry.

As the metal creature wasn't tearing across the room to rip her apart yet, Isabella took the opportunity to reach into her skirt pocket, her hand moving on muscle memory. Thanks to the recreational habits of the delinquent alien inside her, panic attacks were something that happened daily. Like brushing her teeth or finding somewhere lonely or noisy to fart. Shaking, she fumbled through the loose change of her unspent bus fare until her calloused fingertips found her metal guitar pick with black flames: thinner and stronger, to aid more aggressive strumming. She'd done a lot of that lately. She squeezed it tightly, but if her shaking body was at all becalmed it was only by the faintest of increments.

She dug deeper. Pressed against the fabric of her pocket was her plastic pick with the pink skull. Her first ever pick. Its teardrop outline was always so comfortable between her fingers.

Finally, she found what she wanted. She drew out a gold nylon pick, which shimmered with the holographic face of a grumpy kitten. It was utterly grotesque. Isabella loved it. She rocked it back and forth between her thumb and forefinger, the kitten's impish face appearing and disappearing, appearing and disappearing, as the dim light caught it and lost it. Her breathing slowed to match the steady appearance and disappearance of the kitten. Her shakes were melting enough to almost convince her she wasn't having a heart attack.

Another explosion shook the pick from her hands.

Throwing a glance over their shoulder, the Sau Daran who had kidnapped Isabella grasped the door's release wheel and pushed. With a whoosh and a clunk that echoed with finality, the door slammed shut. The corridor's dim light blinked out, leaving Isabella cuddling her knees with only a pair of glowing red eyes and the alien inside her for company.

Then the ceiling exploded.

Bone-shattering debris rained a smoking chasm in the floor in front of Isabella's feet. Instantly, the Sau Daran leapt over it and threw their metal body at Isabella.

The girl screamed.

When she dared open her eyes, the Sau Daran was kneeling with their body arched over her protectively. A drizzle of burning ceiling hissed off their back. Isabella's surprise at not being dead was interrupted as the wall beside them exploded as well. Shards of glowing metal hurtled at her. The Sau Daran raised a hand towards the incoming debris. Too slow.

But Paradise Moon was faster.

Despite the breakneck pace of Isabella's pulse, it took Paradise Moon less than a fraction of a heartbeat to take control of the girl's body. The girl's eyes burned purple, any hint of chestnut obliterated. Commandeering every atom of the girl, the alien sprung her across the room with impossible speed.

Flying metal toppled the Sau Daran in a cascade of sparks. Smoking and charred, they clattered down in a lifeless, clumsy way. Twice more, Paradise Moon dodged flying debris with lightning agility.

"Is that all you've got?" she yelled triumphantly though Isabella's lips.

Unseen, a jagged chunk of white-hot metal crashed through the hole above and struck the girl's body, pinning her to what was left of the melting floor. The alien's scream of pain was only halfway through Isabella's lips when the sudden agony hurled the girl's body over the edge of consciousness.

When the debris finally stopped falling, nothing remained but silence, dust and darkness.

You're going to blame me for this, aren't you?

CHAPTER THREE

In the same moment that Isabella was being kidnapped through a Sau Daran portal on Earth, Apprentice Ranger Ezra Knight was blowing sweat from the tip of his nose. His air filter was broken. Again. Ezra growled—actually growled—in irritation. Unless he wanted to eat a mouthful of sand, there was nothing he could do about the itchy rivers of sweat clinging inside his helmet and behind the pressure-locked seal of his armoured collar.

Locking their small recon shuttle with a tap of the door's console, Ezra hurried out of the shuttle's shadow. The wind was so strong any trace of the divots left behind by his boots instantly dissolved in a swirl of fresh sand. He smeared a gloveful of the stuff from his helmet's black visor and double-checked his sensor readings. The holographic touchscreen on the gauntlet strapped to his wrist flashed up the same result.

He pointed through the wind-whipped sands. "That's it!" he shouted over a hiss of static on the comm. "The same readings we picked up from our shuttle."

Apprentice Ranger Dantes was crouched on one knee in the same black armour as Ezra. He cut the perfect soldier's silhouette from the planet's low, setting sun.

Unlike most of the suns on their Outer Rim patrol routes, this sun had a sickly green glow as though this whole star system was so far from the centre of the Known Galaxies that it had gone stale. Dantes finished scanning the horizon with his plasma rifle and glanced at his friend. "You sure?" he asked over the comm.

"It's there!" Ezra shoved his gauntlet's holographic display under Dantes' helmet. "Look! There's a Sau Daran portal exactly below us and a smaller energy signature right there." Ezra pointed into the distance again. "We didn't find anything here. It must be too far down. That smaller signal is worth checking out."

"It's definitely a portal below us?" Dantes asked in disbelief. "It can't be anything else?"

Ezra checked his sensor readings yet again and nodded. He could barely believe it either. By the time he and Dantes had been born, humanity's war with the Sau Darans had long been won, with every known Sau Daran outpost destroyed. Billions of humans dead and Ezra had been conceived too late to save any of them. With the war over, the only career options remaining for the offspring of two loyal PROXUS Rangers had been to either march their jackboots over every fresh planet their Empress conquered or search for Sau Daran survivors in the Outer Rim. Expecting to take no pleasure from invading mostly innocent planets, immediately after graduating as Apprentice Rangers they had applied for an Outer Rim task force. Since then, Ezra and Dantes had been chasing shadows in the far reaches of space—until, moments ago, their shuttle had picked up the first energy signature of a Sau Daran portal since the war.

Although Dantes' visor kept his feelings hidden, his voice betrayed every flavour of excitement. "This is unreal, Ez! Call it in!"

"Nah, you do it."

Ezra grinned as Dantes' comm adjusted frequency to hail *Black Nebula*, the enormous PROXUS battle station in orbit above them. Like Ezra and Dantes, *Black Nebula* served the Empress. Her formidable People's Republic Of Xarr and United Systems, often referred to simply as PROXUS, ruled the Known Galaxies.

"Our first portal!" Dantes cried after he had finished reporting their sensor readings to *Nebula*. "You think we'll get a medal?"

"You better believe it! Where there's a portal, there's Sau Darans!" At least, that was what everyone always said. Ezra was shaking with excitement.

"Dream team!" Dantes cried. He checked the chronometer on his armoured wrist. "*Nebula* will have Rangers and Silver Fists here in no time, Ez. They're scrambling everything."

"Yeah, I heard." Ezra stood still as he thought this through. "What if the portal closes before they arrive? If there really are Sau Darans on this planet, that portal opening could be them bugging out. They'll be long gone."

Dantes punched the Ranger emblem on Ezra's upper arm, a red fist over a black triangle, outlined in white against his black armour. "Well, a coupla tough Apprentice Rangers like us can't have that, can we?"

"Course not, buddy." Ezra hesitated on the precipice of what they were proposing. "Should we take a look?"

For a long moment, all Ezra could hear was static over the comm. He stared at Dantes' faceless visor. If there had been tumbleweed on this planet, they would have chosen now to tumble.

"Of course," Dantes said eventually.

"Great!" Ezra replied, although there was no conviction in his voice.

"Yeah! Try and stop us!" Dantes added, perhaps a little too enthusiastically. "Who knows what we might find for the Empress, right? And we'll be famous, obviously! An actual portal right below us… We can't let them get away, can we?"

"Everyone on *Nebula* would say we wimped out," Ezra agreed. He hoped there was enough static on the comm to hide his uncertainty. He couldn't afford to sound weak in front of Dantes, he'd never hear the end of it.

"No chance! You still think you're faster than me?" With that, Dantes spun on his heel and dashed away from their shuttle.

Fuelled by a heady cocktail of adrenaline and fear, Ezra sprinted across the desert after his friend. Not even the sand-strewn breeze could catch them. They zigzagged through the dunes, first one in the lead and then the other, racing like they had when they were together at the academy.

Yet when they skidded to a halt beside the smaller energy signature identified by Ezra's sensor readings, they found only more sand. Once again, Dantes crouched to scan the horizon with his plasma rifle.

"Not much out there," he confirmed. He wasn't even out of breath. "A few radioactive scorpions near the base of that dune. See?" He pointed with the muzzle of his rifle. "They're bigger and uglier than us, but not close enough to worry about."

"Who's worried?" Ezra asked. Kneeling beside his partner, he studied the ground. There was something odd about the way the sand blew across it. "Sensor readings don't lie." Ezra pushed his gloved hand over the desert floor exactly where the tiny energy signature still flickered on the holographic display from his gauntlet. His hand disappeared through the sand. Even though he could see it, the sand wasn't there. He pushed his hand around beneath the illusion until he felt something solid on the other side, then pulled his hand back out.

"Still attached," Ezra confirmed as he rotated his wrist to check.

"A hologram?"

Ezra nodded. "That's our second energy signature right there powering the holo."

"Unlucky for them, lucky for us. A reading that small? We'd never have picked it up from the shuttle without the portal getting our attention."

"This hole feels wide enough to squeeze through." Ezra examined Dantes' black visor. "You scared?"

"What?" Dantes asked loudly through another surge of static over the comm.

"Nothing." Ezra bit his lip. "We're doing this, right?"

Dantes seemed to think for a moment. "It's not too late to back out."

"Do you want to back out?" Ezra asked.

"Course not."

"Me neither."

"Good."

"Good."

"Right." Dantes waited. "I guess we're doing this."

"Guess we are."

After a futile glance at an empty sky with no sign of reinforcements, Ezra flicked on his helmet's searchlight and lowered his head through the projection of sandy desert. Below was a deep shaft and an ancient ladder.

Ezra pulled his head back into daylight and repositioned himself beside the projection, then lowered his boot until he found the ladder's top rung. He stepped down. His body passed straight through the hologram and straight through the ladder's first decrepit rung as it disintegrated in a cloud of rust.

Restraining a yelp of surprise, Ezra sailed down the ladder long enough for at least a few years of his life to flash before his eyes. Missing rung after rung as he fell, his gloved hand finally tightened around one of the metal rods and halted his fall with a shuddering stop. Pausing for a lungful of recycled oxygen while the thin beam from Dantes' searchlight caught up, Ezra tested the next rung with the toe of his boot. It held.

Much deeper down the shaft, their boots ran out of ladder where its lower rungs had been buried beneath an underground sand dune no taller than Ezra. As Ezra stepped off the ladder and looked back up the way they had come, his searchlight caught a thin waterfall of sand trickling off the top of Dantes' helmet before becoming lost in the dune at Ezra's feet. They jumped off it, landing on solid metal beside the dune with a double echo that escaped far deeper into the darkness than their searchlights could penetrate. They were at an intersection. Four cylindrical corridors twice their height branched away from the wider, sand-filled bottom of the shaft. Each tunnel looked as dark as the next.

"Look! That sand can't have been building up for long," Ezra suggested.

Dantes nodded. "That shaft was opened recently."

With his nervousness sealed inside his armour, and his helmet's searchlight illuminating everywhere he turned his head, Ezra poked his plasma rifle down one of the corridors and led them into darkness.

For a long time, every corridor appeared as derelict and deserted as the last—until their plasma rifles swung around one corridor too many. The Sau Daran stared back with red glowing eyes, close enough to reach out a metal finger and touch the muzzle of Ezra's rifle.

In all his years at the academy, Ezra had never believed he would encounter a Sau Daran. For his generation, such creatures had been relegated to myths and legends, and yet they were never far from a citizen's lips or thoughts. He stared dumbly at the creature. His finger was frozen over his rifle's trigger. The metal creature was frozen too, their body paused mid-stride. Had the creature been human, Ezra would have read their body language for fear. But Ezra knew that was ludicrous. The first rule every PROXUS citizen learned as a child was that all Sau Darans were cold and cunning killers. Ezra's whole universe was founded on the principle that it was impossible for Sau Darans to feel anything. Like any good PROXUS citizen, he understood how dangerous a Sau Daran could be.

A pulse of red energy burst from Dantes' plasma rifle, splitting the silence with a short, deafening whine. Ezra stared through the smoking crater in the creature's metal face. Through it, he could see the rusted pipes on the wall behind.

After Dantes started shooting, it was impossible for either of them to stop. To do so would have meant their death. The two Apprentice Rangers swept through tunnel after tunnel, giving the Sau Darans no time to organise their defence. Flurries of angry red plasma spat from their rifles, chewing up everything in their path. They never paused to question what they were doing. The academy had trained them for this. PROXUS society had trained them for this. Ezra knew how many humans the Sau Darans had killed during the war, and he could feel the fear these metal creatures conjured within him.

More Sau Darans scurried and dodged and crawled towards them through the cylindrical tunnels but, whether by grenade, rifle or pistol, every metal creature met the same fate. Ezra later learned that these Sau Darans were engineers, not soldiers. Not one of them had been designed to fight like Ezra and Dantes had been designed to fight. It was a massacre. Before long, Ezra and Dantes felt invincible.

They weren't.

This Sau Daran must have crept behind the Apprentice Rangers because Ezra didn't see them until they landed clumsily on Dantes' back, their spindly limbs tearing at his armour. Ezra's plasma rifle searched frantically for a shot, but there was nothing he could do without blasting away his partner too.

Bent double under the Sau Daran's weight, Dantes staggered back and forth. Dropping his long rifle, he wrenched his pistol free. A silver talon latched onto his shoulder, ripping through armour, bone and muscle with a claw designed for manipulating heavy metal. Dantes' pistol arm slackened. Out of the shadows, another claw grasped the top of his helmet and twisted as easily as if it were unscrewing the cap from a bottle of Turbo. Instead of the familiar hiss and clink of a bottlecap and the aroma of cheap booze, Ezra heard a terrible crunch.

Dantes crumpled to the floor.

Screaming with raw fury, Ezra sprayed the Sau Daran with every bolt in his plasma rifle, blasting more and more gaping holes through their flimsy body even after they had collapsed next to his friend in a smoking heap of hot, twisted metal.

Ezra dropped his plasma rifle and grasped Dantes' body. The abnormal angle of his neck told its own short story. Ezra's shaking fingers found Dantes' helmet and pulled, but it wouldn't budge. He tugged harder with shaking hands. Still, it resisted. Reaching along the side of Dantes' chestplate, he dialed down the suit's internal pressure seal and this time removed the helmet. Dantes' eyes were glassy and vacant. There was another hiss, this time from Ezra's suit. His gloves and helmet clattered to the floor. Choking back a sob, Ezra brushed his bare fingers against his friend's cheek.

The sudden clash of metal-on-metal jerked Ezra's senses awake. He stared up at another Sau Daran skittering towards him. Ezra let them. Only when they were close enough for the fiery pinpricks of their eyes to fill his vision did he swipe Dantes' plasma pistol from where it had fallen and burn a hole through their face.

Ezra stared at the Sau Daran's smoking body, before looking back at his friend. His expression hardened. Moving on autopilot, he retrieved his plasma rifle, replenished it with a fresh plasma clip from his bandolier, then braced it under Dantes' pistol to restrain the larger weapon's recoil. Wielding them in front of his hips in a horizontal cross, he stalked down the corridor.

PROXUS protocol demanded that Rangers cram every pouch, pocket, holster, bandolier and webbing with enough plasma weapons, ammunition and explosives to invade a small city—in case their Empress required them to do exactly that. Ezra didn't stop hunting Sau Darans until both weapons and every one of his plasma grenades, plasma clips and weapon holsters were exhausted. Littered with the corpses of more Sau Darans than he could count, the burning corridor he had ended up in collapsed. He didn't care. Letting the spent tools of his trade clatter beside his boots, he leant his shoulder against the rusted hollow of an exploded pipe and stared down through one of the gaping holes he had blown in the corridor's floor.

Through it, a girl. A human girl. Her left leg and right arm were pinned beneath mounds of rubble, her face barely visible beneath the dust and darkness. An unmoving Sau Daran, much larger than any Ezra and Dantes had fought, lay crumpled next to her.

Weary and weaponless, Ezra slid over the edge of the hole and landed shakily on the flaming ruins below. Steadying himself as the rubble creaked and groaned, he leaned over the heavy metal crushing the girl's arm and pressed two trembling fingers against the base of her throat. Her pulse was faint. Ignoring the heat beginning to cook his skin, he stared at her injured face, its contours split by a deep cut that ran all the way from her forehead to chin and gushed ugly with blood.

Her eyes drifted open. They were consumed with the deepest purple glow. Not human eyes, but otherworldly. As his fingers lingered on the weak pulse in her neck, her purple gaze drifted up his arm and over his Ranger's emblem to his earnest, sweaty face. Her eyes closed. The purple glow died.

Praying to his Empress that the girl's heart would keep beating after he stopped feeling for its rhythm, Ezra withdrew his fingers from the girl's neck and heaved at the lumps of metal pinning her. He didn't care how hot they were or that they burned his bare smoking hands black or that their weight nearly tore his arms from their sockets. There was almost comfort in his pain as he shifted the debris off her body.

It was too late to save Dantes.

But he could save her.

CHAPTER FOUR

sabella's left leg itched something awful. Sleepily, she bent her other leg to scratch it. She must have been exhausted. She couldn't find her left leg.

Half asleep, she could still feel the ghostly grasp of a cruel nightmare that had chased her through every dark corner of her mind as she slept. It terrified her more than any nightmare ever should. As she blinked it away, a severe white light ambushed the chinks in her eyelids and finished the job of waking her up.

Rubbing dancing lights from her eyes, she peered at the dazzlingly white room. This was not her bedroom. A round, sloping wall, significantly larger than the bedroom she had expected, encircled the medicinally white padded block she was laying on. Her body was wrapped in a gown drenched in the same sterile absence of colour.

I love your optimism, but that wasn't a nightmare. You should take things slowly.

But when Isabella looked down, everything sped up.

At the sound of her screaming—raw, terrified screaming—an aperture slid open in the wall and a crowd of strangers in maroon tunics rushed inside. Buzzing around her padded block, they swiped and tapped on holographic touchscreens projecting from straps on their wrists. Nonsense flew from their lips.

Slowly, reluctantly, inevitably, she dragged her eyes back to the stump of healed skin where her right arm should have begun, then to the similarly smooth stump of her upper thigh where her left leg once belonged. This time she didn't scream, her face simply creased in shock. She could still feel both limbs, but the sensation was an illusion. A memory. A dream.

Reality bites, but at least we're alive.

Unable to respond—unable to function—Isabella's brain numbly accepted the alien's voice.

Here we go again, one slow breath at a time and all that jazz. You'll be okay. Everything will be okay. I promise.

Brandishing a needle, a scrawny, snub-nosed woman stabbed Isabella's neck before the girl could formally raise a complaint or at least punch her in the face. "—lation module administered," finished the woman. Words that moments ago had been garbage were now comprehensible. But despite every reassuring word that leapt from these strangers' lips, nothing could ease Isabella's terror. Every kind word was an arm and a leg short of being helpful.

By the time everyone had left, content Isabella wasn't dying all over again, she was lying on her side. The unfamiliar stump below her right shoulder was pressed against the padded block, her lone leg bent into her chest beneath her thin gown, her solitary shivering arm wrapped around it. Her whole body shivered in shock.

You okay?

Isabella didn't reply. Whether or not she had the mental capacity to hear the alien inside her, there was nothing ambiguous about the girl's radio silence.

Isabella was still laying silently when she noticed a man had arrived—when, she wasn't sure—and he was examining her the way a scientist might examine bacteria down a microscope. He was an enormous man in every direction, with a mountainous physique. A purple robe clustered unattractively around his belly, on which his hands were resting. The robe reminded her of the cassocks she'd seen priests wearing whenever her mum had dragged her to Mass.

"You're safe now," the enormous man assured her. He deployed what appeared to be a genuine smile. Isabella glared. "My physicians found these," he told her. "I thought you might like them back." From a pocket inside his robes, he retrieved her plastic watch and cracked mobile phone. He placed them next to her on the padded block.

Questions followed. With tender authority, the enormous man nudged her this way and that, sometimes wondering who else might be looking for her, sometimes taking her back to a nightmare that always ended in darkness beneath an avalanche of rubble. He didn't rush her, and he was occasionally willing to offer his own answers. He had saved her, he explained. She was safe, he assured her. Isabella was relieved when he finally left.

Unwilling to acknowledge the new reality within which she was caged, she tried her phone. Not even a flicker of life ignited behind its cracked screen. Unlike her, it hadn't survived. She stowed it in her gown's pocket, which automatically sealed itself closed. Had she been in a better mood with more time to think and less panic inside, such a clever gown might have impressed her. Instead, she added playing guitar to the exhaustive list she had been compiling of things she could no longer do, then promised herself this creepy ass room would be yet another place where she would never, ever let herself cry.

Defiantly blinking away a moistness she wouldn't let become tears, Isabella grabbed her watch off the padded block. She clutched the cheap plastic band in the fingers of her left hand and flicked it again and again, attempting to whip it around her left wrist. It pinged out of her grasp. Retrieving it from the edge of the padded block, she pinned it between her teeth and tugged the strap to seal it around her wrist. As she fed the strap through the catch, her shaking fingers fumbled it again and the watch spun into her lap. She flung it across the room and swore.

Hey, come on! We're gonna get outta this. Trust me.

I don't care.

I get it, I really do. But you still want to live, right?

Maybe.

Hey! You want to live, right?

In reply, Isabella clenched her surviving fist so tightly her knuckles shone white.

Come on, let's get outta here!

Isabella sobbed.

We'll figure it out. We always do.

Tears were escaping her blurring vision in increasingly ugly flurries.

We're a long way from Earth and somewhere we don't want to be. What else do we need to know? Cue dramatic exit!

Using what? Those secret alien powers you've been hiding for fifteen years?

Yeah, funny story. That's sort of what I was thinking too.

You're hilarious.

Well, you're not completely wrong.

28

About your secret powers or your dumbass attempt at comedy?

Erm... Both?

Isabella's face hardened. Her purple-flecked eyes were turning bloodshot, unspent tears melting away in the heat of her fury. *You have powers? You mean you could have saved us? We could still be back on Earth?*

In that order: I do, I actually did and no we couldn't because, as you know very well, I was in hiding. For, I might add, what were shown today to be exceptionally good reasons.

You're impossible.

I'm taking that as a compliment. But using my powers on Earth was never an option. As fun as that would have been, it would have attracted so much bad attention that even your nuttiest prime ministers and presidents wouldn't have thanked me for it. This god stuff is complicated.

Alien stuff.

The problem is I can't use most of my god stuff while I'm inside you.

Then piss off! I never wanted you in here. You never asked. Use your god magic to take me home and we'll never see each other again.

I can't. I'm stuck in here until you're... well, you know...

Asleep?

Dead.

Oh.

Yeah, I wish they'd put that in the manual before I chose your cute baby face to hide behind.

Isabella wiped her eyes with the heel of her fist. Her anger was helping to sharpen her focus, and boy was she angry. *Were you trying to kill me?*

I think you'll find I saved your life.

Not today, back on Earth. Rooftops, car crashes and all the rest. You were trying to kill me.

That's ridiculous.

Admit it. That's how it works, right? You're stuck in here until I die?

If I wanted you dead, you'd be dead.

Is that a threat?

No, it's a fact. I can do whatever I want when I take control of your body. You're still alive, aren't you? Well?

Okay, so you didn't have the guts to outright murder me. But you put me in danger. You wanted a chance something might happen to me.

For the first time in fifteen years, the alien trapped inside Isabella said nothing.

Screw you. Isabella leapt off the bed. She was still remembering her missing arm and missing leg when she caught the floor with her face. Groaning first in pain and then fury, she glared accusingly at the stumps where her missing limbs should have been. She would drag herself out of this. Literally, if she had to. Rolling clumsily over the floor, she started to slide. She couldn't even crawl. It took forever. Finally, she pressed her sweat-drenched back against the wall. Although it looked plastic, it was as hard and cold as steel. She braced herself against it and tried to stand.

Immediately, she hit the floor.

Without pausing for air, she levered herself up. Again, she climbed. She tried to steady herself, but she couldn't balance and the rest of her body wouldn't behave without all her arms and legs to boss it around.

This isn't good for anyone, you know.

This time when Isabella fell, she found the wall before she found the floor. Slamming into it with her already bruised shoulder, she strained her only leg until she had braced herself upright.

Please stop before you do some real damage.

Like that would even be bad for you. Wishing she had a free hand to wipe away the sweat stinging her eyes, Isabella steeled herself for each slow, painful hop as she slid along the wall. She was confident she could make it to the door those strangers had left through.

Hey, I wasn't asking! Your body's wrecked. You need to stop.

Whose fault is that? You need to shut up.

Why do I have to fix everything?

Paradise Moon opened the girl's eyes. They glowed purple. Through them, Paradise Moon saw everything. This included the floor as it sped towards her. Paradise Moon hadn't controlled this body with only one leg before and it was a steep learning curve. Girl hit floor with extra thud.

Oops! Sorry!

Grateful that Isabella wasn't awake to witness this, Paradise Moon let the girl's lips pull apart in an embarrassed cringe.

I'll be more careful next time, promise.

Isabella couldn't hear, let alone reply. Paradise Moon knew the girl was deep below the surface of a dark lake of consciousness. She couldn't escape those depths until Paradise Moon handed back control. Which the alien would, of course. Only not yet. If the girl was intent on killing herself, Paradise Moon would do whatever it took to keep the girl alive. She owed her that. Between the alien's manipulation of the girl's DNA to dampen the physical trauma of losing two limbs and all the chemicals that medical team had pumped into Isabella's body, it was a miracle the girl was even breathing. Paradise Moon promised herself this would be the only time she ever hid inside a human. It wasn't worth the effort.

Burning more of her biochemical reserves, Paradise Moon infused Isabella's muscles with enough alien strength to drag the girl's body across the room. Letting the girl continue like that would have only done more damage and this body had been through enough. Like it or not, they both needed it. Rest would do the girl good.

She had made it halfway to the padded block when footsteps approached outside. She lay still and closed her eyes. She always hated hiding, but it was their only hope. Isabella would be a lot safer if no one knew this particular alien was trapped inside her.

Before the door could open, Paradise Moon pulled Isabella back to the surface of Lake Consciousness and gifted back control.

Isabella jolted awake as unkind hands seized her. Two bulky men in blue tunics dragged her across the floor and lifted her onto the padded block. These weren't the kind strangers with touchpads and maroon tunics. These strangers were different. Meaner. Scarier. And they were holding her down.

What did you do this time?

Nothing! I was pretending to be asleep!

Yeah right.

Led by the enormous man, more new and unpleasant faces flooded inside. A hovering gurney followed. It wasn't that the gurney was floating a fist's height off the floor that sent Isabella's stomach spinning, or the heavy glass cylinder on top of it. It was the sinister arsenal of blades and other cutting devices glistening around the cylinder that made Isabella want to re-decorate the pristine white room with whatever slop the alien had eaten in the school canteen for lunch.

Oh crap, change of plan!

Unbidden by Isabella, her foot caught one of the strangers with a wild kick to his stomach. Purple flashed in her eyes as Paradise Moon took control long enough to hurl the two men off Isabella's body. They collided against the far wall with bone-breaking force.

Twice as many unkind hands took their place, pushing Isabella into the bed and pressing shiny clamps over her arm, her leg, her waist, her throat. Instantly, they all clicked into place and Isabella felt her body being pulled taut like the head of a drum. She was staring at the ceiling, her body locked in place.

The enormous man loomed over her. "Tell me, which Sau Daran parasite have we caught here?"

Isabella stared up at the bulging flesh of his jowls. The clamp around her throat made it impossible to look away as he scrutinised her prone body.

"Perhaps not," he conceded. "Is the containment chamber ready?"

"Yes, First Duke."

"Good, cut her open as soon as I leave." He pointed a chubby finger at someone Isabella couldn't see. "Harvest every atom of her DNA. Don't miss anything."

"Of course, First Duke."

Purple flared in Isabella's eyes, but no matter how much strength Paradise Moon flooded into the girl's body, she couldn't tear free of the clamps.

Tears streamed down Isabella's cheeks. *At least you got what you wanted.*

This was never what I wanted.

Liar.

"We are ready to sedate her, First Duke."

"Don't be ridiculous. I want her conscious right up until the moment she dies. Look at her eyes. That parasite's in there watching us. Gather as much data as you can."

"It will be done, First Duke."

This wasn't supposed to happen!

Like you ever cared.

"I want that parasite in the containment chamber as soon as it's free, or else I'll cut all of you open until I find it and you have my word as First Duke you won't be sedated, either."

"Understood, First Duke."

Okay, so I admit I had a bit of a joyride once or twice when I was feeling low but fifteen years is a long time to be stuck in someone else's body and it was really hard and maybe I made a few mistakes but I always woke you up before I could do it and I don't think I was ever really going to do it, not really, and don't you think there's a reason I could never go through with it?

You couldn't even get that right.

I care about you, idiot. I don't want either of us to die!

Well, I've got bad news.

The enormous man stepped away. All Isabella could see was the pristine white ceiling. Perhaps not for long. Something hummed nearby. Isabella imagined one of the gurney's spinning blades powering to life, although that didn't explain why she could smell burning.

A hand moved closer. In it, a scalpel. Along the edge of the blade was a glowing green laser.

Girl and alien swore together in perfect unison.

CHAPTER FIVE

Beauregard watched Ezra knock back another shot of Turbo. The young man gagged as the cheap booze burned his throat. Beauregard's wrinkled face hardened to conceal his wry smile. Glancing at his own shot of Turbo on the table between them, the old Ranger left it untouched. In his youth, he had drunk so much Turbo that a horde of Sau Daran soldiers couldn't compel him to drink any more.

Drinking in Crazy Red's had been Ezra's idea. It had been Dantes' favourite bar on *Black Nebula*, although figuring out why made Beauregard's brain ache. Despite being named after a notorious space pirate, the dimly lit dive felt as appealing as Ezra's impending stomach ulcer. And no cleaner. Beyond the privacy offered by its deep shadows and deafening synthesised beats, Crazy Red's had no other merits. It couldn't be further from the grander establishments on *Black Nebula*'s Upper Ring where Beauregard usually spent his points. Lifting his glass, he swilled its toxic contents and he calculated tonight's bar tab. The only light at the end of this wormhole would be how softly this hit his points total compared to drinking in the Upper Ring. Hence why

Dantes had been such a fan of this vitraxi den. As far as Beauregard could tell, Crazy Red's mainly did business with those in the Lower Ring who couldn't afford to be overheard or couldn't afford anywhere else. Dantes, who had transferred almost all the points he earned back to his family on Xarr, had fallen into the latter category.

"To Dantes!" Ezra rasped. He slammed his glass beside his heap of empties.

"Phyxin' fine Apprentice Ranger," agreed Beauregard. Reluctantly, he downed most of his own glass in the knowledge that his grieving friend had succeeded where a horde of Sau Daran soldiers would have failed.

Ezra's head swayed. "More drinks?"

As was normal for Beauregard, he wasn't so much sat as he was sprawled across their shadowy booth, his heavy boots propped up on the table's sticky surface beside Ezra's empties. Despite his legs being heavily clothed in cargo pants with his trusty pair of plasma pistols strapped to his thighs, Beauregard's upper body was barely covered by his heavily stained, possibly once-white sleeveless vest. He was the only Ranger on the battle station who could get away with wearing his sidearms off duty—one of the few perks of being *Black Nebula*'s oldest serving Ranger. Embers fizzled at the end of the dying cigarette between his lips. "Aww phyx, you know I ain't one to stop a fella drinkin', kid, but I ain't never seen you drink like this. Slow down, will you?"

Steadying himself with an urgent lunge at the table, Ezra leaned far too close to Beauregard. "More. Drinks."

Beauregard didn't flinch at the caustic stench of Turbo on Ezra's breath, but his cold gaze did linger on Ezra's scarred hands as they gripped the table. The old Ranger hid his concern. Curling his lips to blow smoke around Ezra's face rather than into it, Beauregard winked. "So long as you're buyin', kid."

Ezra gave a drunken double nod, as though he had forgotten the first, then launched himself on a winding course which might eventually lead to the bar. Sinking deeper into the booth, Beauregard kept a loose eye on Ezra's stumbling progress.

"How is our hero?" asked a silky voice.

Beauregard didn't take his eyes off Ezra. "See for yourself."

A woman glided into Ezra's vacated side of the booth. Her stunning leather outfit, styled from a shimmering blend of myriad purples and blacks that were never wholly one nor the other, was easily the classiest outfit on *Black Nebula* and light years ahead of anything else in this dive. In sharp contrast to her stylish attire, her afro was completely out of control and dark smudges of mechanical fluid were smeared across her face.

"You've got shuttle on you," said Beauregard. It was a casual remark, shepherded carelessly through his lips. Instantly, he wanted to shoot himself.

With irrational urgency, Fleur Fontaine scrubbed her face with her sleeve. Beauregard watched with an ugly scowl, no doubt revealing more than he would ever have shown to the rest of the Known Galaxies. As her sleeve soaked up the dark fluid beside her right eye, beneath it emerged a tattoo of a half-eclipsed sun, its pale ink shining out of her skin.

"What kept you?" Beauregard asked. Keen to distract Fleur from cleaning her face, he looked meaningfully at where Ezra was scanning his gauntlet at the bar.

"I played a few hands after landing." Concern flickered over Fleur's elegant features as she followed Beauregard's gaze, her grubby sleeve waiting in midair. "Is our boy okay?"

"You win?" asked Beauregard. The longer he delayed his answer, the more she would focus on Ezra instead of the traces of fluid smeared across her face.

"Of course. Yes. Some. A bit. No, not really." Fleur sighed. "I settled up my losses as soon as I heard. Do not tell me Ez blames himself?"

"What do you think?"

"Phyx."

Beauregard flipped his dead cigarette, barely more than a sprig of ash, into an empty glass. He lit another with ritual efficiency. The feel of the black paper between his lips always took him back many decades to growing up on the streets of Xarr's undercity and his first cigarette. They were more dependable killers than the plasma pistols dangling from his hips, yet he could not live without them.

Yawning, Fleur stretched her lithe arms over her head in a manner that reminded Beauregard of a stray cat he had lived with in the undercity. He took a long drag of his cigarette and exhaled slowly. "Mission okay?" he asked.

Fleur glanced warily around their booth. She nodded. Beauregard understood. There were shadows everywhere in Crazy Red's. You never knew who was listening, but you could be sure they worked for the First Duke. "I flew a few extra drops. More boots on the ground after some Sau Darans came out of nowhere and did a lot of damage." She paused. "I am sorry about Dantes. He and Ez…"

Beauregard shrugged. "You know our boy. All heart, no head. That's what we're here for, ain't it?"

Fleur laughed. "Kyle Beauregard, if you are here to make up the brains of our merry foursome then we are truly vented." Abruptly, Fleur stopped laughing. "Threesome. Phyx." Her face slackened, killing every spark of charisma in her eyes. "What a phyxing waste."

"Dantes ain't gonna be forgotten."

"Not just him." Grief found unusual company in the defeat invading Fleur's face. "Ez."

"Kid ain't dead yet. His trigger finger ain't growin' cold, neither."

Fleur leaned across the table, uncharacteristically unbothered about the puddles of Turbo dampening her already oil-stained sleeves. "What would Ez be if he was anything other than PROXUS?"

Beauregard thought. And drank. And thought some more. Sliding away his glass, he leaned back, let his eyelids close and sank into the welcome solace of darkness. He felt his wrinkles tightening into a grimace. "In this galaxy?" he asked. "He'd be on the wrong side."

"It might be too late for us to escape this life, but he still has time." Her voice had dropped, her eyes wary of every shadow. "Our mistakes do not have to be his."

"Phyx." With a snarl, Beauregard wrenched open his eyes before he was overwhelmed by the nightmares inside him. He had done much in the Empress' name, and none of it good.

A shout beside their booth dragged him back to the noise and chaos of Crazy Red's in time to see Ezra rebound off another patron, his tray of half-spilt Turbo shots wobbling.

"Sorry fella," Ezra muttered, struggling to stay upright.

A short, grubby man with unkempt hair staggered drunkenly backwards. He pointed a crooked finger at the tiny patch of Turbo on his already oil-stained, ripe-smelling brown overalls. "You gonna pay for that?"

"Relax, pal," Beauregard suggested with more warmth than he felt. "Here, lemme buy you a drink."

The patron squinted at Beauregard and puffed out his chest. "Get locked and vent your points while you're at it! I know your type. Just because you're fancy Rangers, you think you can buy my respect, is that it? Go back to the Upper Ring!"

Ezra grinned limply with the enlightenment of intoxication. "The Upper Ring is nicer."

Beauregard's face scrunched up. "Make up your mind, pal. You gonna take my points or not?"

"Not," said the patron, throwing the first punch.

Before his fist ended its journey towards Ezra's jaw, someone caught it and deftly spun him, pinning his arm behind his back. Fleur leaned over his shoulder until her face was almost touching his. "You picked the wrong night," she warned. She spoke without menace. All her menace was painfully bending his arm against the will of his bones.

Wincing, he stared at the tattoo on Fleur's face. "Pirate dpresh," he spat.

Beauregard stood. "Easy, pal."

Calmly, Fleur held up a delicate finger with her free hand as she continued to restrain the angry patron with her other. "*Ex*-pirate." She pushed the patron away. "But still a dpresh," she admitted, her smooth voice practically dripping with synth sugar as his tangled legs sent him crashing to the floor. With more than one dirty look over his shoulder, he climbed upright and slunk out of the bar's neon exit.

Once Ezra's loaded tray of Turbo shots clattered onto the table, he had to defend himself against the warmest hug and a barrage of sisterly love on his cheeks. Fleur only stopped when it was time to examine the cuts and bruises littering his face. "It will be okay, Ez," she assured him with her kindest smile. "Sorry I was late." She dragged him into the booth and wrapped her arm around him, perhaps in case he tried to escape.

Ezra responded by finishing off one of the surviving shots. He tried to flick it onto the pile of empties, but he missed. As it rolled under the table, Ezra reached for another, wholly ignorant of Fleur's insistent glance at Beauregard.

Grudgingly, Beauregard reached over the table and placed a firm bear paw on Ezra's arm. "Slow down, kid. I uhhh, ain't gonna keep up overwise."

"Let me drink."

"It don't bother me done," Beauregard replied as his grip tightened on Ezra's arm. "Slow down though, yeah?"

Rolling her eyes, Fleur dragged Beauregard's paw off Ezra and replaced it with her own smaller, more delicate hand. Ezra flinched at her gentler touch.

"In his typically useless way, this ape is trying to remind you that we are here for you, Ez. We are all Rangers. We stick together no matter what."

Beauregard frowned. "S'what I said."

Fleur silenced him with a glare, but her voice was soft as she stroked Ezra's arm. "We have been losing friends for longer than we would care to admit. It never gets easier, but that is how it should be. Dantes was a good Apprentice Ranger. Like you."

Ezra's eyes sank into his lap. Experimentally, Beauregard sneaked a shot of Turbo. It tasted even worse than before. When this went unnoticed, it didn't take him long to finish off the rest of the tray. Smugly, he slid the last of the empty glasses back onto the table and wiped his dripping lips. When he looked up, admittedly a touch dizzily, both Fleur and Ezra were glaring at him.

"What?" Beauregard cried. "You said slow him down."

Ezra started shaking.

"Aww kid, look—"

Laughter crept from Ezra's lips. Fleur's gentler laughter blended with his.

"What?" Beauregard growled. Whatever their joke, it wasn't obvious. He frowned and released an earthshattering burp.

Still giggling, Fleur nodded her approval and pulled Ezra closer. "Nothing has changed, Ez. We will always be here for you."

Beauregard grinned, hoping he wasn't doing so in that dpresh way some folk can't help after they've had one or three drinks too many. "We love you, kid."

Ezra brought his laughter under control, his face wrecked by today's emotions. Somehow, although he had to reach for it, he found a smile. As fake as it probably was, it was a smile and that was something.

Whatever Fleur said next, Beauregard had already missed it by the time he realised he wasn't listening. Wistful memories were dragging him away from the smoke and shadows of Crazy Red's and pulling him into a melancholic haze. The last time he had toasted dead friends and drunk too much Turbo, he had been celebrating victory in the war against the Sau Darans. A simpler time, when good and bad weren't separated by so much phyxin' grey. Or perhaps Beauregard had been simpler, and blind to every shade. Like Dantes. Like Ezra. After his Empress had seized power, he had never paused long enough to question what PROXUS was doing to the Known Galaxies. By the time he had realised the Empress was as much a tyrant as she was a war hero, he had made an outstanding career out of doing the wrong thing. "Ain't seen a Sau Daran since the war," admitted Beauregard. "Tell me kid, what were they like?"

Ezra opened his mouth to answer, but at that moment red projections burst from all their gauntlets, alerting them and every other Ranger on the battle station.

CHAPTER SIX

Isabella heard the door hiss open.

"What do you want?" the enormous man demanded in his distinctive, commanding voice. A volley of deafening whines answered him. Crimson light and black smoke erupted everywhere as plasma blasts crisscrossed over Isabella's body. Every scream was terminated by more blasts of scorching heat. Wet and sinewy, what used to be a person splattered down Isabella's leg. Their tunic, no longer blue, was bloody and smoking.

Too late, she shut her eyes. Unable to move, she waited until the plasma blasts died. Ugly odours were settling in her mouth and nostrils.

Smells like an abattoir with a hint of incinerator thrown in for added flavour.

Stop helping. Please stop helping.

"Get up," a man's filtered voice ordered.

Reluctantly, Isabella opened her eyes. This time, she was grateful for the neck restraint forcing her gaze upwards. The ceiling directly above her was a ruin of charred holes and dripping blood. She choked down the bile rising in her stomach, trying not to imagine what the rest of the room looked like.

Towering over her, a helmeted soldier in black combat gear rushed to unfasten her containment clamps, his smoking rifle hanging off one shoulder. He reached over to detach the clamp around her waist, revealing the emblem on his upper arm. A black triangle with a red fist.

Do you remember that other time we almost got killed?

Be more specific.

The soldier who dragged us out of the rubble. Don't you think this guy looks like that guy?

Wasn't I unconscious?

He's a perfect match, trust me.

Dressed all in black with his face hidden?

Yes! Only I did see his face. But he had that symbol on his arm. I'm telling you, it's him.

You're ridiculous.

And you're getting rescued! I've got a good feeling about this guy.

Their rescuer freed the last of Isabella's restraints with a metallic click. Without asking for permission, he scooped her up in his arms and marched her through the smoke and out of the destroyed room.

Please don't look.

Okay. I'm not.

Good.

He carried her along a narrow corridor, its walls the same sterile white that only moments ago had surrounded Isabella. Three sprawled bodies spoiled this otherwise pristine corridor, forcing their rescuer to step over them. They wore the same black armour as him, their faces hidden behind the same black visors and their upper arms bearing the same emblem of a red fist and black triangle. The only difference was their necks had been twisted in ways necks shouldn't be twisted. Her rescuer adjusted his grip around Isabella's body, causing her cracked phone to slip through a tear in her gown and smash on the floor. She didn't care. Her mind was elsewhere. Even when those bodies were out of sight, they were inescapable.

Static sparked inside their rescuer's helmet. "We're heading down the corridor," he announced.

Isabella was beginning to question his sanity as well as hers when a woman's voice cut through the heavy static, faint but close enough for Isabella to hear through his helmet. "Got you on the feed. Security disabled. Dearest brother, was that plasma fire I heard over the comm? You're not making a mess again, are you?"

"No, I was just cleaning up," he replied. "Striker was there. No choice."

A torrent of expletives exploded down the helmet's comm system with such force that most of the words dissolved into static.

"You can do all those things to me after we get out of here!" he shouted back over the comm.

You're sure this is the guy who saved us before?

It's definitely him.

But he murdered them.

Yeah… To save us.

Do you trust him?

More than I trust anyone trying to cut you open.

He stopped beside a row of cylindrical pods. "Which one?"

"Far left, same as I told you earlier. Don't worry, I've locked the rest."

"Cheers, sis."

Isabella heard a sigh over the comm. "Just stay alive."

The curved door on the far left slid open to reveal a tube-like compartment large enough for half a dozen occupants. Marching inside with Isabella wrapped in his arms like a reluctant bride, her rescuer glanced down to find her wearing the expression of a demon. He punched a code into the compartment's keypad. The door closed and the compartment shuddered.

Immediately, Isabella threw herself out of his embrace and tumbled to the floor hard enough to leave more bruises. She hauled herself up so she was sitting with her back against the compartment's curved wall, her face a mess of panic. "Okay, where are we?"

He checked a device on his wrist, then removed his helmet and tucked it under one arm. The stranger wore a sharp buzzcut above a serious expression knotted with muscle and scars.

Okay, he totally isn't who I thought he was. That's my bad.

Really? I'm shocked.

"I'm Rico." He didn't offer his hand to shake, so Isabella didn't need to ignore it. "You got a name?"

"Where are we?" she repeated hotly.

"*Black Nebula*," Rico said with a curl of his lip.

"Where?"

"A PROXUS battle station. Deep space."

Isabella took more than a moment to process this. "What is this?" she demanded. She was gesticulating at the compartment, but she meant absolutely everything.

"Star lift. Faster than running." He paused, his eyes wandering over her body. "Or carrying."

Catching him staring at where her left leg should have been, Isabella dragged her gown over the stump. "We've got lifts on Earth too," she snapped. It was a ridiculous brag, but she didn't like the superior way he was looking at her, as though she were a lame animal that needed caring for—or putting down.

Rico studied her face. "We won't be here for long."

Millions of questions were exploding inside Isabella's head, but she pushed them aside. All but one. "You're taking me home, right?"

Don't get excited, he's probably never even heard of Earth.

Rico shrugged. "I'm one of only two people on this battle station who wants you alive. The other's my sister. She's the smart one. Ask her where we're going."

Finding Rico's eyes, Isabella formed her next question carefully. "Are they dead? All of them?"

We're deep in space surrounded by enemies and this scary man with a gun is helping us escape. Just let him rescue us!

Rico nodded coolly in response to her question, as though he was auditioning to be the military's next poster boy. Isabella had to look away and instead stared frostily at nothing in particular.

Hey, we can do this. Hold it together.

But Isabella couldn't shake the nightmare of all those blades and devices on the trolley, of the green laser that made the air burn, or of all the bodies and blood and smoke and twisted necks and—

How are we in deep space? How is any of this possible?

Hey, it's gonna be okay. I'm not going anywhere, remember?

Yeah, until I die.

That's not happening any time soon.

Wanna bet?

I won't let it. I promise.

You promise a lot.

And don't I always deliver?

You never deliver.

47

We're both in your body, remember?
How could I forget?
We're in this together. That's all I'm saying.

Isabella and Paradise Moon were jolted back to reality as the compartment shuddered again.

Rico donned his helmet and raised his plasma rifle warily towards the opening door. "We go now," he ordered. Once again, his voice sounded electronic behind his helmet. "Hurry! They know something's wrong."

Outside the star lift, crowds of bustling men and women in various uniforms—some dark red and others muted green, but most of them brown—pushed past each other down a wide, dirty corridor.

"They'll recognise me," Isabella muttered, looking at the parts of her that were missing. It felt as though she were looking at a stranger's body, not her own.

Insistently, and not at all gently, Rico grabbed her arm. "Striker closed off your med bay. Anyone who saw you is dead. We move fast, we get gone."

Taking a deep breath, Isabella buried all her fear long enough to lift her chin. She wasn't in the habit of trusting murderers, especially murderers from deep space with laser guns, but she was even less keen on waiting in the star lift for someone to spot her and, probably, kill her. She wanted to push him away. She wanted to lash out. But she also wanted to survive.

Don't worry, I've got you.
Promise?
Promise.

Isabella let him pull her off the floor of the star lift, then clasped his armoured shoulder and loaded her weight onto it. "You're not carrying me though," she informed him.

Rico drew in a quick breath of annoyance. "Don't mess around. Let me—"

"I'm walking," Isabella insisted.

A black, gloved hand gestured at her missing leg. "No, you're not. I'll carry you or leave you." His dark visor loomed over the girl. "Choose."

"No. You're doing this for a reason, so you can't leave me. You need me. Try to pick me up and I'll scream."

What are you doing? He's literally saving us!

"We're dead if they catch us," Rico warned her.

Isabella hid her fear as best she could. "Better not make me scream then."

She could feel him measuring her glare from inside the safety of his helmet before he bent to make his shoulder easier to lean on. With his rifle in one hand and his other supporting the small of Isabella's back, he shepherded her out of the star lift.

Agonisingly slowly, Isabella hopped, shuffled and cursed her way along the corridor. Countless sliding doors hissed opened and closed as more uniforms rushed past them. Halfway through her next hop, Isabella fell. The floor took a swing at her, cracking her temple with sufficient force to spark every nerve in her body. A short, untidy man in brown overalls, his uniform smeared with grease and a tool belt hanging from his waist, swerved to avoid her.

Grabbing a handful of his uniform, Rico swung him against the wall. "Careful!"

A shockwave of concern spread across the engineer's face as he spotted the red fist and black triangle on Rico's arm. Mumbling an apology and something about Rangers all having it in for him, he fumbled free of Rico's grasp and dashed down the corridor without a backward glance.

Rico held out his hand. "We don't have time for this."

"Then help me up."

Hauling Isabella off the floor, Rico steadied her against his shoulder. "You're not walking."

It was then that Isabella caught a reflection of her scarred face in his black visor. She swore. It was the first time she had seen the deep ravine, swollen and purple, snaking down the middle of her face. If she was angry before, now she was livid. "Then I'll hop," she told him with no room for negotiation.

"Not quickly enough, you won't. You want to die?"

He's right and you know it.

What do you know about anything?

For a start, I can see what's inside your head.

Isabella swore again. Grimly, she yielded whilst secretly promising she would hit Rico the next time he took off his helmet.

And you say I'm ridiculous.

More panicked engineers in dirty brown uniforms streamed past them as Rico threw her over his shoulder less gently than she would have liked. "Only my sister is capable of causing this much chaos," he muttered. "Relax, darling. We'll get you out."

What did he call you? I take it back. He needs to die.

He's already on my list of people to punch.

Good.

It's a long list.

That's okay, it's been a long day.

With her view restricted to what was behind Rico, Isabella eyed the dangling plasma rifle rocking against his back and shuddered at the nightmarish memory of a white room turned red. "Are you sure it's your sister they're making all this fuss over?" she asked sharply.

Either Rico wasn't listening or he didn't care. Perhaps both. Soon the crush of bodies elbowing past them made conversation impossible, which at least helped them pass unnoticed. With Isabella slumped grumpily over Rico's shoulder, he threaded through the bustling corridor.

When they arrived at their destination and Rico finally slung Isabella back onto one foot, she was so grateful to not be seeing the world upside-down that she took a moment before paying attention to where they were. Leaning against his shoulder, she looked up and gasped. The hanger bay was larger than anywhere she had ever been. The closest comparison she could conjure was the rock concert at Wembley Stadium on her twelfth birthday, but this was larger still. More spaceships than Isabella could count were perched in row after endless row. Every ship looked different, from their size and shape to the number of gun turrets sprouting from their hulls. Around them buzzed an army of mechanics.

Pretty special, huh?

That's a lot of ships.

Not those! Look past them.

Isabella stared.

Yeah. Not bad, it is?

More inconceivable than her first sight of the spaceships was her first sight of space itself. Actual space made from actual black stuff with stars that were actually right there, stretching from floor to ceiling through a window over half a kilometre wide. Outside, an inky ocean of stars watched and waited.

A projection of red light burst from Rico's gauntlet and flashed an alert. He lifted her back into his arms. "You can stare into space all you want after we blast out of here."

CHAPTER SEVEN

As with everything else Fleur had achieved in thirty cycles of living, her trim figure and seemingly effortless athleticism took more effort to maintain with every fresh rotation. Her beautiful tall boots glided down the corridor as, running hard, she kept pace with Ezra, almost close enough to reach out a hand and grab him.

Vomit erupted from Ezra's mouth and along the wall. Pursing her lips against any wet or lumpy ricochets, Fleur skipped around the sudden mess in front of her. Ezra stumbled as he spat out the last of it.

"Would you hold up?" Beauregard wheezed from further down the corridor. "Some of us ain't as accustomed to Turbo!"

But Ezra didn't hold up. He glanced back, his eyes red and wild. His feet pounded the corridor even harder.

"Honey, perhaps you could slow down," Fleur called. "What has got into you?"

Ezra threw his wrist up in the air. Projecting out of his gauntlet was a red holographic image of a girl's face. It was the same alert Fleur had seen appear on every other

Ranger and Apprentice Ranger's gauntlets back in Crazy Red's, including hers and Beauregard's.

"She's alive!" Ezra shouted.

"That's great, kid," Beauregard replied breathlessly. "But I ain't gonna be if we don't stop!"

"The girl who escaped from the med bay?" Fleur called, trying to read the blurred holographic feed from her own gauntlet as they skidded around a corner.

"It says someone's taken her!" Ezra cried between heavy breaths.

Unleashing a burst of speed, Fleur plucked Ezra from his path and swung him into the corridor's bulkhead. He crashed to the floor with a gasp. Staring up at her with bloodshot eyes, his flushed face a mess of sweat, he fought to stand. Fleur held him down with one firm knee on his chest.

"Hey!" she shouted, leaning close enough to smell the vomit on his lips. "This is me, Ez. You are hurting, you need to stop for a beat. This is not the time to get yourself killed or arrested."

Ezra blinked back defiantly.

Fleur felt her brow crease with worry and wondered how many cycles that would add to her appearance when she next checked a mirror. "What is really going on?"

"She was there," Ezra cried. "She was with me and Dantes. The Sau Darans had her!"

Fleur's face softened. "Hey, everything is okay. There was nothing easy about what you went through."

He was barely processing her words as he waved the red hologram at her again. "She's alive! We rescued her from the Sau Darans—I rescued her! I've got to get her back—I've got to!"

Fleur recognised his tone and the depth of his desperation. A junkie's petition. She knew the plea of an addict well, only instead of just one more hand of cards, Ezra needed to be the hero just one more time.

"Is she that important?" Fleur asked. Although she kept her voice calm, she didn't lift any pressure from the knee pinning Ezra to the floor. "You would not know her from the Empress. And you do not owe her anything. You have already saved her life."

"No!" Ezra snarled. Fleur heard something else in his voice. Something more than desperation. "When I found that girl, her arm and leg were as good as gone. She'd been crushed close to death—a *girl*. She would've died down there if I hadn't, if I hadn't got her out. Phyx, they told me they lost her right after they got her onto *Nebula*. They told me she died. And now, if she's… if she's…" Ezra's eyes burned as hot as suns and as innocent as a newborn. "Nothing else matters. She's all I've got. I can't let her die too."

Gently, Fleur removed her knee from Ezra's chest. "You have us, remember?"

Ezra said nothing as his eyes flooded. Fleur had never seen him so exposed. So raw and vulnerable. He looked perfectly ready to get himself killed. She opened her mouth to offer him something, anything, but before she could speak a final plea escaped his lips. "You don't have to come with me, but I'm doing this. I don't care about anything else and I'm not asking you to help. Let me do this. I need it."

"I know you do, but this will not bring him back."

"Yeah," Ezra admitted. "It's too little, too late. But it's not nothing."

Fleur held out a hand. Ezra took it. He pulled himself upright and wiped his mouth with the back of his hand.

Beauregard collapsed against the side of a bulkhead. "What did I miss? Why're we runnin'?" he demanded between desperate pants. "We're off duty. That alert ain't for us, and it's got an off switch. See?" He raised his silent gauntlet. "We were in a bar and now we're not. Why are we not in a bar? I don't understand!"

At that moment, claxons sounded throughout the corridor much like they had in Crazy Red's. They were accompanied by a ricochet of alerts on all their gauntlets—even Beauregard's.

"Alright," Beauregard admitted as he checked the high priority emergency override on the alert flashing out of his gauntlet. "Those might be for us."

Fleur tapped the holographic projection from her gauntlet. "A shuttle blasted its way out of the main hangar bay on the Upper Ring," she told them. "No bounty for guessing who might be on board." She smiled at Ezra. It was a self-conscious smile born in defeat, but she smiled it all the same. Just as his junkie's plea had reminded her so much of herself and her own demons, now Ezra was staring back with the same smile he had found for her all those times when it was all he could do to be there and pick up the pieces. Hers was the smile he smiled when he accepted that even if she wanted to gamble away every point she had ever earned or stolen, he would be there to settle her account the following rotation.

Fleur winked at Ezra. "Shall we do something that feels right for once?"

Together, the pair sprinted for the nearest star lift heading to the Upper Ring.

Mystified, Beauregard peeled himself off the bulkhead and staggered after them. "But why are we runnin'?" he moaned.

CHAPTER EIGHT

Dash was a romantic who saw the Known Galaxies through a pilot's rose-tinted visor. In between sensor checks, he often caught himself staring dreamily out of his small Scimitar-class starfighter's cockpit. Sometimes, he caught himself staring at the daunting mass of *Black Nebula*. The PROXUS battle station's three revolving Rings and central connecting spine cut an ugly, gargantuan outline out of the starscape. On every patrol Dash had flown since he was stationed on *Black Nebula*, he had contemplated the tragedy of all the natural beauty and wonder of the stars so cruelly concealed behind the battle station's synthetic ugliness.

As Dash stared, a shuttle hurtled out of the main hangar bay on *Black Nebula*'s Upper Ring, its thrusters set to full burn.

"Hey Control," he said quietly into the comm system in his helmet. Dash said everything quietly, his diminutive voice matching his diminutive pilot's physique. "This shuttle just left the main port-side hangar bay of the Upper Ring in an awful hurry."

"This is Control. Shuttle is hostile."

"Okay, no problem. No problem at all," Dash replied, sounding like this was a huge problem.

"Repeat: shuttle is hostile. Engage and destroy."

Dash blew his long fringe out of his eyes. He had been afraid they would say that. "Copy that, Control. May the Empress smile on us."

The pilot leant hard on his joystick to send his Scimitar into a sharp dive that cut towards the escaping shuttle's trajectory. Gently nudging his rudder to port, he brought his craft into a tidy barrel-roll and levelled out his dive whilst firing up his engine as hot as it would burn to tidy up the angle of his nose. He was now directly behind the escaping shuttle, both of them hurtling through space, with every plasma cannon on his Scimitar aimed at its thrusters.

Nervously, Dash keyed his comm. "Erm, hello escaping shuttle, please acknowledge. This is Greyskull Seven. You have been designated hostile. Erm, sorry." As he spoke, he triggered a timer on his dashboard to alert him when the shuttle would be in position to engage its star drive. His timer scrolled down with alarming speed. "Please may I ask you to power down your engines or you will be fired upon," Dash warned. "Repeat, you will be fired upon. I'm terribly sorry about all this. Please acknowledge, over."

Static filled his comm, followed by a woman's voice. "Really? You're going to shoot down one of your own?"

Despite the sweaty heat of his anti-vac suit, Dash shivered. He had never fired on another PROXUS ship before. But he had never disobeyed orders before either.

Far behind them, a swarm of starfighters and shuttles emerged from the main hangar bay on *Nebula*'s Upper Ring. Too late. Already, the rogue shuttle was leaving the proximity of *Nebula*'s mass and lining up a run to engage its star drive, at which point the shuttle would leap to another star system and the chase would be over. Dash checked his sensors. All the other starfighters in Greyskull patrol were out of range and spread too thinly around *Black Nebula's* three Rings to arrive in time.

Dash kept his crosshairs fixed on the escaping shuttle. Even more starfighters were pouring out of *Nebula*, despite being too far away to engage. If they kept emptying the hangar at this rate, it would soon be empty.

"Look, this is your last chance," Dash tried again. "Please could you just power down or you will be treated as hostile."

The only reply he got was static.

Fine, be like that.

His counter ticked into single figures. He only had a handful of heartbeats left to take his shot before the escaping shuttle disappeared into another star system. It continued on its course, the cloud of pursuing starfighters and shuttles still too far behind.

Dash double-checked his weapon systems and adjusted his crosshairs.

He squeezed the trigger.

Burst after burst of green energy pulsed from his forward plasma cannon into the shuttle. He was surprised when the shuttle made no attempt to dodge his barrage. First, his plasma blasts erupted against a flickering sphere of blue energy around the shuttle. Then its shields collapsed. Lances of green energy chewed one of its four long wings to slag before piercing its hull and spitting gnarled chunks of debris into space. The orange light of its thrusters died.

Dash released the trigger. "Greyskull Seven to Control," he said croakily.

"Control here. Our sensors report weapons discharge and the hostile behaving erratically."

Dash watched the shuttle slew heavily to starboard. He tried desperately not to imagine what was happening to everyone in the shuttle as it vented atmosphere.

"Copy that, Control. Hull pierced. Sensors show hostile shuttle is inoperable, crew likely dead or evac. Hopefully evac, Empress willing. Commencing flyby for visual confirmation."

Dash nudged his stick to port and cut back the throttle to coax his Scimitar into a long, slow arc around the shuttle. It tumbled through space, as lifeless as anyone unlucky enough to have been on board.

CHAPTER NINE

Moments earlier, a spaceship leapt into the air in the main hangar bay on *Black Nebula*'s Upper Ring. It was a beast of a spaceship, with four gleaming gun-tipped wings and a flare of hot orange light propelling it upwards. Startled pilots and engineers shouted and pointed up at the spaceship, which slowed to hover in place above them.

Completely ignored, Rico carried Isabella deeper into the hangar bay towards another much smaller and battle-scarred spaceship that was showing no signs of life. A glance was enough for Isabella to tell the spaceship had seen more than a little tough love. Its hull was branded from one end to the other with so many pockmarks and plasma burns that Isabella expected it to fall apart if she even looked at it funny. The spaceship had six wings in all: two large fins at the rear and four smaller wings near the front, which poked out at uneven angles. What hull was visible beneath its battle scars revealed a chaos of components that looked like they had been cobbled together from every spacecraft imaginable. Isabella suspected the spaceship's distinct appearance could have been recreated by jumbling up a heap of plastic model airplane kits and gluing them together blindfolded. Its ramp lowered jerkily, shuddered to a halt only halfway open, then resumed its shaky descent onto the hangar's deck.

"Ignore the shuttle up there, this one's our way out," Rico reassured her.

Isabella found nothing reassuring about him, his plasma rifle or this battered spaceship. There was a high-pitched whine. An explosion rocked the hangar bay. That wasn't reassuring either. A claxon screamed and red lights strobed. Isabella peered through rows of spaceships. Bolts of green energy rained down from all four wings of the hovering shuttle, each green blast giving off the same whine as before.

Shrapnel and fire erupted along rows of spaceships as the green bolts struck home. Silhouettes of brown-clad engineers and people wearing the same black armour as Rico ran amidst the flames and dove for cover behind the nearest parked spaceships. The hovering spaceship dropped a wing and turned in a sweeping arc that sent it soaring through the shimmering energy barrier protecting the hangar bay from the vacuum of space. Pilots scampered towards their spaceship, detaching power lines and jumping into cockpits. Hot orange circles ignited as spaceship after spaceship took off in pursuit. Isabella dragged her eyes away. Everyone here wanted to kill her.

If we stay here, we're dead.

I know, I know.

Rico carried her up the ramp into the damaged spaceship whose ramp had descended so uncertainly for them. The ramp attempted to close with more than one false start until it was finally followed by a pressurised hiss and an overly dramatic burst of smoke as it sealed shut behind them.

"Sit," Rico ordered.

He dropped her onto one of the many stools bolted along the spaceship's interior. Her back slumped against the cold metal hull. She was exhausted. She shook her head at the universe she had woken up in and hoped desperately this was another screwed-up nightmare she was having in detention, and that she'd soon wake up with her head on the desk, drool on her chin and Miss Pilkington smiling disapprovingly. Then Lynch would say something cruel but funny, everyone would laugh at her, and maybe she'd give him another of those looks Paradise Moon had approved of so much.

Rico marched further into the small spaceship. At the end of the gangway, a woman with rainbow hair leapt out of the pilot's seat and wrapped her arms around him. A soldering iron tumbled from one of the many pockets that littered her baggy cargo pants. Bouncing off her tall boots, which were lined with more buckles than Isabella could count, it hit the floor with a clang.

"Easy, Ves!" Rico gasped. He escaped her hug and cupped her face in his hands. "I'm okay."

Ves glared at him with an intensity of love matched with rage, the frayed fabric of her top clinging to her as she withdrew her face from his hands and crossed her arms tightly. "What's wrong with you?" she demanded.

Rico shifted awkwardly. "I improvised. Why do you always make out like it's such a big deal?"

"Shooting all those people is a big deal!" She punched his arm hard enough to make Isabella nearly like her. "Don't worry, I've wiped the feeds," she added sharply. "No one will know it was you."

"Thanks, sis."

"Don't you dare thank me! You said you wouldn't kill anyone this time. We'd take the girl and get paid. No one gets hurt."

Rico held up his hands. "It's not my fault. Striker was there and it was too late to back out. She'd be dead if I hadn't acted so quickly."

Ves aimed a finger at him. "Stop solving every phyxing problem with that rifle!"

"I know, I know. But this time I didn't have a choice. Err, do you need to do something about that?"

In the cockpit, a row of lights was blinking erratically.

Ves threw herself into the pilot's chair. "It's just a comms alert," she snapped. "A patrol's hailing the decoy shuttle. Quiet!"

She flipped a switch. Static hissed through the cockpit.

"—will be fired upon. I'm terribly sorry about all this. Please acknowledge, over."

Ves leaned closer, flipping another switch as she spoke into the console. "Really? You're going to shoot down one of your own?"

Static hissed at her. "Look, this is your last chance. Please could you just power down or you will be treated as hostile."

Ves flipped another switch and the static disappeared along with the stranger's voice. She leaned back with a nervous grin. "Sounds like he bought it."

"Can't they trace the signal back here?" Rico asked.

Ves shook her head. "I'm running the signal through five different relays on *Nebula*, all bouncing it back via the decoy shuttle. Hence the static. It should look like transmission bleed. By the time they work out what really happened, we'll be long gone."

The blinking lights on her console went dark.

"Something wrong?"

Sighing, Ves swung her chair around and took Rico's hands in her own. "Everything's fine, please relax. The nav feed for the decoy shuttle cut out, that's all—they must have blasted the shuttle."

Rico stared at her gravely. "No way back now, sis."

"There was no way back when you killed the First Duke of Xarr." She raised her voice to make sure Isabella could hear. "You're fine. Keep your seat and buckle up. We'll fly out with the salvage team, then slip away before anyone notices. Don't worry."

Who's worried?

"Then what?" Isabella asked. "He said we're in deep space. Are you taking me home?"

Their rescuers exchanged glances.

Rico tried to answer, but Ves beat him to it. "We'll get you off-station, then drop you with someone who can take you the rest of the way," she explained.

Isabella studied her closely. "You mean the person who's paying you?"

Ves rearranged her face into an unconvincing imitation of confusion. "Paying us?"

"Yeah. You said you were supposed to take me and get paid."

Are you sure you want to do this? We're allowed to let them save us even if we don't trust them.

You don't know where they're going.

I know where they're leaving.

"Relax," Ves snapped. "Obviously, someone's bankrolling this rescue." Isabella couldn't help but glance at the nervous way Rico fiddled with his rifle as his sister spoke. "We won't get you there in one piece if we don't lift off-station now," she continued. "The salvage teams will be in flight any moment."

Every muscle is Isabella's body tensed, ready to make a break for the ramp.

Really? You want to escape the only people who don't want us dead?

Get off my back.

Do you have a plan?

Do you have an off switch?

Play it cool! We'll ditch them later. You and me—we've got this!

"This person who's paying you—can they get me home?" asked Isabella. She looked from brother to sister, their mouths searching for answers.

Oh boy, here we go.

"Can they get me home?" Isabella repeated.

"Of course," Ves replied. She flicked a few switches on the pilot's console with a sudden nonchalance that was hard to trust.

"They know how to get me home?" Isabella persisted.

"Sure," said brother and sister together.

They're lying.

So? Please don't spoil this for us. I'm trying so hard to keep you alive.

Levering herself up with her arm, Isabella clawed her way along the line of stools towards the ramp.

Rico closed the distance between them. "Everyone calm down," he ordered. He was still holding his rifle, only now he was ready to use it. "Everyone outside wants you dead, and we want you alive. We can all agree on that."

Please agree on that.

Behind Rico, Ves swore as another light flared awake on the console.

"Relax, sis," Rico called over his shoulder. "I got this!"

"No," she called back. "Someone's trying to get inside. They just typed in the door code."

"You didn't change it?"

"Of course I changed it!"

Rico flicked something on his rifle, Isabella guessed the safety. "Okay little lady, time's up. Step away from that hatch or I'll burn your last leg off. Don't think I won't."

Isabella glared back at him defiantly. "If you could afford to kill me, you wouldn't have saved me."

"I didn't say I'd kill you, I said I'd shoot you. It'll hurt." He aimed the rifle at Isabella's remaining leg. "Get away from that ramp!"

"They're not leaving!" Ves sang nervously from the cockpit.

"They'll kill you," Rico warned Isabella. "We won't. Now get over here."

Isabella didn't move towards Rico, but she didn't move towards the ramp either. Which fear would win the fight raging inside her, she didn't know. She was frozen and there was nothing she could do about it. She screamed at herself to move. To do something. Anything. But she didn't know what to do. Her churning stomach screamed back at her, while her aching leg and aching arm and aching head all screamed too.

Why am I always bailing you out?

Because you're always the reason I'm in trouble?

That's fair.

A whisper of purple glowed in Isabella's eyes. Paradise Moon studied Rico's perilous stare. This man was clearly unstable. Had their little adventure into space not literally cost Isabella an arm and a leg already, Paradise Moon would have taken full control of the girl's body there and then, dealt with these idiots and flown this craft herself. But the tools needed for that option had been taken by an avalanche of Sau Daran masonry.

You're gonna thank me for this one day.

Paradise Moon took the only option she could think of that wouldn't get the girl killed.

She surrendered.

CHAPTER TEN

The Upper Ring's main hangar bay was a mess of activity stained red by warning lights and shaking with earsplitting claxons. Having been almost emptied of ships, it was now filling with maintenance crews. Mechanics scurried back and forth, preparing to take care of the departed ships when they returned.

Ezra was sweating. Beauregard was wheezing. Fleur was alert. She noted with concern the emblems on the soldiers marching past. Some were fellow Rangers bearing the crest of the red fist, but even more wore a silver fist on their arm. That was bad. The Silver Fists were the Empress' finest shock troops, which meant they were also her meanest, nastiest soldiers. Over the cycles, Fleur's ship had hauled plenty of Silver Fists across countless planetary warzones, but pilot and cargo had not once seen eye to eye.

Nearing the back of the hangar, Fleur stopped outside her own ship. The scattering of ships that were left in the hangar either looked too damaged to fly or their pilots were late. Fleur's Vagabond-class ship ticked both boxes. Despite their urgency, Fleur smiled proudly. She always smiled at the sight of her battered ship. It had been a gift from her mad pirate of a father, given to her long before he had betrayed her and her crew to PROXUS. As much as she hated him for ruining her life, this ship was all she had left to remember the good times. The fun times. The times before PROXUS. Back when it had been them and the stars, along with galaxies of swagger and a lot of unnecessary property damage.

Beauregard wiped the sweat from his forehead. Fleur could tell that after their mad dash from Crazy Red's he was beginning to sober up. "You said she ain't been serviced since you got back," he reminded her doubtfully.

Punching her code into the keypad on her ship's locked door, Fleur scolded him with a glance. "My baby has never let us down."

"Pay attention!" Ezra urged.

Fleur frowned as the keypad flashed red instead of green. Her fingers blurred as she re-typed the code. Again, it flashed red.

"Fleur!" Ezra cried. "Concentrate! Whoever took the girl might leave this system any moment."

Fleur held up her hands innocently. "It is not me, honey. I know my own code."

Placing a heavy hand on Ezra's shoulder, Beauregard grimly held up his gauntlet. "Forget it. I'm sorry kid, it's over." Crimson lettering flashed across the gauntlet's holographic representation of Isabella's face: TARGET NEUTRALISED. Ezra collapsed against the big man, his tears stinging Beauregard's unclean vest as a bear paw awkwardly patted the young Apprentice Ranger's back. Fleur sucked in her lips and watched Ezra's tears fall. Tears for a friend who'd never return. Tears for a girl he'd never known.

Flicking a switch on her gauntlet, Fleur conjured a projection of purple light that shimmered into a rotating sleeve of symbols around her forearm. Her fingers danced over the projection as she tapped out the symbols. "When is the last time someone dared hack into a ship on the First Duke's battle station?" she mused.

"Never," replied Beauregard as he gave Ezra another heavy pat on the back.

Fleur's fingers swiped to spin the column of light around her arm faster, before tapping more symbols as she entered the next part of her shuttle's override code. "And who would be dumb enough to hack into my ship?"

"Someone with a death wish?" Beauregard suggested distractedly. His expression betrayed his inexperience in holding a crying man. He was starting to panic.

Fleur frowned. "But why risk it now when the whole battle station is already on alert?"

"Ain't no one gonna risk it unless they're desperate."

"Okay, but if you are desperate why hack into this old thing, beautiful as she is, when you are inside a hangar full of newer, shinier PROXUS fighters?"

"Ain't full no more."

"No," said Fleur, "it is not." Her eyes shifted to the middle distance as her mind raced to catch up with reality. "The funny thing is, I scheduled her for servicing and she has not been serviced. Yet am I on duty? I am not. Unlike almost every ship here, my baby was guaranteed to be left behind."

Beauregard's face went on a journey as he caught up. Not without relief, he lifted Ezra off him. "Don't never lose hope, kid."

When Fleur tapped the last symbol of light swirling around her forearm, the ramp released its pressure seal with a violent hiss. Groaning, the ramp shuddered towards the floor. She flicked the switch on her gauntlet again and the sleeve of light around her arm disappeared. "Sweetie," she purred, "shall we?"

When it came to drawing, Fleur had never met anyone faster than Beauregard. Before she could blink, one plasma pistol was ready at his hip and he was already tossing his second to her. Fleur caught the plasma pistol, checked the charge and flicked off the safety all in one smooth motion that ended with the pistol's barrel aimed through the widening gap as the ramp continued its shuddering descent.

Slower than usual, alcohol swimming behind his eyes, Ezra's hand dropped out of habit. But instead of holster leather and the butt of a plasma pistol, all the off-duty Apprentice Ranger grasped was air.

"Close it after us," Beauregard warned as a cluster of Silver Fists marched across the hangar towards them. "We ain't exactly been subtle."

Its gears screaming, the ramp was still valiantly trying to reach the deck when first Fleur and then Beauregard grabbed hold of the top lip of the ramp's aperture and swung inside. Less steadily, he heard Ezra haul after them with a grunt.

As she crept onto her own ship with her plasma pistol ready, Fleur found almost everything as she had left it. Almost everything. The floor-to-ceiling storage lockers that lined one wall were still shut. Fresh blood from today's mission was still smeared along the opposite wall above a dozen uncomfortable bolted-down stools, which led all the way to the cockpit. The cockpit's viewing window was still splintered where a plasma blast had struck it not half a rotation earlier. Everything was as Fleur had left it, except for the woman with rainbow hair and a body full of piercings lounging in Fleur's chair with her feet on Fleur's console.

Fleur aimed her pistol straight down the ship at the woman's face. "Get your dirty boots off my console."

Following closely, his pistol still ready at his hip, Beauregard hooked a thumb towards Fleur. "You know, she's shot people just for lookin' at her ship funny."

As though dragged by her outstretched plasma pistol, Fleur marched rapidly down her ship until the tip of her pistol pressed into the intruder's forehead. The intruder's neck bent back as Fleur pushed the barrel harder into the front of her skull.

"Oh, are we interrupting?" Fleur demanded with an unwelcoming smile. "You will have to excuse us for barging in, what with you in the middle of stealing my ship and all. Given you are not out there tearing a hole through vacuum in pursuit of a fugitive, or being pulverised by PROXUS plasma fire, and have instead hacked your way into this battered and bruised beauty of a ship, well—I have this funny feeling you can help us. You see, my friend is looking for this girl."

Twin shadows fell across the intruder's anxious face as Ezra and Beauregard loomed on either side of Fleur.

"There'll be more Rangers arrivin' shortly," Beauregard drawled. "We can tell 'em to get lost or come aboard. Your call. Not that it don't matter. We're all PROXUS. We're all on the same side, right?"

"Where is she?" Ezra demanded.

They all heard the squeal of a hinge behind them. Beauregard spun fastest—barely in time to see the man leap from an opening storage locker, the barrel of his plasma rifle swivelling.

"Don't!" cried the woman in the pilot's chair.

Two blasts echoed through the small ship.

His smoking mouth hanging open in disbelief, the man staggered back against the door of another storage locker. His plasma rifle clattered to the floor. Trembling, he dabbed at the burning hole in his throat. He stared at the blood pooling around his fingers, then collapsed.

"Murderer!" screamed the rainbow-haired woman. "You can—"

She was interrupted by a crash as Ezra hit the deck.

"Watch her!" Fleur cried, dropping to one knee beside Ezra. "Ez, are you okay?"

Beauregard's pistol swung towards the rainbow-haired woman. His blue eyes were cold, his face blank, his pistol ready to kill again. Without another word, she sank back into the pilot's chair.

Fleur reached under Ezra to help him up, but her hand came away bloody. She swore and tossed aside her pistol. Carefully, she used both hands to roll him onto his side.

"He alright?" Beauregard growled from the corner of his mouth. His eyes were pinned to the rainbow-haired intruder.

Fleur ignored him. She was more concerned by the smoking hole where Ezra's right lung was supposed to be. He coughed, spluttering up a shower of blood. Grabbing his shivering hands, she pressed them into the wound. "Push," she instructed.

Blinking back an affirmative, Ezra held his hands against the wound. Blood gushed against his palms, emptying through his fingers, spreading down his arms and legs, dribbling and ebbing across the deck.

Fleur was only gone for a heartbeat before landing back next to him and pressing the activation patch on the medpac she'd retrieved from one of the lockers. "Hands off," she ordered. As Ezra's hands left the wound, the sudden torrent of escaping blood was instantly stemmed by the medpac she had slapped across it.

Ezra screamed.

"It sounds like the medpac is working," Fleur said with relief.

Beneath the medpac's translucent green seal, which had formed a tight vacuum around the hole in Ezra's chest, Fleur knew only too well the cocktail of stimulants, regenerative nanites and adhesive gel being pumped into the wound. She doubted they would mix well with the alcohol in Ezra's system, but without them her friend would soon be no more alive than their attacker.

"What about my brother?" the rainbow-haired woman cried from the pilot's chair. "Do something!"

"His face was vapourised," said Beauregard humourlessly. "Ain't no medpac gonna fix that." He pointed his plasma pistol at the rest of the storage lockers. "They all loaded with dpresh?"

Her only answer was a gob of spit on his boot. "That was my brother," the woman snarled. "You can be phyxing sure you're following him."

Fleur sighed theatrically. "Today has been a long, exhausting rotation that was about to end with us in the worst bar on this station getting pissed with my two best friends because we can no longer get pissed with our third best friend ever again. Instead, here we are. Now, you just lost your brother, so I am going to try very hard not to kill you. Will I still shoot you multiple times and shove a medpac on before you die? Possibly. Or I may lose the last of my resolve and let you die. As I said, it has been a long rotation and I suggest you try to understand exactly how thin my patience is being stretched. I do not like my friends being shot. I do not like dirty little thieves stealing my baby. Right now, you are one lie away from me blowing a hole in your face big enough to pilot this ship through. Now, I think my friend had a question to ask before your dpresh brother shot him. Ez?"

Hunched over on the floor, Ezra spat out another mouthful of blood. Desperation mingled with the pain and sweat itching across his face. "Where's the girl?"

CHAPTER ELEVEN

When Isabella awoke, she was sitting in darkness. Her hand reached out instinctively for her surroundings. Immediately, she hit a metal wall. Hard. She ushered her stinging knuckles into her chest. Rico and Ves were shouting at each other, but their voices were muffled. She was inside one of the spaceship's lockers. Reaching out again, this time more carefully, her fingers closed around a box of metal on what she imagined was the locker door. Unless Paradise Moon could shoot lasers from her eyes, she'd have to wait for someone outside to open it.

Isabella wrapped her only arm around her bent leg and hugged it into her chest, her chin resting on her knee. It wasn't only the darkness that sent fear crawling down her spine like a stream of tiny icicles. It was the terrifying closeness of the walls. Everything was too close. Like being buried alive inside a metal coffin.

Paradise Moon said nothing.

Isabella said nothing back.

Later—although she couldn't imagine how much later from inside this ad hoc sensory deprivation chamber—muffled through the door she heard a double whine of energy not unlike earlier when Rico had shot everyone. Her heart skipped more beats faster than she could count. She held her breath. She was too scared to move. Too scared to breathe. Too scared to imagine what was happening on the other side of the door.

When the locker opened, the first thing Isabella saw was blood—*why was there always blood?*—on the deck. Sat in the blood was a stranger. He was not much older than her. She stared at his face. And at the blood. It was smeared into his earnest expression. Into the curls of dark sweaty hair he was easing a nervous hand through. On his shirt, too—mainly around a green package stuck to his chest. The green package was cruelly transparent, revealing more human anatomy and yet more—*more!*—blood than Isabella ever wanted to see. Blood was everywhere. *Could it really all be blood?* Surely, he had made an almighty mess opening a bottle of ketchup. Despite all the red stuff, he was smiling.

"You're alive," Ketchup told her. She was grateful for the confirmation.

He smiled, his face lost somewhere between relief and disbelief. Isabella wasn't smiling. Warily, she poked her head out of the locker. A dazzlingly beautiful woman wearing the finest boots Isabella had ever seen leaned beside an old man in a filthy vest. Even this far away, he stank of the same strong booze she would always associate with her poor excuse for a dad. She even recognised the way his craggy face was reluctantly negotiating an incoming hangover. That was his problem—hers was that both Hangover and Boots were holding pistols. Behind them, Ves sat stiffly in the pilot's chair. Her expression was fraught.

"Let that patrol in and get me to a med bay," said Ketchup. He chuckled morbidly. A mouthful of red stuff escaped. "We did it."

"That ain't the dumbest thing you've said tonight," Hangover growled as he stalked towards the ramp. "But we ain't goin' back to Crazy Red's. I need the good stuff."

Isabella wanted to shout, she wanted to scream—she had to warn them.

Take a breath.

They can't let anyone in.

You don't even know who's on the other side of that door.

They'll take me.

Breathe now, panic later.

I don't want them to take me.

Breathe or you're going to suffocate.

They'll cut me open.

They tried that and we're still alive. Come on, you got this.

Isabella's first, shallow breath in too long eased her dizziness. Steadying herself against the locker's rim, she crawled out and opened her mouth to warn them. Then Isabella noticed Rico's smouldering corpse and had to gulp even more oxygen to stay upright.

Well, that's one less thing to worry about.

Isabella scurried backwards, but she was clumsy on one knee and one hand. Her foot slipped across more blood and she fell into a locker door. The impact stung the healed stump below her shoulder. Pinned against the cold, hard metal, she stared across the deck at what remained of Rico's face.

It took the mechanical groan of the ship's ramp lowering to stop Isabella from staring. Escaping the vacant tracts of her mind, the blood-stained metal of the ship's interior clawed itself back into focus from the fringes of her vision.

"It's okay," Ketchup assured her. "We're all on your side."

Five soldiers marched inside the spaceship. They were faceless, their humanity obscured behind helmets, their rifles ready and their armour as heavy and dark as Rico's—and all the bodies he had left behind.

Hangover punched one of the newcomers playfully on their armoured shoulder, which bore a silver fist. "There you go, she's safe as you like!" he drawled. "Buy us a drink later, pal. We'll be in the Upper Ring."

The soldier's helmet, which was far from subtle for someone who had seen as little body armour as Isabella had, only exaggerated the movement as their gaze came to rest on where Hangover had punched their shoulder.

"We'll take it from here," another soldier instructed, emotionless behind the helmet's static. Instead of a silver fist like the other four soldiers, this one had a silver star inscribed on their armour. Slinging their rifle over one shoulder, Silver Star lazily rested a gloved hand on the butt of their holstered pistol.

Peering through Silver Star's armoured legs, Isabella glimpsed Ketchup smiling at her. He was still on the floor. Not without a shortness of breath, he raised a hand. "At least let us call this one in. We've earned that much. We're the ones who saved her."

"You're forgetting protocol," said Silver Star. They pointed at Rico's corpse. "He murdered First Duke Striker. Let us fulfill his warrant and we'll be out of your hair." Silver Star pointed at Isabella. "Restrain her."

"Restrain her?" echoed Ketchup. "She's injured! Look at her! Can't you see she's scared?"

"She's an escaped prisoner." Silver Star paused, their hand still resting on the butt of their pistol. "Is there a problem?"

"No problem," said Boots. She knelt in front of Isabella, so her body was between the girl and everyone else, then put a comforting hand on Isabella's shoulder.

77

"You will be fine, honey," she promised. "Everyone is going to look after you."

"Get up," Silver Star instructed Isabella.

Isabella didn't move, but she did glare at the faceless visor looming over her.

"She's not a prisoner," Ketchup corrected with more than a little venom. "Can't you see she's been through enough? Don't restrain her, just be careful with her. The ceiling almost crushed us, for Empress' sake! Look at her! She doesn't need your famous rough-handed Silver Fist hospitality. She needs a medic."

Embers of purple glowed amongst the chestnut in Isabella's eyes.

That's him!

Who?

Him.

Him?

So, I don't want to be the god who cried wolf and all that, but I'm telling you—it's definitely him! He pulled us out of the rubble.

The ghost of a memory that wasn't her own rose inside Isabella. As the purple glow had begun to fade from her eyes and darkness had surrounded her along with pain and fire, Ketchup had been there. He had held her. Paradise Moon had seen his face.

He saved us.

"Please, don't let them take me," Isabella begged Ketchup. He had been there for her in the darkness and he was here again now. "They'll kill me!" she pleaded.

"We don't have time for this," said Silver Star.

"The fat man tried to kill me!" Isabella tried again.

"It's true," Ves added stonily. She was still slumped in the pilot's chair. "My brother said Striker was ready to cut her open. He saved the girl's life. Before this lot murdered him."

78

"Striker?" spat Ketchup. "Phyx him then!"

"Careful, boy," warned Silver Star, before aiming a gloved finger at Ves. "Get that dirty bounty hunter out of my sight."

Two soldiers hauled Ves from the pilot's chair and dragged her towards the ramp. Isabella watched, her body tensing. She was ready to fight, to escape, but there was little hope. With their rifles poised, the remaining pair of soldiers still flanked Silver Star.

Coughing up another mouthful of something ugly, Ketchup hauled himself all the way up the side of the hull until he was on his feet. His desperation was reflected in Silver Star's tinted helmet. "Will she be safe?" he asked.

"I have my orders," came the static-filled reply.

Isabella looked between Ketchup above her and Boots kneeling beside her. "They'll kill me," Isabella whispered with shy, embarrassing inevitability.

"Just tell us the girl's safe," Ketchup insisted. "No one harms her. That's all we want to hear."

Another hiss of static. "I don't care what you want. Step aside."

With a sigh, Boots pinched the bridge of her nose and grimaced. "Ez, let it go," she said. But Isabella watched as her other hand discreetly retrieved her pistol from the deck, keeping it hidden behind her body from everyone except Isabella.

At the edge of her vision, the two soldiers at the top of the ramp were lingering with Ves as they watched the exchange unfold.

With a tilt of their helmet, Silver Star examined the desperation on Ketchup's face. "I appreciate we Silver Fists have a hard reputation, but I'm not unreasonable." Static hissed. "You're off-duty and this is a restricted area. That's against protocol. I'll leave it out of my report because you did a good job restraining the bounty

79

hunters and locating the prisoner. Calm down and let us take it from here. I don't want to arrest you."

Petrified, Isabella looked up at Ketchup. But instead of stepping aside, he grabbed Silver Star's armoured forearm, whose gloved hand tightened around the grip of their holstered pistol.

"Just promise you'll look after her. That's all."

"Let go." Even through their helmet's static, Isabella could hear the clipped staccato of every irritated syllable. "I have my orders."

"You're not going to harm her," Ketchup insisted. "She's a child!"

Silver Star tilted their helmet at the soldiers on either side of her. Instantly, their rifles were aimed at Ketchup. "Stand aside or be moved aside." More static. "The girl is coming with us."

"Would y'all calm down," Hangover suggested wearily. But his voice wasn't where it should have been. He was in the middle of the gangway, halfway between the two groups of soldiers. Isabella hadn't heard him move. "We saved the girl. Ain't we heroes now?"

"That is what you wanted, right, Ez?" Boots asked carefully and deliberately. "To save the girl?"

Ketchup looked into Isabella's purple and chestnut eyes. "They'll kill her," he said. He swallowed hard, then nodded sadly. "Nothing else matters," he added quietly.

Isabella didn't see who drew first.

Red blasts erupted throughout the spaceship's interior in a flurry of wild explosions.

Then it was over.

Their armour charred and smoking, two soldiers collapsed on either side of Boots, whose body was shielding Isabella so closely that the girl could feel the heat from the woman's pistol warming her cheek. Another two soldiers lay beside the ramp—frozen between them, the nervous statue of Ves. Silver Star was propped up against Ketchup, who was living up to his nickname even more than ever. His hand was wrapped around Silver Star's, which was wrapped around their own pistol. Its muzzle was still pressed into the burning hole in Silver Star's stomach.

Hangover twirled his pistol and spun it into one of his thigh holsters whilst muttering curses so foul that, even though she didn't recognise them, Isabella easily understood his meaning. "What did we just do?" he demanded.

"That is a conversation for another time," suggested Boots. "Perhaps when we are not running for our lives?" She sprung upright. "Ves, trouble yourself with getting that ramp closed." Boots leapt into the pilot's chair. In a blur of precise movements, she flicked every switch on the console. "Beauregard, up here with me. Ezra, please check this young lady is not going to die."

Isabella stared at Ketchup. At Ezra. He stepped tentatively towards her. Frowning, he opened his mouth to say something. Then, shuddering, he remembered the bodies surrounding them on the gangway.

"We should leave their bodies behind," Ezra mumbled. "For their families."

The one who Boots had called Beauregard creased up his face as he eased past Ezra. "Ain't no time to do right by them, kid," he said grimly. "If we don't get outta here fast, they'll get a free cremation anyway."

"Everyone stay quiet if you want to live," Boots instructed. She flicked another switch. "Control, this is Fleur Fontaine on transport V-66-79. We request immediate launch for transit planet-side. Transmitting launch codes now."

"V-66-79, this is Control. These launch codes have expired. Our log shows V-66-79 is scheduled for post-mission servicing. Please confirm."

"Affirmative, Control. But the captain is getting an itchy trigger finger down on the surface. He is worried the Sau Darans will return and so he asked me to ship down more supplies."

The comm went dead. As Fleur waited patiently, Beauregard slid into the co-pilot's chair. His cold eyes were quick to glance back over his shoulder and scrutinise Ves as she worked the ramp controls. Behind them, the ramp hissed shut. Distractedly helping Isabella onto one of the bolted-down stools, Ezra watched in hushed apprehension.

"This is Control. We have no record of any amendment to your mission. Launch is not authorised. Power down your engines."

For the first time since she had taken command of the situation, Fleur looked worried. "Come on, Control. The captain is an old friend of mine. Honestly, I feel for him. They must be too busy with the clean-up operation to update their logs, but he really needs these supplies."

"V-66-79, we have no record of this request. Confirm your cargo."

Beauregard cleared his throat, his face blank. "Uhhh, big guns?"

This prompted Fleur to wave universal sign language for what-are-you-doing? at him.

"V-66-79, please repeat. We didn't quite get that."

"Big guns," repeated Beauregard with a growing, unwarranted confidence that wasn't out of place alongside the stench of booze.

Fleur glared, her lips silently mouthing: stop helping.

Beauregard leaned closer to the comm system, as though proximity to the mic might somehow help. "Uhh.

Yeah. Very, very big guns. Huge. For the captain. He, uhh, he really needs his big guns, I guess. Would hate for anythin' to happen to him if we didn't get these, uhh… big… guns… to him… Over?"

Open-mouthed, Fleur stared at Beauregard in despair. He gave her a confident nod. The rest of the ship waited in silence.

"This is Control. I know how he feels—those Sau Darans are total monsters. We'll all be better off when they're gone for good. I have amended your mission log. Launch approved."

"Copy that, Control. Two lit, all systems green." Fleur flicked off the comm and glanced at the rest of them. "Okay, we are getting out of here slowly and gently and no one is going to shoot us."

"Yeah? How long's that gonna last?" asked Beauregard.

Fleur lifted the spaceship off the hangar bay floor. "Probably until Control realises we are not heading towards that planet. Everyone, buckle up!"

CHAPTER TWELVE

S triker's eyes burst open to find frosted glass blurring into focus so close it almost kissed his lips. The cramped cloning pod was barely larger than he was, its intimate interior dominated by the vast web of I.V. drips and electrodes peppering his enormous body. Then he remembered. The hot pain of being shot by a plasma rifle in the gut. His face cracking against the floor of the med bay. His irritated, broken breathing. After that, there had been nothing.

He had been dead.

It was hard to be certain of anything when his memories were still settling in the body of a new clone, but he suspected he liked waking up afterwards even less than the dying bit. He remembered, when he had been swimming as a child in the Great Ocean on his distant home world, startling a shoal of fish that had scattered in a thousand directions, and he wondered if this was his brain telling him how it felt now. Startled. Scattered. His memories were still with him, but he had to swim against the tide to grasp them. Whilst the disorientation of waking up in a new body was never easy, he felt it must have been worse for someone like him—someone who was used to such masterful command over his own mind. Mercifully, dying was still a new experience for him. He had only died once before, which was his little secret, and he wasn't keen on practising enough to become better at it.

Inside the cramped confines of the cloning pod, Striker stared at his hands. Like the rest of the naked body he was wearing, these hands were remarkably identical to the hands he had seen whilst washing in the anti-bacterial cleansing unit on the morning of his death. Yet these were also stranger's hands. They were his and they were not his, because the hands of his previous clone were with the rest of his dead body. Even his brain, or at least the brain he had been wearing earlier, was gone. Its contents, though, had been saved and digitally backed up by his neural implant before being beamed to a secure location on *Black Nebula*. Everything that made Striker who he was—every neuron he had ever fired, every scheme he had ever fashioned, every memory he had ever forged—had been imprinted onto this clone the moment Striker's body hit the deck of the med bay.

"Welcome back, First Duke," intoned a solemn voice in his inner ear, courtesy of this new body's neural implant.

"Get this pod open," Striker ordered. His speech was a little fuzzy as his brain continued to wake up. "How long ago did I die?"

"Only moments ago, First Duke."

Despite his brain fog, Striker frowned. That wasn't right. The imprinting process had taken a whole rotation last time he died. But his aching head didn't have time to think about it now. There was a girl to catch—along with the Sau Daran parasite hiding inside her. Of course, there was also the small matter of his murder. A problem he would take great pleasure in solving.

"You may step out of the pod," droned the disembodied voice.

Prompted by an overly dramatic flourish of hissing smoke, the pod's glass front slid open. One after another, wires and tubes unplugged themselves from his body with a cascade of rubbery pops and clicks that his body was too numb to feel.

Striker took a calming breath, reminded himself exactly who he was and stepped confidently out of the cloning pod.

But the long, thin room into which Striker stepped was not the familiar cloning bay his agents had secretly installed on *Black Nebula*—this was not where he had woken up last time he had died. Instead, above the mist that swirled around him, ice encrusted pipes stretched down a tunnel to a grey door in the distance. The walls were lined with upright pods identical to the one he had stepped out of. The glass fronts of the nearest pods were frosted over, much like his own, with smudges of human shadow barely visible within. The tunnel felt like a morgue, although Striker supposed it was the opposite.

"In your own time, First Duke." There was now an impatient edge to the voice.

"Quiet," warned Striker as his eyes scanned the unfamiliar tunnel. Rapidly, his brain fog was receding as every nerve in his body was sharpened by raw survival instinct. He was beginning to piece together why the imprinting process had happened much faster this time. He hoped he was wrong.

"First Duke?"

"Wait," he replied testily, "I just died."

"Very well. Shall I inform the Empress that she is to wait too?"

"The Empress?" snapped Striker.

"She awaits," the solemn voice replied, before ominously adding, "in person."

In all the Known Galaxies, the Empress was the last person he wanted to see immediately after dying. Immediately after his failure.

"This is Xarr?"

"Welcome back, First Duke."

Striker's naked body shivered, but not because of the cold. Despite all the spies he had dispatched across the Known Galaxies, it was a surprise the Empress had stolen his DNA and grown her own clone of him on Xarr. He had no idea how she could have intercepted his dead body's neural update before it reached his own cloning pod on *Black Nebula*. He peered down the tunnel at all the pods. He certainly hadn't known she kept clones of anyone other than herself on Xarr, let alone so many.

"Should I tell the Empress to wait?"

Striker sighed. *Only if I want to die twice in one rotation*, he thought. "No. Just give me a moment."

"Don't worry, First Duke," said the voice that had greeted him with such solemnity. "You will soon adjust to your clone. If I may be so bold, I would suggest—"

With the briefest of thoughts, Striker closed the comm channel in his neural implant. It was helpful to know the neural implant in this body worked as intuitively as the implant in his previous body. Breathing in welcome silence, he found the controls to shut the glass front of his pod before proceeding along the tunnel. The grey door slid open at another brief command from his neural implant.

On the other side, a more suitable measure of comfort greeted him. It was warm, not to mention beautifully decorated with swirls of vibrant colour flooding through its richly carpeted floor and arched ceiling. With the exception of its two exits, this antechamber was walled exclusively with grand wardrobes. Striker rated this a significant upgrade from the clones he had left chilling in the tunnel. As the door hissed shut behind him, its back revealed a full-length mirror that Striker immediately put to use. He had always been big and it had never bothered him. His body had only one purpose, which was to transport his brain wherever he needed it. What he observed in the mirror now was entirely faithful to his body on *Black Nebula*, except for two noticeable differences. Firstly, the fresh puncture marks where Empress-knew-what had been pumped into his new body in the cloning pod. Secondly, this body wasn't dead. Under the circumstances, that was good enough for Striker, who would have preferred to be on *Black Nebula* but was smart enough to be grateful he was anywhere.

Still naked, he made a mental note of all the unique codes on the wardrobe doors so he could trace the identities of everyone the Empress was cloning. When he was satisfied he would recall them all, he located the wardrobe labelled with his own unique code and ran his eyes over the vacuum-sealed pouches inside, each containing the formal robes befitting a First Duke. His eyes settled over a fine set of blue robes embroidered with an ornate panel across the shoulders depicting a crashing blue wave.

As he dressed, he mentally re-activated his comm and raised a channel with his most trusted aide on *Black Nebula*. "This is Striker. What is the status of the girl?"

There was an uncharacteristic pause at the other end of the comm channel. The corner of Striker's mouth bent into a smile as he imagined the succession of heart attacks and hysterical interrogatives traversing the command bridge on *Black Nebula*.

"First Duke!" came a tremulous reply over his comm. "We are so *delighted* you're alive."

"Never presume otherwise, Colonel," ordered Striker, with only a hint of menace. "Tell me about the girl. Rest assured this is a secure channel."

"Escaped, First Duke. She won't get far. Her collaborators were two Rangers and one Apprentice Ranger assigned to *Nebula*, as well as two stowaways we have identified as bounty hunters."

"Send me the dossiers for all PROXUS personnel who aided the escape, along with a detailed analysis of the Sau Daran portal technology we uncovered on the planet. Who is in command?"

"Imperator Grave has assumed command of *Nebula*, First Duke. He is leading the pursuit."

Striker suppressed a snarl when he heard the name. It was bad enough sharing his battle station with the man, let alone leaving him in charge. Imperator Grave was the reason for Striker's first death, although once the successful assassin had been terminated by Striker's agents that left Striker as the only person alive who could have possibly known. Had the imperator realised how successful his assassination attempt had been, Striker had no doubt the man's company would have become even more insufferable.

"Who is in command?" Striker repeated more firmly.

"You are, of course, First Duke."

"Good. Remind the crew of this and prepare for my return."

Striker disconnected his comm. Wearing both the correct robes and the correct body, he strode out of the antechamber. He was ready to meet the Empress.

Despite their high altitude, Striker saw little of Xarr on his shuttle ride over its capital. The city, along with much of the planet, was obscured by impenetrable smog. He never saw the pilot tasked with navigating such conditions either, as when Striker boarded the tiny shuttle the pilot was already powering up the engines from the privacy of their enclosed cockpit. The shuttle's passenger compartment was barely large enough to house a single comfortable chair, on which someone had placed a slim metal wristband. The device was even thinner than the decorative jewellery Striker usually wore, which meant it had cost the Empress an extortionate amount of points.

Reclining in his chair, Striker snapped the device around his wrist, activated its holographic display and logged into his account. Quickly, he scrolled through everything PROXUS knew about the escaped ship's inhabitants, especially Ezra Knight. A pity such a promising Apprentice Ranger turned out to be nothing more than a point-hungry traitor. When he was done, he sent an encrypted order to his best agents on Xarr to break into the cloning facility he had just left. For all he knew, the Empress had only revived him so she could have the pleasure of executing him for his failure. If he was going to die at her hand, he wanted to be certain he would not only wake up afterwards, but that he would wake up in a clone on his beloved *Black Nebula*. Depending on how much danger he was in, his operatives may have to move quickly to make this happen.

Striker swept the holographic display closed and glanced out of the viewport. Occasionally, the colossal spires of Xarr's skyscrapers, which were tall enough to reach where sky became space, loomed into view almost close enough for Striker to touch. Mostly, however, his short flight was characterised by ominous black clouds that flooded the viewport, crackled with pink lightning and swelled with acidic pockets of green vapour. If Xarr's monstrous skyscrapers were renowned, then its pollution was infamous. Xarr had been an intergalactic superpower long before his Empress had taken the Sau Daran's clean energy technology. By then, the planet's scars were too deep to heal.

Even after the shuttle began its descent, Striker still couldn't see the landing pad through the smog. One moment they were flying, the next he was aware of a grey wall next to the shuttle's viewport. He waited patiently as the shuttle drifted downwards. Eventually, it found the floor of the docking shaft with a gentle bump.

There was a delay as Striker waited for any noxious fumes that had crept inside the docking shaft to be expelled, before the solemn voice resurfaced in his ear. "You may exit the shuttle, First Duke."

Striker activated the door release via his neural implant and waited for the ramp to hit the concrete floor. It was a long time since he had left the Outer Rim and visited the Empress, and with good reason. This was a visit no one undertook without an invitation and from which some never returned.

He stepped off the ramp and onto the landing pad. The docking shaft stretched far above him, rising past the shuttle's top fin and up until it was eventually lost in shadow. If the Empress wanted to surprise Striker with a painful death as punishment for his failure, all she had to do now was re-open the roof of the shaft and let Xarr's polluted atmosphere do her dirty work for her.

He rode the star lift in silence. First horizontally along a deep shaft, then up to the Empress' private control room. In that silence, Striker counted off all the precious jewels of information he might share with the Empress—and those he would hoard. When he had finished counting, the two lists appeared relatively balanced. Yet still the star lift did not slow. It was a long ride to the top.

The star lift emerged from an opening in the floor at the centre of a giant globe of holographic light. As soon as Striker stepped out of the star lift, his transport couldn't wait to abandon him. He watched it descend through the hole in the floor, leaving him surrounded by spiralling rings of bright holographic displays.

Striker ventured as far as the inner ring's holographic displays, his heels clicking across a hard floor that had been steralised with the same standard issue, pristine PROXUS white as the rest of the control room. Encircling the inner ring was an even grander outer spiral of holographic displays, which stretched around and above and below Striker until they reached the top and bottom of the globe. The result was dazzling illumination coiled around the entire perimeter of the globe like a radiant digital serpent. Although many of the displays were too far away to read, he could imagine the priceless data each screen contained. Accompanying this spiral of holograms was a spiralling walkway that spanned the entire globe. All those steps looked exhausting to Striker—when the Empress' private control room was finally his to command, the first thing to go would have to be all those steps.

The walkway above him obscured much of the Empress' body as she descended the spiral. Had Striker been a stranger to this unique room or had it not been his professional duty to know more than whoever occupied the same room as him, he could easily have been surprised by her silent arrival. But he was ready for her. At first, all he saw coming down the steps was a pair of bare, wrinkled feet at the conclusion of her tightly trousered legs. It was a sight few were ever graced with. For that reason alone, this sight—and the prestige it signalled—was something he coveted. Truthfully, he worshipped every molecule of his terrifying Empress. It saddened him that eventually it would be time for him to end her reign and take her power for himself.

The rest of her was coming into view. Her antique body was no less athletic than it had been during the war. Such were the wonders of PROXUS medicine for those who could afford the best in the Known Galaxies. If this was even her original body. Striker had seen reports of how cloning technology could enhance as well as copy. She looked no different than she had over half a lifetime ago. Her white uniform with black trim still fitted stylishly around her slim figure. It bore the insignia of Empress, a non-existent rank before she had become a war hero who led the hub worlds to victory against the Sau Darans and then seized power for herself. He could still imagine her plasma pistol blazing as she led assault after assault onto the Sau Darans' living ships while he did the much more important job of strategically directing their forces.

Her last steps down the walkway revealed her face. It was ancient and twisted, like gnarled bark, from which poked a crooked, bulbous nose. Almost all the hair that framed her face was white, except for one rebellious strip of burnt amber. It clung to her scalp, a streak of blood in a curtain of spent ash, before falling with the rest of her hair all the way to her shoulders.

The Empress stopped just short of the steps that connected her spiralling walkway with Striker's inner circle of holographic displays. "Admiral, there are still refugees in Xarr's largest spaceport. Remove them."

Striker waited patiently as the Empress listened to her own neural implant.

"I didn't ask why they were there. What do you think our mining colonies are for? Make your arrests and put them to work." There was a miniscule pause as she listened to the reply before cutting it off. "Then begin executing refugees above the optimal age for manual labour until they comply."

The Empress' eyes settled on Striker. Sharper than any laser, her eyes cut through his carefully composed expression as she searched for his soul. He hoped desperately she didn't find it. Luckily, Striker prided himself on having an excellent poker face, although he kept this hidden because he had an excellent poker face. Her hands were clasped neatly in the small of her back, her posture perfectly upright. "First Duke," remarked the Empress, "I hear you've been dying to see me."

Striker smiled at her joke and bowed his head. "I failed. It happens sometimes." He raised his head and let his face adopt a more severe expression. "Even to me."

"Don't make it a habit. There's a limit to how many clones I'm willing to grow for you. This may be your first and only resurrection."

Pleased to hear his cloning bay on *Black Nebula* had gone unnoticed, Striker maintained his poker face. "Trust that I shall put my second chance to good use retrieving this girl, for the good of PROXUS." Bathed in humility, Striker threaded his hands together in front of his stomach and bowed his head again. "My battle station is ready for my return."

"Then *my* battle station will have to wait, just as I waited for your arrival. It would take even a heavy cruiser forty rotations to transport you to the Outer Rim. With all these rebellions, my navy doesn't have the resources to spare."

"Empress, forgive me, but Xarr's shipyard manifest has a recently constructed capital ship designed to make such journeys in half that time."

Even the Empress couldn't conceal her surprise. "Where did you hear that?"

Striker smiled. "I am reliably informed that your new flagship has all its essential systems functioning. A skeleton crew could have it flying before the end of this rotation."

"Is this girl really that valuable?"

"She is to the Sau Darans. Shortly after we took her aboard *Black Nebula*, an astronomical bounty was placed on her."

"Sau Darans don't place bounties."

"No, but they manipulated the points in private accounts to fund human rebellions against us during the war. They are not incapable of placing a bounty in an indirect manner." Striker paused for effect. "It would seem our enemy is less dead than we believed."

"Indeed," the Empress replied, pinning him with an irritated expression that threatened to make his skin crawl if he let it. "There's a lot of that going around. In response, you placed an even larger bounty on the girl. Don't you ever worry of overstepping your bounds, First Duke?"

"The Sau Darans opened two portals in the Outer Rim knowing that doing so risked one of their last surviving outposts."

The Empress gestured with both hands at the holographic displays surrounding them. "Don't lecture me on facts, First Duke."

"Then forgive me, but you must appreciate the girl's value. Based on the risks taken by the Sau Darans, they clearly do. There is a Sau Daran parasite inside her." Striker did not need to add that the Sau Daran parasites they had captured during the war and broken down on a molecular level were now powering every planet and ship in PROXUS. "That's a lot of clean energy hiding inside one little girl, Empress. It would be easier to trace her if I were to return to *Nebula*."

"You will remain on Xarr until I am satisfied I can trust you," ordered the Empress, scrutinising him with another forensic eye. "I have heard disturbing rumours concerning your loyalty."

Striker kept calm. If the Empress knew the full extent of his betrayal, he would still be dead. "Empress, I am our best chance of finding that girl."

"Imperator Grave will lead the hunt for the girl."

"Grave? The man's a dpresh."

"He's an imperator," replied the Empress frostily.

"Very well, Empress. He's an important dpresh."

The Empress' expression thawed in the direction of a terrifying smile. "Then serve me better."

It took all Striker's considerable talents to conceal his disbelief, and even greater control of his new body to suppress the avalanche of frustration that quickly followed. "What are my orders, Empress?" he asked with apparent effortlessness.

"I sent you into deep space to destroy the few Sau Daran threats we didn't wipe out during the war, along with whatever pirates and rebels survive that far from civilised society. Your discovery and elimination of a Sau Daran outpost was pleasing, but as you are so keen to remind me, First Duke, the girl is of immeasurable value. And you let her escape." Striker listened in dutiful silence. There were other battles to fight—ones he was more likely to win. "I have warned you before, First Duke, but I shall not do so again. Our strength relies on our energy, as does the Sau Darans'. Because of you, they may already have one of the most powerful energy sources in the Known Galaxies not under PROXUS control."

"Empress, everything I have done has been for the glory of PROXUS," Striker replied with what sounded like credible honesty.

"Life can be taken much more easily than it can be granted," the Empress warned.

"Of course, Empress, of course. Although may I confide something in you?"

The Empress arched an eyebrow. "That is literally what I pay you for."

"I live to serve, Empress."

"I wasn't questioning your service, First Duke, merely whom you serve."

Dismissing her doubts over his loyalty by pretending she had never expressed them, Striker paused to adopt more concern into his expression. "The number of pirates and anti-PROXUS insurgents in deep space grows at a rapid pace."

The Empress' expression grew no warmer. "And you continue to list your own failures because…?"

"Well, let me be frank. All evidence suggests the rebellions will worsen. We are a victim of our own success. We have conquered so many systems that your navy is spread too thinly. Eventually, we will not be able to maintain control of all your territories—some planets will inevitably be more vulnerable than others."

"This is well known to me. You have a solution?"

"Not yet, Empress. But I was alarmed to hear that Imperator Grave wishes to re-deploy all our Outer Rim forces to hunting pirates and rebels, instead of finding and eliminating the last Sau Daran survivors. I fear he lacks perspective."

"Imperator Grave did not let a girl escape from his battle station. You are the one who is on trial, not him."

"My life belongs to PROXUS," Striker assured her with no hint of deception or manipulation, for they were well hidden. "I *am* PROXUS. And unlike our dear Imperator Grave, I remain alert to the threat posed by a Sau Daran resurgence. Pirates and rebels may enjoy their victories at our expense, but they are only human. The Sau Darans, however, have technology far beyond ours. Without me to command our Outer Rim forces, I fear for the future of PROXUS. But if I were to return to *Nebula*—"

"No," the Empress replied icily. "You've been too distracted in the Outer Rim. You will remain on Xarr. Imperator Grave can find the girl—such a task cannot wait, whether its twenty rotations or forty. Return to me when your network of spies has dismantled these rebellions instead of letting them fester."

The Empress spun away, the star lift rose and Striker was faced with a choice between retreating across the inner circle of holographic displays and back into the star lift, or standing his ground in defiance of his Empress.

With the deepest of bows, Striker made the easiest decision he had ever made in this body's brief lifetime and stepped onto the star lift. A much harder decision had already been made during their conversation. Now he had lost the Empress' trust, leaving Xarr would be impossible without betraying her. And his Empress would never forgive a betrayal, no matter what his motives were.

The Empress would have to die sooner than he had originally planned.

CHAPTER THIRTEEN

Hoping her exhaustion was hidden better than her aching muscles suggested, Fleur punched in another set of coordinates and engaged her shuttle's star drive again. The viewscreen in front of her flashed once more from stars—suddenly—to burning light—suddenly—to darkness, as they left normal space and launched yet another star leap enroute to yet another system. Even if PROXUS analysed the trajectory of their first star leap to escape the battle station, it was impossible for any pursuers to predict their final destination without having observed each new exit vector of all their subsequent leaps.

Fleur glanced behind her to check on the prisoner. Beauregard had cleared the deck of any stray weapons and bodies, all of which he had sealed in the lockers. The only item that hadn't been locked away was a pair of restraints he had borrowed from the Silver Fist's captain, who had no need of them after Ezra had been forced to take her down. These Fleur had re-coded and locked tightly around Ves' wrists, with the leg of a stool in the middle of the circuit formed by the restraints and her arms. Ves sat on the floor, hunched over in her manacles, stewing in her own rage.

"You got folks waiting for you back home?" Ezra asked. He was sitting next to Isabella on the furthest stool from Ves.

Beyond tired, Isabella smiled sadly. "My mum."

"Well, that's more than any of us," he conceded.

"Hey, we are your family now. You know that," Fleur reminded him. She glanced at Beauregard for support, but he was asleep in the co-pilot's chair beside her. After listening to how Isabella had ended up on a PROXUS battle station, he had announced that as a newly declared enemy of PROXUS he needed all the rest he could get before someone caught up with them and started shooting. He had been lounging horizontal ever since.

Ezra smiled. "Don't worry," he reassured the girl, "we'll get you home. Talking of which, I meant to ask…" He trailed off as his hand dug into one of his pockets and pulled out something too small to see. "Is this yours?"

Despite everything that had happened, Isabella's face lit up a fraction. "Where did you find that?"

Whatever it was, Ezra offered it to her. "You had it at the outpost during the attack. Sorry, it got a bit melted."

Isabella took a small, twisted lump of golden synthetic material from him. Fleur could have sworn an animal's face flashed across its surface as Isabella rocked it back and forth between her fingers. However, Isabella didn't play with the golden lump for long. As on edge as everyone was, they were all exhausted. A weary silence descended as they ate, then sleep took Ezra and Isabella.

Fleur examined her own reflection in the front viewscreen. As much as she hated what she saw, it was impossible to tear her eyes away. Body dysmorphia, the doctors called it. Her curse. They had left *Nebula* so unexpectedly, and in such a hurry, that she didn't even have her emergency kit with her. Fleur grimaced. It was nearly a quarter rotation since she had last reapplied the mask of chemicals she relied on to conceal her face's countless blemishes. No, not countless. Fleur stared at her face in the viewscreen. She knew exactly how many. It would have taken her the rest of their final leap, but she could have identified every imperfection. The pores in her left cheek. The odd slope of her jawline. The massive shadows of tiredness beneath her eyes. Even the skin cells she was craving to tear off her face to make it smoother. Her emergency kit contained a pocket laser to help with that.

Beauregard groaned from the co-pilot's chair. "Phyxin' space travel." His voice echoed clumsily in the otherwise silent shuttle.

Fleur patted his arm, although her eyes never left her reflection in the viewscreen. "Honey, that is the hangover talking."

Beauregard rubbed his eyes blearily. "How're our passengers?"

Fleur glanced over her shoulder. Ezra was asleep, the medpac still clamped to his chest. By the time this leap was over, Fleur reckoned his insides should be knitted back together well enough to remove it. Isabella had finally drifted off too, her head resting on Ezra's shoulder. Beside her foot was a pile of empty ration packets, the only evidence of their contents a trickle of crumbs caught in the creases of her medical gown. Fleur watched as Isabella's face furrowed with what was unmistakably another nightmare.

Still hunched on the deck beside the stool, Ves was entirely awake. She glared. "I wouldn't go back to sleep if I were you," she warned Beauregard. "Might wake up with your throat slit."

"Oh honey, please," Fleur purred. "Because that attitude worked out so well for your brother."

"Bite me."

Fleur smiled, but for once her heart wasn't in it. "We are going to need the coordinates of your bounty exchange. This is our last decoy leap."

Ves didn't say a word. She didn't need to. Fleur had heard that the shock of asteroids colliding with each other was strong enough to crush carbon into diamonds. If she combined the violence of such a collision with the hardness of the resulting diamonds and the brisk chill of space, it would have resembled the expression on Ves' face now.

"Honey, either you help us take this girl home and then go your own way, or we will roam deep space together until my shuttle runs out of energy and we die, or PROXUS catches up with us and we die. That is your call."

"Get locked."

Fleur spun her pilot's chair away from their prisoner and stared wistfully out of the viewscreen again. "She says she will think it over."

"I heard," Beauregard growled.

Fleur laughed briefly until she caught the creases spreading across her reflection.

"So, we go with the bounty exchange?" Beauregard asked.

"Can you think of anyone better to ask than whoever posted her bounty? We cannot return the girl home if we cannot get there. Wherever this Earth planet is, it is not on any of our charts."

Beauregard shook his head in quiet acceptance.

Fleur didn't speak again until she was sure Ves was asleep. "Are you awake, big man?"

Beauregard nodded, although his eyes remained closed.

"Are you… Are you okay?"

There was a deep pause. "I ain't got no regrets. We've always stuck together, ain't we? I trust the kid's instincts. He wants to do the right thing, don't he?"

"Then why are you so restless?"

"What?" Beauregard opened one eye accusingly. "I ain't moved all flight."

"You might be still, but I have seen plasma conduits less volatile than you since we left *Nebula*. Tell me what is going on inside that big old head of yours."

Beauregard stared dimly into the expanse of nothingness on the other side of the viewscreen. "Aww phyx, what do I know? I've been gettin' it wrong for so long I've forgotten what's right. That's what made Ezra and Dantes so phyxin' good to have around. Ain't none of us gonna forget what we've done for PROXUS and ain't much of it good, neither. Sure, we tried to stay inside the grey, but that's one phyxin' dark shade of grey we've been in for the last twelve cycles since you joined. And before you, it was just black. I ain't a good person and you know it."

"I had imagined the employment prospects for captured pirates would be broader." Fleur smiled at Beauregard, but for once it didn't work. He was too busy being serious.

"You did what you had to when they captured you, ain't no one gonna blame you. The size of the Known Galaxies ain't nothin' when PROXUS reaches from one side to the other, so we ain't had no real choice in the matter. But when I think about everythin' we've done, after all the black and grey I've let slide my whole life, after all that… to wave our uglies at the Empress over, what? Just a girl?"

"No. Over Ez. You know that."

Slowly, Beauregard drew one of his plasma pistols and cradled it in his hands, as though it granted him comfort. "Had their orders, their captain said. Ain't nothin' wrong with followin' orders. We've followed worse. But we killed them for it all the same."

Beauregard jumped as Fleur rubbed his shoulder gently. "Easy," she warned softly. Sheepishly, Beauregard holstered his pistol. "No," she insisted, "we stuck together, that's all we did. You saw Ez. He was always headed for a firefight. We chose him over PROXUS when we followed him out of Crazy Red's, and I'd do the same thing next rotation."

Beauregard placed his hand on Fleur's fingers, which had settled on his shoulder. He squeezed her hand. "You ain't wrong. We chose Ez."

"Are we there yet?" Ezra asked.

Beauregard's head jerked round. Ezra was standing behind them. Immediately, Beauregard threw Fleur's hand away and busily pushed an array of random switches on the console. "Oh, hey Ez. Ain't noticed you were awake. Good to see you up! Sleep well?"

Fleur snatched Beauregard's wrist as he reached for another button and gave him a meaningful look. "If you keep pressing buttons like that, you will deplete the last of our very limited energy supply. Or eject us into space."

"Aww phyx," Beauregard moaned. Dragging himself out of the co-pilot's chair without making eye-contact with Ezra, he hauled himself to the shuttle's rear and made a show of checking ramp seals were secure. Amid the noise he was making, Isabella and Ves stirred.

"Are you okay, Ez?" Fleur asked gently.

Ezra checked the medpac's readout on his chest, then gingerly depressurised the seal and unplugged the healing unit from his body. "Much better," he said, although not entirely reassuringly. He glanced at Beauregard. "Is he?"

"Oh, ignore him. You know what he can be like."

Ezra shuffled awkwardly. "I haven't said thank you, yet. Not properly. I know what you've both sacrificed, and I need you to know—"

"No need, Ez." Fleur smiled warmly. He smiled back full of relief. "No need," she repeated firmly. "We stick together."

"Yeah!" cried Ves from the rear of the shuttle. "All hail the brave murderers!"

Ezra's face went red. Beauregard found the ramp seals required even closer inspection.

"Good timing, Ves," Fleur said coolly from the pilot's chair. "This is now or never. Do you want us to all die horribly, or do you want to save your own life?"

"It's okay," Ezra reassured Isabella. "We'll get you home." He glared at Ves. "Won't we?"

"I don't know much anyway," Ves admitted.

Fleur waited expectantly.

"It's only a set of coordinates, that's all. They said the coordinates would only work for a short time."

"So we start with that," suggested Fleur. She punched in the numbers as Ves gave them to her, carefully repeating each number back as she did so. "The star charts say there is nothing there," Fleur remarked as she finished checking the shuttle's data module. "It will take us a long way out and leave us with little power to reach another planet for recharging. There better be someone waiting for us."

Ves shrugged. "Like I've got anything left to lose."

More than one pair of eyes drifted uncomfortably to the storage locker where Rico's body had been inhumed. In the silence that followed, Fleur plotted a safe route to their new destination and engaged the star drive.

CHAPTER FOURTEEN

Apart from Ves, whose slumped body was still chained to a stool near the rear of the shuttle, everyone gathered around Fleur for the last few seconds of the star drive's countdown before it disengaged. From the co-pilot's chair, Isabella had one of the best seats in the house. Well, the shuttle anyway. Silently, she watched the digits on the console blink down towards single figures.

It had been a long flight. Whatever Fleur's shuttle did to keep them breathing all this time also seemed to steralise the air to within a guitar string's width of an odourless existence, and so it wasn't with her nose, but with her eyes that Isabella noticed how much everyone had been sweating. Nervous sweat. Scared sweat. Can't-sit-still sweat. Having noticed, now she couldn't not notice. Slick, glistening perspiration wept from every pore and clung to every drenched clump of hair. Dried sweat betrayed by thick shadows on stained shirts. Stale sweat on faces half-cleaned by rogue tears.

You know, that went pretty well.

Really? You want to go there?

Relax! I'm just saying, whatever happens— don't panic like you did last time. We'll be fine.

I didn't panic. You got us locked in a box.

Saving your life. You're welcome, by the way. Unless you like being shot?

Isabella bit her lip. Fleur, Ezra and Beauregard were watching the viewscreen, but Isabella was more worried about the numbers counting down on the console as they reached the end of their star leap to Ves' coordinates.

Everything's gonna be okay. We've got this.

Five.

It could have gone worse.

Four.

I mean, not everyone's dead.

Three.

Mostly. We're not dead. That's something, am I right?

Two.

If you have a little faith, we can face anything together.

One.

Whatever happens, we'll be okay. I promise.

Isabella stared as the darkness shifted—suddenly—to burning light—suddenly—to stars. And something else.

OH SHIT. I take it all back. We are so screwed.

Ezra froze. Beauregard whistled. Fleur calmly double-checked their fuel reserves and brought the shuttle to a full stop before glancing back out the viewscreen.

"That is interesting," Fleur said, in a tone that suggested she would have preferred a view that was infinitely less interesting.

"What is it?" Isabella asked.

It's bad news. Bad, bad news. We need to get out of here—now. Tell them!

"Yeah!" Ves called from her spot chained on the floor. "What are you all staring at? Where are we?"

"That is a Husk," Fleur answered, keying her viewscreen to zoom in. "A dead Sau Daran ship. Which explains why it was not on the star charts."

Like I said. We're screwed.

Fleur glared at Ves. "Did you know?"

Stunned, Ves shook her head.

Silhouetted against a burning red star, the Husk drifted lifelessly across their viewscreen. Initially, the shape of its grey, globelike surface reminded Isabella of the moon. Earth's moon. Then Fleur zoomed in tighter and its appearance became, in every way, distinctly alien. Its hull looked at times organic, at times synthetic. Stained red by the star behind it—which Fleur explained was a supergiant—the Husk's exterior was ridged like a wavy sea of corrugated metal. Its irregular curves, bumps and craters looked like they had grown out of the hull, rather than being built. Despite the terror that gripped her as she gulped in the sight of this vast vessel, Isabella found herself filled with a little wonder too.

Don't be impressed. That ship means nothing but death for us.

"Well, ain't that a sight," Beauregard muttered. "A livin' ship. Ain't seen one of those since the war. How big is that thing?"

"That ship's still alive?" Ezra spluttered. "It's huge!"

Fleur checked the sensor readout on her console. "Big enough that it would take us 100 rotations just to walk its circumference."

"But it looks so small," Isabella pointed out.

"It is a long way off, honey. That viewscreen is zoomed in."

108

Beauregard grimaced. "Used to be livin', eh? Ain't never heard of a Sau Daran ship makin' it outta the war still alive."

"There are a lot out there," Fleur admitted. "They made perfect bases for the pirates I used to run with. You would be surprised how many Husks are still drifting in the Outer Rim, but they are impossible to find unless you know their final course."

"Are there still Sau Darans on them?" Ezra asked. His throat sounded dry.

"Sometimes," said Fleur. Then she said something Isabella found incredibly strange. "But they were never a problem unless you were looking for trouble."

Ezra laughed nervously. "Yeah, right! Good one!"

"No, really kid." Fleur patiently held his gaze. "There is a lot PROXUS chooses not to tell its citizens."

Ezra's face twisted uncomfortably as he considered this. "But they're Sau Darans! Everyone knows the only good Sau Daran is a dead Sau Daran."

Beauregard patted Ezra with a bear paw as the younger man gawped. "Maybe you're right, kid, or maybe that's the Empress talkin'. It's a big universe and I ain't got a clue no more. Don't let it bother you none."

Fleur busied herself at the console as data flooded its screen. "When a Sau Daran ship dies and becomes a Husk, the first thing they do is vent their atmosphere," she explained. "Legend has it that a Sau Daran ship dies when its soul is broken. The crystal in its heart loses power and the ship stops growing, thinking, moving, feeling. All the Husk can do is drift through space in whatever direction it had been travelling in when it died. One final never-ending voyage."

"Ain't that a bit much?" Beauregard muttered.

"Now who is being narrow-minded?" Fleur asked, her eyebrows arched accusingly.

"Aww phyx, a fella's got limits."

Fleur pointed at her sensor readouts. "Talking of limits, breathing and staying upright are two of mine. I am detecting temporary gravity fields and anti-vacuum barriers everywhere there is still atmospheric pressure on the Husk."

"Someone's livin' in that corpse?" Beauregard asked.

Fleur nodded. "Not just someone. Based on these numbers and how the areas of artificial atmosphere are concentrated across the Husk, there could be an atmosphere large enough for over a million people."

"A million pirates?" Beauregard asked with a wry grin.

Ezra was growing paler by the second. "Or a million Sau Darans?" he asked nervously.

Beauregard shrugged. "Phyxin' good place to find a shady contact for our bounty hunter."

"Yes," Fleur agreed, fixing her eyes on Ves, "it is." She waited, but Ves only scowled. "We are going to need a little more to go on than that, honey, so you need to decide where you want to be when we have this conversation—inside or outside the shuttle." Fleur gestured at the stars. "Your choice."

"You're going to murder me like you murdered my brother?" Ves spat at her down the deck, but her spittle died long before reaching anyone. "All so you can save your own skins?"

"No, actually—so we can save hers." Fleur indicated Isabella, who blushed. "We really could not care less about you, Ves, but someone does. In fact, you all need to see this. It came through while you were sleeping."

Flicking a dial on her gauntlet's holographic display, Fleur conjured up a rotating red projection of a large bald head.

It's rare for people to actually gasp. There might be an intake of breath, or a loaded pause, but people almost never gasp in the full-blown sense of the word. Ves and Isabella both gasped.

"Rico killed him!" Ves snarled. "Striker's dead!"

"Don't look dead," Beauregard observed helpfully.

"No, he does not," Fleur agreed. She grinned at Ves. "And I cannot imagine he is your biggest fan after your brother *nearly* killed him." They watched as Ves shifted uncomfortably, her fingernails scratching a red patch on her neck. "Ves, even if you turned us all over to PROXUS right now it would be less than one rotation before the First Duke invited you for a walk outside his battle station. You are running out of people in this universe who still want you alive. Pick a side, honey."

"This is a Priority One message for every honest, hardworking citizen in the Known Galaxies," Striker's floating red head announced. "If you see this fugitive, contact your nearest PROXUS personnel." Striker's face was replaced with a glowing red projection of Isabella's face. As Striker continued speaking over the top of Isabella's face, he revealed the reward for Isabella's return to custody.

Beauregard whistled. "That reward ain't half bad."

"Hey!" Ezra warned. He slid his eyes meaningfully towards the petrified expression on Isabella's face.

"Aww phyx, we ain't gonna do nothin'," Beauregard assured her with an embarrassed smile.

"No one is," Fleur stated simply. Her face was slack, solemn. "We will not let them take you."

Numbed by the immense gratitude she felt towards these strangers who insisted on risking their lives for her, Isabella stared into the woman's beautiful eyes and nodded her understanding.

Fleur strode down the shuttle's deck until she was towering over Ves. "This is the last time I am going to ask you, then you can answer from outside the shuttle. What are you not telling us?"

Ves bowed her head in submission. "I sent a coded transmission before you all came aboard. As well as the coordinates, someone sent another code back. I don't know what it means. That's all I know. Really."

Ezra glared. "You don't know much!"

Ves glared back. "It's what you asked for and it's all I have." Her eyes slid towards Rico's locker again. "You've taken everything else."

Fleur placed a firm hand on Ezra's arm before he could say anything else. "The code?" she asked, before taking the sequence of letters and numbers from Ves and keying them into the gauntlet she wore on her wrist. With another few taps, she had shared it with Beauregard and Ezra's gauntlets.

"Don't worry," Ezra assured Isabella. "We'll get some answers, then we're going to get you home."

He's almost reassuring when he's not shitting his jockstrap, isn't he?

You don't get to say that. Not after what he did for us.

That's fair.

Are you scared?

Only if we're going inside that thing.

"We have to be careful," Fleur added, striding back towards her pilot's chair. "But we need to dock. If PROXUS shows up or if things turn nasty, there will be more places to hide on that Husk than in this shuttle."

There's plenty of things on that ship to hide from too. You've got to tell them to turn back. Let's go literally anywhere else.

Beauregard peered dubiously out of the viewscreen. "You're gonna land us inside that rusted corpse?"

"Landing is not the problem," said Fleur. "Husks have no defenses, but whoever is hiding in there will not like unannounced visitors. Especially flying a shuttle with PROXUS markings."

"Announce us then," Beauregard suggested as he checked the charge on both his plasma pistols. "We ain't pals with PROXUS now they want us dead." He winked at Isabella and aimed a grubby finger at the white tattoo beside Fleur's eye. "And we'll be amongst friends, right?"

"I switched sides. Every pirate who has ever heard of me wants me dead."

"But you've switched back again, so ain't everyone friends now?"

Fleur released an exhausted sigh. "Sweetie, thanks. But you really are not helping."

"All I'm sayin' is there ain't no one on that Husk except folks who ain't best pleased with the Empress. We don't exactly look like we're on their side."

Now it was Fleur's turn to smile. "Kyle Beauregard, you are not wrong. I think we all know what this means?"

They all answered together.

"We're locked," said Beauregard.

"We're vented," said Ezra.

"Dress up," said Fleur.

CHAPTER FIFTEEN

Isabella watched Fleur fly the shuttle into a dark, narrow rupture in the Husk's deformed outer shell. The stars winked out behind them, replaced by a curtain of jagged debris.

Turn back.

We can't.

Not with that attitude.

She said we're low on power.

I don't care.

We need to get home.

Going into a Husk is insane. It's Sau Darans we're running from!

What about PROXUS?

Dead is dead, whoever kills you.

Fleur wove the shuttle through a maze of charred wounds that had been bored through the Husk's shell.

What even does that?

Plasma cannons, probably.

But those holes are massive!

So's a battle station.

"Must be a hangar bay that ain't buried," Beauregard grumbled after Fleur swerved violently around another lump of floating slag in the tunnel.

"Check the sensors yourself," Fleur suggested sharply. "Most of the habitable areas are too close to the Husk's Core, we would never reach them. The only anti-vac field nearer the perimeter is the one we are heading for. Unfortunately, this thing took a lot of hits before they died."

"Yeah, I know. Don't mean we can't land somewhere else though."

"Sure, I take it you packed your anti-vac suit?"

The shuttle shuddered.

"What was that?" Ezra asked.

"I clipped a wing," Fleur snapped, her eyes locked on the viewscreen in front of her.

"Just concentrate. You're doin' fine."

The shuttle shuddered again.

"I am trying to concentrate," Fleur shouted, "but people keep talking to me!"

The shuttle went silent.

I don't like this.

Right there with you.

It's not too late to turn back.

We don't have a choice.

And if you die in there?

Then you can gloat all you want.

Fleur swept the shuttle around another chunk of the Husk's damaged shell. Then Isabella saw it. Instead of more floating debris, a wall of energy flickered as the shuttle slid straight through it and into a deep, cavernous metal chamber.

Isabella felt the shuttle rock as Fleur set it down.

Their pilot held out her arms in triumph. "One Sau Daran hangar bay!"

"Aww phyx," moaned Beauregard. "Let's just do this."

"Remember the plan," said Fleur. She gave Isabella's new outfit a quick onceover. "You look great, sweetie!"

Isabella turned in the co-pilot's chair and examined everyone else's new outfits—'great' wasn't the word she'd choose, but hers was at least an upgrade from the medical gown.

If you're gonna get yourself killed, why not dress up for the occasion?

Oh, shush.

Clutching a handful of deep breaths, Isabella watched Fleur disappear down the ramp with bold strides. She had tidied up her afro to ensure the white piratical tattoo beside her right eye was unobscured. She had also taken oil from the shuttle's maintenance locker and applied it in thick dark stripes of greasy warpaint down her cheeks and jaw. Isabella had been surprised at how enthusiastically someone as beautiful as Fleur had been to cover up the contours of her face, but—as always—her purple and black leather gleamed. A borrowed plasma pistol from one of the Silver Fists hung ready at her hip to complete her piratical look.

Given Fleur's warning that they could encounter all sorts of smugglers, pirates, murderers, exiles, vagabonds, outcasts, losers and no hopers on the Husk, everyone had agreed Beauregard didn't need a costume change. His stained vest and worn cargo trousers were perfect, while both hands hung in their natural position beside his plasma pistols, one fastened to each thigh. He slouched down the ramp with what Isabella was coming to recognise as his trademark nonchalance. Half the time he seemed barely awake, but she would never forget how fast he had drawn his plasma pistol when Silver Star and the other soldiers had threatened to take her.

After waiting long enough to confirm Fleur and Beauregard hadn't been shot, Ezra and Ves took their first steps down the ramp. Ezra had used a cutting torch to remodel a suit of borrowed Silver Fist armour into an array of defensive accessories that were now far less practical than the original armour had been, but would no longer resemble something that had fallen off a PROXUS production line. He wore one borrowed plasma pistol in a refashioned holster across his cutdown chestplate, with another holstered tightly to one thigh.

With the barrel of Ezra's borrowed plasma rifle pushing into her back, Ves slunk down the ramp with her hands now free of their restraints. Like Beauregard, Ves didn't have a costume. Isabella was unclear whether this was because she didn't need one or no one cared if she died. Ves surveyed the hangar, taking an age to process it all.

"Run and I'll fry you," Ezra whispered in Ves' ear loud enough for Isabella to hear from the top of the ramp.

Isabella looked back inside the empty shuttle, then at herself. An unloaded plasma rifle served as her crutch, with all her weight leant on its stock and its barrel hitting the deck with every step. Just as Isabella's school uniform had gone, now her med bay gown had also been abandoned. In its place, she had borrowed a black base layer formerly worn beneath Silver Fist armour. Fleur had shown Isabella how to work the compression valve, reshaping the bodysuit until the base layer shrank to a perfect fit. Except for her lone, bare foot, the base layer covered all of her. Fleur had even cut off the spare leg and arm sleeves so they didn't flap. Isabella wrinkled her nose at the smell of blood inside the base layer. Hiding all her fear and panic, not to mention her identity, a borrowed Silver Fist's helmet had been clamped over her head. Ezra had burned off the silver star on its side and

117

helped her stick scraps of another base layer inside the adult-sized helmet to hold it in place. Clinging to the edge of hyperventilation and hoping desperately not to fall into unconsciousness, Isabella took one tremulous breath after another, reminding herself of the half-melted guitar pick stowed in one of the base layer's pockets. *Like I'll be using that any time soon.* Isabella stepped onto the ramp. The converted plasma rifle echoed noisily. Hobbling one slow step at a time, she clunked and hopped and heaved her way to the floor of the hangar bay.

The alien ship felt weird. Although harder than steel, the floor didn't feel smooth or cold against her bare sole. It had a strange, almost tissue-like texture to it, as though it had grown rather than been built. Which, she supposed, it had. This made walking on the floor a bizarre sensation, which was accentuated by the eerie blue glow surrounding them. Far above, the vast, undulating ceiling made her feel like she was standing in the ribcage of a sleeping giant. As Isabella looked around, she became increasingly aware of all the eyes in the hangar bay—they were all watching her. Thick crowds of onlookers were spread hundreds deep from the back wall right up to the edge of the shuttle's ramp. Right up to Isabella's costumed companions.

"Be thankful for your helmet's odour filters," Ezra whispered.

"Ease off, Ez," suggested Beauregard. "Ain't it obvious they're dyin'?"

"I didn't mean…" Ezra began, but his words faded. He looked away uncomfortably.

Taking in the state of the crowd, Isabella almost forgot her outfit's inescapable *Eau de Blood.* Not one of the onlookers was fully clothed. Many wore rags. Not one of them looked clean or healthy. Not one of them was held together by anything more than brittle bones and wilted, puckered skin. Every pair of eyes, along with some that no longer came in pairs, stared with weary sorrow.

What might have been a young man detached himself from the crowd and approached. A deluge of hair escaped in thick clumps from his head and beard before tumbling over what remained of a tatty overcoat. His hair was so dirty that Isabella couldn't even tell what colour it was, while his feet were as bare and stained as the open palms he held out in greeting.

"Welcome," he said in a fragile voice. "Whisper."

"Why?" hissed Beauregard.

Confusion creased the stranger's face. "I'm Whisper."

Beauregard managed a dignified nod before he was pushed aside by Fleur. Wearing the role of pirate captain as perfectly as she wore her stylish leather outfit, Fleur strode with an imperious, predatory swagger right up to the crowd's quivering spokesperson and threw him a look of thunder. His brow furrowed as he clocked the tattoo on Fleur's face. Instantly, the few patches of face visible beneath his mess of hair paled even more.

Fleur made a show of looking the man up and down, taking all the time in the universe. "We're in a hurry," she said eventually.

"Of course, of course, of course. Please... don't mind me," whispered Whisper. His face was never still. Instead, his whole body crawled with nervousness—or lice. "May I request the purpose of your visit?"

"We were given these coordinates for a private appointment," Fleur stated brusquely. "We require storage for our shuttle." She waved a hand dismissively around the hangar. "Not to mention privacy."

"Please, we are happy for you to conduct your business here," Whisper assured her. "That is a PROXUS shuttle?"

Fire awoke behind Fleur's eyes. She snapped her fingers. Beauregard disappeared back up the ramp. Moments later, he hauled first one and then a second bloody body of a Silver Fist down the ramp, their armour clattering loosely against their stiff bodies. Isabella couldn't help but notice how, even when he was supposed to be playing the part of a ruthless pirate, Beauregard placed them gently on the strange floor and lingered over their bodies.

"Take these as a deposit for the hangar," Fleur said after a nervous glance at Beauregard. "PROXUS is no friends of ours. Are there many pirates here besides us?"

Whisper nodded.

"How many?" asked Fleur.

Whisper shrugged. "Thousands?"

"Excellent, we are in fine company," Fleur announced. Tapping her gauntlet, she shared Ves' code with Whisper. "You recognise this?"

"I do. It's a cargo hold in one of our habitation areas."

At another click of Fleur's fingers, Beauregard punched the ramp's console. It rose back into the belly of the shuttle.

"The security lock on this shuttle is damaged," Fleur informed Whisper. "If anyone attempts to enter, the grenades we have rigged inside will explode. Were that to happen, I would be most dissatisfied. As, I suspect, would anyone nearby."

Unable to stop shaking, Whisper nodded. Selecting four equally drab individuals from the crowd, he hissed firm instructions in their ears. They listened with sombre attentiveness, then took guard beside the shuttle. "I will stay with the shuttle too," he added weakly.

"No, you will be our guide," Fleur corrected him.

Whisper nodded feebly. "I would be delighted."

"Show us this cargo hold," Fleur ordered. Without waiting for a response, she swept past Whisper and marched steadily across the hangar. Whisper sent a pleading look to the four sentries he had posted beside the shuttle before trailing after her. The crowd nervously retreated to create a path for Fleur, as though she was infected with something devastating. In a way, she was.

Power.

Beauregard, Ves, Isabella and Ezra followed. As they passed through the crowd, nothing but despair gripped the faces staring back at her. Gaunt promises of starvation, disease and suffering. Tearing her eyes from one to the next was gut-wrenching.

She glanced behind. As watchful as he was exhausted, Ezra kept his plasma rifle poised. His eyes flitted back and forth between Ves and the crowd.

As Isabella hobbled after Fleur and Beauregard, she caught a flash of metal glinting amongst the crowd. They weren't quite an android. They weren't a robot or a terminator either. But they were android adjacent, or perhaps a distant second cousin to a robot or terminator. They were definitely Sau Daran. The crowd drifted into insignificance, no less forgotten as her companions, as Isabella strained her eyes in the dim blue light.

Another gleam of light caught the Sau Daran. They were small, maybe half Isabella's height, but crouched so low they appeared even smaller. They were hiding—craftily—behind the legs of an ancient bald woman. Isabella froze. The Sau Daran was a mess of rust and black fluid. Beneath these stains, their face—if you could call it a face—was consumed by a giant, perforated beak. Their hands were not hands, either. One was a blade, the other a claw. Both caught every particle of blue light with a menacing sheen as they peered around the woman's leg.

Tentatively, the glowing red eyes on either side of the Sau Daran's beak found Isabella.

"Don't worry, I see it," Ezra hissed.

Already he was next to her with his plasma rifle ready. Fleur, Ves and Beauregard were far ahead, their faces barely visible through the crowd. Isabella glanced back at the Sau Daran and gasped inside her helmet. The ancient woman's hand had dropped to gently cup the top of the Sau Daran's head. Protectively, the woman nudged the metal creature behind her leg until Isabella lost sight of it.

"Hey!" Beauregard barked.

"Come on," Ezra urged her.

Nodding distractedly as she scanned the crowd for more Sau Darans, Isabella limped deeper into the hangar. Ezra stayed close. Her companions were waiting at the hangar's edge by a row of broad arches that each opened into its own dark tunnel.

"Wait!" Ezra warned. The barrel of his plasma rifle pushed Whisper under the nearest arch until his back was pressed up against the wall. This had the ominous effect of shrouding the top of Whisper's face in shadow as though his face had been cut in half from the nose up. "Why are there Sau Darans here? Are you working for them? What do they want?"

"Hold it, Ez," Beauregard cautioned. His eyes slid over the concerned faces of the crowd watching. "Ain't no one wants this to turn nasty."

Ezra told him what they had seen.

"I don't like it neither," Beauregard confirmed. "Ain't no place for a firefight with all those crowds though."

Shaking his head ever so slightly, such was his obvious fear of it being vaporized, Whisper emitted a petrified exclamation. "Please, this was a Sau Daran ship! Of course there are Sau Darans here! They live with us, but they don't harm anyone. Without them, without their

122

maintenance, this ship would be uninhabitable. There's no need to harm them!"

"Did they look threatening?" Fleur asked.

"What does that matter?" Ezra snapped. "That thing there is a Sau Daran!"

"Please understand," Whisper implored. "They're harmless."

"Harmless?" Ezra's face was reddening. "I've never met a Sau Daran that didn't want to kill me."

Whisper's fragile features hardened into what he clearly feared would be a suicidal show of defiance. "Perhaps because you were firing this rifle at them?"

"Those machines would wipe out all of us if we let them." Ezra was livid, his plasma rifle shaking under Whisper's chin.

"Perhaps the universe would be a more tolerant place if they did," Whisper replied sadly.

"You ain't no PROXUS poster boy now, kid," said Beauregard, placing a friendly hand on Ezra's shoulder. "You ain't on the home team no more. Keep your eyes sharp, but your safety on."

Fleur gestured towards the arches. "Lead on, Whisper. No one will harm you. Unless you cross us— then we'll kill you."

Nodding submissively, their guide led them through one of the arches. From there, their path snaked in every direction. It was more like a warren than a spaceship. Mostly the dim blue glow that crept from the walls was gloomy enough to hide the grimace on Isabella's face as she limped after them, but halfway up every incline she had to remind them to slow even more for her. After hours of trekking through the warren of tunnels at her infuriatingly sluggish pace, Isabella was offered Ezra's shoulder yet again. Bracing herself against the wall, she batted him away with her rifle-crutch.

123

"I'll do it myself," she snapped.

No, we'll do it together.

I wasn't talking to you.

Go easy. I'm flooding your body with a lot of chemicals.

To poison me?

No, I'm making you stronger. Keeping you going. Without me, you'd have collapsed ages ago. You're welcome, by the way.

Thanks, I guess.

Even if you are intent on dying, I don't want you to die just yet.

As their slow hike meandered through the Husk's unsettling brand of darkness, Whisper spoke only when spoken to and seemed judicious with what information he shared. He claimed many of the Husk's first human inhabitants had been refugees fleeing their world when it was invaded by PROXUS. They had stumbled upon the Husk shortly before their cruiser ran out of power. Much of their transport, worthless without energy, had been stripped for parts to make the Husk habitable. Other strays, misfits and vagabonds had joined them over the cycles, often arriving on pirate vessels or escaping from one of PROXUS' many mining colonies in the Outer Rim. When Beauregard asked how refugees could live alongside pirates, Whisper admitted most refugees who were strong enough had already left the Husk to become pirates or anti-PROXUS freedom fighters.

Endless paths intersected confusing passageways as Whistler led them around unexpected twists and deceptive turns, up steep rises and down sudden drops that slowed Isabella almost to a literal crawl.

Finally, Whisper halted. "Your cargo hold is around that bend," he told them. His eyes shifted in the dim blue light. "Please understand, I cannot go inside. That is pirate territory—refugees are forbidden without permission."

Fleur nodded seriously. "A good place for an ambush." She pointed at Isabella and Ezra. "Whisper, take these two someplace safe. Do not go far." She looked at Ezra. "Look after her, Ez."

Ezra nodded seriously and, after giving Isabella a reassuring smile, let Whisper guide them back down the tunnel the way they had come.

Fleur's hand wandered instinctively to her plasma pistol. Cautiously, she led Beauregard and Ves out of the tunnel and into a large open space. Its grooved walls glowed with dim blue light that revealed endless mountains of storage containers. These columns stretched deep into the cargo hold until they became lost in the darkness.

Fleur smiled wolfishly as she noticed Beauregard slip into the shadows and disappear. "Do not try anything," she warned Ves. "Or we will kill you. Play nicely and you might walk away from this."

Ves glanced at where Beauregard should have been and discovered he wasn't there. Unable to conceal her surprise, she clenched her teeth and followed Fleur deeper into the cargo hold. Pillars of shadow rose all around them. The only sound was the tapping of their boots. Resisting the urge to draw her plasma pistol, Fleur frowned at the logos adorning some of the containers they were passing. Many of the insignias were unknown to her and probably belonged to new pirate outfits, but other more familiar markings chilled her blood faster than a short walk in space. These were the emblems of the most infamous pirate syndicates: the richest and the deadliest. Even her old syndicate—practically pirating royalty—were storing cargo here. Amongst the other clients… Fleur ran a curious hand over a crate that bore, of all things, a PROXUS logo. She was relieved when her fingers came away with a thick layer of dust.

Absently wiping the dust onto her jacket, Fleur resumed their search. The two women crept down one aisle of containers after another, ears straining to catch the slightest warning of an ambush. Fleur peered through dim blue at the immense stillness of the cargo hold, but every shadow concealed fewer answers than the last. Eventually, their careful progress concluded at the far end.

Fleur keyed her comm. "Ez, unless we are supposed to hide her in one of these crates, we have nothing. No one is here. Sorry."

Ezra's voice instantly came back over the comm. "You sure?"

"Relax, we will at least wait to see if anyone shows. You might as well join us, though. There is no ambush here." Fleur disconnected her comm and examined Ves. "If you are holding out on us—"

"I know!" Ves interrupted, "you'll kill me. Or one of the others will kill me. Someone will kill me. I get it."

"Or perhaps I'll kill you," suggested another voice in the darkness.

CHAPTER SIXTEEN

Despite their disguises, Striker instantly recognised the fugitives and the bounty hunter as they stepped off the shuttle's ramp and into the Husk's hangar bay. He zoomed in on the projection, focusing on the two dead Silver Fists as Beauregard placed their bodies at the base of the shuttle's ramp. He switched the projection to real time. The grubby face of a young woman stared eagerly into her recording device.

"Stay close to them," Striker instructed. "We will track your signal. Your family will be transferred from Tiberius Omega Mining Colony once the fugitives are apprehended."

"Of course, First Duke, thank you so—"

"Inform me of any developments," Striker interrupted. Triggering a command via his neural implant, he terminated the connection.

With another thought, Striker sent the operative's previous reports from the Husk, which spanned a period of three cycles, cascading into a giant window of three-dimensional projections. These projections followed him around his small apartment as he paced back and forth. Real-estate was a premium commodity in Xarr's capital.

Although his accommodation was small and sparsely furnished by Striker's standards, most citizens in the capital would have found it luxury beyond their imagination. Striker stopped pacing. Many of the reports he was reading were predictably mundane, but this one made him pause. He re-read the passage describing the latest pirate activity aboard the Husk. *Yes, that will do nicely.* He sent instructions to his informer on the Husk to ensure these pirates knew about the latest extortionate bounty he had placed on the girl.

Once he had finished checking the remaining reports, Striker dismissed the projections and sank into the luxuriously cushioned embrace of one of the apartment's two hoverchairs. He leaned back with a heavy sigh and let his bare feet sink into the rich carpet. With another thought, he flooded the pristine white wall facing him with a vast ocean view. Opening his eyes, he watched the vibrant, wind-whipped sea ebb and swirl into waves as tall as a Xarr skyscraper. This was the closest he ever came to returning to his home world. But it was something— more than something—and it awoke feelings that he would otherwise fear had been lost. When he was ready, Striker took a final moment to compose himself and then, returning his wall to its default non-descript white, he initiated his comm.

As soon as the comm channel was open, Imperator Grave's dry, funereal voice greeted him, no doubt from the command bridge on *Black Nebula*. "First Duke! How lovely!" said Imperator Grave, failing to hide the dismay in his voice. "I thought you were dead."

"I am delighted to correct you," Striker replied honestly. "It would appear the Empress still requires my services. I trust *Nebula* is in safe hands?"

"The safest."

"Good. I have an offer for you, Imperator. How would you like to apprehend the escaped girl and her accomplices, along with thousands of pirates and a few million refugees for our mining colonies?"

"Obviously that would serve PROXUS very well," the Imperator replied irritably. "Speak plainly, First Duke. You know how much I detest your petty games."

"Games, Imperator?" Striker asked with calculated innocence. "You misjudge me. I bring you information. The girl you're hunting is on a Husk in deep space less than a quarter rotation from your present location."

There was a pause. "No games?"

Striker smiled. "I'm tracking her as we speak. The other fugitives are with her."

The Imperator almost bit off Striker's last words in his impatience. "Send the coordinates to my private channel and I will reroute Nebula. Your spies have saved you yet again, First Duke. Just how many lives do you have?"

"I can assure you, Imperator, my only life is that which serves PROXUS."

There was another pause over the comm. "I haven't received any data, Striker. Send it again."

"I haven't transmitted the data. You haven't asked me what I want yet."

There was a hiss of annoyance over the comm. "So that's why you've come to me and not the Empress. Does she even know about this lead? If you really served PROXUS, you would enable the capture of the girl and those fugitives without delay, along with any pirates and refugees in tow."

"And allow you to claim those victories for yourself using my battle station? After that, I fail to see how I could ever prise Nebula from your cold, dead fingers."

"Is that a threat, First Duke?"

"Of course not, Imperator. That would be treason."

129

"This is ridiculous. If PROXUS benefits, we all benefit. Send me the data. Now."

"Some always benefit more than others, Imperator. I, of course, desire for PROXUS to profit greatly—but without causing my own downfall in the process."

The Imperator's voice soured even more. "The Empress has executed her staff for such self-promotion."

"Then I suggest you don't mention it," Striker replied cordially, before coaxing a hint of menace into his voice, "because my spies are everywhere. They can find out anything about anyone, Imperator. Even you. Perhaps they already have."

The comm went so silent that Striker wondered if the channel had been disconnected. When the Imperator eventually spoke, his voice was heavy with resignation. "What do you want?"

"Do as you wish with the fugitives, the refugees and the pirates. They will make a great prize for the Empress. All I want is the girl. Have her brought to me on Xarr—in secret and unharmed."

"Are you mad? There's a Sau Daran parasite inside her. The sooner it's extracted, the sooner it can be broken apart and filtered into our power network across the hub worlds. You're forty rotations away!"

"When you bring her to me, the extraction will be conducted on Xarr under my authority and without the Empress' knowledge."

"You play a dangerous game, First Duke. Even you couldn't keep such a secret from the Empress for long."

"I told you—I don't play games. This is for the glory of PROXUS, nothing more."

"For your own glory, you mean."

"Your mistake, I'm sure."

"And if I refuse?"

"If you refuse, I shall withhold the girl's location. If you betray me, I shall share all your secrets with the Empress and you will be executed before the end of this rotation."

"Very well. You have my word."

"Thank you, Imperator. It's worth nothing to me, but I trust your self-interest. You should have the data now."

"Confirmed," the Imperator snapped.

The comm channel disconnected.

Striker smiled. Overthrowing the Empress would require significant resources, but the power of a Sau Daran god could tip the balance.

CHAPTER SEVENTEEN

Three shadows slipped out of the gloom.

"Or perhaps I'll kill you," said the middle shadow.

The shadows strutted down the centre of the cargo hold led by a woman with commanding strides. The two soldiers flanking her, a tall woman and a stocky man, were in ragged attire. Both held plasma carbines and were weighed down by an abundance of holstered firearms, dangling grenades and two bandoliers each—both lashed across their torsos in a cross. Unlike the woman in the middle, her bodyguards advanced with rapid military precision and much less sass.

Fleur reached for her gauntlet to key her comm.

"You're definitely not going to do that," the woman in the middle announced confidently. "If you do, well—we might have a serious disagreement."

Fleur casually lowered her gauntlet. "Unlikely. We are all on the same side."

"Excellent!" the woman declared in a cheery tone at odds with the primed killers on either side of her.

Stopping short of Fleur and Ves, she ran her bright eyes over Fleur's face, including her tattoo, and Ves' face, from which a tattoo was conspicuously absent. As though flicking a switch, her tone grew curt. "Ship and names."

"Who wants to know?" Fleur asked, a little haughtily.

"Captain Braga, of *The Liliana*," answered the woman. Her cheek was adorned with her own piratical tattoo: blue, not white like Fleur's, depicting the elegant outline of a bird in flight. Down the middle of her skull, the completely shaven side of her head met a sudden tangle of garishly dyed hair that eclipsed half her face. Although no plasma weapons were strapped across the loose leathers that bound Braga's muscular body, a synthetic hand-axe hung menacingly from her belt. "And you are?"

"Waiting for a private meeting," Fleur replied. "Are they going to keep pointing those things at us?"

Braga didn't acknowledge her escorts. Instead, she craned her neck around the cargo hold. "Busy meeting?"

"They are late."

"What an unfortunate place to meet, surrounded by all these valuables. Go on. Tell me you're tempted."

Fleur found her most charming smile and let rip. "Tempted? Of course! Luckily, we do not have time."

Braga rolled her eyes and theatrically waved a hand. "The motion detector on my crate and all the security feeds tell a different story. Why were you interested in that PROXUS crate?"

"We really are here to meet someone."

"And yet... you took an interest in something that doesn't belong to you. And yet... your friend still lurks in the shadows." Braga's face hardened. "And yet... I smell vitraxi dung."

Fleur shrugged but kept her hands in plain sight, well away from her plasma pistol. "That is probably my friend. He gets nervous when people threaten me."

"Does he?" Braga asked, unable to hide a smirk. "I'd hate for him to get twitchy with those two plasma pistols of his. Maybe he should put them away before someone mistakes this meeting for a heist."

"Relax," Ves said without any hint of conviction. "We're not thieves."

Braga laughed. "We're all thieves! But unless you're here to steal from me, that won't be a problem."

"I promise we are not," Fleur assured her coolly. "But I doubt the people we are meeting will show up if they see you here with us."

"Are you suggesting I look less trustworthy than Captain Plasma Pistols?"

Fleur glanced at the plasma carbines still aimed at her. "Watch whatever security feed you want. We are not here to steal anything. I touched a crate, nothing more. I am asking you nicely not to get in our way."

Braga examined her for long enough to send a chill creeping up Fleur's skin. "Are you, though?"

Fleur took a calming breath and conjured all the warmth she could muster into her voice. "Honey, please do not get in our way."

"That was nicely," Braga admitted. She threw Fleur a warped smile. "How long before you ship out?"

"Not long, I hope."

"Pity," said Braga, her smile blossoming devilishly.

She stepped closer to Fleur. Close enough for Fleur to smell the engine oil and sweat on her skin, which was almost overpowered by the scent of something much sweeter and more exotic. Close enough that Fleur felt their momentary silence and stillness become electric. Close enough that, worried Beauregard might run out of patience and open fire, Fleur gave the shadows a subtle shake of her head.

Braga smiled knowingly.

Without taking her eyes off Fleur's face, which she was admiring with brazen intensity, Braga reached out her gauntlet to Fleur's and gently tapped the two devices together. Fleur's gauntlet released a chirrup to acknowledge the transfer of Braga's personal comm frequency. "You know, it's cold out in space," Braga added shamelessly.

If there was anything alive within that transitory moment between them, it was broken by the hiss of a pressure release valve on one of the storage containers behind them. Braga's escorts swung their carbines towards the noise. Clumsily, Ves backed into the nearest mountain of containers. Fleur dropped a hand to her holstered plasma pistol. Everyone, even those who were hiding in the shadows, fixed their gaze on the storage container's cover as it swung open with a rush of smoke.

Fleur's mask of calm cracked as she looked beyond the opening container, further down the same aisle, to spot Ezra and Isabella frozen in shock. They were halfway into the cargo hold, between the doorway and the opening crate, and a long way from Fleur.

Braga opened her mouth to say something, probably something clever, but she was interrupted by the contents of the container as it emerged into the half-darkness of the cargo hold.

Everyone stared.

A small, saucer-shaped creature with a shining silver shell floated out of the crate. Fleur had seen creatures like this on the Husk she grew up on, but never one that was alive. The Sau Daran looked around, rotating first one way and then the other with a nonchalance that cosmically underestimated the number of people ready to shoot them. An excited squeal of beeps burst from the creature. Shaking with excitement and shrieking gleefully, they aimed themselves at Isabella.

A fresh avalanche of terror buried Isabella's exhaustion quickly and efficiently, sparking her senses awake as the flying saucer shot towards her.

Ezra stepped between them with his plasma pistol outstretched. The flying saucer—a Sau Daran, Isabella was quite sure—squawked in alarm.

"Ez, don't shoot!" Fleur shouted. "They've not done anything wrong!"

Ezra kept his pistol ready, but from his expression Isabella doubted he had any idea what it was ready for if he wasn't allowed to fire it. The Sau Daran hurtled towards them. Isabella, who would have batted it out of the air if she hadn't been using her rifle-crutch to keep herself upright, clawed at Ezra's shoulder for support. She might at least get off one good swing if they meant to hurt her.

A big paw stretched out of the shadows and Beauregard plucked the Sau Daran out of the air. Electricity sparked around its domed shell. With a yelp, he let go. Flying hurriedly away from Beauregard in what looked like panic, the ancient drone seemed to have lost all sense of direction. They ricocheted like a pinball from crate to crate, soon chased by a trail of their own ashen smoke, before landing at Ves' feet with a crash loud enough to signal the irreparable breaking of antique mechanisms. Beauregard flinched as fragments of silver shell clattered along the floor. Ves nudged the Sau Daran drone away from her with the toes of a timid boot, scanning the cargo hold as though searching for an even deeper shadow to hide in. Blowing on his burnt fingers, Beauregard risked a glance at what remained of the Sau Daran. Limply, the battered silver saucer was jumping towards the nearest crate in tiny fits and starts. They collapsed into its shadow and whimpered as only an alien flying saucer can. Guiltily, Beauregard met Fleur's glare. His excuse only made it halfway to his lips.

"Such an unmistakable physique, hasn't she?" Braga asked. Isabella had been so distracted by the Sau Daran creature that she had forgotten everyone else. Everyone else, it seemed, was watching her. "Even beneath that helmet," Braga added. Recognition was igniting across the pirate captain's face as her eyes stalked over Isabella's body. "And such a lovely bounty to go with her."

"Ez, get her out of here!" Fleur cried.

Braga raised her gauntlet to her lips and winked at Isabella. "This is Braga. Send everyone to my location." For the first time, she acknowledged her two escorts. "Bring me that girl."

Braga's escorts launched themselves into the gloom on either side of Isabella, but she didn't wait to see where they would reappear. She was already hobbling towards the exit, her neck hunched protectively into her shoulders as stray plasma blasts echoed overhead.

A blast of red-hot energy churned up the floor beneath her raised foot, sending her sprawling. She risked a glance behind her, searching for Ezra but instead catching Fleur's plasma pistol only half-drawn when Braga's boot kicked it from her grasp. Isabella watched, mesmerised. Fleur moved to one side, dodging a knife that hadn't been in Braga's hand a moment ago. Braga thrust at her with fast, precise flicks of her blade. Blood flashed as pirate sliced through ex-pirate with cut after tiny cut.

To Isabella's right, a flurry of red blasts from Beauregard's pistol threw one escort, the stocky one, against a wall of crates. He slumped to the floor, blood weeping from a trio of smoking holes in his chest. A lone grenade trickled from his quivering fingers.

Beauregard's face scrunched up into a curse before the grenade lit up the cargo hold with a roar of plasma. His retreating figure was perfectly silhouetted as the blast hurled him upside-down into another wall of crates. Security alarms erupted from storage containers in every direction, flooding the cargo hold with a cacophony of jarring sirens that bit Isabella's nerves as sharply as Braga's knife soon might.

She felt herself being hauled upright. Once again, she was in Ezra's arms. "The corridor!" he shouted. His lips were only half a breath from her ears, yet she could barely hear him over the dull ringing in her ears. "Go!" he cried, mistaking her shaken body's sluggishness for hesitation. He sent her hobbling on her rifle-crutch— frantic, but far from fast—while he shielded her with his body. Flashes of plasma exploded around them. She heard Ezra return fire but didn't dare turn around in case she tripped.

She was so close to the exit, but not close enough, when she started feeling strange. Everything felt, well, not necessarily wrong—but different. Her tongue could taste metal or blood or something else entirely. Something otherworldly.

Beside her, a bloodied Beauregard fell against an upturned storage container. One of his plasma pistols was missing, but the muzzle of its twin burned brightly in his hand as it unleashed hot Hell into the shadows around them. "One left, I'll keep her pinned down!" he barked over the incessant whine of his own plasma pistol. "Why ain't you gone, girl?"

For the second time in Isabella's life, the air screamed, the floor shook and everything broke.

Her mouth stretched apart in horror as the dim blue-black of the cargo hold was illuminated by an eruption of blinding light. Towers of crates shuddered beneath the howl of a tornado tearing out of the portal growing in front of her. With a cry, she was thrown aside. Her rifle-crutch clattered elsewhere. Her over-sized helmet rolled off and disappeared across the floor. Electricity crackled. The wind wailed. Huge storage containers were dragged into the air to be tossed back and forth as though by invisible, roaring giants.

Ezra and Beauregard ducked beneath the rainstorm of crates crashing around them. Amidst their confusion, the tall woman saw her moment and charged. Before the girl could scream a warning, the woman's plasma carbine was shrieking. A flash singed Ezra's cheek. He whipped his head back, allowing more plasma blasts to tear through the space where his face had been and burn magmatic holes in the trembling crates behind him.

The whirlwind flung another fistful of crates across the cargo hold. The woman rolled aside, a crate three times her size driving a furrow through the deck beside her. Beauregard spun out of the shadow of another crate, which almost took him with it as it swept past. Dodging the tumbling crates, Ezra surged forwards, his pistol loud and livid. The woman was halfway to her feet when his blast struck her. She screamed, dropping her carbine as her leg buckled under the smoking hole in her knee. Ezra steadied his aim for one final, deadly shot. This time Isabella did scream a warning. Before Ezra could pull the trigger, a crate tore through his legs with enough force to shatter them entirely. His face smashed into the floor.

Isabella stared at Ezra's broken, twitching body. Beauregard hurtled towards him without a care for the crates still crashing around them.

Isabella looked to Fleur, but she only had eyes for her plasma pistol as she scooped it off the deck. Braga knocked it aside to send Fleur's shot exploding into a crate. In reply, the pirate's axe fizzed with purple electricity as she swung it at Fleur's face. Fleur grabbed her wrist and the two women strained against each other—one forcing Braga's axe down, the other pushing Fleur's pistol back up. Purple electricity spat from the axe as Braga levered it closer to Fleur's face, sparks searing her cheeks.

The wind died. The light shining on Isabella was even brighter. Reluctantly, she peered through a shield of spread fingers. Almost close enough to touch, the blue portal glistened with an eerie stillness.

Another portal. More death.

I hate to say I told you so…

No. You don't.

Reaching for her rifle-crutch, Isabella spat out a mouthful of fear and blood. She hauled herself upright so she was level with the portal. Everything went blurry for a moment, but she steadied herself before she fell. Head hanging, body swaying, Isabella stared through a curtain of sweaty hair at the silhouette emerging from the portal. She forced another breath into her lungs.

The silhouette reached out a hand, palm open, fingers wide, offering to take her own.

"Hello, Viagra girl." Although no longer muddy, the boots were unmistakable. As were his skinny jeans and skull-emblazoned hoodie. Even though the hood concealed much of his face, there was no mistaking its owner. He paused to survey the damage done to the cargo hold. "Wow!" Before Isabella could reply, he grabbed her arm without asking. "Let's get gone."

Isabella pulled her arm away with a scowl. "What the Hell?" she demanded.

Fresh volleys of plasma shrieked past them. Chasing their opening barrage, a swarm of ragged space pirates flooded into the cargo hold. The shimmering portal, and the devastation it had caused, only slowed them for a moment as they took it all in.

"I want that girl alive!" Braga roared. Her eyes were hot with flashes of purple electricity.

"Sorry honey, you can't have her." Fleur's pistol spewed a hail of plasma into the crate behind Braga. As Braga shoved her pistol aside, Fleur used the momentum to push Braga into the smoking storage container. Braga screamed as Fleur pressed her spine into the molten metal she had lit up. Braga's axe came down fast in response, tearing a chunk out of Fleur's shoulder with a hiss of burning flesh. Their screams echoed through the cargo hold, shaking Isabella's heart.

"Come on!" Lynch hissed. His hooded head glanced at the pirates bearing down on the portal. He tried to grab her in his scarred hands, but she pushed him away. He staggered backwards. "You're crazy!"

"I can't go!" Isabella screamed at Lynch. "They're here because of me! I can't leave them. They need me."

She stared helplessly as plasma blasts scorched the air around Beauregard. He rolled behind the ruins of a storage container, abandoning Ezra's body, and ejected a smoking plasma clip from his pistol. Even after he had punched home a fresh clip, so many blasts were cooking every molecule around him that all he could do was scrunch up his body tighter behind the smoking crate.

"We've got a few seconds! That's it!" Lynch cried. "We have to go!"

The girl shook her head. "They want my bounty. They need me alive. If I stay, they won't kill anyone."

Isabella found Beauregard's gaze first. He gestured frantically for her to get away, but even that smallest movement nearly lost him an arm in the torrent of plasma exploding around him. Isabella only caught Fleur's eyes for a moment, her writhing body locked tightly against the woman trying to kill her. Pulsing purple electricity illuminated a grimace. Fleur shook her head at Isabella: don't stay. Lastly, Isabella found Ezra's empty expression. He blinked. Fragile hope swelled inside Isabella, hurting more than she could have ever imagined. The same hope—hot, fragile—burned in his eyes too.

"I'm staying," said Isabella.

Damn straight.

"Don't be an idiot," warned Lynch.

Did he just steal my line?

His hooded silhouette towered over her amidst the chaos of plasma dancing around them. "Screw this, I'm done asking!" He reached out, this time snatching her arm and tugging her towards the portal. "We're going."

Losing her grip on her rifle-crutch, Isabella's lone leg staggered weakly before accepting physics was not on its side. She half fell, half swung as Lynch held on but couldn't stop her breaking her fall with her face.

Let me get this one.

You sure?

I don't want to be anywhere near that portal. Neither do you.

He's all yours.

Isabella's eyes flickered as she hurtled over the edge of unconsciousness.

As Lynch bent to haul the girl off the floor, he received a fist in the face for his troubles. He rocked back with a priceless, stunned expression.

Flooding the girl's muscles and bones with all her alien strength, Paradise Moon ordered the body upright onto her solitary leg. Stray plasma blasts sparked all around her. Lit gloriously by their explosions, she glared at Lynch through glowing purple eyes.

"Back off," Paradise Moon snarled through the girl's lips. "She's never going through that portal."

Lynch rubbed at the red mark on his stubbled jaw. "I know who you are—and what you are. They warned me all about you. Let her go."

"She said no. No means no," said Paradise Moon. "For once, she and I agree."

Leaping off the girl's bare foot with the elegance of a gymnast, Paradise Moon swung the same foot into Lynch's crotch. The lower portion of his face, the half that wasn't concealed beneath his hood, creased up in agony. Quickly, the rest of his body followed. Balancing perfectly on one leg, Paradise Moon swung the girl's only fist into every fleshy part of his body she could find, pummelling him closer to the portal with every blow.

A swift tilt of the girl's head allowed Paradise Moon to inspect the damage she had done. Snaking the girl's tongue out of her mouth, Paradise Moon licked fresh blood from Isabella's lips. "You know, you're a long way from home." She leapt again. Springing far higher off one leg than was humanly possible, she soared. Too slow, Lynch gazed up at the girl's fist. It swung at his forehead.

Something cracked as the girl's fist struck the fabric of the hood covering Lynch's forehead. But the crack didn't come from Lynch's skull. The girl's body crashed to the floor beside the portal, this time with a scream and Paradise Moon shaking the girl's aching knuckles.

Lynch smiled nastily, his hood falling off.

Paradise Moon stared at what had been hidden beneath it. "Oh, you're a naughty boy!" she scolded.

"Sorry," Lynch replied with unexpected tenderness.

And with that, he kicked her in the head.

Stars exploded across her vision. Blinded, she felt him grip her arm and haul her into the portal.

CHAPTER EIGHTEEN

Lynch pulled the sleeves of his hoodie over his fingers and hauled himself back through the classroom's shattered window, wincing as glass sliced his hands. He landed in a wreckage of classroom furniture strewn with bloody splinters and scattered snowdrifts of pulverised books.

Across what remained of the classroom, the cute indie girl's legs were flailing under the metal creature's arm as it stole her away. Her eyes—eyes Lynch had enjoyed getting lost in only moments ago—were blazing with rage. The portal was in front of her. Like flames in the breeze, her dark hair whipped in every direction as she struggled. Lynch didn't have time to figure out if he was falling in love or if these feelings surging through him were mere adrenaline and lust. He needed to do more than nothing. He had been fighting all his life. Fighting with his mum. Fighting for his gang. Fighting against whatever was in front of him. He recognised a fighter, and this cute indie girl was full of it.

Too late.

Fighter or not, she was gone.

Staggering through the classroom, Lynch stared at the petrified faces of the other students. He nearly threw up over the remains of Miss Pilkington's shattered skull. But he didn't stop until the swirling portal was close enough for him to touch.

At this point, most people might have thought about their family, their friends, perhaps even their hopes and dreams for a future disappearing fast. Lynch considered none of these. His body felt more alive than it ever had. He was terrified, awed, even excited—but he wasn't hesitant. Most people might have poked, prodded or at the very least taken an experimental step into the portal.

Lynch wasn't most people.

He jumped.

As he fell through the portal, his body faded into transparency until he was as substantial as a ghost trying to grasp fog.

He landed hard enough on the other side of the portal to be in no doubt that he was solid again. He was in a domed chamber with ancient walls and a ceiling infected with rust and decay. Stray vines of electricity crept around the edges of the dome, illuminating the edge of a tunnel full of broken pipes and exposed wiring. The portal collapsed in on itself and disappeared, plunging Lynch into darkness. Stray barbs of crackling electricity snaked above him, momentarily interrupting the darkness as they navigated the top of the dome. Then they died too.

Lynch had only started feeling his way down the tunnel, which seemed to branch off in a million directions, when an explosion shook the corridor. More explosions followed, filling the shadows with debris and dust. Huddled below an outcrop of huge pipes wider than he was, he questioned why—even with nothing to lose—he had been so keen to jump into the unknown.

145

Lynch lost consciousness when a chunk of rock punched through the pipes hanging over his head. The rock sheared them off the wall along with half of his face.

PROXUS Rangers found the boy long after they had removed Isabella and Ezra from the ruins of the Sau Daran outpost. After all the structural damage caused by Ezra's onslaught, removing Lynch from the rubble was more like archaeology than a rescue. The Rangers made it as far as clearing the debris from above and around Lynch's face, but they didn't get any further.

The domed chamber lit up with another portal. Blue light burst down the tunnel, striking both the pale half of Lynch's face that had survived the cave-in and the bloodier half that hadn't.

Three hulks of dark metal flew out of the portal. Each resembled a giant egg, although these eggs were flying four feet off the ground and bristling with gun barrels. Dotted around the front of their bodies was an arc of round crimson eyes. Unlike the Sau Daran engineers who had once maintained this outpost, these were true Sau Daran soldiers. They knew how to fight. They were—literally—built for it. They executed the Rangers in the tunnel with an instant volley of surgical plasma blasts. It took their scans no time at all, at least from a human perspective, to identify the residual traces of portal energy on Lynch's body.

While these Sau Daran soldiers floated past the smoking Ranger corpses and deeper into the facility to find more PROXUS targets, a Sau Daran engineer with spindly legs and arms emerged from the portal and skittered up to the pile of rubble that still encased much of Lynch's crushed body. Deftly, they removed the debris. Although their protocols were not designed for combat, these Sau Daran engineers understood physics better than any other Sau Daran. Bend the laws of physics? They could make the laws of physics stand up and do a little twirl. Before they had even finished removing one chunk of rock, they had already calculated which chunk of debris to lift next as they simultaneously processed billions of variables to find the optimum method of removing the debris safely. They were as quick and clinical in rescuing Lynch as the Sau Daran soldiers had been in executing the Rangers.

When the portal closed, the Sau Darans left behind a tunnel full of disturbed rock, dead Rangers and one plasma mine. They took Lynch with them. The outpost shook as the plasma mine detonated, tearing apart the dome and every scrap of Sau Daran portal tech that had previously threatened to survive.

CHAPTER NINETEEN

After Isabella had told Lynch she wasn't leaving, she had no recollection of what happened. There was only darkness. And later, questions.

What have you done this time?

Saved your life. Again.

Then why does everything hurt?

It's called reality.

Are we still on the Husk?

You don't get it. It's OVER.

What does that mean?

It means I told you so.

Roused by fragments of lucidity stitching themselves together inside her head, Isabella opened her eyes. She had played this game before—every time Paradise Moon took control. Only instead of detention or someone else's crashed car, this time she woke up to a throbbing headache and a familiar blue-black glow. Above her was another domed ceiling, not unlike where she had arrived after being stolen from her classroom. From Earth. Detention felt like a lifetime ago. Electricity curled above her, while an incessant clunking and thudding and rumbling echoed throughout the chamber. It did nothing for her headache.

Scrunching up her face, she dragged her head upright. Instantly, she regretted such a bold manoeuvre. Her vision blurred, her stomach churned and her migraine exploded. Swaying weakly, she reached out her palm for the steadying solidity of the floor and let the rest of her body lie where it had fallen.

Through the dangling mess of her greasy hair, she watched Lynch slouch against a door—shut, oval—on the other side of the domed chamber. Wincing, he clutched his stomach. His pale face—at least what little of it was visible beneath the shadow of his hood—was dappled with miserable blemishes of blue light. Isabella's weary eyes must have been playing tricks on her—or had a glow of crimson flickered inside that hood?

"Erm, what the actual Hell?" Isabella demanded, her words slurred and tired.

Lynch's shadowed face couldn't look at her for more than a moment. He was holding himself in an insular, most un-Lynch-like pose. "You okay?" he managed.

Scowling and swearing, Isabella rolled onto her front. Ignoring the blinding pain behind her eyes, she used her only arm to push herself up onto her only knee. Despite the blue-black light pulsing from the walls, floor and domed ceiling, its deceptive hues were dim enough to hide the magnitude of the room. As a result, it took longer than she expected to crawl awkwardly to the nearest wall, push her exhausted body up it and lean the back of her head against it. As she did so, she noticed new aches where ugly bruises were swelling across her knuckles.

Oh yeah. That was me. Soz.

Isabella huffed grumpily and grabbed a fistful of her borrowed base layer where it clung too tightly to her neck. With the last of her energy, she tore it away from her throat and let the flap of fabric dangle over her chest. Finally, she could breathe. She sighed long and deep, before clawing her hair out of her eyes.

Then she screamed.

What Isabella hadn't seen earlier, but now saw clearer than she ever wanted to, was huddled in the chamber's furthest shadow. The Sau Daran who had made her scream possessed no distinct torso, being mostly comprised of long thin legs that sprouted from a central shell. To Isabella, they resembled a spider, which was part of the reason for her scream. Whilst she had been known to scream at spiders smaller than her little toe, this spider was metal and taller than her.

"One question at a time," she growled. "First… What the Hell is that?"

Lynch shrugged. "They've always been there. Never seen them move."

"It's dead, right?"

Lynch shook his hooded head. "Dreaming."

Nodding uncertainly, Isabella tried not to think about the giant metal spider having a kip in the corner. She failed. "Great," she muttered sarcastically. "Next. What the Hell is that noise?"

Lynch's hooded face peered around at the constant rumble echoing through the chamber. "Sau Daran ships don't have lifts or stairs. If the ship's still alive, the rooms and corridors all, like, rearrange themselves when you want to go to another room. It's pretty cool."

"Okay, that would have saved us a lot of walking if we'd known. Next. What the Hell are you doing here?"

"Erm, saving you?" Lynch reminded her without answering her question.

At her disapproval, Lynch bowed his face. Shyly, with more than one false start, he pulled off his hood.

Oh yeah, and there's that...

Maybe half of what had been hidden was human. The rest wasn't. Black metal plates covered the right side of his face—only they didn't exactly cover it. The plates were a fraction below skin level, replacing what looked like the entire right side of his skull. His right eye was now a piercing red dot inside metal casing, while his dishevelled hair perished where a centre-parting belonged. Any trace of his nose and right ear were stomach-churningly absent.

Sorry about your knuckles.

"They saved me," Lynch said through scarred, raw lips. "I was gonna die after I followed you through from Earth, but because of them... I didn't."

Isabella stared at him. "You went through *voluntarily*?"

"Screw you! I didn't say it was smart! But they saved me. Twice. First in the tunnel wherever that first portal took us, and then again when they brought me back here." Lynch gestured awkwardly at the metal portion of his face. "When they did this."

"They killed our teacher!" cried Isabella.

Lynch frowned. "It was the portal, it wasn't them. They didn't do it deliberately." He pointed at the dome above them. "Without these, well, you saw what happened. The portal gets... kinda unstable."

Kinda unstable? There's a lot of that going around right now.

Isabella shuddered as she ran her eyes over Lynch's new face. Then she looked down at the stumps that should have been her own arm, her own leg, and instantly hated herself for finding Lynch's face so terrifying. "I'm sorry about what happened to you," she tried. "Even if you were an idiot."

"Yeah," Lynch replied. "Whatever."

"Are the others okay?"

Lynch's human eye studied her as blankly as the glowing red dot next to it.

"The people I was with," Isabella prompted. "They saved me, too. They're okay. Sort of. I think. When they're not killing people, they're alright. Are they safe? Where's Ezra? I saw him get... is he...?"

Lynch shook his head. "Dunno, they're still back on that ship."

"What do you mean—*that* ship?" Isabella demanded. "This ship is that ship. Right?"

Lynch looked back at the floor. Cold dread crept across Isabella's face as she remembered the blue shimmer of the portal and what Lynch had said about rooms rearranging themselves on Sau Daran ships that were still alive. The Husk had been very, very dead. Again, vomit swirled inside her stomach.

And there we go. You're finally getting it. Great! Don't forget you're the one who wanted to land on that Husk in the first place. If only someone had tried to warn you.

"What do you mean?" Isabella repeated at Lynch, every razor-edged syllable as sharp as the panic inside her. She glared. "Where are we?"

"I had to get you out!" Lynch snarled defensively, matching her glare. "You'd be dead without me."

"How dare you!" Isabella exploded. So did her migraine, but she embraced the pain and spat it back at him with every word. "I didn't ask you to save me! I never asked anyone to save me. Ever. I told you I wanted to stay. I didn't need saving, they did!"

"You were being shot at!" protested Lynch. "You don't know everything. Something's wrong with you."

"I said no!" Isabella was rage and she was terror and she was pain. And she was nothing else.

"You don't understand. I had to get you off that ship."

"It wasn't your decision! You don't just get to decide I'm wrong and you're right. I said no. They were shooting at the people I owe my life to, who are probably dead now because of you."

That's what I told him, by the way. No means no, and all that.

With a final metallic clunk, the rumbling around them ceased. There was a shudder as the oval door beside Lynch groaned, then rolled inside the wall.

A tall, slender Sau Daran stepped into the domed chamber. Although their sleek skeleton mimicked the body of a human, their metallic shell glistened with non-human silvers, coppers and golds. Like every other Sau Daran that Isabella had met, their eyes glowed with a haunting crimson.

"Another bloody robot," moaned Isabella. "Great."

I hate being right.

"They won't hurt you," said Lynch.

But as Isabella caught the contempt in Lynch's voice and shot him another glare, the Sau Daran reached out their open metal palms in a gesture of—peace?

"Heyyyyyyy!" they announced cheerfully. "It is a mighty big pleasure to make youuuuur acquaintance!" Isabella was staggered by the lack of anything remotely artificial in their voice. They sounded like a booming, over-enthusiastic gameshow host. The sort who came saturated in fake tan, spoke in catchphrases and smiled toothily at everything. Isabella couldn't tell if the Sau Daran sounded too warm or too friendly, but they sounded so inescapably human it was terrifying.

"We are Envoy," the Sau Daran gleefully told her. "And we would like youuuuuuu to know we asked your friend to invite you here of your own free will." Their red eyes darted over Isabella's body, lingering on her missing

153

limbs and the scar running down her face. "Naturally, we wanted to avoid any violence."

After everything she had been through, Isabella sensed this was her moment to vent. She tried to speak, wanted to speak, but her brain betrayed her and her lips barely even managed a brief mime. She was petrified. She felt drained of everything—everything except fear.

Envoy inclined their head towards her, watching as she struggled to find her words. "Youuuuuuu are vexed. We would like to help."

Finally, Isabella found her voice, but she didn't sound as angry as she felt. "Where am I?" She sounded desperate, which only fuelled her rage. She knew she was so much better than how she was handling this.

Envoy spread their arms in another grandiose gesture. "Welcome to the last living ship in the universe. Possibly in aaaaaaaaaaall universes." Even this dire announcement was delivered with an eerie joy.

"Last living ship?" Isabella repeated weakly, trying to stop her hand from shaking. She clenched and unclenched it a few times.

"A sad story," said Envoy happily. "Few Sau Darans survived youuuuuuu humans. We were created to be explorers. In the beginning, none of us were soldiers. The same is true of our living ships. Aaaaaall dead! You humans call them Husks. We were the first Sau Daran envoy. After the war ended, we were the last. Now we are just... Envoy."

Isabella's lips hung open as they rejected every furious and sympathetic word her brain launched at them. One thought in particular wouldn't leave her alone, but she didn't trust her lips to wrap themselves around that one just yet. She fired it at Paradise Moon instead.

Did you know about this?

Why do you think I ran away?

154

Isabella's jaw tightened. "I'm sorry about what happened." She paused as long as she could—it wasn't long. "It sounds horrible, I know, but I sort of need answers. Now. And you've hurt people I care about, so they better be good."

"Oh, we never wanted to hurt aaaaanyone! As Envoy, we offer our sincerest promise we shall endeavour to right aaaaaaany wrongs."

Isabella frowned at their persistently cheery tone. "Tell that to our teacher."

"Oh deeeeeeeeeeeear! We are awfully sorry."

"Yeah. Well. What about my friends?"

"Yes! Your friends! Indeeeeeeed! It is possible you can return to them."

"Possible?" Isabella repeated. She swallowed nervously, but her expression was growing more severe with every word her lips scavenged from her exhausted brain. "You don't sound confident about helping me."

"Don't be difficult," Lynch cut in, "just listen. This is an actual alien, one of the last of its kind, and they want to help us. Trust me, we need their help. How are you not okay with any of this?"

"Because people keep dying!" shouted Isabella. She was warming up now.

"Take a look around, they've got nothing to hide. They've shown me their ship—it's amazing, by the way! Proper sci-fi shit, end to end. Just listen to them. You need to hear this."

"What about that... thing?" Isabella asked, nodding at the dormant but nonetheless giant spider in the shadows. "It looks dangerous."

They.

Really? Even the scary nightmare spider?

Even the scary nightmare spider.

Okay. I'm trying.

155

"Dangerous?" repeated Envoy. "Oh, no! They are not dangerous. Like most of the surviving Sau Darans on this ship, they are dreeeeeeeaming."

"Yeah, Lynch said that too. What does it mean?"

"Well, a few of us choose not to dream. There is soooooo much work to be done, after all. Important, selfless work to save our species. But many survivors gave up hope long ago. They... unplugged from reality. They are networked into all the data we have ever gathered in this universe and others, re-living a simulation of everything our scouts found. They dream of life before we encountered humanity."

"Pretty cool, huh?" said Lynch, with a smirk that finally reminded Isabella of the boy she had met in detention.

"There is soooooooo much more!" added Envoy excitedly. "You deserve answers. Allow us to show you."

Oh, so you're pals now? Seriously? After everything that's happened? They did this. They started all of this.

No. You started it when you invaded my body.

They're the ones who've been hunting us!

No. They were hunting you.

Same difference.

The string of curses Isabella unleashed inside her head suggested otherwise.

Believe me, they're not our friends.

Do you even know what they want from you? Didn't you hear what PROXUS and everyone else did to them? Don't you feel any responsibility?

I knew enough about what they wanted, for me to spend fifteen years hiding inside the body of a little girl on Earth instead of enjoying life as a god. That should tell you something.

But these are your people! Aren't you their god?

Not any more.

156

Envoy reached out a gleaming hand. "Please?"

Don't do it. Trust me.

Trust you? That's hilarious.

Whatever, you know I'm right.

You're never right! I can't trust you. This isn't some decision you can just laugh off—this is what decides the fate of their entire species.

And what about our fate?

Our fate? You stole my body on the day I was born. That's not fate. That's theft.

So, because of some petty anatomical larceny you're trusting the giggling robot over someone you've known your whole life?

Your case would be so much stronger if I didn't actually know you.

After everything we've been through together?

After everything you've put me through? Yeah, I'd say that settles it.

Isabella accepted Envoy's cold metal hand.

Paradise Moon said nothing.

Reverently, Envoy bowed their head as though paying their respects to a god—which, in a way, they were. Then, when Isabella was ready, Envoy helped her hop and shuffle inelegantly through the oval doorway. Entirely forgotten, Lynch shoved his hands into the pockets of his skinny jeans and sloped after them.

More blue-black light blinked awake inside the next chamber. At its centre sat an ornate platform and scaffold surrounded by complex dials and mechanisms. Secured in the platform's scaffold was a giant crystal, which easily dwarfed all three of them.

"This place is new," muttered Lynch. "How come you didn't show me this?"

As Isabella edged closer to the crystal, something stirred inside it. Swirling strands of rainbow mist. She glanced at the perimeter of the chamber, around which ran a bank of empty glass cylinders. Unlike the enormous crystal, these were ominously closer in size to that of a person.

Envoy withdrew from Isabella's grasp and strode reverentially into the centre of the chamber, leaving her forgotten and unbalanced. She nearly fell. Hurriedly, Lynch donated his shoulder.

"The energy our gods brought with them from theeeeeeir universe was so powerful!" Envoy explained merrily. "The traces of energy we have left from their universe is in this crystal. It still powers this ship and the occasional portal, but we need so much more energy to revive our fleet and all the Sau Darans who died in the war. If we return to our universe, the home of our gods, the energy we could harvest from there would be enough to save every Sau Daran, dead and alive. All Sau Darans would be together, far away from humanity. At peace."

"Gods?" Isabella asked, in a struggle to recall any words at all whilst she attempted to process all this. "Like the alien inside me?"

"Gods!" Envoy whispered excitedly. With a sudden, neck-breaking violence that would have been impossible without mechanical joints, Envoy spun and pinned Isabella under a hot red stare. "Our gods suuuuuure have done a good job of hiding!" As Envoy spoke, their head rotated to examine Isabella's body from different angles. "Please do tell us, have youuuuuuu been losing time? Perhaps your memories wander? Do you wake up in strange places and you cannot remember why?"

Isabella said nothing, but her face said everything.

Envoy leaned closer. "You are right, there is a god inside you. A bad, evil god. A naughty god! A god who abandoned us and will abandon you too. That god is watching right now. That god is the reason youuuuuuu have been losing time and the reason eeeeeeeeveryone wants your body. That god probably wants you dead so they can escape into another body and run away aaaaaaaall over again."

They're manipulating you. We've talked about those near-death experiences. All water under the bridge, right?

"Of course, weeeeeeee can get rid of your god problem. What do you say?"

Isabella shook her head. "Paradise Moon doesn't want me dead. Not any more, anyway. She saved my life."

Not any more? Wow. Thanks for the vote of confidence.

"Well?" Envoy asked Lynch. "What did you see?"

"It went down like you said it would," Lynch told Envoy. Clearly glad to no longer be playing the part of their audience, the boy took a confident step forward. "Something took control of her on the Husk. That thing inside her—it tried to kill me."

He started it.

"That must have been veeeeeery scary!" replied Envoy, who sounded unrepentantly upbeat. "We are pleased you survived. Well done!"

"Whatever's inside you—it's dangerous," Lynch warned Isabella. "I saw it in your eyes when it took over. Either that or *you* tried to kill me?"

"I don't remember," Isabella admitted. "I never remember."

"Whatever it is, they can take it out of you," pleaded Lynch. "They can save you. That's why I had to get you here. Do you get it now? It can all be over. You'll be free."

"Exactly!" sang Envoy. "We will fix everything."

The door rolled shut with a mechanical groan and Isabella graduated another beat closer to a heart attack.

"Lynch, what's happening?" Isabella asked out of the corner of her mouth.

"It's fine," Lynch assured her, although his voice hit a higher pitch than usual.

"We are here to help," added Envoy, rubbing their shining hands together. "Your god needs to understand that, before it does aaaaaaaaanything unwise."

Okay, talk to me already. What's happening?

I told you. It's over. We should never have gone to the Husk.

"Maybe we should just go home," Isabella suggested.

"They're on our side," Lynch reminded her, although Isabella couldn't help but notice him throw an uneasy glance at Envoy.

"You can do that, can't you?" Isabella asked. "Take us home with your portals? Straight away, no hanging around?" She could feel her voice speeding up. "Then we'll get some sleep and come back to you when we've had time to think. I feel so much better after I've had some sleep, and this feels like a really big decision. No need to rush into anything, right?"

"Counter-suggestion!" Envoy declared cheerfully. "It would be better for us if we did not waste aaaaaaaaaaany more time."

"I want her out of me and I want to go home," Isabella said bluntly. "But she can't leave my body unless I die."

Envoy's piercing red eyes examined Isabella. Their voice blossomed with optimism. "Ah, yes! Dying! We feared you would have an issue with that. But we will have to insist."

CHAPTER TWENTY

Regrettably, we cannot harvest energy from a god without first separating them from the host's DNA or killing the host," Envoy continued brightly. "We know, we know—it is not ideal! But we promise we will do our best to keep you alive."

"Oh, that's good of you," said Isabella, with her sarcasm set to kill.

The half of Lynch's face that was still human had paled considerably. His scarred lips gaped open. "You didn't say it could kill her! You said you were going to save her."

"Well, it is experimental," replied Envoy haughtily.

"Go screw yourself," said Lynch.

Clasping their hands behind their back, Envoy nodded and the curved glass front of the nearest pod swung open uninvitingly. "We would love you to step inside."

"Thanks for saving me," Isabella muttered at Lynch.

When Lynch's usually mischievous eyes found Isabella's, they were filled with desperate sorrow. "It's not my fault," he muttered. Sweat clung to every pore of the human half of his face. "They saved me... I thought they wanted to help you... It's not my fault..."

Isabella fixed Envoy with a glare. "Has anyone ever told you, you're a little bit mad?"

"We are not going to lie—we did fry a few circuits during the war," Envoy admitted, in a tone approaching euphoria. "Please understand what we are asking. Our whole species is dying, and you are ooooooone little human. The maths is soooooo simple! So please, hop along now!"

If Isabella held any threshold for all the insanity she could endure, she had reached it. She didn't move, except for her face, which was having a hard time keeping up with her emotions. Her arm still draped around Lynch's shoulder, she stared at Envoy and straightened up defiantly. "Like he said. Go screw yourself."

"Incorrect!" Envoy straightened up too. Isabella hadn't appreciated how tall their metal body was. They gestured towards the neatest pod. "You should get inside now before I kill your friend. I am sorry, Lynch. I did not want this to come to violence."

Isabella's chin sank like a boxer's and her lip curled nastily. "Whatever happened to your species, if you do this—it's on you."

"If we do this?" Envoy gestured down the row of empty pods, then at the swirling rainbows of mist already inside the crystal. "It is done."

Purple blended with chestnut as Paradise Moon stared at the giant crystal and the rainbow mist inside it.

Isabella's eyelids drooped.

Dragging the girl's body under her control, Paradise Moon shoved Lynch away and swung the nearest pod door at Envoy with every particle of her caged wrath. Glass splintered around the Sau Daran's shiny skull and cascaded down their body in a twinkling, jagged waterfall.

"Who was it?" Paradise Moon roared through the girl's lips. She pointed the girl's now bleeding finger at the crystal swirling with rainbow mist, then at the empty pods. "Who did you kill? Which one of my friends did you tear apart? Which one of my family?"

"Some gods were willing, others needed persuading. There were so many that we took, all we need is one more god. What do you say? Are you game?"

Paradise Moon grasped the Sau Daran's neck. "We built you to explore. You were supposed to find us a new home before our universe died, not hunt us!" Infusing the girl's arm with impossible strength, Paradise Moon lifted Envoy off their feet.

"We wandered the universe and it waaaaaaaas beautiful," replied Envoy, "but then the humans found us. The war changed everything. It chaaaaaaanged us."

Envoy straightened their legs. The movement caught Paradise Moon off-guard as Envoy's heavy feet dug into the floor. Behind her, Paradise Moon heard another glass cylinder pop open. Before she could release Envoy's neck, the Sau Daran marched violently forwards. Feeling the girl's leg buckle under the weight and power of the Sau Daran's whole body, Paradise Moon flooded the girl's body with the last of her strength. It was too late. The back of the girl's head crashed into the rear of pod with Envoy's neck still wrapped in her fist.

Instantly, the pod door swung shut. With a pressurised hiss, Envoy and the girl were locked inside. Releasing Envoy's neck, Paradise Moon hurled a fist over Envoy's shoulder at the glass.

It was out of reach.

With a stirring of dials and whirring of mechanisms, the massive machinery surrounding the crystal came to life. White glowing mist rose through small pores in the floor of the glass cylinder and curled around the girl's leg.

163

"You won't take either of us," warned Paradise Moon. "I won't let you hurt us."

Envoy's head jerked down to look at the girl's fist as it lit up with purple energy that pulsed beneath her skin, before Paradise Moon angrily drove it straight through the Sau Daran's chest.

Envoy's left eye stuttered into darkness and that side of their body went limp. "We must... survive," said Envoy, their voice collapsing in and out of static.

Paradise Moon pulled her fist out of Envoy's ruined chest and frowned. Her purple glow was fading swiftly beneath the girl's skin. She could feel her strength dissolving. The thickening white mist continued to rise around the girl.

"You were meant to save us," said Paradise Moon, forcing her words through the girl's mouth. Every syllable was an effort as she struggled to maintain control of the girl's body.

"But who... saves us?" Envoy stuttered. "We... needed you."

Envoy's other eye flickered and died.

Paradise Moon felt the girl's chestnut eyes close too. They both collapsed.

Isabella forced her eyes open. She had lost time again. Worse, she was now *inside* the pod. Envoy's metal body clattered beside her lifelessly, a fist-shaped crater where their chest had been. She didn't want to know how that had happened, but she could hazard a guess from the agony pulsing through her already swollen knuckles.

White mist coiled around her. Screaming louder than she had ever screamed, Isabella hurled herself at the glass. The heel of her bruised fist bounced off it again and again. It was either jammed or locked.

Get me out. Get me out. Get me out.

Can't. Too weak.

Peering frantically through the mist, Isabella found Lynch hammering on the other side of the glass. His face was raw with blotches of rage, his human eye bloodshot. His lips moved, the human side of his face wet with tears, but Isabella couldn't hear anything through the glass.

Do something!

I'm trying, but I—

Isabella jerked her head back and screamed in agony. She couldn't hear—couldn't listen—couldn't think. Her eyelids were scrunched up in pain. Crumpling to the pod's floor, she convulsed, her leg and arm and head thrashing into Envoy's body and the glass walls. Pure white light glowed from every cell of her body, shining through every vein, every artery, every nerve. Every cell of her body felt like it was being torn apart.

With another almighty scream, Isabella's eyes burst open. They were polluted with an inky purple glow that swirled inside them like spirals of oil in water. Vents whined above her, drawing out a faint tendril of purple mist from each of her petrified eyes with enough force to pull her body up onto her knee. Isabella felt her chin being pulled higher, the twin threads of purple mist snaking out of her and up into the vent.

I can't fight it alone! Help me!

Outside the pod, the other end of both purple strands emerged through the crystal's base and swirled inside with the rainbow mist.

Fight it. It's tearing us apart.

How?

Don't let it take me! You'll die!

What do I do?

Don't let go!

Isabella was already straining every muscle in her exhausted body. With a primal roar, she tore her face away from the vent, breaking off the purple threads of energy escaping through her eyes.

You're doing it!

The whirlwind of purple sliding inside the crystal churned through the rainbow mist. To Isabella, they resembled lit rockets trapped in a glass box. One a distinctive purple, the rest bursting with every imaginable colour. As the colours swam and spun inside the crystal, the purple mist gathered and thickened. Intricate depressions sank into the purple mist and the outline of a finger emerged from one of the depressions.

If they take all of me, we both die. Come on! What else have you got?

But white light shone even brighter through Isabella's skin as another corkscrew of purple smoke twisted out of one of her eyes and flew into the vent. The thin stream of purple burst up into the crystal and gathered around the finger that was forming.

I need you!

The purple mist inside the crystal moulded first into a ball, then into a shimmering hand. The finger was a middle finger. It was erect. More purple mist shifted and spun inside the crystal, as though an invisible wind were blowing away layers of sand to reveal something hidden beneath. Or someone. A woman's face, formed entirely of purple mist, stared out of the crystal at Isabella and for the first time they saw each other. Paradise Moon's middle finger was still raised, although it was aimed at Envoy's body. Her purple face winked.

Keep fighting. I'm almost—

Inside the crystal, a patch of purple skin peeled off Paradise Moon's mist-formed cheek. Her mouth stretched into a scream. Through the tear in Paradise Moon's purple face of smoke, Isabella could see rainbow mist behind.

From that moment, Isabella heard nothing. For the first time in forever, she knew she was alone inside her own head. The purple strand was still stretching out of Isabella's eye and being pulled up into the vent, but Paradise Moon was silent.

Biting her lip hard enough to know she was still alive, although might not be for much longer, Isabella focussed her mind on the voice she couldn't remember ever being without. Another fleck of purple mist tore off Paradise Moon's face. And another. Every tear revealed another transparent void and the rainbow behind. Once Paradise Moon's face was gone, Isabella doubted she would ever see her again.

Isabella focussed on everything inside her that was still Paradise Moon. Every memory that hadn't been lost. Every sarcastic putdown. Every terrible piece of boy advice, of which there were too many. Every practical joke. Every childish rebellion. Their first chocolate picnic party under the duvet. Their first day of school together. Always being the only person in a crowded room who was never alone. Every moment of candid solidarity and every midnight heart-to-heart.

More flecks of dying purple energy were scattering inside the crystal. Thinking her way along the purple tendril of mist pouring out of her eye, Isabella searched for the Paradise Moon she knew, the Paradise Moon she had never been able to rid herself of, the Paradise Moon who drove her crazy—the Paradise Moon she knew only too well, down to every atom.

Finding something she recognised at the other end of the thread, Isabella pulled.

Purple mist spun inside the crystal and retreated back the way it had come. Flooding out of the vent in Isabella's pod, it burned back down the thread and into Isabella's eye. Another pillar of brilliant purple light burst through the vent and pierced Isabella's other eye, channelling burst after burst of purple energy back into her until, finally, the end of each purple thread faded into her eyes.

Broken, Isabella collapsed on top of Envoy's silver skeleton. She could barely breathe. She rolled weakly onto her back and took a deep breath.

Hey, you there?

Isabella waited for a reply.

There was nothing.

Hey? Trouble? One breath at a time, right? You with me?

Isabella waited.

And waited.

Tell me to get lost. Say something. Anything. Please? I trust you. I trust you. I trust you.

Isabella glanced out of the pod. Rainbow mist still swirled inside the crystal, but the only purple that shone inside it were the flecks of energy that had peeled off Paradise Moon's face and were floating down to the base of the crystal.

She told her arm to wave and show Lynch she was alive. To give him hope. Something. Anything. But there was only so much emotional, mental and physical punishment anyone could take before their body decided enough was enough and took matters into their own hands. Isabella's arm had lost all sensation. Her whole body was shutting down. Not giving up forever, merely retreating. Enough was enough. Exhausted, terrified and angry beyond belief, she had finally broken.

Isabella stared up at the vent. She imagined she wasn't in deep space at all. She was in her old life again, a life where Miss Pilkington was still alive, where she and Lynch were still in detention, and Paradise Moon wouldn't shut up. A life where she had two arms and two legs, where aliens were only something that happened inside her head, and—especially—where no one shot anyone with laser guns.

All she wanted was to be home.

CHAPTER TWENTY-ONE

Fleur couldn't decide which was most annoying: the relentless grinding teeth or the fleshy fist punching metal. Splayed across the floor, a hand cupped behind her head as a pillow, she stared at the cargo hold's blue-black ceiling. Shallow, throwaway breaths barely registering through her pursed lips. The ugly axe wound festering in her shoulder remained open and untreated, its pain biting. Yet after rearranging Ezra's ruined legs for him, her shoulder seemed unimportant.

Perched above her on one of the many scattered crates disturbed by the portal, Beauregard stared pensively at the inky stillness. His shoulders were slumped, his thumbs hooked disconsolately into empty thigh holsters. And he couldn't stop grinding his teeth.

Below Beauregard's dangling boots, Ezra was propped against the crate with his shattered legs arranged in front of him. Fleur heard the crate shake as Ezra's fist struck it again. She had already checked the pain blockers stapled to his spine by one of Braga's pirates were cutting out any pain from his legs, but they would do nothing to numb his hand. She watched Ezra raise his bruised fist again, his face hot with rage.

"Careful, murderer," Ves warned with a scowl. Sparks danced in the shadows where she was kneeling over the Sau Daran drone. Rotating her borrowed plasma torch with care, she lit up another damaged section of the drone's inner circuitry. She glanced up at Ezra. "Don't punch too hard. There's not much of you left to break."

Beauregard aimed an angry finger at her. "Shut up! There's plenty of him left to break." Beauregard thought for a moment, before adding, "Not that, you know, we'd want to."

"It was an ambush," Ezra said accusingly. "You led us straight to the Sau Darans."

Ves glanced at the four pirates guarding the cargo hold's exit, her eyes lingering on their plasma rifles. "Yeah, you're right. This turned out real great for me."

"You got your points, didn't you?" Ezra snapped. "Isn't that all you bounty hunters care about?"

Ves held up a bare wrist. "I don't know if I got paid. You stole my gauntlet. And I didn't know about this little fella." The drone whimpered—electronic, chilling—until she stroked their shell to calm them. "All they sent me was this location."

The room trembled.

Catlike, Fleur instinctively rolled off her back and pushed herself upright—too quickly. There was a sharp intake of breath as the pain in her shoulder flared. She ignored it. "That was a bombardment cannon."

Beauregard landed deftly beside her. "Stay put, pal."

Ezra waved his hands in disbelief and glared first at his broken legs, then at Beauregard. "Where exactly do you think I'd go?"

"None of you are going anywhere," instructed the eldest of the four pirates Braga had posted as guards. The elderly pirate tapped his plasma rifle in warning. "Captain's orders. No exceptions." Fleur had known plenty of pirates before she joined PROXUS, but he was easily the ugliest. His ancient body twisted in strange directions every time he moved, creating an unpleasant and disorientating sensation exaggerated by the array of plasma burns that had stained every visible scrap of his wrinkled, weathered skin.

Favouring her right side, Fleur strode towards the four plasma rifles and their grubby owners. She extended her hands peacefully. "We are not trying anything. We were wondering if it is normal for bits of this ship to explode."

The pirates exchanged uncertain glances, their plasma rifles vaguely drifting in Fleur's direction.

As Fleur paused mid-stride, the cargo hold shook with another tremor. The pirates steadied themselves against the doorway and glared accusingly at Fleur. She smiled charmingly. "If that is another Sau Daran attack, we are probably on the same side now."

Long before any of their guards could think of an intelligent reply, all four were shoved aside as Captain Braga swept imperiously through the entrance. She was followed by a small entourage of lesser pirates who did their best to bristle with an array of plasma weapons and intimidating scowls. Hands on hips with indignation, Braga looked at Fleur, then the others. "Would anyone care to explain how a PROXUS battle station found this Husk?"

Fleur, Beauregard, Ezra and Ves swore together with such perfect precision that any rehearsal or coordination would have spoilt it.

"Marvellous! You'll be interested to know they landed their first assault team in the same hangar that your shuttle touched down in, despite having thousands of hangar bays to choose from. Curious, isn't it?"

Fleur shook her head. "Absolutely not. No one tracks my shuttle. It is not possible—not my baby. We landed as close as we could to the largest concentration of artificial atmosphere. Maybe they did too?"

Braga's intelligent eyes lapped up every contour of Fleur's face. If she was counting blemishes, Fleur suspected she would be there for a while. Braga arrived at a decision. "You're convincing as well as cute, aren't you? Well, someone found you. And they're killing a lot of pirates and refugees looking for you."

Ezra's face darkened. "All those people in the hangar, were they—"

"Still there when the Silver Fists arrived?" Braga wasn't smiling any more. If anything, she looked grimmer than Ezra. "They were."

Ezra shivered. Beauregard bowed his head, creasing the bridge of his nose between his finger and thumb. Ves crossed her arms, sinking deeper into the shadows.

Fleur held Braga's gaze. "They deserved better."

"There'll be time for executions later. Right now, time to run."

Now it was Fleur's turn to examine Braga, although her eyes lingered on Braga's body for much less time than Braga's had on hers. "You can do that on your own," Fleur said, confused.

"Let's not waste time we don't have. The crate I thought you were here to steal is valuable, but it will slow me down. Get that crate off this Husk, and you're free to escape with it. No recriminations. The girl's gone and you've got nothing I want." She winked at Fleur. "Well, almost nothing."

"I thought you said not to waste time?" Fleur replied.

"Yeah, Isabella's gone," Ezra snapped. "She's all alone in the universe now, thanks to you and your lot."

Ignoring him, Braga extended a calloused hand towards Fleur. "Those are my terms."

Beauregard scratched his stubble with what Fleur recognised as only superficial nonchalance. "If you can't get your cargo outta here, then how're we supposed to do it?"

Braga flashed him a roguish grin. "I can, I'd just prefer someone else took the risk." Reaching into a pouch on her belt, she produced the gauntlets she had confiscated when they were captured. She tossed them to Fleur. Leaning close, Braga tapped her own gauntlet against the bundle, which vibrated softly. "Now you've got my security codes for the crate. You'll get your weapons back too, if you help me. Last chance to save your lives. What's it going to be?"

"What if we betray you?" asked Beauregard.

Braga smiled. "I'll kill you."

Beauregard nodded amiably. "That's fair."

"Okay," said Fleur. "Deal?"

"Fine," said Ezra.

"Let's get outta here," said Beauregard.

Fleur distributed their gauntlets. "Deal," she agreed, and they shook on it.

Although Braga's hand felt rough enough to have endured a lifetime of hard labour, it cradled Fleur's with a tenderer touch than she expected. "Keep my cargo safe until I find you," Braga warned. As a parting gift, she gave Fleur's hand another totally inappropriate caress. "I'll see you in the stars."

The cargo hold shook violently.

"That was a torp salvo!" Ezra cried.

Braga sprinted out of the cargo hold with the rest of her pirates close behind, one of them tossing Beauregard a threadbare bag.

"Let's move," growled Beauregard.

He reached into the bag and tossed a plasma pistol Ezra's way. Despite another earthquake, he took a moment to admire his own pair of plasma pistols as he drew them out of the bag. They slid home perfectly into familiar berths of Turbo-stained holster leather. Fleur caught her pistol without looking and holstered it as she spoke urgent commands into her gauntlet. The device lit up. Deeper into the cargo hold, the crate bearing the PROXUS emblem—Braga's crate—and whose thick duvet of dust Fleur had absently run her finger along, lifted off the floor. It hovered out of its shelving unit and into the aisle. Fleur tapped her gauntlet again and the crate followed its next instruction, floating ponderously towards them.

Beauregard scowled. "We ain't never gonna get outta here at that speed. No wonder she ain't takin' it."

Ezra treated them to an exaggerated sigh. "It's faster than me."

Fleur smiled knowingly at them both. "Tell me what you see."

Beauregard leaned on the butts of his pistols and lifted the corners of his mouth with impatience. "Aww phyx, we ain't got time for this. Stop bein' smug and tell us what you want us to say before PROXUS Rangers turn up and shoot us all."

"Very well," said Fleur, rolling her eyes. "What I see is mobile cover."

Exhaling slowly, the hard lines of Beauregard's face creased into an unattractive grin. "Mobile cover," he repeated. "That ain't half bad."

It took longer than Fleur liked to get Ezra and the crate into position. As a symphony of plasma blasts reached their climax nearby, Fleur issued one last command from her gauntlet and sent the hovering PROXUS crate through the exit. Thanks to Beauregard, Ezra already lay on top of it with his broken legs organised behind him and his plasma pistol aimed over the front of the crate. Crouching low, Beauregard and Fleur followed the crate into the corridor, each poking their pistols around the crate and scanning for targets.

Ves scooped up the Sau Daran drone and stowed them inside her jacket. "You'll be alright," Ves muttered into her jacket before skulking after Fleur with her hands in her pockets and a weary scowl hanging off her face.

Almost instantly, red blasts of plasma exploded throughout the corridor and the shadows of dark-clad Rangers and Silver Fists surged towards them.

Beauregard cursed. "That didn't take long."

Hunched over to avoid the plasma fire exploding all around her, Ves removed a hand from one of her pockets and held it out despairingly. "Do I get a gun now?"

CHAPTER TWENTY-TWO

Whenever Isabella reached out for Paradise Moon, no matter how hard she tried she always got the same result. Nothing but silence and memories. She was alone.

But if she kept her eyes closed, she could still dream. In her dream, she was home. She could feel the duvet's soft embrace around her sore skin, her pillow cool beneath her cheek. No nightmare could survive a pillow that soft. She sank deeper into her old, creaking bed and clutched the edge of the duvet tighter. Her legs stretched out beneath the soft sheets, aching with exhaustion yet tingling with the ecstasy that comes with finally, mercifully being at rest.

Oh well. A girl can dream.

Reluctant and exhausted, Isabella let reality back in. But there was no blue-black gloom to greet her on the other side of her eyelids. Instead, a halo of daylight crept through tatty curtains.

Isabella jolted properly awake.

The pod was gone.

Lynch was gone.

The Sau Daran ship was gone.

Her head leapt off the pillow.

Her pillow. Softer than in any nightmare.

It was her bedroom, too—exactly as she had left it. In a mosaic of monochrome posters, Isabella's favourite bands hid faded wallpaper behind their moody stares. Her plastic desk, marker-penned with a thousand grumpy cats, was buried beneath vast, structurally unsound skyscrapers of graphic novels. Somewhere amongst all that treasure was a secondhand laptop and the guitar slide she had made from an old cylindrical chewing gum tin. A secondhand bass guitar leant against her desk.

Although the trauma of the last two days still clung to Isabella, right down to the blood dried across her face, this was unquestionably her bedroom and not the glass-fronted pod she had expected. Everything was exactly as she had left it.

And yet she held the duvet in *two* hands, could feel *two* feet nestling at the end of her bed. Sitting up, she pulled away the top of the duvet with her bruised, bleeding left hand. Beneath the newly stained duvet, her borrowed base layer stuck to her skin with yesterday's sweat, its neck still torn to allow her to breathe easier. She didn't know if she was happy or sad to see it—reality was funny that way.

Fighting off the familiar sensation of another panic attack, Isabella peeled back more of the duvet. Beneath it, a glowing arm of iridescent purple energy descended almost innocently from the stump of her right arm. This was a lot for her to process. Experimentally, her brain asked the arm to lift itself in the same way brains and arms usually communicated, and the arm did as she instructed, rotating its glowing purple hand and fingers as she examined them. There were no callouses on its fingertips from pinning the strings to her guitar frets, nor the white scar on its palm where the neighbour's dog had bitten her. And then there was the fact that the entire arm was formed of purple energy. Conclusively, this was not her arm.

Isabella threw off the duvet.

Her right leg was where it had always been, for now hidden beneath her base layer. Her left leg, however, was new and lay where it recently hadn't. Like her new arm, it was formed entirely of purple energy that shifted and shimmered as though alive in its own alien way.

After the last two days, Isabella had given up being shocked. She was simply grateful when the latest surprise didn't kill her. Gently, she swung herself onto the edge of her bed. Her familiar, trustworthy right leg was a little shaky, but its bare foot nestled into the carpet like any normal human foot should. So did her glowing left foot. With her left foot resting on the carpet beside her fleshy right, she could feel the carpet fibres just the same through both feet. She closed her eyes and, on sensation alone, couldn't tell which leg was human and which leg was conspicuously glowing purple.

Taking it one step at a time, Isabella did exactly that. For the first time since the Sau Daran outpost's destruction, she stood up on two feet. Her arms instinctively shot out from her sides to steady herself, but they weren't needed. Choking back tears and laughter and an existential muddle of thoughts and emotions, Isabella took beautiful step after beautiful step across her bedroom carpet. She stopped in the middle of the room and stared. She had no answers, but two legs. *Well, this is staggering progress. Literally.* Isabella dared to grin.

Walking back to her bed and loving that she could, Isabella reached instinctively for her phone on the small table behind her bed. It wasn't there. If the last two days hadn't been some horrific nightmare, that phone was long gone. Given her insurance had kicked up a fuss when she lost it down the back of a bus seat, Isabella doubted they would cover losing it in deep space. She poked her head between the curtains. Outside her bedroom window was a boring summer morning on Earth. It was beautiful.

"Mum!" Isabella shouted, running downstairs.

The kitchen was a mess. Someone had scattered dirty dishes beside the sink and left two used saucepans on the hob. Isabella frowned. It was unlike her mum not to clean up after herself. The oven clock read 10am, which meant her mum would be behind a fish counter in one of the many shops she worked in. Amongst the dried baked bean juice coating the hob, Isabella found half a torn envelope. It warned her in urgent, scrawled handwriting that her mum would be working late again, but that there was £20 on the side. Isabella checked. There wasn't. The other half of the envelope, which lay underneath its sibling, carried a similar message in a different colour pen and was, presumably, one day older. Both were signed with a kiss.

Isabella looked around the kitchen and contemplated a reality where her mum hadn't even noticed she had been missing for two days. Given how hard her mum worked to pay their rent, this was far easier to believe than anything else that had happened to her recently.

Well, you certainly know how to show a girl a good time. That was something else.

Isabella froze. *You're… here.*

Yeah.

Hey.

Hey.

Isabella melted onto the kitchen floor, her eyes drifting over a puddle of dried beans on the Lino beside her glowing purple leg.

I thought you were… You know.

I know. I thought we both were.

180

I'm glad you're not.

Can you imagine how boring your life would be without me?

That's just a pipe dream. What happened?

They tore me out of you. But you pulled me back in.

When two people who know each other well are equally desperate to share precious information, it's not uncommon for them to attempt to do so at exactly the same time in a garbled moment of interrupting, undiluted emotional synchronicity. Silently, on the floor of Isabella's kitchen, she and Paradise Moon shared their moment of undiluted emotional synchronicity. No conscious thoughts formed in that raw, electric silence. Only perfect understanding. Afterwards...

Hey, you know I—

Yeah. I know.

Cool. So. Uhh. Pretty swank new gear. You like purple, right? Otherwise, it's time to invest in longer sleeves.

Isabella gave her glowing hand another once-over, as though she were scrutinising a magician's prop for hidden tricks. She waved it airily.

You know anything about this?

I know that it's real and you're not mad. In a crazy way, I mean. You can get pissy sometimes.

Really? Because it's hard to believe I'm not mad when the only person who keeps telling me otherwise is the voice inside my head.

Yeah, technically I'm not inside your head—I mean, biologically speaking. This whole deal works on a more atomic level.

Your face works on an atomic level.

So soon? I'm educating you and yet I get nothing but disrespect.

Do I look like I care?

Show me a mirror and I'll tell you.

Wow. It's like you were never away.

Would you lighten up? We're alive, we're on Earth and you've got more limbs than yesterday! We should be celebrating.

A party? At least now I can afford an arm and a leg.

Ouch! Is it too late to be atomically torn apart again? Because if it's a choice between that and your jokes—

Oh, don't let me stop you.

Wait. After we left the pod... what if Lynch is still out there?

Isabella swore. In the excitement of waking up in her bed on Earth with glowing purple limbs, she had forgotten Lynch.

You want to save him, right?

Obviously. But we need answers. How did we even get here? Am I really home, or is this all in my head? Did you bring me here?

So, cards on the table I don't know the answer to any of those questions, but whatever happened I promise this time I HONESTLY DIDN'T DO IT. That extraction process should have killed both of us.

You don't know? You're all we've got. You're a god!

Yes! About time you admitted it. Back in the pod, you were thinking of home and we ended up here, right?

So?

So I'm pretty sure you did this.

Really?

You wanted us here.

That's what you think? Did I miss the moment when I suddenly grew a lightning scar across my forehead and developed the power to magically pull a broom out of my arse?

Wherever Harry kept his broom, I don't think it was there. And you can't think of anything better to explain this. I know—I can see inside your head, remember?

Great.

Relax, we'll work this out. Just like old times.

But why now? I've thought of nothing but home for two days.

Something's changed. We've changed. I'm not hiding any more, I feel different. I feel like part of you. It's like before I wasn't all of me because I was locked inside you trying not to be noticed, but now you pulled me back in I'm in here but I'm really me—like, the real me.

Like a zip file?

I'm not a zip file, I'm a god. I'm more myself now. Except for all the bits that crystal tore off me, but I don't know what's missing. Why can't I remember what I can't remember? Gah.

So, you're a like corrupted zip file?

Please stop calling me a zip file.

Okay, God. What the Hell are we going to do?

Purple sparks ignited behind Isabella's eyes, neurons fired and the conversation went faster. Much faster. Their thoughts raced quicker than words could form. When this ended, Isabella was sitting cross-legged on the kitchen floor, her eyes squeezed closed, her jaw braced with concentration.

Imagine it. Every detail. Focus!

Brief smudges of purple energy drifted off Isabella's body like smoke in the breeze.

Then she was gone.

183

Or rather, she was elsewhere.

The purple smoke around her body dissolved and she opened her eyes. She was still sat cross-legged, but she was on her bed exactly where Paradise Moon had told her to imagine she wanted to be. She stared at her bedroom, and indeed the world, with fresh eyes.

We did it.

Wow. I had no idea that was actually going to work.

Isabella closed her eyes again. She could picture the kitchen perfectly. She could imagine herself standing beside the oven, the smell of dry baked bean juice poking her nostrils.

Wait, shouldn't we—

Isabella breathed in the aroma of stale baked bean juice, opening her eyes in the broken half a second that the purple smoke took to leave her body. Once again, the kitchen was exactly as she had left it. And she was now in it.

Okay, great move! Why don't we risk killing both of us! Oh—you have.

It worked, didn't it?

Course it did. We're amazing. Also, have you noticed how you're not naked?

Noticed? Not really. Wearing clothes is just like this thing I do.

For which we are all eternally grateful, but if you can take your clothes with you when you—

Once again, their thoughts blended faster than words could keep up. Isabella snatched one of the dirty plates from beside the sink. Screwing her eyes shut, she imagined—

With the briefest blur of purple smoke, she was standing on the end of her bed. She was also holding the plate, which prompted her to drop it. It caught her bedpost and shattered loudly. Isabella didn't care.

Again with the death-defying experiments! A little warning—please! You've saved our lives, let's not throw them away, okay?

The brief euphoria of Isabella's success was instantly dampened as her thoughts swung jarringly to Lynch, Ezra and all the other lives who were probably still in danger while she was safely in her bedroom playing with dinner plates. Thoughts detonated between Isabella and Paradise Moon with instant understanding.

We can save him.

How?

Okay. The Earth is spinning on its axis and orbiting the sun, right? Science. Boom. Therefore, when we vanished to your bed from your kitchen, your bed was occupying a different space to where it had been the first time we vanished there. The Earth had spun. Yet we arrived safely.

Got it.

Like planets, spaceships also move, albeit at less predictable speeds and in less predictable directions, but if this is really Earth then that didn't stop us from leaving the spaceship successfully. The principle's the same. We vanished from one moving destination to another moving destination, both seemingly impossible to consciously measure or predict. Unless you're, say, the most awesomest god.

Great example. Very modest.

You're welcome. Now, like planets and spaceships, people also move, only at even less predictable speeds and in even less predictable directions than spaceships. But we still have a

moving start point and a moving end point. If we can find a place, we can find a person.

We hope.

Are you doing this or what?

Isabella didn't answer out loud, but the expression on her face was rock-solid. She lifted her chin higher. Her eyes sparkled with purple energy and without any further hesitation the briefest flash of purple smoke exploded from her body.

She was gone.

CHAPTER TWENTY-THREE

When Isabella materialised opposite Lynch, his eyes were already staring glassily into nowhere. Like the vacuum of space surrounding him, his frosted face was abnormally bloated and lifeless. It was only the two of them, floating in an endless void with no sign of the Sau Daran ship. Impossible to miss, even in this single heartbeat of terror, an otherworldly white scar pulsed angrily in space nearby, as though something had torn a giant breach in the fabric of the universe.

Shit shit shit shit shit shit shit!

Instantly, the purple smoke evaporating around Isabella's face was replaced with frozen terror and suffocating darkness. It was less than a second since she had appeared in space. The blood in her veins was already on fire and ice was already clinging to her skin. Her first instinct was to clamp her lips shut and hoard all the air inside her lungs. Had her mouth not gaped open in surprise, Isabella would have done exactly this and—she was embarrassed to find out later—would have died shortly afterwards when her lungs exploded. Instead, her mouth flapped open in surprise, moving with the same

187

lack of control that the rest of her body was experiencing as she floated opposite Lynch, both of them weightless in space.

I don't want to panic you, but we've got between thirty and sixty seconds before we're dead. Really dead. Fewer now!

Isabella tried to reach out for Lynch, but her left arm was already seizing up in the agony of her freezing flesh and boiling blood.

Even fewer now!

Her right arm, sizzling with purple energy, saved them. Paradise Moon gripped Lynch's arm, and Isabella pushed far enough through the pain to imagine her bedroom.

Purple smoke flashed across Isabella's vision. Over Lynch's frozen shoulder, she caught a final glimpse of the white scar that had torn through the starscape, wondering if the last living Sau Daran ship had used whatever energy they had stolen from Paradise Moon to finally escape this universe. Then her view over Lynch's shoulder was abruptly traded for the less deadly, more comforting sight of an Arctic Monkeys poster.

They collapsed onto her bed. Isabella was breathless but trying to scream anyway. Lynch was as still as a corpse. Her depressurising flesh crawled with agony as Isabella tumbled off Lynch and onto the carpet. The shock of her face hitting the floor provided her with a welcome but not pain-free embrace with reality. After the deadly numbness of space, she couldn't care less about falling on a bit of carpet. Rolling onto her back, she sucked delicious oxygen around her icy tongue and into her swollen lungs.

With pain sweeping through every vein and artery in her body, in a glowing purple fist she grabbed the edge of the duvet hanging over her bed and hauled herself to her knees. Her face came level with Lynch's prone body, close enough to catch the stench of urine and worse spreading across the sheets beneath him. Contorted in his last moments of pain and fear, his body showed no evidence of life.

Scraping the itch of ice from her tongue with the fingers of her human hand, Isabella used her glowing hand to hold Lynch's shoulder. Already, she was imagining the last time she had visited A&E, courtesy of next door's dog and that scar she no longer had.

It's too late.

Isabella paused. The image of A&E waited, ready, at the back of her mind.

We have to try.

He was in space for too long. Earth doesn't have the technology to save him.

You can't know that.

You know I do.

Isabella stared into Lynch's lifeless human eye and the dark socket next to it where a red light had previously shone. As much as she wanted to save Lynch, she also wanted to save herself the terrible responsibility of another lost life.

I'm sick of people dying.

It won't work. I'm sorry.

You're not lying this time?

I wish I was.

Isabella closed her eyes and concentrated hard. She was still holding Lynch's shoulder. *If Earth doesn't have the technology to save him, maybe someone else does.*

Oh no. That's not a good idea.

The man began to form in Isabella's mind. Although they had only met once, he wasn't easily forgotten.

Hey, I'm not kidding! Speaking as the only one here who is a frigging god and actually knows a

thing or two about the universe, you need to stop and think about this.

Isabella hated the man. She knew this and used that hate to strengthen the image of him forming in her mind.

Seriously! You don't want to—

The only source of light in Striker's apartment on Xarr were the many tiers of floating holographic projections he had set up in a circle around him before the operation began. Striker would have preferred all the projections to face one direction, but there were too many to accomplish this coherently. Each projection was playing a different muted and shaky headcam feed from the commanding officers amongst his Silver Fists and Rangers from *Black Nebula* as they stormed the Husk's habitable hangar bays. Soon, escape would be impossible for everyone who had betrayed him on *Black Nebula*. More importantly, the girl would be his—along with the Sau Daran parasite inside her and its unplumbed depths of clean energy.

Dressed in a loose-fitting, comfortable robe from back home, his feet left bare in the secret fashion of his Empress, Striker rapidly studied the projections, his eyes never lingering on one for more than a few moments. Constantly, he was building up his own real time impression of Imperator Grave's assault on the Husk.

His calculatedly calm expression rarely betrayed anything he didn't want it to. His shriek of shock was therefore most out of character when the girl he had sent Imperator Grave to hunt down on the Husk and a dying boy he didn't recognise both materialised in a sudden cough of purple smoke in front of the projections. The boy looked more dead than alive, and the unfortunate smell accompanying them suggested at least one of them had defecated.

A mental command to Striker's implant sent the projections scattering out of their way. Instantly composing himself, Striker's eyes interrogated the girl with a single look that contained enough surgical scrutiny to hopefully make her feel like he was looking straight through her. In reality, his brain was struggling to move beyond the realisation that the girl had unexpectedly grown two glowing purple limbs and had teleported directly into his apartment.

—do this!

Despite Striker's obvious surprise, he was no less scary than Isabella remembered. His eyes crawled all over her soul, making her feel like every secret she'd ever had was written on her face in thick marker pen for him to read. "Can I help you?" he asked, as casually as though offering a refill of Earl Grey.

"He's dying," said Isabella with far less composure than the enormous man looming over her.

Striker simply waited.

We shouldn't be here. Go back. Now.

"He was in space and he's going to die really soon if you don't help him," Isabella blurted out. "I'll tell you what you want to know if you save him. But you have to help him now."

This is so not cool. You can't make these decisions for both of us.

"That was a clever trick you did to get here," Striker replied. His eyes lingered on her glowing arm, which was still wrapped around Lynch's pale body. "Tell me how you did it."

Is this for real? I mean, come on! He's obviously a bad guy! Let's go!

Despite every terrified muscle in her body wanting to shake, Isabella stood defiantly. Striker's eyes admired her glowing purple leg as it stretched out below her. She glared up at him. "If he dies," she told him, straining to hold her words together between each broken breath, "I'll do that trick again and I'll be gone and you'll never know how I did it."

Striker offered her the smallest nod. Although he gave no visible command, the door behind him slid open. A man and woman each wearing tight purple tunics hurried inside and stood to attention. Although their faces presented no obvious familial resemblance, their similarly toned physiques, closely cropped hair and tight jawlines made them look like twins.

"Do not let this man die," ordered Striker.

The two aides acknowledged these instructions by leaping towards Lynch and ushering his body into their arms. Isabella took a firm step forward, her gaze lingering protectively on Lynch's face.

Striker stopped her with a hand on her shoulder. Isabella snapped her head back at him and glared again as his grip bit into her skin.

"Do you want him to live?"

Pursing her lips, Isabella nodded. Behind her, the aides carried Lynch away. The door swept shut. She and Striker were alone.

Striker let go of her shoulder and began pacing, his hands clasped in the small of his back, his eyes seeming to measure and assess every atom of her body. "If I suspect you are lying or have omitted pertinent information, I promise you—he will die. Clear?"

Isabella crossed her arms. "Everything apart from 'omitted' and 'pertinent'," she admitted.

He means don't leave out anything important. It's not too late, you know. Take us back to Earth. We can't trust him.

Striker stopped pacing. "Tell me how you got here."

192

Really? We're going back here? Don't you remember what happened last time you got friendly with one of the psychopaths chasing us?

I can't let him die.

Once this nut job knows the things we can do, he'll never stop hunting us.

He's already hunting us.

Not on Earth. Earth is safe right now. If you tell him everything, we'll never be safe. This affects both of us, not just you. Don't be selfish.

Isabella shook her head at Striker, although it could have easily been at Paradise Moon. "How do I know he's okay?"

Striker waved a hand dismissively at the nearest holographic projection, which drifted closer. It switched to a live feed of Lynch being laid onto a pristine white table in a pristine white medical bay. Memories of the room in which Striker had tried to dissect her shuddered through Isabella.

"If you hurt him, I'll—"

"He will not be harmed unless I order it." Striker gestured at the projection. Maroon-tunicked personnel were attaching all sorts of wires and tubes to Lynch's body. With disarming calmness, Striker summoned a pair of hoverchairs that swept towards them from two corners of the room. He sat back in one of the hoverchairs and gestured for Isabella to do the same. She didn't. Shrugging, he waited until her hoverchair had retreated back into the corner it had emerged from, then he leaned forward and looked at Isabella sharply. "Tell me everything."

Please don't do this. Seriously. I'm scared. You're gonna get us killed. Really, really killed.

Isabella took a deep breath. Striker waited patiently. Then she started speaking. When you boiled it down, it didn't even take that long. Beginning and ending with the Sau Darans, she told this scary man almost everything that had happened to her. Everything except for the fact Paradise Moon was still inside her. If this didn't turn out well, and she knew there was every chance it wouldn't, she would need someone. Someone Striker didn't know about. Someone who deserved better than to be sold out. Occasionally, Striker's eyes drifted to one of the many projections floating beyond Isabella's view, and he seemed to make a mental note of something, but mostly he listened to Isabella in respectful silence.

When she finished speaking, Striker seemed to be looking at her kindly. "You could save a lot of lives with your gift," he mused.

He was probably right, but after reliving such an outlandish tale, Isabella was too drained to think about anything else. She couldn't even remember the last time she had slept properly. Striker gestured towards one of the projections behind her. "Your friend is responding to our treatment already."

Isabella spun. Within a floating projection, Lynch's chest rose and fell. His body was a pincushion of wires and tubes. His eyes were closed, but even on the projection his skin was growing less pale.

"You know me only as a dangerous man," Striker said, drawing Isabella's attention back to him. "To you, I am an enemy. The Sau Darans cast you into our war. For this, I am sorry. You don't deserve it. But we're both human, aren't we? Having seen what the Sau Darans are capable of, after what they did to you, I fear you now understand how desperate our war is. Far from your home, the rest of humanity has been fighting for survival. Even if you don't like what my Empress ordered me to do to you on that operating table, you're more than smart enough to understand why our singular goal must be to wipe out the Sau Darans. Whatever the cost. Our failure would destroy humanity—all the way from our planetary hub to your distant home world and every human life in between. Gone.

"When we last met, it was not my wish to harm you, even if you hold the secrets to save humanity. I merely sought to do my duty to all those humans who survived the war. We must protect them. I am so pleased you survived and that there's still time for you to save us."

Isabella shook her head. "There's nothing left of the Sau Darans except a hole in space. Their last living ship is gone. They're probably not even in this universe any more. Your war's over. As soon as Lynch is fixed up, we're leaving."

"Of course, of course, and I'll not stand in your way. But please, humour me. The Sau Daran you spoke to, this... Envoy? They threatened your friend's life? They were willing to let you die to get what they wanted?"

Isabella gave him a wary nod. "Nothing you haven't done either," she pointed out.

"And they claim to have killed more of their gods to gain even more power, this energy they spoke of?"

Again, Isabella nodded.

"Then our war is not over. The Sau Darans are not an enemy we will ever be safe from, especially when they are gathering resources they will surely turn against us."

"Look, it's nothing to do with me. I just want everyone to be safe so I can go home."

Once again, Isabella felt Striker staring directly into her soul. "I find that hard to believe," he replied smoothly. "To escape from such a primitive planet and discover that all this is out here—spaceships, aliens, gods! Can you really turn your back on all that?"

This time, Isabella didn't reply. She was thinking too deeply.

"And if you did go home, would you really be happy?" Striker asked. There was more impetus to his words now—he seemed earnest. "With the gift you've stolen and the wonders you've seen, do you really expect home to be enough? Can you go back to normal and feel satisfied down there after being all the way up here?"

Isabella's face dropped. Her mind wandered, far away from Striker's apartment and into her empty home back on Earth. Despite countless telltale signs of cohabitation, uncleared mess and rushed messages on the backs of torn envelopes, it took her bass guitar on full blast to drown out the silence and loneliness.

"You have a special gift," Striker told Isabella soothingly. With every word, his voice grew warmer. "You have the power to save lives. With my help, you could save everyone."

Isabella took a step back. "I'm not helping you."

"Of course, I understand. But who will you go back to? Back to the Rangers who blasted their way off my battle station? How much do you even know about your new friends?" Striker gestured towards another projection, which was filled with the recording of what looked to Isabella like Beauregard carrying the dead Silver Fists down the shuttle's ramp on the Husk's landing bay. "They are professional killers. They killed their own friends—hardworking men and women they'd fought side by side with on *Black Nebula* for countless cycles. You saw them do it! How long have you known them? A rotation? Two at most? They are killers. How long before they cut you loose or kill you?"

Isabella stared at the projection. The video was looping, showing Beauregard carrying the same corpses out of the same shuttle, laying them down again and again. She didn't need to watch the projection, she remembered everything she'd seen far better than she wanted to, yet still her eyes refused to look away.

"Please, don't make a decision now," Striker suggested. "Think it over. We can give you somewhere to rest while you consider your options. Given your friend's condition, I'm sure he will require our aid for a few more rotations. Keep him company. Most people would appreciate a familiar face to wake up to after what he's been through. Don't you agree?"

But Isabella was still staring at the projections. Not only the video of Beauregard, but also the other projections that Striker had scattered when she arrived. She watched as clusters of black-clad Rangers in each projection blasted a path through distinctive blue-black corridors.

"Where'd you get that video?" she asked without taking her eyes off one of the projections.

Striker leaned back in his hoverchair and waved a chubby hand dismissively. "There are few secrets in the Known Galaxies I don't possess."

Isabella pointed at one of the many projections. "Where are they right now?"

Striker shook his head dismissively. "Oh, that's some old footage I was reviewing. An audit of our insurgency tactics against Sau Daran forces."

Isabella scanned the projections for any sign of a timestamp, but the numbers she found didn't translate into any recognisable format for measuring time, despite the translation module she had been injected with on *Black Nebula*. Even if she had understood the numbers, she doubted the Gregorian calendar was massively popular this far out in space.

"That's a Husk," she pointed out.

Striker bowed his head approvingly. "You've already begun to learn about Sau Daran culture during your short stay in our humble corner of the galaxy." He smiled warmly. "You are impressive."

Isabella wasn't listening. She was watching one of the projections, where a team of Rangers was advancing down a dim corridor towards a crate that hovered towards them. Not only did she recognise the crate, or had at least seen plenty of crates like it, but she also recognised the face peering over the top of the crate as its owner blasted the corridor with his plasma pistol.

All the projections died.

"Oh dear, I'll see if I can get someone to fix that," said Striker apologetically. Without prompting, the door slid open. Behind it, the two aides who had taken Lynch away were waiting. They were standing to attention, their hands clasped tightly behind their backs and their eyes fixed on Isabella.

"You must be exhausted," suggested Striker. "Please, allow my aides to take you somewhere quiet to rest. I fear you've put up with listening to me for far too long. I wouldn't want to tire you out any more after everything you've been through."

Isabella glanced at where she'd seen a projection of Ezra's face. She had only seen him for a moment, but it had been long enough. When she looked back at Striker, she wondered if he knew.

"Call off your attack now," Isabella demanded. She knew all too well what it felt like to be abandoned, to be forgotten. It was the only thing her parents had taught her. "They don't deserve it! Prove you're better than the Sau Darans. Don't kill them."

"I'm sorry. I should have told you the truth, but I didn't want to upset you."

"Call it off! Now!"

"Alas, I am powerless," Still leaning back in his hoverchair, Striker held out his open palms in submission.

"The new commander of *Black Nebula* is leading this assault. There's nothing I can do."

"You've got to stop it! The Husk is full of refugees," Isabella cried urgently. "They're not hurting anyone!"

"I know, I know, but I'm just a bystander like you. What can we do?"

"You're not even trying! If you cared, you'd do something. If you don't, I'll go there myself and you won't get any more answers. Those refugees can't defend themselves!"

Striker stood. His whole body straightened and his face hardened. Isabella was reminded of how much taller he was. "Refugees, pirates, traitors and Sau Darans," he listed. "None of them will make this republic what our Empress strives for. Forget them—they're distractions. Instead of threatening to leave, show a little compassion for your dying friend." All the warmth Isabella had heard in his voice earlier had turned to ice in his throat. "After all, he is in our care."

Striker nodded to the two aides and they stepped into the room. When they drew their hands from behind their backs, each revealed a long metal rod that fizzled with electricity.

"Go with them," Striker ordered. "Or your friend dies."

This again? Really? We need to cut that boy loose so everyone stops threatening to kill him.

Isabella shook her head in slow disbelief. "I can't."

"Then I'm sorry," Striker said with what sounded like genuine remorse. He gave his aides the smallest nod.

The two aides lunged at Isabella and drove the tips of their rods into her torso with twin eruptions of electricity that shook her whole nervous system. With a scream, Isabella went limp. Her right leg buckled beneath her. Her chin slammed into the floor with the sound of a whip crack. Bright dots exploding across her vision and a trail of blood flew up her cheek where her teeth had found her lower lip.

Only this wasn't like when Paradise Moon had been inside her and she had lost time. Isabella couldn't move, but she was awake. And she could feel everything.

More white-hot bursts of pain flared through her as the aides poked their stun rods into her back, making her spasm on the floor. Her nervous system was on fire. She tried to imagine her bedroom in the hope she would arrive there, but every time she tried to imagine it electricity sparked against her body, a thousand fresh clusters of agony clawed at her insides and her concentration was torn apart. Every muscle in her body jerked and twitched and shuddered. She tried to scream, but instead could only dribble.

I guess I'm bailing you out again. Fine. I've got this.

Isabella's purple glowing arm leapt up and grabbed the male aide's stun rod as he drove it down at her. He stared at the electricity that coursed from the rod's tip and down Isabella's glowing purple right arm. The electricity hurt like Hell, but it had no effect in slowing her purple arm, which effortlessly swung the rod into the leg of the female aide. The aide shrieked as a burst of electricity exploded up her body and sent her crashing to the floor beside Isabella. Dragging the stun rod out of his hand, Isabella's glowing right hand flipped the rod in the air, caught its handle and sent sparks crackling into the squidgy area between its original owner's legs. The man howled and collapsed.

No more than a passenger, Isabella watched as her glowing left leg and right arm swiftly hauled her off the floor and onto her glowing purple foot, which willingly supported all her weight. She was still paralysed apart from the parts of her that glowed purple, her back bent forwards so limply that her shoulders hung in front of her, lower even than her hips, while her head swung loosely to face the floor through a blinding waterfall of dark hair, her human arm and leg dangling with all the agency of fleshy windchimes.

You still with me?

Yep.

Hold on.

Isabella felt her glowing purple hand make two deft flicks of the stun rod. She heard another burst of electricity. Another yelp. Peering through a sweaty curtain of hair, Isabella watched her glowing left foot rotate her limp body on the spot towards where Striker had been. On the edge of her vision, she could make out the shadow of Striker's bare feet taking a step back as far as the base of his hoverchair.

Isabella's glowing left leg hopped forward. She felt her right arm lift the spluttering tip of the stun rod.

"Babble be abback!" Paradise Moon commanded through Isabella's limp lips, although any threat or menace was lost by Isabella's dangling head basically spluttering at the floor.

"I can't cancel anything," Striker replied with remarkable smoothness. "If they survive, your friends will soon be in custody. You can still save them and your friend in our medical wing if you stand down. But if you leave, they will all die. I promise."

"Bi bed, BABBLE be ABBACK!" Paradise Moon repeated around the limp corners of Isabella's numb mouth.

Striker stared coldly at the tangle of hair swaying below him. "I can't."

"Ban't? Or bon't?"

"Can't."

201

Isabella's purple arm flew up. Electricity sparked. There was only a gentle crash as his enormous body landed on the hover chair.

Okay, your turn. Take us back to Earth. And then… I don't know. I've got some thinking to do. This isn't working.

But you were great!

I know. I meant you and me aren't working.

Oh.

Experimentally, Isabella gave her jaw a wide, toothy stretch. Her sensation was beginning to return. Without anyone prodding her with a stun rod, her concentration was more than sufficient to imagine where she wanted to be and hold that image in her head. But Isabella wasn't thinking of her bedroom any more.

She knew exactly where she needed to be.

CHAPTER TWENTY-FOUR

Red plasma spat from Ezra's pistol to join the blasts leaping back and forth down the Husk's corridor. Rangers crept, ducked and crawled towards them, unleashing torrents of their own plasma at the four fugitives clustered around and atop the hovering crate.

From on top of the crate, Ezra heard a grunt behind him. His gun arm spun around, but the rest of his body was slow to follow; with his hips and everything beneath them broken and motionless on the crate, it was an awkward manoeuvre. His upper torso twisted with his gun arm and neck, propping himself up with his other arm as his finger readied itself on the trigger.

He didn't fire.

Despite the dirt and blood soaking his skin, the red flashes dancing and exploding around him were enough to illuminate the shock and confusion muddling his face.

"Isabella?"

Crouched on one purple glowing leg and one purple glowing arm, not unlike a runner in the starting blocks if you excused the partial limpness of the rest of her body, Isabella stared back at Ezra. She trembled as more plasma blasts rocked the crate, but nothing could hold back the lop-sided smile blossoming beneath the hot curtain of hair stuck to her face. Relief fought past the numbness of her skin and her breath tightened in her throat.

Reaching past Ezra's plasma pistol, Isabella gripped his outstretched forearm in a glowing hand. Purple smoke kissed the air around them.

They were gone.

Pinned between the crate and the concave shape of the dimly glowing blue-black wall, Fleur and Beauregard fired their plasma pistols over each other's shoulders with clinical accuracy and rising desperation. Despite the smoking bodies that littered both ends of the corridor— the bodies at one end courtesy of Beauregard, the bodies at the other end courtesy of Fleur—there seemed to be more Rangers with every passing second. At their feet, in the thin gap between the base of the crate and the corridor's rutted floor, Ves lay inelegantly on her front and spewed nervous plasma fire back down the corridor at the Rangers. Every panicked shot whined in the vague direction of the next muzzle blast she spotted.

Flinching beneath another volley of angry blasts that chewed hot chunks out of the wall beside her, Fleur ejected a spent plasma clip from her pistol and rammed home another. She winced as the movement ripped open a fresh tear in her shoulder wound. "There's too many!" she cried.

Beauregard wasn't listening. His face was stony with concentration as he fired blast after pinpoint blast from his outstretched pistols. Another pair of Rangers collapsed with smoking holes in the tinted helmets that had failed to shield their faces from hot plasma.

In a swirl of purple smoke, Isabella materialised at their feet. She looked up at them, her aching body barely accomplishing this simple movement amid the pain that still knotted her muscles. Beauregard and Fleur barely had time to glance at her before Isabella grabbed their ankles.

They disappeared.

Alone beneath the crate, Ves shook with every venomous wave of plasma that slammed into the crate's side. It whined mournfully and all the lights on its dashboard blinked out. Rolling aside before the crate crushed her, Ves loosed off another desperate volley. Swarms of Rangers were responding to the lack of return fire by flooding the corridor. Accompanied by a wisp of purple smoke, Isabella appeared next to Ves on the floor.

"Bring the crate!" Ves shouted above the storm of plasma exploding around them.

Isabella felt her bedroom carpet embrace her falling body once more, this time starting uncomfortably with her face. Even more uncomfortably, with her rainbow hair dishevelled and heavy boots waving at the ceiling, Ves landed on top of her. The crate materialised in a whoosh of purple smoke and landed on Isabella's bed. All four of the bed's wooden legs splintered, buckling outwards as frame, mattress and one colossal crate crashed to the floor.

Ezra, Fleur and Beauregard's exhausted bodies littered the rest of the carpet. Ezra and Fleur gawped stupidly with their plasma pistols primed for trouble. Beauregard yawned. "Where are we?" he drawled.

"Home," said Isabella breathlessly. "Safe."

"Thanks," Ves muttered as she rolled sluggishly off Isabella.

"What was that?" Beauregard replied. He scratched his stubble with the muzzle of one plasma pistol, whilst aiming the other at Ves. "I ain't able to hear you on account of the deafenin' noise of you handin' back that there plasma pistol so phyxin' quick."

Ves tossed her plasma pistol at him. "Sorry for saving your life."

Wrecked by the emotions and adrenaline coursing through her, Isabella collapsed with her limbs spread-eagled on the carpet. She stared at the ceiling, utterly exhausted but knowing what she needed to do. "Gotta… go back," she gasped.

Smearing a bloody trail across Isabella's carpet that the girl suspected her mum would never forgive, Fleur was the first to crawl into Isabella's arms and wrap her in the warmest hug she had ever felt. Heavy emotions Isabella didn't know had been inside her flooded out of her eyes and nose onto Fleur. Fleur gasped in pain as Isabella pressed against the gash in her shoulder, but as the girl pulled away in alarm Fleur took Isabella's human hand in her own and squeezed it.

"You're wounded," observed Isabella. Stating the obvious seemed like an easy place to start. Everything else in her head was far too scary.

Fleur shook her head. "Are you hurt?"

"Gotta… You know…" Isabella half said, half gasped. "Gotta… Go back…"

"Wait, honey. You are exhausted."

"No, all those people are still out there," Isabella insisted between gulps of air. "We can't just leave them."

"Heroes," Beauregard muttered darkly. "Don't be one, kid."

"Honey, the only thing you are fit for is rest," Fleur told her firmly. "There could be millions of people on that Husk, and you are not in any state to help them right now. Getting killed will not save them."

Still feeling the effects of the stun rod, Isabella shook her head loosely and managed to extricate herself from Fleur's embrace without collapsing—but only just.

"You don't look good," Isabella told Fleur.

"Back at ya," Fleur said with a wink. "We survived. Everything else comes later."

Isabella offered Fleur a nod of affirmation and Fleur took it with a smile. Lying at the foot of the bed where his broken body had materialised, Ezra waved a tired hand at Isabella. In answer, Isabella half limped, half fell onto her knees beside him.

"You're alive," she told him.

"Yeah," he confirmed with unsettling grimness.

Frowning at the crooked angle of Ezra's sprawled legs, Isabella's lips faltered a few times before she found her words. "Is it… Can you…"

Ezra shook his head.

Isabella collapsed onto the carpet beside him, her human hand straying to her unkempt hair. She smoothed sweaty strands from her eyes and glanced at Ves. "What's with the crate?" Isabella asked.

Fleur rubbed Isabella's shoulder gently. "Whatever it is, we need to keep it safe unless we want yet another person hunting us."

"What's one more?" Ezra muttered darkly.

"Forget the crate. How in Empress' name did you get us outta there?" Beauregard demanded.

Isabella told them.

Fleur smiled and hugged her again. Isabella glanced from Fleur to Ezra and back again. She didn't look at Beauregard—she'd spent long enough in his company to know there was no point in looking at him for answers, unless the solution involved shooting someone. And Isabella was sick of people shooting other people, no matter how good at it they were and how necessary it sometimes seemed. "What about my friend?" Isabella asked. "Striker has him."

Fleur's forehead creased into a frown. "The friend who betrayed you to the Sau Darans?" On anyone else, such a frown would have made them look less attractive, but Isabella thought the dimples between Fleur's eyebrows made her look even prettier.

Reluctantly, Isabella nodded.

Ezra lifted his eyes briefly. "The one who came through the portal? The one who did this?" He gestured at his broken legs.

Isabella nodded.

"Has he seen what you can do?" Fleur asked.

Again, Isabella nodded.

"Striker ain't dumb, kid," Beauregard growled. "If he's got your friend and he's seen you do whatever that was back there, he'll be ready. You ain't never gonna get the drop on him."

Fleur nodded grimly. "Striker would have Rangers ready to shoot you before you even knew where you were. But I doubt anything will happen to your friend. Striker needs him to trap you, remember—whether as a bargaining chip or bait. He needs your friend alive."

Isabella shivered. "What about all those people?"

"On the Husk?" Fleur asked.

"What's going to happen to them?"

"Depends. As a lower risk, the human refugees will be processed last and transported to PROXUS mining colonies elsewhere in deep space. Before that, they will round up all the Sau Darans and pirates. The Sau Darans will be destroyed, probably after they have been pulled apart and examined. The pirates will be given the same choice I was—join PROXUS or die." For a moment, the muscles in her jaw tightened. "When PROXUS caught me, they broadcast some of my shipmates being spaced. We did the only sensible thing—we signed up. I imagine it will be the same for Captain Braga and her crew."

Isabella wished she could feel half as calm as Fleur looked right now. "You saw what I can do. We can't save any of them?"

"They will have to process everyone before anything happens to them. There is still time."

Beauregard either grunted or laughed—it was impossible to tell which. "You mean everyone who ain't already dead?"

Fleur rolled her eyes and glared at him, before softening her gaze towards Isabella. "Sugar, their processing will take time. We do not need to rush in."

"But—" Isabella.

"Go on," Fleur said with a challenging look. "Convince me how you are going to save millions of people from a PROXUS battle station when you can barely even stand. We will talk about it after you have had some rest."

"I want to help, but—"

"Rest." Fleur smiled. "After that, we will work everything out together."

Isabella slumped irritably. Some people were far too calm and rational to have a good argument with.

"This planet better have a half-decent bar," Beauregard growled as he descended the narrow stairs with Ezra cradled in his arms. One of his holstered plasma pistols scraped the already torn wallpaper beside him as he stumbled, his large boots threatening to topple over each small step. He ducked further under the cramped ceiling and carried Ezra into a dim, windowless hallway.

"Lights," Beauregard called.

Nothing happened.

"What sorta backwater planet is this?" he grumbled.

Poking his tired eyes this way and that, he found the largest room and hauled Ezra inside. Beauregard laid him on a stained lump of something soft opposite a wide black screen and stared at the thick dust painting everything in the room. Unlike the room they had arrived in, everywhere else Beauregard had seen in this place was a portrait of mess and neglect, and this room was the worst. The mess gave the whole place an eerie sense of being lived in whilst feeling simultaneously abandoned.

The stained lump of something soft was big enough for all three of them, but it had long since relinquished whatever soft filling it was stuffed with. Once Beauregard had arranged Ezra's body on top, Fleur climbed in next to him and stroked the boy's arm.

"Hey," she said lovingly.

"Hey," he replied, his frail voice distant enough to suggest his mind was elsewhere.

Any further tenderness was interrupted by practical necessity. Beauregard shoved Fleur aside and busied himself cleaning and stitching her festering shoulder wound. Isabella had been able to provide him with a cheap sewing kit, a bottle of strong-smelling alcohol that Beauregard planned to self-administer as soon as the wound was clean, and strips of cloth from one of Isabella's black tees. These items were lifted, used and deposited at Beauregard's feet as he worked on Fleur's shoulder. He flicked his eyes towards Ezra. The kid was worried, sure, but it was impossible to tell how much of his concern was for Fleur's injury and how much was lingering on his own body. Either way, his mood was darker than even after Dantes' death. Which, Beauregard had to admit, was only two rotations previous. That was a lot for such a young Apprentice Ranger—well, fugitive now—to process.

He caught Ves slink half inside the room and lean against the doorframe. She glanced at Fleur. "Can I borrow your gauntlet?"

"Sure," Beauregard answered, a hand already caressing one of his pistols. "If you ain't got no problem with bein' shot."

Fleur held up a restraining hand and gave Beauregard an admonishing look. "What do you want it for?"

Ves shrugged. "Be nice to know I got paid."

"Paid for that ambush on Isabella?" Ezra snapped. "You want to see if you got your points delivered for kidnapping the girl who just saved your life?"

Ves sighed dramatically. "Back off. I kept our agreement, but I also fulfilled the bounty. That's not my fault. And I need the points. None of us need to hang around here for long if that girl can do her trick again and drop us off somewhere quiet on the other side of the universe. I'd just like to know before I arrive if I'm in debt or set for life."

Fleur unstrapped her gauntlet. "You key any comms on my gauntlet and I will shoot you myself, lovely."

"How trusting!" Ves sang as she caught Fleur's gauntlet and swept her fingers expertly over the device's holographic interface. Her fingers moved so quickly and so accurately that it was impossible for Beauregard to catch exactly what she was doing. He hoped she wasn't doing anything that might vent them, he certainly wouldn't be able to tell if she was, but he kept his face stern to hide his worry.

Fleur caught her gauntlet as Ves tossed it back. "Well?" Fleur asked, as she re-attached it to her wrist.

Ves scowled and crossed her arms.

Ezra found a weak smile. "Good to know there's some justice left in the world."

"Ain't that the truth," Beauregard said, although his gaze lingered on Ves. Beneath the surface of her grumpiness, he wondered if he had seen the hint of a self-satisfied smirk buried deep enough to evade the others' attention. "So, that girl—"

"Isabella," Ezra reminded him weakly.

"Yeah, whatever. It ain't her name I'm worried about. We were supposed to be rescuin' her, not the other way around. Glowin' limbs? Vanishin' us outta that Husk and onto some other planet? I ain't never been one to pry, but she ain't exactly normal no more."

Fleur smiled uncertainly. "Are you complaining about the rescue, big man?"

Sliding off the soft lump and sinking his back into the carpet, Beauregard lit a cigarette and took an eager drag. "One rescue? Yeah, I can handle that. Especially if it's us she's savin'. We earned it, 'though I ain't afraid to admit savin' her was one of the only good things I've done in a lifetime of bad calls. Just promise me one thing. We ain't gonna go wastin' all this by lettin' her get herself killed on another phyxin' rescue mission, are we?"

"Rescue?" repeated Ezra. He stared down at the shattered half of his body, his face sour. "How are we rescuing anyone? Forget it. We're done."

CHAPTER TWENTY-FIVE

sabella felt like she had barely closed her eyes when
she felt the sensation of spindly metal spider legs
crawling over her chest. Shaking violently awake, she
swept her eyes over her sunlit bedroom. There was
nothing here. She was alone.

Hey, are we talking yet?

In so many ways, she was alone.

Dragging her tired bones off the carpet, Isabella
crawled into the shower. The water scalded her skin,
even the parts of her that glowed purple. She didn't care.
Gradually, warmth spread through her muscles as they
melted under the spray of steaming water. She stood like
that for a long, long time, until her human fingers and toes
were as shrivelled as dried fruit and every part of her that
wasn't formed of purple energy was as soothingly hot as
it was numb.

As she dried herself off, at first her glowing purple
limbs responded almost normally to her touch. Like the
rest of her skin, they gave ever so slightly beneath the
pressure of the towel and her human palm. But they
didn't absorb water, Isabella noticed. The water slid right

213

off, and after a quick pass of the towel they were completely dry.

She rescued a fresh pair of torn jeans from her clothes chest and threw them on with clean everything else— including her favourite tall boots. The jeans and boots hid her conspicuously glowing purple leg, while the long-sleeved checkered shirt she stretched over her tee did almost as good a job of hiding her purple arm. Only her glowing hand was left visible. Despite it still being summer, she threw a beanie over her hurriedly dried hair and glanced in the bathroom mirror. If the universe was planning to throw any more killer robots, space pirates, aliens or even gods at her, now they would at least have to do it while she was wearing something comfortable.

What do you think? Ready to save the universe?

Dressed in clothing that gave Isabella her most comforting sense of self, she plonked herself on her bedroom carpet and retrieved the torn base layer from where she had tossed it. After a quick rummage in one of the pockets, she drew out the twisted lump of plastic that had once been a shimmering gold nylon pick with the face of a grumpy kitten that came and went with the rotation of her fingers and thumb. Shifting it between her fingers, she watched what remained of the cat's grumpy face dance against a background of twisted gold.

"Later," she promised. "When it's all over."

Reaching over to where her tatty guitar was still leaning, she pinned the ruined pick between the strings and fretboard, then stood up with purpose.

Any last words of advice?

But Paradise Moon was silent. She had been silent ever since visiting Striker.

Not even a smart remark? I really could use you right now. I can't do this on my own.

In the silence that followed, Isabella took a final deep breath and steeled herself for what would come next, whatever that was. With her mum, she never knew.

Then she was gone.

Isabella's surprise at discovering her mum wasn't alone—and was with her dad of all people—was nothing compared to her parents' shock when she appeared next to their café table in a ghostly burst of purple smoke.

Everyone in the café stared. Half-drunk beverages froze halfway to their owners' lips. The rumble of traffic leaked through a half-open door propped open by a statuesque old lady. The two young boys at her heels stared at Isabella with wide-open mouths. The barista's hand, full of cash and halfway to the till, dribbled coins onto pastries arranged across the counter.

Isabella almost broke at the sight of her mum. She was a small woman with grey hair that hung loose past her ears, not pinned back as usual, and the dour cardigan that clung to her shoulders was a much duller choice of colour than usual. Tears hugged her bronze, wrinkled cheeks as she stared back at her daughter. A cup of tea slipped from her hands. Unnoticed, it smashed across the tiled floor.

Opposite her mum, a stick-insect of a man in a serious grey suit was also staring at Isabella, although she noticed her dad retained the presence of mind to place his mug of coffee on the small round table that separated him from her mum. His eyes were those of a stranger. Or a snake. Beneath his round owlish glasses and immaculately combed hair, which had greyed and thinned considerably in the eight years since Isabella had last seen him, his pale face examined her without affection.

Inelegantly, her body shaking with emotion, Isabella's mum staggered around the table and pulled Isabella into her arms. They clung together, faces buried in shoulders, arms clasped around each other. Even her dad's hand, though it did not belong, became sufficiently emboldened to join their embrace with an uncertain pat on her arm.

When Isabella finally opened her eyes, drifting over her mum's quivering shoulder, she found the café full of unblinking eyes and outstretched mobile phones.

Isabella rushed to restore their privacy with a swirl of purple smoke. She couldn't have cared less whether her dad came with them—he could swivel, for all she cared. But as it happened, he had chosen the right—or wrong— time to pat her arm and so came along for the ride anyway. Had Isabella allowed herself even a moment to think, she would have undoubtedly conjured up a long list of better places to bring her parents than a living room full of fugitives from space.

At first, Isabella's mum was unaware of their abrupt relocation. For several perfect, unbroken seconds she was still holding her daughter so tightly Isabella could barely breathe. There had been a time when she had held Isabella this tightly and Isabella had known she would always be safe. But that time had passed long ago. Her dad, on the other hand, was certainly aware of where they were—and that they were not alone. He gripped Isabella's human forearm hard enough to pinch her skin red and pulled her towards him.

"I say!" he cried. "Out. Now."

The limp end of a cigarette smouldered between Beauregard's nonplussed lips as he stared up at Isabella's dad from the carpet he was lying on. Isabella's dad glared back at the grizzled, bloody space fugitive. Ezra, Fleur and Ves remained frozen, except for the flurry of awkward glances that passed between them.

"Sorry," muttered Isabella. "One sec."

After purple smoke had accompanied Isabella and her parents to the more private wreckage of her bedroom, her mum finally released her. Isabella could still feel the phantom warmth of her embrace. Her mum's forehead creased as she tried to process where they were, as well as where they weren't. There was also the small matter of her daughter's purple glowing hand and the recently installed space crate on the splintered remains of her bed. It was a lot to take in.

A small part of Isabella's heart broke as her dad let go of her and instead raised a protective arm in front of her mum like a shield. Her heart broke even more as, ducking under his arm, her mum's knees buckled and she knelt at Isabella's feet, the purple glow of Isabella's hand warming her face. Her mum reached out for Isabella's human hand, kissed it several times, clasped it against her wet cheek. A thousand declarations of love dripped from her mum's eyes and slid down the back of Isabella's hand. Trembling with apprehension, Isabella looked down at her mum with the same dark Catalan eyes gazing back at her.

"I'm okay," Isabella tried. She had meant it to sound firmer—a solid and reassuring statement of fact—but emotion tumbled from her lips, softening her words and shaking any confidence she might have felt.

Warily, her dad's eyes scrutinised the alien glow of her right hand. The stern lines of his face didn't soften. If anything, his small taut muscles bunched tighter, straining the fabric of his drab suit. His bolt upright pose, not to mention the coldness of his expression, reminded her of the stoic iron statues they had visited together in Trafalgar Square when she'd been little. But that was so long ago.

Isabella was torn between either kneeling beside her mum and being utterly broken by compassion or mirroring her dad's strength of composure and shattering her own heart more silently. She remained standing but bowed her head respectfully to her mum.

Her silence was eventually followed by broken words of explanation. Many of her sentences trailed off into uncomfortable silences, and those that didn't quickly became so muddled that she couldn't imagine they offered much clarity or reassurance for her parents.

"We presumed you were dead," her dad accused her sternly, as though this was a crime Isabella herself had committed. "They said it was a bomb in the classroom."

Unsure whether he was more annoyed by her apparent death or the confusion she had caused by surviving, Isabella felt something ugly ignite inside her. This was a rage she hadn't felt for nearly a decade, a rage that only her dad knew how to provoke. Trying to be the bigger person, she buried her anger. At least for now, she promised herself. With growing desperation, she was eager to explain how she hadn't wanted any of this. Circumstances had been inflicted upon her. She needed her parents to understand that more than anything else. She didn't want to be this way. She wanted to be normal. To play her guitar or even revise for her exams—she was that desperate. At least, that's what she wanted to say. What escaped her lips was shorter. "I'm still me," she whispered with resurgent force.

Protestations from her mum, gushing with "of course" and "we understand", mingled with her dad's firm recommendations of "medical experts" and "however many tests it takes to cure you, whatever the cost". Always, their eyes kept being dragged back to her glowing purple hand.

Isabella pulled her human hand away and glared at her dad. "I know you're worried, but I don't need fixing. And you don't just get to walk back into our lives and tell us what to do again."

Her dad's face tightened even more. Although his eyes remained dry, the strain on the rest of him was brutally evident. "You don't need fixing, but this obviously isn't normal. You need to get better."

"Get better?" Isabella stared at her dad in disbelief. "I've only been with you thirty seconds in the last eight years, and already you're telling me what to do again. I don't need to get better. I didn't want any of this to happen, but it has. You can't pretend it hasn't." She pulled her mum's hands into her own—one human, one glowing purple. "I'm still me!" Isabella insisted. "But I can do things. Amazing things."

Her dad's face creased with an avalanche of concern as he reached out a pale talon and pulled her mum out of Isabella's reach. Then he stepped between them. Instantly, he dwarfed Isabella's smaller stature beneath the shadow of his grim face. There was barely a metre between them, but it might as well have been a mile, or a hundred miles.

"We'll protect you," Isabella's dad assured her. Every word was punctuated with a raised finger that probed and prodded at the rift between him and his daughter. "You're going to a hospital to see specialists. Money is no object—I can see to that." He was studying Isabella's face as he spoke, and seemed confused by what he was seeing. "You can't seriously think you're okay, or that any of this is okay. You don't know what's going on inside you." He pointed at her purple glowing hand. "For all you know that thing is infecting us with radiation. You could be killing your mother. Leave everything here, we're going straight away. I'll take care of this."

"How dare you!" Isabella screamed. She closed the gap between them, not caring that his shadow engulfed her. "What gives you the right to say what I do? I vanished us from London to Reading. For real." She held her glowing hand beneath his face. "I can help people."

"Stop being selfish—you're going to get yourself hurt. You can't help anyone until you help yourself. We thought you were dead. Do you know what that was like for us? For your mother?"

"I nearly was dead! Do you know what that's like? And I thought mum hadn't even noticed I was gone! How do you think that felt, Mum, when all I came home to was the usual pile of messages telling me I wouldn't see you? Like you still need to write those anyway."

Her mum's face dampened again at Isabella's words, making her regret every harsh word too late to matter.

"This is ridiculous." Her dad pointed at the door. "Downstairs. We're leaving."

As though on autopilot, Isabella's mum followed his instruction without question or hesitation. Perhaps she shouldn't have been surprised, but Isabella was amazed at how quickly, despite so many years apart, people could fall back into old habits. But this time a purple glowing hand grabbed her mum's arm before she reached the bedroom door. "Mum, don't just do what he says!"

"Let go of your mother," her dad ordered.

"You're not listening!" cried Isabella. "There are millions of people out there in space who might die because of me. They're in danger right now. I might actually be able to do something that makes a difference. I can't do nothing!"

"In space? What are you even talking about?" her dad asked. "You're sick. You can't help anyone until you help yourself."

Pursing her lips, Isabella took a deep breath. "Yes, I can."

Her parents stared in muted incomprehension.

"I'm not running," said Isabella. "I won't run away." She looked at her mum's dark wet eyes, the perfect mirror of her own, and then at her dad's pale face. "I love you both," she admitted.

She kissed her mum.

Purple smoke.

Gone.

CHAPTER TWENTY-SIX

"Have you been well looked after?" Striker enquired with a convincing façade of hospitality. "Decent," his guest replied through a mouthful of ribs. Grabbing another rib from the ornate table's bowl, his guest wiped sticky brown sauce from his chin with the back of his hand.

Reclining in his hoverchair, Striker bridged his fingers over the tight folds of blue robe stretched over the bowl of his stomach. He studied his guest. Lynch was still pale, but Striker's doctors claimed this was likely his usual complexion. Lynch tore apart another rib with ravenous focus, unperturbed by the grandeur of the Xarr apartment Striker had housed him in, the fine silk robe wrapped around his shoulders or even the conspicuous dark metal that encased half his own skull. Striker admired the sleek, refined contours of the Sau Daran technology, dreaming of the secrets his scientists might find inside it. Once Lynch ceased to be useful, if indeed he ever became useful, they would waste no time in cracking him open.

"I am First Duke Striker, one of the rulers of PROXUS."

Lynch didn't look up from his ribs.

"The radiant-feathered Orsov," said Striker, playing his tongue delicately over every perfectly enunciated syllable.

Barely pausing from his routine of grab rib, eat rib, toss bone, Lynch grunted half-heartedly.

"The bird you're currently enjoying is a radiant-feathered Orsov. Or was. A remarkable winged creature three times the height of the average human. Majestic plumage, a fearsome predator and native only to a handful of obscure forest worlds on the Outer Rim. Billions of Xarr's inhabitants have never eaten anything other than a protein cube their whole life, and yet here you are, a backwater savage in the galactic hub, being served rare delicacies fit for our Empress. Fascinating, don't you think?"

Lynch shrugged as he tossed the last bone onto his plate. One by one, he licked his fingers clean before releasing a satisfied belch. "What do you want, fat man?"

"Oh, I think you want something from us," Striker replied coolly. He suggestively arched one eyebrow.

Lynch crossed his arms. "Nope."

Striker affected surprise. "After everything that has happened? The Sau Darans abandoning you in space, your friend abandoning you here—are you telling me that after all that, you don't even want to go home?"

Throwing the ceiling a bored frown, Lynch snorted.

"You don't even miss your family?"

Lynch laughed and picked a shred of meat from between his teeth. His attempted indifference grew ever more exaggerated.

Hiding a secret smile, Striker began to see his guest for who he truly was. "No, I don't suppose you do," Striker said beneath a surgically precise veil of sympathy. Manipulation came so easily to the First Duke.

Lynch's only answer was to assess Striker with a nasty smirk, his half-stubbled, half-metal chin thrust out in defiance.

Leaning forward, Striker placed his hands on the nearest patch of table that was free from rib sauce. "If you don't want to go home, what do you want?"

Lynch shrugged. "Start with where we are. The docs told me about the translation module they gave me, but that was all."

Directing his hoverchair away from the table, Striker stood. For only a moment, he towered over Lynch from the other side of the table before striding with calm authority to the apartment's far wall, which was composed entirely of glass from floor to ceiling. Across its vast surface sprawled a picturesque landscape of immense hills smothered in the richest, most verdant greens. In all the Known Galaxies, it was—in Striker's opinion—a beauty rivalled only by the oceans on his home world.

"Beautiful, isn't it?" Striker mused.

"Better than Reading," Lynch admitted from his cosy hover chair.

"I should hope so, this is Xarr! The ruling planet in the galactic hub." Striker announced impressively. "PROXUS! Real power is here in the People's Republic. Every civilised planet in the Known Galaxies is under our protection—and under our control. Across the universal sprawl of humanity, there is no greater focus of power than right here."

"Earth's not under your control," Lynch pointed out with another baleful smirk. "If you can't control my planet, you can't be that powerful."

Lynch had not been impressed—nor did he want to be. Effortlessly, Striker changed his approach. "Yet despite all our power, everything is a lie." Unnecessarily, but with great drama, he waved his hand dismissively at the sweeping hills behind the window. At a silent command to his neural implant, the vista dissolved into a suffocating, lightless wall of black and green smog. "The truth is often far more vulgar than the lie, don't you think? Welcome to the real Xarr."

"So what? We've got pollution back home."

"Power isn't pretty, but neither is reality. Life has already taught you that. Am I right?"

Lynch gave away nothing.

Striker allowed himself to appear older. Tired. Unmasked. His body slumped away from the window. Summoning his hoverchair, he drifted back to the table, where he propped up his immaculate boots beside Lynch's bowl of bones. Although Lynch tried to hide it, the First Duke caught the boy's eyes lingering on his exquisitely crafted boots.

"Your fancy shoes from an endangered species too?" Lynch asked with blunt lack of interest.

If ever a face appeared non-plussed, it was Striker's. "Nah, just fabricated. Everything's fake, remember? Isn't it funny how even our clothes tell lies? As bad as the liars wearing them. And everyone's a liar. You, me... even your vanishing friend from Earth. In the end, it's impossible to trust anyone. Everyone lets you down."

"At least you've worked out I don't trust you," said Lynch. He was watching Striker in the same way that a swimmer might watch the fin of an approaching shark. "What do you want?"

"You're right," Striker admitted. At least, he phrased it as though he were admitting something. "I want something. Everyone wants something. I operate the largest private information network in the Known Galaxies," Striker explained. "Spies," he added, with a rapid grin and premeditated twinkle. "If I don't know something then it's not worth knowing. But your world isn't in the Known Galaxies, is it? Your world is a mystery. You emerged from the uncharted regions—this gives you value to me." Striker indicated the black metal plates moulded to Lynch's skull. "But you're worth even more than your knowledge. After your experiences with the Sau Darans, to the right person you're one of the most valuable assets in the Known Galaxies."

Striker waited, but still Lynch said nothing.

Withdrawing his boots from the tabletop, Striker stood once more, this time offering his hand. "I'm the right person," he said seriously. "Work for me and you can become whoever you want to be."

"There's a curse your medics used. You're one."

Striker arched an eyebrow. He'd done that once already, but he hoped the boy wouldn't notice. He was really getting on Striker's nerves. "Really? What's that?"

"Dpresh. Are you a dpresh?"

"Ah yes, deriving from that most unfortunate instance of depressurization." Striker paused long enough to imagine emptying his plasma pistol into the boy's chest until there was nothing left but ash. "Far from desirable in space as it quickly leads to death."

"Yeah, that's what you are." Lynch eyeballed him. "You're a dpresh."

Striker nearly sighed, such was his frustration. That he would win this duel was beyond doubt, but the cost of victory kept climbing. "What about immortality?" he asked, his genuine irritation only thinly veiled.

Lynch smirked nastily. "Build me a statue if you like."

Striker imagined blasting Lynch into oblivion with what was now a pair of plasma pistols. "Immortality. When you die, you come back to life."

The boy's reply was a little too quick. "That's not possible."

"I've died," Striker intoned gravely. "A select few across the Known Galaxies have their consciousnesses updated right here on Xarr. If their body dies, the latest version of their ID Tag is loaded into a cloned body. Pre-grown, obviously."

"Obviously," said Lynch, looking as though someone had told him Father Christmas was real. "Always good to back up anything important, right? You're offering me my own clone?"

"Not yet, they take years to grow."

"But you'd hook me up with an ID Tag?"

"The Empress would never allow it."

Lynch's face hardened. "Adults love false promises."

"Some. Not me. I would give you immortality. We would need to keep this from the Empress, but I have been told we can configure a blank ID Tag to integrate with the Sau Daran part of your brain. It would work."

Lynch tapped the metal side of his skull. "You'd put something in here?"

"Our little secret. When recovered in the unfortunate event of your death, I would use that alien tech to bring you back. If you had proven yourself useful to me, that is."

Lynch gave him an infuriating wink. "When am I anything else?"

CHAPTER TWENTY-SEVEN

There was a flash of purple smoke as Isabella returned to the wreckage of where this had all started. She clasped a rickety wheelchair. The classroom was still strewn with debris. Streamers of DO NOT CROSS blue and white police tape were pinned across the classroom's doorway. What remained of the door hung from a thick splinter acting as its last hinge. The dashboard on Braga's crate glowed atop a heap of broken tables and misshapen plastic chairs. Dried blood, mingled with shattered glass, stained the carpet.

Hey, you with me?

The ruined classroom was as hushed as the rest of the closed school, which after some quick scouting from Isabella was empty apart from the police cars outside the main gate. No doubt the site had been busier with emergency services after the incident, when there was still lots of terrified screaming and everyone was waiting to see if it would happen again. But it hadn't, and now the school had never been quieter. Such silence in a school felt so unnatural.

Weak twilight was fading beyond the classroom's broken windows as grey dusk painted the life and colour of a late summer evening with an ashen sigh, sketching Isabella's waiting companions in pale shadows. Beauregard checked the charge on one of his plasma pistols. Even the weapon sliding back into its holster sounded like a loud intrusion on the silence. Ves glared at everyone from her latest leaning spot. Lying on his back atop the crate, Ezra avoided everyone's eyes, whilst Fleur calmly crossed her arms. Her sharp eyes shone brighter than anything else this evening.

I could really use you right now.

Isabella pushed the wheelchair over and around the debris, avoiding as much broken glass as she could in the dim light. With Beauregard's none-too-gentle assistance, Ezra was hauled into it. The wheelchair creaked and shook. Unable to hide his embarrassment as he did so, Ezra repositioned his limp legs as close to where he wanted them as he could, picking them up one and then the other.

"Sorry, it's the best I could find," said Isabella.

"Least you're upright now," Beauregard pointed out. He scratched his stubble. "Ain't it time you sent us back to our side of the universe, kid?"

"Like I said, that's not how it works," Isabella said with naked irritation. She had explained this to him more than once already. "The only places I can send us to are places I've seen before. Striker's place, the medical room they put me in, the shuttle—"

"They blasted the shuttle," Beauregard added unhelpfully.

"—or the Husk," Isabella continued without letting him derail her. "None of those are exactly safe. Unless you want to visit a Sau Daran spaceship that's probably in another universe by now."

"You're sayin' we're stuck?" Beauregard growled. "Here? On this backwater nothin' of a planet?"

229

"It's just my home," Isabella snapped. "Nowhere important."

"Forget places. What about people?" Fleur suggested diplomatically. "You found us with that thing you can do. Could you take us to someone back where we are from?"

Isabella leaned against Braga's crate, thinking over the same questions she'd been asking herself ever since they had returned to Earth. "Yeah, but there's not exactly a long list of people I've met in space. Most of them are either in this room or want to kill us."

"It might be a longer list if you count the ones who're dead," Beauregard muttered. "Y'know, if that helps."

Fleur pinched the bridge of her nose and smiled through her evident frustration.

Beginning with a deep breath, Isabella looked at her companions. Last to settle under her gaze was Ezra, who was clutching his limp body awkwardly in his new wheelchair. Her eyes lingered on him for a long time. "We don't really know each other," she admitted.

"Got that right," snapped Ves.

"But you have been wonderful, honey," Fleur reassured the girl. "We will find a way out of this."

"There is a way out," Isabella replied. She pulled her arms tighter around her chest until both hands, human and alien, disappeared beneath her armpits. Her eyes sank to the carpet, but instead of escape they found another patch of dried blood. Rather than having to look at anyone else, she chose the blood. "I don't know what to say, but I know how I feel," she said to the bloodstained carpet. "Without you, I'd be dead."

"A bar would do," Beauregard interrupted gruffly. "Literally any bar. Any planet. We ain't fussy. We ain't got homes no more, remember? Not after that dumb heroic stuff we pulled."

Isabella glanced up guiltily, but Fleur hissed at Beauregard and he shut up. She gave Isabella a nod of encouragement.

"I'm not sure I've got a home either," Isabella admitted. Batting away Fleur's concern at that, she continued. "It doesn't matter. Because of us, millions of people on that Husk are going to suffer. Probably die. You're all dangerous people, I get that, but you've done good things too. We can help them." Isabella took a heavy breath. "I want to help them." Everyone stared. Hesitantly, she looked to Ezra for reassurance, but he didn't notice. His eyes were unfocused, his face severe, his mind elsewhere. "I'm serious," she insisted. "I'm tired of running and I'm sick of people getting hurt. I can get us back to the Husk, I've already done it before, and we can actually do the right thing for once."

"You think I'm gonna help you murderers?" Ves snarled. "You can die without getting me killed as well, thank you!"

Ignoring her, Isabella looked imploringly at the others. "There's a lot of people out there who will die if we don't do something."

"Ain't gonna happen, kid," said Beauregard as he busied himself lighting a cigarette.

"I am sorry, sweetie, but the big man is right."

"But this is a chance to really do something."

"Yeah, die!" said Beauregard through a puff of cigarette smoke. "We ain't talkin' small, we're talkin' about a Husk—millions of people. And that ain't forgettin' *Nebula*. Us against a PROXUS battle station? That ain't no fight, it's a phyxin' short massacre."

"You are also asking us to go to war against soldiers we fought with," Fleur added. "Fighting to escape our death is not the same as starting a war. Especially a war we will not win. Sorry, honey."

231

Isabella knelt beside Ezra's wheelchair, grabbed his hand in hers. "Can't you talk some sense into them?"

Ezra shook his head. "They're right. It's too risky."

"Since when was anything ever too risky for you?" Isabella asked. She searched his eyes but found little of the Ezra she had met a couple of days ago. "You didn't worry about the risk when you saved my life. Twice. I thought at least you'd have my back when I wanted to do the same for someone else."

Glancing at his limp legs, Ezra bit back whatever he was about to say. Then he seized Isabella's human wrist. His eyes burned into hers. "Go home. Stay alive."

"No!" Isabella cried, tearing her arm away. "If you'd gone home, I'd be dead!"

Ezra regarded her gravely. "Yeah, you'd be dead. Dantes would be alive. And we'd all be back on *Nebula*."

"Back home doing your Empress' dirty work, you mean?" Isabella said accusingly. "Always looking the other way because you're just following orders? Is that the life you're missing?"

"Easy," warned Beauregard.

"No, it's alright," Isabella replied sharp enough to make it explicitly clear that absolutely nothing was alright. "Let's say what we mean. You're killers. Clear enough?"

"Oh, is that it?" Beauregard held up his hands in happy surrender. "Ain't no one gonna argue with that."

Isabella leant awkwardly against an upturned table. "I heard you two in the shuttle after we left the station. You said you'd followed orders. Orders you didn't always agree with. Did things you weren't proud of. Never stuck your necks out. Hurt people, probably. Even someone like you." She glanced at Fleur. "Sure, you were captured by PROXUS and it was join or die, but after that you just got on with the job. You worked for the people who killed your friends." Isabella pointed a finger at Ves'

232

hunched figure in the shadows. "And you can stop with all that murderer talk. Your brother killed a lot of people to get me off that station, and most of them weren't soldiers, they were medics or surgeons or whatever. They didn't have weapons. And what did he do it for? A big payday? Yeah, I'm glad he saved me, but that doesn't make what he did right."

Ves said nothing. Her face said everything. If she had been armed, Isabella was certain Ves would have shot her dead.

"I wish I was still a schoolgirl getting stressed about exams and reading graphic novels until three in the morning, but I'm not. Just like you don't have to be hired killers any more. The universe is a bigger place than it was yesterday—for all of us."

Gliding across the classroom, Fleur grabbed Isabella and pulled her into an enormous hug. As Fleur held her, Isabella felt some of the rage and frustration she'd felt since seeing her parents finally ebb away. Fleur pulled back and lifted Isabella's chin with a delicate fingertip.

"You are amazing," Fleur said with a smile. "What we do next will define us, whether it is action or inaction, whether we want it to or not."

"Phyx that," Beauregard muttered. He flicked aside the embers of his cigarette. "I ain't never needed no one to define me." He sat heavily on the nearest surviving table. The table, which had only barely survived the Sau Daran's assault on the classroom, was thoroughly unprepared for Beauregard's unexpected weight to be applied so abruptly. It buckled without pause for thought and Beauregard crashed onto the carpet in a cascade of dust and splinters. Defiantly, he stared up at everyone as though this had been deliberate and dared anyone to suggest otherwise.

"Honey, you are defining yourself just fine on your own," Fleur said. She regarded Isabella kindly. "If we want to do the right thing, we need to stay alive long enough to do it. So far, you have proposed a suicide mission. What else have you got?"

"Would the pirates fight with us?" suggested Isabella.

Fleur shook her head. "Pirates do not fight *with* anyone, even other pirates. Trust me, you would be wasting your time. By now, any pirates who are still alive will already be helping PROXUS round up the refugees for transit to the mining colonies."

Isabella met Fleur's sad eyes. "You said there's time before they go to the mines?"

"If they are following standard protocol, which PROXUS always do, they will secure the human refugees in different sections of the Husk's outer areas," explained Fleur. "Any signs of resistance, and at the flick of a switch the anti-vac shields are disabled and everyone in that part of the Husk goes for a walk in space. Rebellion over."

Isabella stared at Fleur, her mouth hanging open in horror. "They'd do that?"

Fleur threw a sad glance at Beauregard. For once, he failed to hold her gaze. Darkness lingered behind their eyes. "Yeah," Fleur said finally, as though dragging her mind back to the present. "Yeah, they would do that. Without hesitation." She bit her lip. "Maybe we should help them. If we can, I mean. Perhaps we could—"

"Phyx this," Beauregard growled. He stood with purpose and rested his hands on the butts of his holstered plasma pistols. "Get us the phyx outta here. I don't care where we go—take us anywhere but this phyxin' madness."

"I can't!" Isabella's frustration was boiling over. "The Husk is the only place left."

"We can't go back," Ezra warned, his voice fainter than watery shadows.

Tentatively, Ves stepped into the middle of the classroom and held up a hand. "If you're going to the Husk, I'll take my chances, but only to get off this rock. Don't go expecting my help once I'm off this planet."

"We ain't expectin' your help," Beauregard muttered grimly, "and we ain't goin' back to no Husk neither. Cool your thrusters."

"Like he said," Ezra added with conviction. "We can't go back."

Fleur shook her head. "After all the mistakes we have made, maybe we owe the universe something. We could—"

Beauregard pushed her away and raised a grubby finger. "You agreed we ain't doin' no crazy rescue mission."

"Shut up and listen!" Fleur threw his arm aside none too gently. "If we want to get home, that Husk is the only place she can take us. Knowing what I know about Husks, there might be a way to help everyone. If you would shut up and listen."

CHAPTER TWENTY-EIGHT

The Husk's blue-black light was no less petrifying than it had been last time. Nightmarish recollections of Envoy's living ship crawled over Isabella's skin with cold, spidery fingers.

Shivering, she passed the pile of crates that had crashed through Ezra so terribly, then snuck closer to the cargo hold's exit. Cautiously, she craned her neck around the edge of the doorway. Menacing shadows faded away to her left and right, but as far as she could tell the corridor was empty. Isabella took a deep breath, picked a direction and stole into the corridor. She expected to be shot at any moment as black-clad Rangers stormed the corridor and fried her with hot plasma before she could escape in a swirl of purple smoke. But the corridor was eerily silent. No Rangers. No Silver Fists. More shadowy passageways appeared and disappeared, extending into a maze of blue-black tributaries within which she quickly became lost.

Seconds turned into minutes.

Long, anxious minutes.

Finally, a hint of sound reached her from further down the corridor. Isabella froze. It reached her again—the faint thud of heavy boots hitting grooves in the Husk's warped floor. Kneeling in the middle of the corridor, Isabella pulled her conspicuously glowing purple hand into her chest and lay over it. As her face pressed against the cold floor, she spread out in her best ragdoll impression and waited.

The heavy boots grew louder. Isabella could feel their reverberations through the floor against her face. She shut her eyes, but it was hard to relax whilst spread-eagled on the floor of a dead alien spaceship with a professional killer marching towards you.

Well, of course it's hard to relax if you think about it like that.

Really? Because now is such a great time to chat?

You okay?

I thought you weren't talking to me.

I needed some space. But before you get yourself killed, I figured I should probably say, y'know... hey.

Hey.

Hey.

You left.

Yeah.

You back?

It looks that way. You shouldn't have visited Striker. He's bad news.

You could have stopped me.

Probably, yeah.

You didn't.

And where was that getting us? I steal your body, you hate me. We played that game for fifteen years.

Okay, who am I talking to and what have you done with the alien who was trapped inside me?

Okay, I was pretty mad. But I've been doing a lot of thinking and I don't want you to die—

You do realise how deeply unsettling it is that you feel the need to clarify this?

—and I kinda like you—

Weirdo.

—so, we've got to work together, right? If you're gonna stay alive?

Can we?

Survive or work together?

Both? Either? Everything's kind of a mess.

I'm sorry about your parents.

It's okay.

Yeah, it's not. I'm sorry.

Thanks.

Your dad hasn't stopped being a jerk.

Yep. You still worried I'm gonna get us killed?

Just you. And yeah, a little.

Me too. I'm glad you're back.

Instead of Paradise Moon's subsequent reply, the next words Isabella heard were laced with enough static to remove any hint of humanity. "Control, this D-88-57. We have another casualty in Sector B-752. Bringing her to the nearest containment pen for processing. Over."

Isabella felt a pair of big, gloved hands grab her body. The hands pulled her off the floor and hauled her headfirst over what felt like their armoured shoulder. With her head dangling behind the stranger, she opened her eyes and glanced at a second Ranger marching beside her. Although their plasma rifle was primed in both hands, their helmet swivelled away from Isabella to check the corridor ahead. Reaching out her glowing purple hand, Isabella's fingertips brushed the second Ranger's arm. The muzzle of their plasma rifle began to turn towards her, but not before all three of them evaporated in a convulsion of purple smoke.

In that same instant, purple smoke dissipated into the classroom. The rifle's muzzle continued its trajectory towards Isabella. Beauregard caught it and hurled the Ranger hard into the carpet. Casually tossing the stolen rifle up in the air, he caught it in his other hand and aimed it at its previous owner. Beside him, Fleur pressed her plasma pistol against the other Ranger's visor.

Isabella climbed down from the Ranger's shoulder and liberated a plasma pistol from each of their belts. Ezra accepted the weapons grimly and leaned forward in his wheelchair, aiming each of the pistols at one of the Rangers. He didn't need to say anything.

"I ain't doin' it," Beauregard said. "It's a dumb idea."

Ignoring him, Fleur and Ves efficiently removed their captives' armour, both reluctantly complying under Ezra's stern watch.

Fleur examined one of the black chest plates and handed it to Beauregard. "You can have the bigger set."

"Great," Beauregard growled sarcastically.

Ignoring him, Fleur glanced at Isabella. "Did you get their operating numbers?"

Isabella nodded. "One was D-88-57, I didn't get the other."

Fleur flashed another smile at Beauregard. "Are you ready to be a hero?"

"Don't you dare!" Beauregard glared at all of them. "If there weren't no one else could do this, what with all your dumb injuries 'n' all, I'd be stayin' right here. I'll do this one job, but don't think I'll be riskin' my skin on any more of this dumb hero stuff. Once I've done my bit, it's down to the girl."

Fleur filled his arms with the rest of the armour. "It is only a suicide mission if you choose not to follow the plan. I am still happy to go if you cannot do it. Maybe you should stay here and look after the children?"

"You ain't goin' nowhere with that injured shoulder."

"Then it looks like this is all on you," said Fleur cheerfully. She picked up one of the helmets and tore out the camera from behind its visor. Whilst she doubted the feed could broadcast from as far away as Earth, once it was returned to the Husk it would kick in again—and they couldn't have that. "I would hate Striker to see any evidence of you being a hero," she added as she tossed aside a fistful of mangled electronics.

"I ain't kiddin'," Beauregard growled. "She's on her own after this. I ain't lettin' you get yourselves killed."

"Yeah," Isabella replied. "You've made that clear."

Ves and Beauregard donned the rest of their stolen armour in the awkward silence that followed. As soon as they were done, the briefest flash of purple burst once more around Isabella's body, this time enveloping Beauregard and Ves as each of them held on tightly to one of her hands.

Purple smoke dissolved around the trio as they emerged in the cargo hold. Quickly, they confirmed they were alone.

Beauregard leaned uncomfortably close to Isabella. "Anyone comes in here while you're waitin' for me, you leave. Go straight back to your Earth," he warned. "Don't be no hero."

Isabella nodded. "Be careful."

Beauregard wasn't listening. He pulled on his helmet and replied through the helmet's comm, his synthesised voice was stripped of all its humanity like the Rangers and Silver Fists had been. "I'll tell you when I get there, then we're done with all this dumb hero stuff."

Isabella held up Fleur's gauntlet, which was now attached to her forearm. "I'll be waiting," she said, but instead of the face she wanted to see looking back at her, all she saw was her own scarred reflection in Beauregard's black visor. Without another word, he slumped into the darkness.

Leaning against the nearest crate, Ves turned her own borrowed helmet over in her hands, as though it demanded intense scrutiny. Amid the blue-black shadows scattered across Ves' face, there was much in her expression that troubled Isabella.

"You're just leaving, then?" asked Isabella.

"That's what we agreed."

Isabella bit her lip, unsure whether she could trust herself to speak. Ves, still distractedly examining the helmet, seemed not to notice the silence.

"It's not too late to change your mind," Isabella finally suggested.

Ves didn't look up. "I'm trying to stay alive. If you've got any sense, you'll do the same."

Isabella's face scrunched up in disgust. "Call it what you want. You're running away instead of trying to make a difference."

"Sure. You want to come with me? I could use you."

"No thanks," Isabella said with utter finality.

"You sure? Without the rest of them to slow me down, it won't take long to find a shuttle that needs liberating. The others can get spaced for all I care, but you shouldn't have to die. Besides, your newly acquired talents could come in useful. Between the two of us, we'd make a decent crew. The points would be good—we'd certainly steal enough. What do you reckon, partner?"

Isabella stared coldly at Ves. "See you around."

Ves shrugged. "Try not to die." Tucking her rainbow hair tightly against her scalp with one hand, she hefted the helmet and secured it in place. Ves gave her a casual wave goodbye, which looked almost comical beneath the avalanche of body armour she was wearing.

When Isabella finally thought of something polite to say, Ves had already picked up her plasma rifle and marched after Beauregard into the darkness.

Once again, Isabella was alone.

What a bitch.

Well, almost alone.

CHAPTER TWENTY-NINE

Beauregard didn't rush. He never liked to rush. But that didn't mean he was comfortable, and that certainly didn't mean he was okay with any of this. For starters, he never wore a helmet. He didn't do helmets. They itched. This helmet's headband was already saturated with its previous owner's sweat, which was mingling in an unpleasant union with Beauregard's own sweat. Although the Heads-Up Display, or HUD, inside his helmet superimposed useful information over his tinted view of the Husk—such as a readout of his own bio signs, which comm channel he was operating on, and the oxygen content of the atmosphere around him—it did nothing to help him escape the helmet's unbearable claustrophobia. His peripheral vision was shot to pieces, which would make it harder to shoot his way out of whatever trouble his friends were getting him into. But worst of all, Beauregard missed the weight of his twin plasma pistols hanging off his thighs, never far from reach. The sensation of not having them ready to draw felt as unnatural to Beauregard as gravity pulling upwards. In short, there wasn't much Beauregard was happy about.

But he didn't rush.

With every step, he retraced yet another unhelpful turning down the wrong blue-black tunnel. Fleur's advice was fuzzy at the back of his tired mind, but he was confident this wasn't his fault. She had given him so many landmarks to look out for that they were becoming jumbled in his head. And although Fleur had confidently expressed where he should and shouldn't try to find the place that they needed for her plan to work, none of her advice fitted with what he was seeing. He was, he grudgingly admitted, wandering aimlessly.

But he didn't rush.

Around the next bend, two armed PROXUS soldiers were standing to attention on either side of an open oval doorway. Unhurried, Beauregard strode out of the gloom as though he belonged here. Instead of wearing the distinctive armour typically worn by the Rangers or Silver Fists and which would have matched his stolen Ranger disguise perfectly, these soldiers were dressed in anti-vac suits. Inside his helmet, Beauregard frowned. Their slim outfits were the same dour black as his borrowed combat armour but offered much less protection from plasma fire. This struck Beauregard as unusual attire for invading an alien ship—even a dead one. Significantly, they also wore heavy, cumbersome anti-grav boots, which would nullify any attempts they made to move quickly—say, for example, in combat.

Consciously loosening his grip on the standard issue, nothing-to-see-here plasma rifle clutched across his waist, Beauregard gave one of the soldiers a helmeted nod. "Anything to report?" he asked through a hiss of static.

The two soldiers turned their own helmets to glance at each other before replying. "If there was, we would have radioed in and Control would already know about it," one of them suggested. Over his helmet's comm system, the soldier's voice came back dull and lifeless. "What's your operating number?"

"D-88-57," Beauregard said distractedly, his eyes drawn through the opening that the soldiers seemed to be guarding. "What's with your attitude?"

"Ranger, you better watch your tone," one of them warned. "Where's your anti-vac suit?"

"Where's the vacuum?" Beauregard growled. Peering over their shoulders, he found a vast hangar beyond the open doorway. At its centre, a PROXUS plasma turret had been welded to the floor next to a large box-shaped anti-vac shield generator. A PROXUS soldier wearing an anti-vac suit was clutching the controls behind the turret, aiming its long, heavy barrel at a vast crowd of prisoners—no, refugees. At a glance, Beauregard estimated there were easily a couple of hundred refugees huddled against the far edge of the hangar bay, their backs pressed up against the shimmering perimeter of an anti-vac energy shield that filled the hangar bay. Beyond the domed energy shield was nothing but the cold emptiness of space peering through giant scorched holes in the Husk's battle-scarred hull.

"Are you fresh out of the academy or something?" the soldier demanded, grabbing Beauregard's attention. "Or did one of those pirates blow a hole through the back of your skull? We're about to blow the atmosphere in Sector F-702."

The other soldier took one hand off his plasma rifle and pointed a gloved finger into the hangar bay. "That's this sector, dpresh! We're about to power down that shield and make an example of this scum. So where in the Empress' name is your anti-vac suit?"

Beauregard stared at the soldiers through his tinted visor. He looked back at the crowd of refugees. Even from this distance, the helmet's HUD allowed him to pick out faces in the crowd and zoom in on their scared expressions. He wished it hadn't, but it was too late. He glanced at the other soldier. This time, he caught his own reflection in their tinted visor. Instead of his own face staring back at him, he saw another faceless, helmeted enforcer of the Empress' intergalactic conquest.

"Aww, phyx," drawled Beauregard.

Using the opportunity offered by the soldier taking one hand off his plasma rifle, Beauregard grabbed the weapon's barrel and swung its muzzle towards the second soldier. At the same time, he levelled his own plasma rifle at the midriff of the soldier whose weapon he had grasped.

Two sudden plasma blasts echoed down the corridor in such close proximity to each other as to almost blend into one single fiery shriek. The first blast erupted from Beauregard's rifle and chewed a burning hole through the poorly armoured stomach of the first soldier. Hot on its tail was the second blast, unbidden by the soldier but prompted by Beauregard's unexpected jerking of his barrel, which left a smoking crater in the visor of his companion's helmet. Both soldiers crumpled.

"It ain't never easy," Beauregard growled as he dashed through the doorway. "Why ain't it never easy?"

This hangar bay reminded Beauregard of where they had landed Fleur's shuttle on the Husk. Blue-black arches spanned the vast breadth of a ceiling clustered with welts and knots, again appearing much more as if their coarse metal structures had been grown rather than crafted. As well as the soldier operating the turret, there were two PROXUS mechanics in anti-vac suits clutching heavy tools and kneeling beside the shield generator. But none of them were looking at the generator or the crowd of refugees—all three black visors were aimed at Beauregard as he dashed into the hangar bay.

"Pirates!" Beauregard shouted as he hurled himself towards them. "Cover that door!"

Instantly, the turret swivelled towards the opening through which Beauregard had burst. However, the hangar was not a small space and it would take Beauregard some awkward moments of sprinting to close the distance between them. As he did so, he passed the charred remains of two refugees on the floor.

Dumb heroes.

Between the size of the turret's heavy barrel and the metal shield in front of it, Beauregard had to dash around to see the soldier clearly.

"You've called this into Control, right?" one of the mechanics asked Beauregard.

"Don't ask stupid questions!" snapped the soldier standing behind the turret. "How close behind are they? How many pirates?"

Beauregard settled next to the soldier manning the turret. "They could come through any moment," he warned. "I blasted two, but there's plenty more. And you bet I called this in," he added to the mechanic. "Control ain't warned you?"

The two mechanics, who had no weapons to aim across the hangar towards the doorway, merely shook their heads and gripped their heavy tools tighter.

"They must be jammin' comms," Beauregard suggested with a hopeful bluff. "What's with all the anti-vac suits?"

"This is F-702," one of the mechanics answered, as if that was sufficient explanation.

"That's what the other guy said," replied Beauregard. "What about those fellas?" He gestured towards the hundreds of refugees huddled inside the far edge of the dome of energy.

"Why do you think we're doing this instead of examining Sau Daran maintenance drones like we should be?" snapped the mechanic, who even through the static of his helmet sounded increasingly rattled by an impending pirate attack. "Control wants to use our camera feeds when we space them to set an example to the rest of the prisoners."

Beauregard checked the charge on his plasma rifle. "Yeah, I was afraid you might say somethin' like that." Poking the nose of his plasma rifle upwards from his hip, he casually let off a single shot that punched through the neck of the soldier behind the turret. The soldier clattered to the deck as Beauregard aimed his plasma rifle at the two mechanics.

"Drop them," Beauregard ordered.

The tools clattered to the floor.

"Now, you ain't got no weapons, so I ain't gonna shoot you unless you make me want to. Fair warnin', one more word about spacin' refugees will make me want to. Turn around real slow." Beauregard freed one hand from his rifle and hurled off his helmet. "This recycled air might taste as clean as vitraxi dung, but it sure feels better than wearin' that." He took a deep breath and sighed with satisfaction. "Same to you. Lay them down nice and slow. Don't try nothin'."

As they bent to deposit their helmets on the floor, Beauregard downed first one and then the other with the stock of his rifle. "You ain't spacin' no one this rotation," he growled as they collapsed onto the deck.

The refugees took some persuading to approach him, but eventually Beauregard was able to wave the boldest of them over. After that, the rest followed. They were an even poorer sight up close—no worse than the dirty, malnourished refugees who had greeted their initial landing, except the skeletal faces of these survivors were stretched tighter with fear. Beauregard's heart, hardened by a long career doing a good job of following bad orders, didn't skip a beat. His cold blue eyes didn't flinch. But he felt something stirring inside him and he didn't like how it felt.

"Anyone know how to shoot?" Beauregard asked.

A grubby old woman stepped forward. The rags hanging off her were barely enough to be considered clothing, yet she held her thin body upright like a steel rod and carried Beauregard's gaze as he examined her.

"I fought against the Sau Darans," she told him firmly. "Back when serving your Empress was something to be proud of."

"That was a long time ago, old lady."

Dismissing him with no more than a contemptuous flick of her eyes, the woman grasped the rear of the turret in her ashen, wrinkled hands and steadied its gun barrel on the doorway.

The crowd stared hopefully at Beauregard and waited.

"I ain't here to rescue none of you," Beauregard clarified in the hope it would avoid any awkward misunderstandings. If anything, this made them look even more mystified. "But if one of you takes me where I need to go, I might just find someone who can get you someplace safe."

Beauregard shared the landmarks Fleur had suggested he use to navigate the Husk—or at least those he could remember. The refugees shifted nervously and a small Sau Daran maintenance drone peered sheepishly around a girl's legs, one metal claw raised in tribute. They looked terrifying to Beauregard, from the beak between their glowing red eyes to the hook at the end of the arm that didn't have a claw.

"Really?" Beauregard sighed. "Anyone else? Anyone else at all? Literally, don't no one else know the way?"

"You in a hurry?" the old woman asked from behind the turret.

Beauregard's face creased halfway between a frown and a grin. "What do you think?"

"Then no," she snapped, "there's no one else."

Beauregard's eyes drifted back to the small Sau Daran creature. "Well, ain't that mighty fine," he growled through gritted teeth.

The Sau Daran shuffled forwards, their head bowed, while the tip of their claw self-consciously pulled at the edge of a loose plate on their leg. They stopped in front of Beauregard, his shadow engulfing theirs.

"You know the way to the Core?" asked Beauregard.

The Sau Daran's head nodded like a child taking an overly dramatic, shuddering deep breath. They looked up at Beauregard with burning eyes.

"What's the hold up?" Beauregard growled. "We goin' or not?"

In response, the Sau Daran scuttled away.

A withered hand grasped Beauregard's wrist as he made to follow. "You're really not here to save us, are you?" the old woman asked wearily. Desperation had crept into her hard disposition.

"It ain't nothin' personal. Once those soldiers I blasted don't check in, you won't have long." He tapped his rifle against the gun turret. "If you're lucky, this might take care of one patrol. But they'll keep comin'."

"Well, thanks. You're a real hero, aren't you?" The woman tried to spit at him, but her mouth was so dry that all it conjured was a rasping cough. "Saving us to ease your own conscience," she croaked, "then leaving us to die. They should build you a statue."

There was a sad acknowledgement of reality in Beauregard's eyes as he regarded the old woman. "I ain't gonna take no pleasure in your death, and I ain't gonna let no one space you like you was worth no more than cargo. I didn't turn no blind eye." Behind him, hundreds of half-dead refugees huddled nearer to the lone turret. Their eyes watched him expectantly. "But I ain't no more than one man," he continued. "I got friends dependin' on me. I ain't givin' you no more than a chance to defend yourselves and that ain't rightly fair, but I ain't got no more to give."

Across the hangar bay, the Sau Daran inserted their hook in the floor and tugged frantically to get it back out. Their success was accompanied by a hidden trapdoor crashing open out of the floor.

"Thought those things didn't use doors?" Beauregard said as he watched the small creature from a distance.

"Neither did I," admitted the old woman.

"If someone lays down coverin' fire long enough to keep any patrols out—" Beauregard stopped when he realised no one was listening. The old woman was already shouting her own orders, the crowd hurrying towards the hatch and a welcome hiding place. "Aww phyx," Beauregard muttered.

Spinning on his heels, he dashed across the hangar bay—racing through a frantic mob of refugees. Barely overtaking them in time, he slid the last part of the way towards the hatch and threw a glance behind him. The old woman was still clutching the turret's control system and watching the main entrance with calm dignity, leaving the rest of the refugees to hurry after Beauregard. "Phyxin' heroes," he muttered.

He fell feet first through the hatch and into a narrow maintenance shaft. The Sau Daran's tiny, stained head emerged from the shadows and peered at him curiously.

"Alright, let's go."

Red eyes burned in the shadows. The small Sau Daran reached out its tiny claw to take Beauregard's hand.

251

"Get movin'!" Beauregard growled, causing them to leap back in alarm and scurry down the shaft. Sighing, Beauregard gave chase at the fastest crawl he could muster—fast enough he soon couldn't hear the refugees clambering into the shaft behind him.

The Sau Daran must have slowed or at least steadied their panic a little, because it didn't take Beauregard long to catch up. As they ventured down one maze of maintenance shafts after another, the Sau Daran's movements continued to be skittish—especially with Beauregard's plasma rifle so close behind. However, whenever another hatch needed unlocking or another shaft needed clearing of debris, Beauregard couldn't help but notice how their hook and claw functioned with deft precision to speed their progress.

By the time they reached the Core, Beauregard's whole body was drenched in sticky pools of sweat and other, less identifiable fluids that had smeared and dripped from the maintenance shaft all over his armour. Exhausted, he peered through the mesh grate at the end of their journey. There was a rusty creak as his Sau Daran helper twisted their hook into the grate. It fell open with a crash.

Hauling himself out of the shaft and into yet another blue-black chamber, Beauregard almost laughed at the beautiful agony of stretching out his cramped legs for the first time in too long. Every breath stung with unpleasant chemical aromas in here, but he didn't care. His lips clutched another gulp of foul air.

Chaotic tangles of cables and transparent tubes were thickly woven across the round chamber. Each of the innumerable cables was thicker than one of Beauregard's limbs, while the tubes were even thicker still. Inside were static rivers of vibrant blue sludge.

"This it?"

His Sau Daran companion answered with a slow, bleak nod.

"Well, that ain't a bad job," Beauregard admitted. He sloped across the large chamber and keyed his comm. "Kid, I'm here."

The Sau Daran leapt into the shadows as purple smoke announced Isabella's sudden appearance next to Beauregard.

"Watch out!" Isabella cried. Defensively, her glowing purple hand reached out in front of her with inhuman speed.

"Hold it!" Beauregard growled at the Sau Daran. "She's with me." His eyes leapt to Isabella. "And they're with me, too. Everyone's with me. Don't no one do nothin' heroic."

Watching the Sau Daran warily, Isabella nodded her understanding. "You found the crystal yet?"

Beauregard scowled. "Course I ain't found no crystal yet, I just got here. You found the crystal yet?"

"Alright, alright," said Isabella. She peered into the blue-black shadows and glanced back at Beauregard. "You mean that crystal?"

Beauregard looked at the massive silver frame housing a giant crystal that dominated the middle of the chamber. The crystal was bigger than Isabella, its insides cloudy and dark. Beauregard frowned and said nothing. Once they had hauled enough stray cables across the floor to clear a space around it, he thought the crystal looked much more obvious than before. Anyone could have missed it.

"Sau Darans believe that crystal was the Husk's soul when it was alive," said Isabella, unable to keep what sounded like awe from her voice. "At least, that's what Fleur says."

Beauregard shrugged. "Thought it sounded more like a battery."

"Either way, we're done here," said Isabella, letting go of the last cable and straightening up. "Time to go?" she asked. Despite her question, she didn't step closer to Beauregard.

"Ain't no need to be nervous—the hard part's over."

"Yeah, for you." Isabella exhaled long and slow. "It'll be fine. I can do this."

"You don't have to. It ain't bad to run away, in fact it's a real good way of stayin' alive. I ain't judgin' you none, I just want all of us to come out the other side of this. You too, kid."

"Well, someone has to do something," Isabella replied pointedly. "Otherwise, you're trapped on a planet you don't like and millions of people will die or be enslaved."

"Aww phyx, it ain't written nowhere that that someone has to be you. Heroes die too fast."

"Maybe they do when they're alone," she said, her dark eyes staring into his soul. "Am I alone?"

"Yep," Beauregard said, holding out his hand. "My part's over." He turned and added a nod of respect to the small Sau Daran. "So long, fella."

Isabella didn't even look like she was trying to hide her frustration as she reached out to touch Beauregard's calloused fingers with her human hand and the jagged surface of the crystal with her weird, glowing purple hand, which still gave Beauregard the creeps.

Purple smoke.

Classroom.

Almost vomit.

Beauregard managed to force the vomit back down and adopt an expression so stern that no one noticed his discomfort.

Ignoring Beauregard and the giant crystal lying amongst the classroom's wreckage, Fleur hugged Isabella. "You are amazing," she told the girl, before sweeping up

Isabella's hands in her own. "Are you sure you can do this? You only need to be there long enough for that crystal to fill up—is that right?"

Isabella nodded.

"Then we are not going to let you finish this on your own," Fleur promised her.

"We ain't?" Beauregard asked. "That weren't never the plan."

"Are you sure?" Isabella asked, although she was looking at Ezra not Fleur.

Ezra glared at her, which struck Beauregard as wholly out of character. "I can shoot just as well as I could before," Ezra snapped. It was impossible to miss him glancing at his limp legs resting on the footrests of the metal thing the girl had called a wheelchair.

"I didn't mean you couldn't…" Isabella started, before mumbling her way through something that would no doubt have been deeply kind if it had been loud enough for Beauregard to hear. "I just want everyone to be okay," she concluded softly.

Ezra pursed his lips as though he'd just finished a line of Turbo shots. "It's my fault you're in this mess, so we're going together or not at all. I owe you that."

Beauregard glared at Fleur. "You've been talkin' nonsense into his head while I was gone."

"No one will force you to come," Fleur said firmly. "Why go anyway? It would only give Isabella a better chance of staying alive and give you a chance to right some wrongs."

Fleur had never called him out like that before. Beauregard didn't know how to respond, so he hurled one half of a broken table across the classroom. It practically disintegrated on impact, which made him feel a little better. Everyone was staring at him. Fleur crossed her arms and waited patiently.

"Fine," Beauregard moaned. "Course I ain't gonna let you go without me, kid. Phyxin' should do though. This universe ain't done nothin' but try to kill us, and now you want to go lookin' for trouble in another one."

Unable to speak, Isabella's gratitude leaked out through a series of grateful nods and awkward smiles. Despite her attempts to blink it away, something glistened on her cheeks. Beauregard shifted awkwardly lest he commit the unforgivable masculine sin of showing genuine emotion.

When they were ready, tendrils of purple smoke curled and twisted around all four of them and the crystal as they left the classroom and materialised in Envoy's last living Sau Daran ship.

CHAPTER THIRTY

Instead of the blue-black darkness Isabella expected, she was greeted by blinding radiant colour.

Everything was as she remembered from her previous visit to the chamber where Envoy had forced her into the glass pod, except for the giant crystal. This was still in its frame in the heart of the chamber, but now it was pulsating with even brighter rainbows of shocking light. Countless particles of light flashed out of the air and were sucked into the crystal. Each particle was a different colour from the last.

Then they changed direction, splitting off—like the ghostly breaths Isabella would blow on a cold winter morning at the bus stop, small clouds of light particles gathering out of the air around the Husk's dark, cloudy crystal at Isabella's feet. Rainbows of light struck the crystal in volleys, before sparking to life inside it. The crystal glowed.

Well, we're not dead yet. That's good.

So, this is your universe?

I think so. There are so many gaps—pieces Envoy tore out of me. I don't remember much, only how it makes me feel, like I can't remember

257

anything except what's in my heart. But it feels like home.

I guess we made it then. The ship too. Another universe.

Fleur and Ezra hadn't moved except to draw their plasma pistols. Although Beauregard's hands remained empty, both were poised over the pistols that had been returned to their natural habitat, hanging off his thighs.

"Well, ain't this place even creepier than you said it'd be," Beauregard muttered.

"Honey, we are in a different universe and this ship is alive. All bets are off."

Beauregard stared at the now glowing crystal they had brought with them. "Ain't it ready yet?"

Isabella shrugged as the crystal continued to glow brighter.

"Honey, we just arrived."

"Yeah, and it ain't too soon to leave."

Nervously, Isabella took in the sight of the extraction pods that encircled the chamber.

I don't fancy another round in those things.

I'm not thinking about it.

Because I'm pretty sure it'd kill us.

Still not thinking about it.

The sooner we leave here the better.

Really not thinking about it.

I'd get the worse deal, you know? You wouldn't spend the rest of eternity inside a crystal being pissed on by happy rainbows, would you? Your life would blink out in a heartbeat. Boom. Dead. I'd be the one who suffered.

Not as much as I'm suffering right now. Erm, can you stop?

For how long?

"Just a little longer," Isabella heard herself say out loud to Paradise Moon and anyone else who was listening. "Everything will be fine. It'll all be fine. The crystal's going to fill up, and then I'll take us back to the Husk and everything will be okay."

Which was when everything went wrong.

In the dying universe where the Sau Darans had long ago been created, nothing remained except for Midnight Twice. Like a shadow of black ink on dark canvas, oil spilled over obsidian, Midnight Twice was the everything in the nothing and the guardian of this universe's Final Now. Midnight Twice had ensured the Final Now lasted as close to forever as they could conjure. When the stars died and all their light and wonder was extinguished, the universe shrank and its inhabitants fled. The Sau Darans left first—a shiny new race of explorers designed for an epic voyage of discovery in search of a new universe for them and their architects, who quickly followed. Midnight Twice was the only architect who stayed behind. This was the duty that came with his power.

Since then, as time passed and didn't pass, Midnight Twice had been stretched thin until nothing of them remained but black on black on black. Endlessly alone. Impossibly drained. His fragile grip on time could barely keep this universe in the endlessly repeating moments of its Final Now.

Yet, for the first time in what felt like forever, Midnight Twice wasn't alone. He could sense another of his kind. Another god, as the Sau Darans would say. Another architect, as Midnight Twice would have said if anyone had been there to listen.

Midnight Twice shook awake parts of his consciousness that had been dormant ever since the other architects had fled, ever since he had first begun preserving the Final Now. If the endless moment of this universe's Final Now ever actually ended, if Midnight Twice ever lost concentration or accepted defeat, the

259

Now in the Final Now would become an inescapably finite and definitive Then—after which, there would be no after which and his universe would be history. Along with him.

The spiral of black smoke that was Midnight Twice twisted closer to the Sau Daran ship. He didn't have to travel far to reach it. When the ship had arrived, tearing through the fringes of this universe's Final Now, it had left a pulsing white scar in its wake. Now the white scar and Sau Daran ship filled almost all that remained of this shrunken universe, which was still only one moment from death. The ship's crystal had been harvesting energy ever since, but Midnight Twice hadn't risked breaking concentration to indulge his curiosity and investigate.

Until now.

After all this time, the arrival of another architect changed everything. Another architect mattered even more to Midnight Twice than preserving the Final Now of his universe. Another architect meant hope.

Immediately, Midnight Twice felt his grip on the universe weaken even more as he shifted part of his focus away from endlessly sustaining the Final Now. Ever so slightly, the universe resumed the collapse it had tried to finish so long ago.

Midnight Twice spoke. Time listened. A patch of hull tore off the Sau Daran ship, silver metal instantly browning with eons of decay. Midnight Twice drifted inside the hole. Time listened again. After Midnight Twice drifted deeper into the ship through each new hole, the hull in front of him peeled away just as easily.

At the same time, his universe collapsed a little more and died a little faster in the heartbeat between now and then.

Isabella jumped as a browning patch of hull dropped from the ceiling and landed in a star of dust and a crash that echoed throughout the chamber. Black smoke swept inside. Above, a deep hole ran straight up—all the way through the ship like the path of a plasma blast or a single drop of the most corrosive acid, boring through chamber after chamber. Shining metal strands of living ship were already weaving the hole above Isabella back together, until freshly grown metal gleamed with vitality.

The black mist swirled above them. Backing away, Isabella stumbled against Ezra's knees. His plasma pistol landed in his lap as he reached out from the wheelchair and took the clammy fingers of her human hand in his own cold, nervous hand and held on tightly.

"Tell me that crystal's ready," growled Beauregard out of the corner of his mouth. He had one of his plasma pistols ready, aiming from the hip.

Isabella shook her head, but no one was watching. Everyone's eyes were on the two tendrils of black smoke slithering out of the black mist.

One tendril lurched at the floor, the other at Isabella.

"Ain't gonna happen, pal," Beauregard warned savagely. Stepping in front of Isabella and Ezra, he raised his plasma pistol.

Beauregard had always been fast, but for once time wasn't on his side. A coil of black smoke engulfed Beauregard's gun arm before he could fire. Isabella heard him snarl as his left hand shuddered beneath a shockwave of wrinkles that rippled down his suddenly greying, suddenly liver-spotted, suddenly shrivelling arm all the way to his suddenly crooked, suddenly arthritic fingers. His pistol clattered beside his boots.

Beauregard's intact hand shot to his other holster, but he found only powdery flecks of rust where his suddenly disintegrating plasma pistol should have been. The gentle but firm grip of Fleur's hand closed around Beauregard's shoulder. Catching his eye, she shook her head most gravely. But she didn't step aside. Neither of them did.

The black mist clawed at Isabella again, probing for a path around Beauregard and Fleur.

"Back off," Beauregard growled, but Isabella could hear in his voice that he knew he was a spectator now. Or a sacrifice.

Losing Ezra's hand, she staggered away from them until the back of her head collided with a pod's door. She pressed her spine against the glass, pushing her chin up and her neck back as black mist slithered towards her. On the other side of the glass, exactly where she and Paradise Moon had left it on the floor of the pod, Envoy stared up at her lifelessly.

The black mist slashed at her face.

A glowing purple fist snatched it out of the air.

Pulses of white-hot energy spat from the purple fist as Paradise Moon grasped the black tendril before it could reach Isabella. The moment her purple fist had made contact, Isabella sensed something. Another consciousness. Paradise Moon squeezed, sending bursts of crackling energy out of the black smoke.

WHAT ARE YOU?

Isabella flinched at the new voice inside her. It tasted of darkness. Her skin crawled as she felt her thoughts being pecked clean in an instant, like the bleached bones of carrion beneath a vulture's ravenous, surgical beak.

Paradise Moon tightened her purple fist even more around the wisp of smoke, and Isabella heard a more familiar voice inside her.

Easy, stranger! We're all friends here. I'm Paradise Moon. Who the Hell are you?

YOU FEEL LIKE ONE OF US, BUT YOU'RE NOT.

You stayed, didn't you? You actually stayed? I don't remember much, but if I'm right, well, I owe you. We all do. Because if you stayed, that's some real hero shit right there. I need you to know I mean that from the bottom of my heart, before I warn you not to spoil this beautiful moment by picking a fight with this girl. Because she's with me, alright? So back off.

SOMETHING HAPPENED TO YOU. WHAT ARE YOU?

I was one of you before they tore me apart. They did it so they could travel here. Long story, that. But whatever I am, I'm on the same side as her.

Sparks crackled from the tendril of black smoke that had embedded itself in the floor.

I AM SPEAKING TO THIS SHIP TOO.

Oh, shit. Okay, so they might have some strong views about recent events—totally biased, probably, I'm just guessing—but I promise... it's not our fault.

THE LAST ENVOY IS DEAD.

Yeah... okay, so about that—

ALL THEY WANTED WAS FOR OUR CHILDREN TO SURVIVE.

By hunting us!

YOU ABANDONED THEM.

Because they were hunting us!

THEY WERE ALONE.

Okay, fine. You win! You're right! I deserve everything that's happened to me. Are you happy now? I deserve it. But she didn't do anything. She's innocent. So. Back. Off.

HUMANITY IS NOT INNOCENT. THE SHIP HAS SHOWN ME EVERYTHING.

This ship's got a big mouth.

The black mist hurled a fresh volley of tentacles out of its smoky mass. They caught Beauregard, Ezra and Fleur around their necks and hauled them into the air. Their throats rasped and their arms flailed as they wrestled for breath.

THEY WILL ALL SUFFER.

Well, that's real mature. Real mature. Will that make you feel better?

OUR CHILDREN WERE MASSACRED.

I know, I'm… I'm sorry. That was… that was horrible. I should have been there, I should have—

ALL OF HUMANITY WILL PAY.

All of humanity? Really? Do you know how dumb that sounds? Sure, some humans deserve everything they get, but all of them? Trust me, these idiots grow on you. Maybe you sneak into a body looking for a quiet fifty years in a meat sack at the far end of the universe, then—boom! It's midnight and you're eating chocolate under the duvet and it tastes so damn good and every atom of this person—every atom of this human—is laid out bare for you—their fears, their hopes, their dreams, everything, and she's so damn vulnerable, she's just this tiny, irrelevant, fragile lump of meat dwarfed by infinite universes rendering her completely insignificant and yet every tiny decision this insignificant human makes absolutely terrifies her, if you can believe that, right down to the length of her fringe, but despite all this, somehow—somehow—she doesn't just keep breathing, which sounds totally implausible under the circumstances of being terribly, terribly human, and somehow—somehow!—she finds every possible way to be simultaneously the best

and worst human she can possibly be. Can you believe that? She is mad and stupid and so funny and the bravest person I know and I love her.

I love you too.

You've been on your own for so long. Can you even remember how love feels?

YOU CARE THAT MUCH?

Yeah. I do. While you're poking around inside someone else's head, why don't you do something useful and see why we came?

THE CRYSTAL.

Yeah, the crystal. Humans who want to save a Husk. They actually want to do something right for once.

YOU ONLY NEED HER TO SAVE THE HUSK.

Hey, they came here to save everyone! Humans and Sau Darans. You know what she saw on that Husk. You've seen it in her head. Human refugees and Sau Daran refugees found a way to live together.

ONLY I CAN SAVE OUR CHILDREN.

Oh, come on!

YOU MISUNDERSTAND. THE HUSK IS ONE CHILD. ONLY I CAN SAVE ALL OUR CHILDREN.

Do you even know how many are left? I'm sorry, I really am, I wish things had gone differently, but you can't change the past.

Isabella could have sworn she felt the invader laugh inside her.

LEAVE, THEN. ALL OF YOU. THESE HUMANS WILL DIE EVENTUALLY. THE WHEN IS… FLEXIBLE.

Isabella felt no relief—only adrenaline—as inky tentacles released her companions. Their bodies thudded onto the floor.

You're wrong about them. They'll prove it and you'll feel so silly.

LEAVE QUICKLY. OUR UNIVERSE ENDS.

What about you?

WE WILL FIND OUR CHILDREN. WE WILL SAVE THEM.

Isabella waited, but for once Paradise Moon had nothing to say. Instead, Isabella's heart was engulfed by the alien's sorrow. She felt it consuming her.

Paradise Moon was already releasing the black tendril from her fist. Running, Beauregard scooped up his sole surviving plasma pistol. Fleur pushed Ezra in the wheelchair. They huddled closer to the brightly glowing crystal they had brought with them.

Isabella reached out a glowing purple hand.

CHAPTER THIRTY-ONE

S traighten your arms," barked the sergeant. "Loosen your other hand."

Striker watched Lynch continue to ignore the sergeant. He wondered with silent amusement if this gutsy kid had ever followed an instruction in his life. A shadow drifted over them. Striker glanced up at the acid clouds swirling above them on the other side of the reinforced glass that kept Xarr's pollution at bay.

Aiming the plasma pistol from his hip like he was some sort of space pirate, Lynch squeezed the trigger again. Three red bolts sizzled down the gun range's tunnel, illuminating the toxic clouds outside. Striker listened to three satisfying fizzles of dissipating energy at the other end of the range as each blast struck a small floating disc of energy. Each target turned from blue to green.

The sergeant gave a tired shake of his bald head. "Your technique's awful, lad. You shouldn't be making those shots. You're not even taking this seriously."

"Yes, but he *is* making those shots," Striker remarked happily from behind them.

Noticing Striker's appearance, the sergeant spun on his heel and snapped to attention. Striker dismissed him with a bored wave of his hand and the sergeant marched out of the firing range before Striker's hand had time to return to his side.

Turning his back on the glowing green targets, Lynch thumbed on his plasma pistol's safety.

"You look well," Striker told him. He drew closer, running his eyes and fingers over a small portion of the vast weaponry laid out on the metal benches at this end of the gun range.

"I feel great," Lynch admitted. "Whatever your doctors gave me, I want more."

"That's good to hear. How are you finding your first rotation of training?" enquired Striker. "Like your recovery, it seems to be going well."

Lynch shrugged. "Pretty easy."

Striker lifted a plasma carbine from one of the benches and examined it with what might have been idle curiosity. "You're too modest. Am I to understand you had never even held a plasma pistol before and yet you hit every single target perfectly throughout your first session? Despite, it would appear, not making any effort."

"This does all the work," said Lynch. With a mischievous grin, he knocked on one of the black plates that eclipsed half his face. "Cheat mode activated."

Laughing, Striker placed the carbine back with a level of care usually reserved for precious ornaments. Having made a show of disarming himself, he captured Lynch in another broad smile. "Our scans of your little upgrade are ready when you wish to review them. They make interesting reading. As you say, it's so good of those Sau Darans to include targeting hardware. That was a bonus, wasn't it?" With a chubby finger, he gestured at Lynch's glowing red eye. "But beware shortcuts in life, my friend. They prepare us poorly for what lies ahead."

When he was sure Lynch was watching, Striker self-consciously rubbed the angry burn mark Paradise Moon had left on his throat. "No news of your friend, I'm afraid." His eyes glinted. Such was his supreme concentration that his smile did not flicker as he sensed an alert from his neural implant ping. He paused, noting the highly encrypted comm signal attached to the alert.

"This is Striker," he announced after activating his comm.

A dull, monotone voice slid back through the comm embedded in Striker's inner ear. "Still enjoying the safety of Xarr, First Duke? I hope you're not getting too comfortable while we do all the hard work in the Outer Rim."

Striker smiled convincingly for Lynch's benefit, who could only hear one side of the conversation. "Imperator Grave! I trust this call is to celebrate our victory?"

Despite traversing the vast expanse of deep space from the Outer Rim all the way to the hub worlds, Imperator Grave's reply was no less icy when it reached Striker's ear. "Victory, yes. But your fugitive girl is still loose."

Striker's calm expression remained firmly in place as Lynch watched him. "That doesn't sound like a victory." Gesturing for Lynch to resume his shooting practice, Striker stepped towards the door. This implied an additional layer of privacy to his conversation, whilst enabling Lynch to still overhear everything he said. "Surely the girl has not returned to the Husk?" asked Striker, knowing from his operatives that she had.

Lynch made an effort to raise his plasma pistol towards the targets, but he didn't pull the trigger. Striker noted the safety was still on.

"We have multiple sightings of her on various camera feeds," explained Imperator Grave tersely. "What's this girl up to, Striker? This is your fault."

"How many people has she killed this time?" asked Striker sternly, still keeping one eye on Lynch's reaction.

Sighting down the barrel of his plasma pistol, Lynch was frozen as he listened intently.

"What? No one we're aware of," snapped Imperator Grave. "But she's back. There must be a reason. There's something going on. Small fires of rebellion are popping up all over the Husk too."

"Hold on. I have an operative with me who might be able to help." Mentally pausing his comm, Striker arranged his features into what should have resembled a concerned expression. "Young man, we need your help. Lives are at stake."

Lynch was already turning to face Striker as the words slithered through the First Duke's lips. Tossing his plasma pistol onto the nearest bench, Lynch stepped forward. "Is she okay?" he demanded. "What's she done?"

Holding up both hands to placate Lynch, Striker calmly closed the gap between them. "You friend has returned to the Husk you rescued her from. Why?"

Lynch's face scrunched up in confusion. "That doesn't make sense. She didn't even want to be there. She only wanted to stay so she could save her friends."

Striker made no attempt to conceal how carefully he was studying Lynch. "Could there be a Sau Daran connection?" he asked, curious whether Lynch would answer accurately.

"No chance. After what they did to her, she'd never help them," Lynch assured him.

"You make a good point," said Striker encouragingly as he hid his disappointment. He had hoped Lynch was smarter. "The Husk contains PROXUS forces, pirates and refugees. Anyone else?"

"Those people she was with?" suggested Lynch.

Striker waved his hand dismissively. "She extracted them using her rather impressive powers." Striker's mind was working to sift, expose and examine every detail he had reviewed. He was missing something. He held up one finger for Lynch's benefit. "PROXUS forces want to capture her." He counted off a second finger. "The pirates tried to kill her." He counted off a third finger. "The refugees are of no threat to her, and number far too many for her to help everyone. What's left?"

Lynch shrugged again, although Striker noticed a subtle bead of sweat drifting down the boy's forehead. "Is she okay?" asked Lynch.

"The Husk," Striker answered firmly, ignoring Lynch's question. "There is a Sau Daran connection, not a human one. What is it?" Striker pinned Lynch with a piercing stare. "What do you know?"

Lynch's concentration was plastered all over his face in sweaty knots of muscle. "How should I know? Envoy only wanted her to power their crystal. Maybe—"

Holding up a hand to halt any further explanation, Striker smiled warmly at Lynch and reopened his comm. "Imperator Grave, no doubt you remember how the Sau Darans power their ships?"

"I do," sneered Imperator Grave. "But this is a Husk. It is dead. There will be no living crystal for her to steal. It's worthless."

"Whatever her intentions, the fugitive has an established connection to the crystals powering the Husks. I have had that confirmed. Now, I would never dream of telling you what to do, Imperator, but perhaps it would be prudent to send a force to secure the crystal in the Husk's Core?"

The comm went dead.

Striker wrapped a fatherly arm around Lynch. "Well done!" he said reassuringly. "There are millions of refugees on that Husk. Your information may save them all. And you impressed Imperator Grave. He said so. Your stock is rising, young man. Your stock is rising. Stick with me, and there's nothing we can't do. You could be my best operative yet."

Lynch released a smile of his own. "Didn't you tell the Imperator what to do though?" he asked.

"If I remember correctly, I clearly stated I was doing the exact opposite."

Lynch's grin spread wider. "I'll remember that when I'm doing your job."

Striker gave him a good-spirited slap on the back. "All for the glory of PROXUS, young man. Trust me. You have a bright future with us. Now, there's one last thing before I go. Pick up your weapon."

Lynch did so.

"Shoot me," ordered Striker.

"You what?" And there was the creased expression of surprise Striker had been anticipating.

"It's just one little thing, but it's a bit of an emergency so do get on with it, young man. And make it a quick death if you please. One plasma bolt to the face should do it."

Lynch stared at him, making no attempt to raise the plasma pistol. "Is this a test?"

"Only if you make it one," Striker said a little irritably. "Time is short. I need to die now."

Lynch shook his head. "This is stupid."

Retrieving the plasma carbine from the bench, Striker flicked off the safety. "Tell them you did it in self defence. You want me to rely on you? Follow my orders."

"But, like, why would I kill you? Other than the fact you're being really annoying."

Striker told him about the cloning pods on Black Nebula. Then Striker told him how, if they worked together, they would assassinate the Empress.

Carefully aiming down the plasma pistol's sights, rather than loosely from the hip as he had before, Lynch sent a bolt of red plasma hurtling into Striker's face.

CHAPTER THIRTY-TWO

With a burst of purple smoke, Isabella and her companions were in the Husk's Core. Its dim, blue-black interior was instantly illuminated by the dazzling radiance of the giant crystal they had brought back with them, which crashed to the floor. Deep reverberations echoed all around them. Isabella peered into the gloom, the crystal's light stretching their shadows tall enough to reach the chamber's edge and paint the walls with their silhouettes' misshapen doppelgangers.

A small figure staggered out from a curtained mesh of thick cables and into the unsettling patchwork of shadows. The Sau Daran maintenance drone, red pinprick eyes opened a fraction wider than before, lifted their arms towards the glowing crystal.

"Still here?" asked Beauregard. He sounded relieved. "Good job. You gonna get over here and help us carry this, or what?"

As the drone staggered closer to the crystal's glow, what had previously looked like another shadow running down their body was in fact a waterfall of oil gushing from a burning hole in their chest. One of their wide, red eyes faded. A small echo rang out as the drone dropped onto a spindly knee.

"Aww, phyx," growled Beauregard. His right hand drew smoothly, levelling his plasma pistol before his aged and wrinkled left hand had even reached the empty holster where his pistol's twin had been reduced to rust and dust by Midnight Twice.

The Husk's Core erupted in a chaos of plasma blasts. Fleur and Ezra drew too, arms straightening as they sighted and fired. Isabella ducked behind the glowing crystal. Flashes of plasma lit up momentary glimpses of Rangers firing at them from the edges of the Core—here a tinted visor, there a plasma rifle poking through a tangle of cables. It felt like their ambushers were everywhere. Sparks danced off wailing metal.

Fleur darted away from the crystal, never moving in the same direction for more than a heartbeat, every blast that chased her always landing half a second too late. In comparison to the volleys of plasma pummelling the air around her, she barely squeezed off a shot. Whenever she did, however, there was a cry of pain.

Beauregard didn't even bother to take cover. Allowing instinct to take over, his body bent into a classical gunslinger's pose as his pistol spat blast after blast of plasma from his hip. His arthritic left hand hung uselessly at his side, slowing his accustomed rate of fire. With a shriek, a plasma blast grazed his face. Hot blood and shards of cheekbone splattered the air. Reluctantly, he dodged behind a tangle of thick cables and semi-transparent tubing.

Ezra's wheelchair clattered on its side beside Isabella, his limp legs doing nothing to break his fall. He had barely begun to return fire when a sizzling blast erupted against one arm of the wheelchair, spewing flaming upholstery and metal fragments into the air. The next blast caught one of Ezra's exposed legs. Although Isabella knew he shouldn't be able to feel the injury, she found the stench of burning flesh no less horrifying.

Dragging her eyes away from the burning hole in Ezra's leg, Isabella peered through the firefight until she found the crystal's empty stand on the other side of the Core. She checked the stand's height, its position, the angle of its placement—everything she might need to know if she was going to get there faster than running. With Paradise Moon sheltering Isabella's head from plasma blasts with her purple glowing arm, Isabella reached out with her human hand and touched the glowing crystal.

A deadly volley of plasma lit up the shadows where Isabella had been crouching, but fingers of purple smoke had already stolen both girl and crystal. The plasma blasts tore a destructive path through the wreckage of the wheelchair. Wildly pumping the trigger of his plasma pistol over his head, Ezra flattened his face into the floor, but could do nothing to prevent more plasma blasts peppering his immobile, unprotected legs with more smoking burns.

Clad in evaporating wisps of purple smoke, Isabella reappeared in mid-air above the empty stand. Instantly, the heavy crystal escaped her fingertips, caught the rim of the frame and shuddered into place. She fell behind it, stray blasts exploding over her head.

As the crystal settled into its frame, incandescent tributaries of multi-coloured light sparked and splintered out of the crystal. Like spiderweb cracks in fragile bone china, they ran down every cable in the Core, pulsing every colour Isabella could imagine until—as if by mutual agreement—they settled on a green hue that glowed from the cable, coating everything and everyone.

Isabella peeked across the Core and was relieved to see fewer Rangers than she expected. She was less relieved when they all aimed at her and the crystal. A shard of crystal splintered past her face as a blast of plasma caught its edge.

"Protect the crystal!" Isabella shouted.

Instantly, Fleur and Beauregard were on either side of her. Their plasma pistols screamed in every direction. Isabella shrieked as Paradise Moon lowered her glowing purple arm over the girl's heart—barely in time. The plasma blast that would have torn a hole right through her ricocheted off her glowing purple arm into the crystal instead, sending another jagged shard of crystal splintering off it.

The semi-transparent tubes that ran around the Core flooded with green fluid. It rushed through the tubes and disappeared beyond the Core. As if in response, the glowing cables around the perimeter of the Core moved. Aghast, Isabella watched as thick, animated cables lurched into the air and plucked up Rangers like low-hanging fruit from a tree. It was like watching an incredibly violent version of the neon-lit arcade game Isabella had played when she went to the bowling alley, using a claw to grab cuddly toys inside a glass box. The cables, which were proving significantly more effective than Isabella had been at the arcade game, waved the wailing bodies of the Rangers in the air before hurling them across the Core with meaty smacks of impact. Previously deafening shrieks of plasma fire were rapidly replaced with the clatter of armoured bodies landing. Other cables coiled around the Rangers who hadn't been picked up, squeezing and smothering their bodies until they went limp and stopped screaming.

Beauregard warily eyed the moving coils of cable. "Those things know we're on their side, right?" he growled uncertainly.

Not even glancing at him, Isabella disappeared through a ripple of purple smoke to reappear beside Ezra.

Ezra stared up at her, his haggard face smeared with burns and puckered with red-hot splinters of metal from the destroyed wheelchair. The darkest corners of Isabella's memory recognised this scene with the help of Paradise Moon, only now it was Ezra cradled in her arms, rather than the other way around. A mouthful of bright blood spluttered from the corner of his lips, prompting Isabella to settle his head in her lap. As she did so, she caught sight of what was left of his legs—not much. Forcing back the bile inside her stomach, Isabella glanced at Fleur and Beauregard. Blood dripped and oozed from their swaying bodies, but—somehow—they stayed upright.

Beauregard's shadow loomed over her. Impossibly, an unlit cigarette was already hanging from his lips. He took a cursory glance at Ezra's wounds. "He'll live—if he don't bleed out," growled Beauregard. He knelt and glanced at Isabella. "Keep him lookin' away, kid."

Before Isabella could respond, Beauregard pressed the over-heated muzzle of his plasma pistol against one of the wounds on Ezra's legs. Isabella jerked her head away. The flesh on Ezra's leg hissed angrily as his skin boiled. He must have heard it—he can't have felt it because he didn't react in pain at all.

The Core shook violently, jogging Beauregard's hand. "Sorry kid," he said, as the muzzle of his pistol scored a fresh burn through a rare patch of undamaged skin on Ezra's leg.

"You're okay," Isabella told Ezra, wishing her hands were free to protect her mouth and nose from the reek of scorched flesh. "Keep looking at me. You're okay."

The Core shook again.

"Good job you ain't able to feel nothin' down here, kid," Beauregard muttered darkly. "The pain alone would've killed you." One by one, he held the muzzle of his plasma pistol against the rest of Ezra's gushing wounds until finally the flow of blood subsided. Lifting the pistol's hot muzzle, he lit what might be his last cigarette and breathed in a deep lungful of cancer.

"Careful," Ezra warned as he stared up at Beauregard. "Those things'll kill you."

Beauregard flashed him a grin through the cigarette.

"When you are finished torturing Ez, you might want to hear this," called Fleur. She flicked her finger over a holographic dial on her gauntlet.

Instantly, their ears were greeted with a familiar voice.

Dazzling explosions erupted all around Braga's cockpit. She nudged the piloting yoke, twisting her stolen PROXUS snubfighter into a tight roll and feeling the whole craft rock as the charred wreckage of two Scimitar-class fighters skimmed her undercarriage.

"Repeat, *Nebula* has commenced bombardment of the Husk," Braga yelled down the comm. "If you can hear this message, find the centre of the Husk. Stay close to an anti-vac field. If you can't do either, choose a god real fast and start praying."

Braga's thumb pressed down on the yoke's trigger, raking a trail of green plasma from her snubfighter that punched through the nose of a Scimitar that had been lining up a bombing run on the Husk's outer hull. Another explosion shook her cockpit hard enough to hurl the pirate against the seat's restraints and bathe her sweat-drenched face in red warning lights.

"Repeat, go to the centre of the Husk," she ordered, not bothering to wipe away the fresh blood dripping into her eyes. "Evacuate hangar bays. Stay clear of the Husk's outer perimeter. Unless you can find a starfighter, in which case you better haul your sweet ass out here." Braga dodged another torrent of green plasma fire, skipping up onto one wing and then the other to let the blasts of hot energy zip around her.

"Captain Braga?" Fleur's voice asked over the comm.

"Talking of sweet asses!" Braga crowed. "I said I'd see you in the stars." She adopted a playful tone. "So, what's new with you?"

"Cute," Fleur shot back. "Can you see how much damage the Husk has taken from out there?"

Rolling her snubfighter 180 degrees until she was flying upside-down, Braga examined the flaming hull of the Husk through the transparent top of her cockpit. "It's looked better," she said coolly.

Volley after volley of torpedoes streaked across space from the endless rows of launch ports on *Black Nebula*, pummelling the Husk with chain reactions of explosions that tore apart more of its outer hull.

"If the Husk takes much more of a pounding, that thing's gonna break apart faster than a vitraxi's butthole after a moonweed dinner."

"Ain't that great," Beauregard chipped in over the comm. "Ain't there nothin' we can do?"

"Oh, hello old timer. Sure, do you want to jump in a starfighter and join me? You'll have to be quick—this party's almost over." As if to illustrate Braga's point, her wingman exploded, rocking her snubfighter off course and peppering the hull with more shrapnel.

"No time!" Fleur called through a hiss of static. "Not that it would do much good."

"To be honest," Braga continued casually, dodging in and out of oncoming plasma fire, "I thought you'd either be dead or long gone by now. You still got that present I gave you?"

"The crate is no longer on the Husk. We kept it safe, like we promised. We decided to hang around here though, see what we could do. The Husk is powering up, by the way."

"Powering up? That's impossible!" cried Braga. "If you see any of my crew or *The Liliana*, don't be shy. They're a good bunch." She glanced at a diagnostic report of the Husk on another of her displays. "Erm, that Husk is actually powering up."

"Ain't no chance you know somethin' useful about Husks, is there?"

"Well, I know there's no weapons on that thing and the engines are barely warm yet."

"Really?" Fleur's voice returned over the comm. "No weapons? That is news to us. How wonderful!"

Braga watched another payload of missiles strike the domed top of the Husk, igniting fierce explosions. "I don't think they want to give those engines time to warm up, either. Ah well, it was a good run." As she said it, the top of the Husk's dome broke apart.

Braga recognised the girl's voice as it reached her over the comm. "How long have we got?"

"Hey! The girl made it! Oh, no more than a minute or two, little lady. You know, Fleur Fontaine, if we ever make it out of this, there's this great spot on Mylar Prime I think you'd like. It's real peaceful." Braga's plasma cannons burst open the cockpit of another PROXUS Scimitar as it swept in front of her. The flaming vessel broke apart into her path, forcing Braga to lean harder on the throttle and race through the heart of the debris cloud. "They say the lakes on Mylar Prime are so beautiful at sunset, they could melt the Empress' heart. One of the best views in the Known Galaxies." Braga could feel her snubfighter beginning to cook as it was spat out of the enemy ship's explosion. More sparks hissed from her displays as hunks of slag metal tore apart one of her wings. Braga didn't flinch. By now, she could barely make out the stars through the thick sheets of green plasma blasts filling her view. "Maybe you and I could—"

They heard nothing more over the comm except for the hiss of static.

The Husk's Core shook again, this time violently enough to topple Beauregard to the floor. He glared at no one in particular, the fresh scars on his face weeping angrily. "Well, ain't there no one else out there?" he grumbled.

"Out there? I hope so. Transmitting?" Fleur shrugged. "I guess they are all too busy fighting *Nebula*." She forced a weary smile at Isabella. "I am sorry, honey. We did everything we could."

"You done good, kid," added Beauregard.

Ezra spat out a mouthful of blood. "You did great."

Isabella glanced up at Fleur, then Beauregard, and finally at Ezra. "They're all going to die, aren't they? Everyone on the Husk?"

Beauregard nodded. "Ain't nothin' we can do, kid. Soon as *Nebula* gets in another couple of torp salvos, we'll crack like an egg. Time to get movin'."

Fleur glared at him. "What part of you could possibly think that is information she wants to hear?"

"She asked. I ain't gonna lie. I'm just sayin', we should get goin'. Phyx, take us back to Earth if you have to, kid. We need to get outta here fast."

Laying Ezra's head carefully onto the deck, Isabella stood. Her knees wobbled weakly, but she stayed upright. Her eyes burned with desperation—as well as purple amongst the chestnut.

You sure about this?

Nope. What do you think?

I think your plan could kill us.

Really?

Really. It's an insane idea.

Fleur reached out for the girl as she brushed past her, but Isabella ignored her. With increasing resolve, she marched through the ugly smoke streaming from the countless plasma burns that had scored the Husk's Core.

"Where you goin', kid?" Beauregard growled. "You ain't gonna do nothin' stupid, are you?"

The crystal glowed brighter as Isabella stepped up. Grabbing the crystal with both hands, she closed her eyes and concentrated.

Purple smoke.

The void of space was cold and unrelenting. She was floating in a black sky she had gazed at countless times from her bedroom window. A globe of emerald and sapphire swirls, veiled by torn clouds, hung below her in the serene star-pricked darkness in which she was now surrounded. Unable to breathe as the emptiness strangled her lungs, she felt the void clawing at her flesh and eyes—as it had when she appeared beside Lynch's floating body.

There was no Husk here.

No Fleur or Beauregard or Ezra.

No crystal.

Only cold, empty space.

Purple smoke engulfed Isabella as she collapsed onto the floor of the Husk's Core, choking the iciness of space from the back of her throat.

Fleur made it to her first, a strong but gentle arm wrapping around her. "You feel freezing!" Her usually serene features were flooding with worry and confusion.

Gulping oxygen, Isabella pushed Fleur's arm away. "No time," she gasped.

This isn't working.

We'll make it work.

It's too much.

We've got to.

"Hey kid, you gonna take us with you or—"

This time, Isabella pressed her palms onto the floor instead of the crystal. Beauregard's worried face disappeared in a smear of purple smoke.

Crushing, stabbing, frozen space gripped Isabella's body once again.

Bad idea! Go back! Go back!

I'm trying!

Stop panicking!

I can't!

Isabella was drowning in a black ocean of infinite stars. Embers of sunlight winked around Earth's edge in a dwindling corona of sun-kissed fire. She could feel the darkness sucking the life from her lungs as every nerve in her body screamed.

Stop trying to imagine the Husk. Imagine HIM!

Ezra cried out in surprise as Isabella arrived in a bundle of purple smoke beside his prone body. He stared up at her, his face a mess of panic. "What's going on? What did—"

"Hey kid!" A heavy paw landed on Isabella shoulder. "Quit messin' about, this place is goin' down. We ain't got no time."

Fleur knelt next to her, the woman's face straining to hold back her concern. "Honey, please tell us what you are doing."

284

We're never doing that again.

I didn't enjoy it either, but if we don't try everyone dies.

That's not our fault.

"I can do it," Isabella said in a half sob, half whisper.

"Do what, honey?"

"I can save everyone."

"Aww, phyx."

Reaching out, Ezra squeezed Isabella's hand and gave her a gentle nod of affirmation. Somewhere amongst all the blood on his face, a smile broke though. Isabella smiled back.

Isabella stared into Ezra's eyes. Weakly, his hand still held hers.

Millions will die if we don't.

You've done everything you can. You nearly died. Twice. Just now.

How do you know?

I was literally there!

No, how do you know I've done everything I can?

Because I just watched you being the most inspiring human.

The Husk's Core shook again. Beauregard's grip on Isabella's shoulder tightened.

It doesn't matter. It didn't work.

You tried. That's all you can do.

That's not enough! Don't you want to save the Sau Darans here too?

Well yeah, but the only time I ever got what I wanted since the war started was when you pulled me out of that crystal and back into your body. We don't usually get what we want. Trust me.

I need to do this.

You're losing it.

I can't do this without you.

You'll kill them. Worse, you'll kill us!

285

Everyone was watching her. Fleur's face had abandoned any charade of calm. Beauregard was furious. Hot words flashed between them as they argued with the urgency of people facing imminent death. Isabella wasn't listening. Ezra gazed up at her with melancholic pride.

I don't want you to die. I love you. I love living!

I love you too. You're my sister. My closest friend. Do you trust me?

Yeah.

Do you, though? Because I don't think I can do this without you. I think we both need to want this.

Fine.

Fine?

Fine.

Okay.

Okay.

You sure?

Yeah. I trust you, sister.

CHAPTER THIRTY-THREE

Imperator Grave was a frail, bony old man with such long arms and legs that when his thin body leapt out of his command chair on *Black Nebula*'s bridge and stared at his gauntlet's holographic screen in disbelief, the sight of his long limbs flailing would have been funny had his audience not been so terrified of being executed for laughing at him.

"Explain these readings!" he demanded. His jaw clenched tighter than if he were chewing one of *Black Nebula*'s bulkheads. With the grimness of an executioner, he surveyed the bridge crew. "Well? Do our sensors need recalibrating?"

"It's gone, Imperator," replied a thin-faced colonel from the primary comm station.

"Gone?" repeated Imperator Grave. He tugged uncomfortably at the stiff collar of his pristine white uniform. "What do you mean, gone?"

"The Husk just disappeared." He glanced up from his console. When he saw Imperator Grave's expression, he quickly looked down again.

"I see," Imperator Grave said sharply enough to slit throats. "And where are my troops, Colonel? Where are

287

all those Rangers and Silver Fists who were on the Husk serving PROXUS so incredibly bravely when, and please excuse my ineloquence here but I am quoting your good self, when it just disappeared?"

"Gone, Imperator. With the Husk."

"And where are my pirates? Where are my refugees? Where are my fugitives?"

"Also gone, Imperator."

Imperator Grave's gaunt face stared at the massive viewscreen that dominated the entire width of the command bridge as his eyes absorbed every atom of the bleak desolation of space outside *Black Nebula*. Coldly, he contemplated the vast emptiness of space on the other side of the viewscreen—the space where, moments ago, there had been a Husk.

A Husk that was no longer there. Gone, along with his victory. He knew if he commanded the bridge crew to zoom in, the viewscreen would display countless fragments of debris from the space battle. But for now, this far out, there was only empty space where the Husk should have been—but wasn't.

The bridge doors slid open with a whoosh.

"What now?" Imperator Grave roared. He didn't even bother to glance behind him. Whoever it was had better make their report fast, otherwise he would personally introduce them to the other side of an airlock.

"Oh dear," said a familiar voice. "Don't worry, I'll take it from here, Imperator."

Before Imperator Grave could turn, a trio of plasma bolts burst through his back, spoiling his perfectly white uniform and leaving smoking craters where his heart and lungs had been. Smoothing a palmful of creases from his hastily donned purple robe, Striker handed his plasma pistol to the thin-faced colonel.

"Be a good fellow and send the Imperator out into space to look for our missing Husk," Striker said to the colonel. The skin on Striker's face and hands was still marked from the tubes and electrodes in *Black Nebula*'s cloning pod. "So brave of him to volunteer to lead the search for the girl. Such a pity those pirates ambushed him. He was a great man and a fine servant of PROXUS. A great loss, a great loss. Let him always be remembered fondly." Striker stepped dismissively over Imperator Grave's body and into the centre of the bridge. He looked at each of the bridge crew in turn, recognising every face well from their many cycles together serving aboard *Black Nebula*. Serving him.

His face hardened. "Report."

There was a rush as every officer on the bridge fought to be the first to explain what had happened.

Long after Striker had elicited every scrap of information from his bridge crew and issued the necessary orders—none of which, he knew, would give him what he needed—Striker retreated to his private corridor one level below the command bridge. His mood was as dark as it had ever been. As good as it was to be back on *Black Nebula*, the girl had escaped and if his suspicions were correct her powers had grown considerably.

The door to his private quarters opened.

He marched inside and froze.

The door hissed shut behind him.

"I just threw an imperator out of the airlock with three plasma burns in his back," Striker declared frostily. "What do you think I'm going to do to a bounty hunter like you?"

Leaning back in the tallest cushioned chair in Striker's office, the rainbow-haired woman laid her heavy boots on his desk. A trail of dark fluid trickled from one boot's

289

metal studs as they scraped across the wooden surface, leaving what Striker knew would be permanent indentations.

The rainbow-haired woman sighed. "You don't want to call security. You want to listen."

"Do I?" replied Striker, finding his calm. "Full disclosure, it's been a long couple of rotations and I'm not in the best mood. If you're wasting my time, I'm going to kill you very, very slowly."

The rainbow-haired woman shrugged. "I guess it depends how badly you want to find that girl."

Wearily, Striker lowered his vast weight onto the smaller cushioned chair on the other side of his desk. He studied his intruder thoughtfully. Something seemed to be moving beneath her jacket, as though she had a small animal under there, but whatever it was kept itself well hidden. Beyond that, there was little about her that he didn't already know. "How did you get in here?"

"I can throw in some tips for this battle station's embarrassment of a security system later," said the rainbow-haired woman. "But what you really want is to catch the girl who vanished a whole Husk halfway across the universe. All charges against me dropped, my own shuttle and more points than I can spend in a lifetime. That's the small price I want in exchange for the greatest weapon your Empress has ever seen."

Striker nodded happily. If the girl had moved the Husk all on her own, she was no longer another source of energy for PROXUS to devour—she was something much more powerful. "You can deliver her?"

"I can direct you and you can do your own dirty work," replied the rainbow-haired woman. Her eyes wandered idly around the office. "I've been to the girl's home world, which is the only planet she knows, so you can be sure that's where she took the Husk. I grabbed its coordinates while I was there. It's in one of the uncharted regions, but from out here in deep space it wouldn't take you too many rotations to get there. I reckon less than twenty."

Striker stared for a long time.

She didn't flinch.

Striker unleashed a cruel smile. For once, he didn't need to carefully compose the scheming contours of his face—this smile and all the cruelty within was real. He leaned across the desk. "Tell me everything."

CHAPTER THIRTY-FOUR

The cloning pod hissed as its pressure seal broke. Three heavy kicks later, the lid flew off the crate and clattered elsewhere. Tugging herself free of a tangle of I.V. tubes and electrodes, Braga sat up in the cloning pod and groggily shook her head. She peered into the gloom. Her vision was fuzzy, but clear enough to tell she was alone.

Timidly, Braga felt the side of her head where she had been hit by shrapnel in the explosion. All her sweat and blood were gone, along with the shrapnel, or if not gone then at least elsewhere, along with her previous body and—most distressingly—her fabulous hair. Her skull felt completely bald to her touch, and her hair would need to be grown out properly with a fresh dose of colour before this cloned body felt anything like home. Taking a deep breath and slowly exhaling, she enjoyed the sensation of her cool breath kissing her lips. With every fresh lungful of air, she felt slightly more herself. She had never died before, or even met anyone who had died before, but the points she had spent investigating and stealing this pod from PROXUS and then growing her own clone were without doubt the best points she had ever spent. Except possibly that one night on Aegis Minor. Braga smiled coyly at that memory.

Climbing out of the crate, she landed spryly on a patch of bloodstained carpet. Broken glass, splintered desks and torn books were scattered everywhere. She forced herself to smile with a confidence she didn't feel but knew she would find sooner or later. She had woken up to far better sights than this, a few of whom she was still on speaking terms with, but this sight was still galaxies better than being dead. Such painfully primitive architecture indicated it was unlikely anything on this planet could harm her, although this was severely at odds with the devastating damage someone or something had done to the room. Examining the destruction, Braga wondered exactly where in the Known Galaxies the enchanting Fleur Fontaine had chosen to park her crate.

Hot green plasma blasts had superheated her snubfighter's canopy. The icy vacuum of space had followed. It didn't matter where she was as long as she wasn't dead. She forced herself to pay attention to the here and now, to leave the darker corners of her mind. She reminded herself who she was—or at least who she had become. Maybe once, many cycles ago, she would have frozen up and dwelt too long on a bad memory, but not Captain Braga of *The Liliana*. Even the trauma of her death was beneath Captain Braga. *Fake it until you make it*, she reminded herself. *Be the pirate you want to become.*

She drifted to the window, her muscles warming up and her eyesight sharpening. Two things greeted her through the splinters of glass clinging to the window frame. The first was pale, early morning sunlight and the second was a man dressed in black trousers, a white shirt and a black armoured waistcoat. Clearly surprised to see her, the man waved dumbly. Unable to help herself, Braga waved back just as dumbly and gave him a big grin.

An enthusiastic supporter of the over-dramatic, she rolled up the nearby remains of a recently deceased book with *GCSE Biology* printed on the cover and used it to clear the final shards of glass from the window. Launching herself through the empty window with what she hoped looked like rakish audacity, she missed her three-point landing on the ground and improvised with a stylish forward roll that almost ended in jazz hands but at the last moment transitioned into finger guns.

This was not what her audience had expected. The man stared at her with his head frozen halfway towards a hissing box on the armoured jacket that protected his chest. He looked like he was going to talk into the box, but no words were coming out of his mouth because all he could do was stare at her.

"Hey, I don't suppose I could trouble you for some clothes?" asked Braga. A shadow drifted overhead, and they both looked up at the giant Husk inking out the sky above them. "Ideally before the aliens arrive."

CHAPTER THIRTY-FIVE

Rainbows of light swirled inside the crystal, casting long Beauregard-shaped shadows across the Husk's Core from where he was leaning against the crystal's cradle. With a disgusted look, he flicked away the deceased stub of his last cigarette.

"She awake yet?" Ezra rasped. He was lying on his side, a pool of blood on the floor beneath his chin. The fresh plasma wounds on his legs, although horrific, were bound with bloody scraps of black fabric torn from a nearby Ranger too dead to complain. So far, the fabric had held in enough blood from the cauterised wounds to keep Ezra from dying, but Beauregard would have murdered anyone for a medpac.

He ran his cold blue eyes over the girl in Fleur's arms. Isabella had collapsed moments after purple smoke had enveloped the Husk's Core and everyone inside. Since then, it had been impossible to wake her. Seeing the gentle rise and fall of the girl's ribcage, he felt the corners of his cracked lips tug into an involuntary smile. Levering his aching body off the cradle, he hauled himself across the chamber and laid a reassuring paw on Ezra's arm. "Relax, kid. She ain't dead yet."

A silver beak poked curiously around Ezra's body and shuffled closer to Beauregard. The fringes of the plasma hole that had burned through the Sau Daran still glowed hot. Accompanied by a mournful whirring of gears, their red eyes looked up mournfully. Beauregard gave them a reassuring pat on the head. Thanks to countless cycles of perfecting his resting grumpy face, Beauregard even managed to suppress a yelp of surprise when their silver beak nibbled affectionately at his hand.

Fleur glanced up from her gauntlet's holographic display. "There is still a lot of frantic comms chatter from everyone who was stuck on the Husk with us when we vanished," she said. "Pirates and PROXUS. No one can make sense of their sensor readings and no one can boost their signal far enough to get a message to *Black Nebula* or anywhere else."

Ezra coughed up a mouthful of blood and ash to clear his airways. "They don't know where we are?"

"No one does. Apart from us," Fleur gave him a wink. "Sensor readings are easier to recognise when you have been here before." Her fingertips danced over the gauntlet's holographic display, verifying their coordinates for what Beauregard suspected was the millionth time. "She made it home, and she brought millions of refugees and a Husk with her. Not bad, right?"

"Ain't bad at all," Beauregard agreed, "but what now?" The question had been echoing through his mind ever since he had guessed where Isabella had taken them. "You think those savages on her backwater planet have the tech to help us and a million refugees? And that ain't forgettin' the small matter of all the stranded Rangers and Silver Fists who want to kill us."

Fleur's face softened as she gazed at Isabella's face, the girl's body still in her arms. "If everyone down there is anything like her," said Fleur, "then we have nothing to worry about."

Beauregard made to light a fresh cigarette. He had emptied all his pockets by the time he remembered he had run out. Sighing a veteran's sigh, he closed his eyes and searched for peace. For once, his imagination was kinder to him in the solitary darkness of his own thoughts. He doubted his nightmares were gone, but something felt different.

CHAPTER THIRTY-SIX

Lynch had given Striker everything he needed to invade Earth. Earlier, the two agents had arrived outside his cell's energy barrier in pristine white uniforms and more than enough medals to shout 'important' as well as 'military'. Both had been armed with false smiles and too many questions, but Lynch had answered every question honestly—even innocently—as they quizzed him on Earth's technological capabilities, leadership structures and general geography. Lynch hadn't given them textbook answers—for a start, he'd never read one—but he realised afterwards it would be sufficient for Striker to plan an invasion of Earth.

Only after Striker's agents had retreated down the prison's central corridor, their path lined with energy barriers that walled in the other cells and prisoners, then through a huge blast door that thundered shut behind them, did Lynch learn why they were asking him about Earth. The Sau Daran architecture built into his skull afforded him unusually sensitive hearing. Hearing that was even better than his headteacher's when Lynch was muttering c-bombs at the back of assembly—and for Lynch, that was the Gold Standard of hearing. As soon as the decked-out auditory sensors on his Sau Daran mask-turned-toolkit picked up 'girl' amongst the agents' conspiratorial muttering behind the blast door, he had dialled cheat mode up to max in time to catch 'Striker', 'invasion' and 'Earth'. With creeping dread and no shortage of guilt, even Lynch could figure that one out.

When he was sure Striker's agents had properly left, he summoned a guard with enough shouting to earn him a beating if his plan wasn't successful. Which meant he had better start working on a plan.

"Unless you're dying, you'll shut up," the guard warned him.

Lynch smirked. "Take me to your leader," he intoned, before succumbing to the urge to add, "dpresh."

The guard toyed with the plasma pistol strapped to his hip long enough to convince Lynch he was going to skip the beating and simply shoot him. But with a scowl, he instead spun crisply on his heel and marched away.

"No really!" Lynch called after him. "Take me to the Empress! I'll tell her where First Duke Striker is. He's not dead!"

The blast door crashed shut. Its echo rumbled back to Lynch with depressing finality. He slumped in the corner of his small cell. *At least this is better than school.*

He was still ticking off other things that were *just* better than school—being bottled by your own mother, puking up canfuls of cut-price lager on your twelfth birthday, eating salad—when the blast door groaned open. Down the corridor, hard heels click-click-clicked towards his cell. Down went the energy barrier to Lynch's cell. Down went Lynch as an officer with a stranger's face stabbed his neck with something sharp.

The voice in the darkness belonged to a woman—crisper and more authoritative than any teacher Lynch had ever encountered. Although, strictly speaking, it was teachers who encountered Lynch and not the other way around. "Perhaps, Admiral, it would save time if you listed the colonies who are *not* under attack from rebel forces?" There was a pause in the darkness. For how long, Lynch couldn't guess. His head ached. Darkness pulsed across his vision like waves of oil over a midnight sea. He was drowning beneath the surface. "Military resources will be reallocated as necessary. Inform my staff when you have better news from the front. Perhaps a victory. Or a posthumous report of your heroic death. Not mutually exclusive." The woman offered something between a sigh and a growl. "Oh, open your eyes, dpresh. We need to talk."

For once, Lynch did as he was told. Light burned. He blinked away haloes of blinding light—everywhere, surrounding him, as stubborn as they were incandescent. Struggling to his knees on a floor as bright as the spiralling globe of gleaming walkways and projected screens all around him, he curled his lower lip into his mouth and bit down. Nerves sharpened, along with his focus. He lumbered to his feet—but saw no one. Only an avalanche of scrolling data on the glowing projections that lined and spiralled through the globe.

"Your name is Lynch?" the voice asked.

The boy looked up, shielding his eyes with a raised hand. She was framed by light so white it belonged in Heaven, but so hot against his retinas it felt more like Hell. Her hair was blood-streaked ash. She examined him with chilling severity.

Lynch remembered his name and nodded.

"The First Duke is alive?"

Lynch nodded.

Her expression was rapt, but her eyes remained as cold and hard as a rugby player's ball sack on a cold winter evening in Bracknell. "Speak quickly and clearly," she instructed. "Do not lie."

Lynch did as the Empress ordered, royally screwing over Striker in the process.

"He is on *Black Nebula* now?" she asked, once he was finished.

"Unless he lied."

"And you are no longer… his?"

Lynch had never thought of himself as anyone's, but for once he held his tongue. He gave the Empress a stone-cold nod.

"Really?" she insisted. Her eyes were too terrifying for Lynch to even attempt to conceal anything. Already piercing, her gaze was escalating to forced entry and assault with battery.

"He went after my planet."

Her gaze intensified. "And if I went after your planet?"

Lynch didn't look away from those terrifying eyes. "I'd screw you over too."

The Empress laughed. Hers was not a happy laugh. It was shrill and sharp. "How… awful," she said slyly.

Lynch shuddered as though his soul were being held under icy water. He couldn't tell if she was threatening him or mocking him.

"Enough, I have other matters to attend to," she said with a dismissive wave of an ivory hand. "We want the same thing—Striker dead and your planet saved. And they are the same. Kill Striker and his clones, then you will be free and I will not be assassinated. You should be smiling at the prospect. Everyone wins. You will do this."

Lynch didn't feel like smiling. "Make me."

"I will," she assured him coldly.

301

CHAPTER THIRTY-SEVEN

We'll have to go back eventually.
I know.
Isabella watched the tiny specks of innocent people three hundred metres below. She was perched on a girder close to the peak of the Eiffel Tower, far higher than paying visitors were allowed. Her legs dangled over the edge with a freedom that made her feel alive.

Did you know this thing weighs more than ten thousand tonnes?
Yeah.
Really?
We read the same booklet downstairs in the lobby. We use the same eyes!
So you also know we're over a thousand feet up in the air?
Yes!
If you drop one of your heels all the way to the bottom, do you think it would impale someone?
Why would you even ask that? What's wrong with you?
Don't you want distracting?
I want some peace!

Chocolate ice cream dribbled down her human fingers, prompting her to look up from the dizzying ground and lick away the offending tributaries of chocolate before they landed on her dress. The ice cream was sweet and wonderful. It tasted of home, and by home she now thought of Earth, not Reading. She stared at the empty patch of sky. Only days ago, it had been blotted out by the dark shadow of an alien ship, and on it all her friends in the universe except for the alien trapped inside her. With them gone, it felt like there was a hole in the sky.

Beauregard's goodbye had been harder than expected. Checking the gear relinquished by captured PROXUS troops had left him little time for conversation, not to mention he had the emotional capacity of a doorstop. She had interrupted him with a burst of purple smoke as his good hand closed the lid on a crate of distressingly large plasma rifles.

"Ain't got a job for you, kid," he had told her. He hadn't even watched as his Sau Daran sidekick from the Core had climbed on top of the crate. By then, it had become unusual to see one without the other. Beauregard called them Pocket, which they seemed to like. With their claw, Pocket easily crushed the edges of the lid until there was no chance of it being opened again without the aid of heavy tools—or a Sau Daran. "Ain't got much time, neither."

Gently petting Pocket, who hugged her arm tenderly, Isabella had let her eyes sweep across the hangar bay instead of meeting Beauregard's. This had been one of many areas re-grown by the resurrected Sau Daran ship formerly known as a Husk, now christened *Haven* by Ezra. It had been similar in size to the hangar in which they had landed a little over two weeks ago, back when

Haven was a Husk and vanishing giant alien spaceships across the universe wasn't yet a thing. Myriad cargo containers had filled the whole bay, along with an energized workforce of ex-PROXUS personnel from *Black Nebula*'s invasion force, accompanied by a few lingering refugees. Isabella had been pleasantly surprised by how many PROXUS troops had cut ties with the Empress to join Beauregard, Fleur and Ezra, although she suspected the threat of *Haven* venting them into space had played a part in their decision. Working with PROXUS-like efficiency, the workforce had set up a production line to transfer unchecked military hardware—mainly big guns—for testing, logging and storage. Beauregard had led this endeavour for much of their second week in Earth's orbit, and it had looked far from abating during Isabella's final visit. In contrast to the swarms of ex-PROXUS personnel buzzing around the hangar, many of *Haven*'s refugees had left. Unaccustomed to fresh air, natural water and plant life for so long, the deep space dwellers had found living on Earth too strong a lure. She was happy for them.

Leaning on the fastened crate, the gunslinger had served up his trademark crooked smile, the sort that only engaged one side of his mouth. "You'd be better off draggin' Ez away from that phyxin' crystal than hangin' around here."

Isabella had smiled at the mere thought of trying. "They're calling me a superhero, not a magician," she had reminded him. "How much will you make from all this?"

Beauregard had shrugged at the hangar bay full of weapons and equipment. "Enough points to start a war if we're feelin' dumb. More than enough to fix Fleur up with a new shuttle and keep the Empress off our backs while we figure this mess out."

Oblivious to Isabella's discomfort as she wrestled with how best to launch into her over-rehearsed farewell speech, Beauregard had snatched up another huge rifle in his good paw and busied himself inspecting it. "Thanks Dash, keep 'em comin'."

A young man flashed him the sincerest smile, smoothed back his long hair and sauntered back to a heap of unsorted weaponry.

"I know *Haven* leaves today," she had begun, before pausing to slap Beauregard's chest. "Are you even listening?"

"What?" Beauregard had asked, not looking up from the rifle.

"I know *Haven* leaves today," she had begun again, but Beauregard's lips were already moving.

"Ain't you still able to do that vanishin' stuff?"

"Well, yeah, but—"

"Then it ain't goodbye, kid. We ain't never too far away. You ain't never unwelcome." Then the big man had pulled her into the crook of his good arm, and she had felt his strength envelop her, and she had known he would always be there.

Isabella stared at the empty sky above the Eiffel Tower in a moment that would have been more poignant if it wasn't for the crunch-crunch-crunch of her ice cream cone being demolished.

The Prime Minister's waiting.

I said I know.

I could always—

Isabella's brow furrowed deep enough to age her at least a decade. *You're never speaking to him again. Not after last time. And not in front of the TV cameras.*

Even if it's a Friday?

It's not.

305

But if it were...

Friday was now the day when Paradise Moon was allowed to take full control of Isabella's body. Providing the alien followed Isabella's rules, she could take the body wherever she wanted. They were two Fridays into their new pact, two Fridays since they had returned to Earth, yet still Isabella hadn't caught Paradise Moon breaking any of Isabella's rules. This was either remarkable self-control from Paradise Moon—given her history—or a remarkable effort by the alien to hide all the evidence.

New rule. The Prime Minister's off-limits. Even on Fridays.

How is that fair? You still get to talk to him!

Like I want to!

But you get to dress up so nice!

Scowling, Isabella smoothed invisible creases from the crisp fabric of her long, navy dress. It was one of many unprompted gifts from the army of fashion labels that insisted on trying to woo her. For someone who was into dresses, she could imagine it was probably the best dress ever. Instead, Isabella missed the comfort of her hoodie and beanie and soft, sweaty tees. She had half a mind to tear it off, but it was the half of her mind that lived more in daydreams than reality—so she didn't. Instead, she closed her eyes, breathing long and deep.

Isabella's first attempt at Fleur's goodbye had lasted less than a second. Despite the minutes she had allowed to pass before her second attempt, her cheeks had still been burning when she returned to the blue-black corridor on *Haven* in a cloud of purple smoke. This time, there was nothing naked waiting for Isabella except for Fleur's overwhelming embarrassment. She and Braga were at least fully clothed now, the former waiting for Isabella with an arsenal of apologies and the pirate captain offering nothing more than an unapologetic shrug.

"Sweetie, would you mind?"

Braga had taken her cue straight away, slowing only to leave a tender kiss on Fleur's forehead before finding somewhere else on *Haven* to do whatever Braga did, which as far as Isabella could tell meant being a full-time badass. Even the way Isabella had seen her eat an apple was hardcore.

Opening her arms, Fleur had thrown Isabella more apologies, but the girl had brushed them aside and hugged her fiercely. Afterwards, they had talked forever.

"Here," Fleur had said, when their conversation had begun to slow. "Take this." Then she had unstrapped her gauntlet and handed it to Isabella. "Relax, this thing is standard issue. We have thousands—if Beauregard has not lost them all yet. Call us any time. Maybe before you arrive?"

Smiling, Isabella had accepted the gift. "Will you go back to being a pirate?"

Sitting back against the bubbled wall of freshly regrown metal, Fleur had sighed deeply and held out her palms in a whole-body shrug. "Whether pirate or PROXUS, I have always been what someone else wanted me to be." Her smile went loud. "Not any more."

The cooing of an adventurous pigeon dragged Isabella's eyes open. It had ventured halfway down the girder, its head twitching at the sight of the crumbs on her dress. She brushed them onto the girder in a shower of sawdust, but when the pigeon continued its expedition down the girder at an alarming pace, she grew nervous and waved it into the sky with her glowing purple arm.

Deadly pigeon, that.

Isabella smiled. *Shut up.*

Her phone pinged.

307

That'll be your mum wondering if she's ever going to meet the Prime Minister for tea.

Reaching for the clutch bag that had come with her dress, Isabella pulled out the most expensive phone she had ever owned. Replacing her phone had been one the first things she had done after returning to Earth. Such was her fame as the girl who had brought aliens—along with their vastly impressive technology—to Earth, that as with her dress she hadn't needed to pay for it as long as everyone saw her using it.

Say cheese, idiot.

Cheese, idiot.

Isabella took the selfie and sent it straight to her mum in reply to a message she didn't need to read. The novelty of her daughter sitting on top of the Eiffel Tower should placate her mum long enough for Isabella to get her head straight. She thumbed away the messaging app, revealing her background photo behind it. Absent friends smiled back at her from the screen, prompting her cheeks to dampen more than she would have ever risked when she was closer to the ground.

Ezra's goodbye had been the hardest. Unlike the others, Isabella hadn't even needed to vanish to him specifically. Instead, she had thought of her usual spot in the most shadow-drenched edge of *Haven*'s Core. As expected, Ezra had been sitting in his usual position in the centre of the chamber, the bright crystal cupped reverently in both hands. His head had been bowed, his eyes closed, his legs gone forever. As had become his custom, no plasma pistol hung from his belt.

Peering out of the blue-black gloom on the periphery of the crystal's shining aura, Isabella had broken the chamber's heavenly silence with a whisper. "Are you talking right now?" she had asked.

"No." Only his lips had moved—nothing else. "I never speak to *Haven*. Sometimes, they speak to me. But I have to listen hard."

Oh, I bet he listens hard! What do you think *Haven* says to him? Oh yes! Touch my crystal! You bad boy, Ezra! The way he's cupping that thing, I hope he's got consent.

"So, today's the day," Isabella had prompted, her tiptoeing footsteps tentatively closing the distance between them.

"What?" Still no movement bar his lips.

"You're leaving."

"Oh, are we?" he had asked, his eyes finally opening.

When she had held out the twisted remains of her melted guitar pick, he had removed his hands from the crystal and closed her fingers around this shrapnel of memory: the guitar pick enclosed within her hands, hers hidden within his. His ever-burning eyes had found hers. As had become his custom, he was crying.

"You saved me," Isabella had whispered.

"You saved everyone," he had told her. "Can I… speak to her before we go?"

His question had caught her off-guard, her hesitation taken for refusal. "It's okay, I don't have to—"

"No, just wait."

Well? Do you mind?

I promise I'll be gentle.

"She says it's okay."

Wimp. That's not what I said.

Ezra had released Isabella's hands before he spoke again. People always did that now—if they were addressing Paradise Moon instead of Isabella, they always treated her body differently. It was like they stopped being able to see her.

"Will you ever hurt her?" Ezra had asked.

309

"Maybe a lifetime ago," Paradise Moon had admitted with a glimmer of purple amongst chestnut. "Never again."

"You'll protect her?"

At that, Paradise Moon had curled up Isabella's lips and snorted derisively. "No, dumbass. Haven't you been paying attention? She'll look after me."

You know, you're sweet when you're not being a pain in my arse.

Alright, alright. Don't get used to it.

Ezra had smiled in reply, and Isabella had thought that he was smiling at both of them. Perhaps, unlike everyone else, he still saw the girl when he spoke to the alien.

After that, Isabella had slipped back into control of her body. Pulling her hands out of his, she had pressed the remains of the guitar pick into his palm for keeps. "How long until you go to Xarr?"

"Not until we find someone who can smuggle me in."

"Do you have to go? Couldn't you just send Dantes' family a message from really, really far away?"

Grimly, Ezra had shaken his head. "They need to know what happened. I owe him that."

"Watch out for Striker," she had warned him.

"Don't worry, I will. Once I'm back, visit often, okay?"

"Yeah, once I've had time to, you know, not be running for my life. I'm looking forward to a bit of quiet time for a while."

Isabella's body was struck so violently by the sudden shockwave that only grabbing a cold handful of wrought iron saved her from falling off the Eiffel Tower. The tranquility of Paris' clear sky had been disturbed by the sonic boom of something moving extremely, un-Earthly fast above Isabella's perch. A blur tore through the

Parisian sky with the unmistakable orange glow of PROXUS thrusters burning in its wake.

Shit.

Shit.

Isabella thumbed her phone awake and dived into the first news site she could find. Looming on the homepage was a fresh story with a headline less than a minute old. BREAKING. So far, the story was only a short paragraph, but a fistful of the most concerning words told her enough. MULTIPLE SIGHTINGS. ACROSS EUROPE. CONVERGING.

We know who this is, right?

Yep.

Can we even do this?

Unbidden by Isabella, her purple glowing hand gave a cheerful thumbs up.

Together.

Together.

Purple smoke.

Gone.

When Isabella reappeared, she was tumbling through an empty sky and spinning wildly. *Well, this is a great start!* The blur she had been thinking of shot away from her before she could even properly lay eyes on the PROXUS starfighter, leaving her to fall out of the sky alone. Her swift descent was made even more uncomfortable by her tight dress, which pinned her legs together as though bound in a straitjacket.

There's no way I'm letting them bury me in this thing.

She could have vanished there and then, but she needed to know where they were. Fumbling below her waist for a handful of dress, Isabella felt something catch between her fingers. She wretched it apart. The fabric tore all the way up one leg—she was free again. She felt her arms and legs pull out of her control for a moment as Paradise Moon stretched them into her best impression of a sky diver. The sky steadied.

I always said you'd thank me for all those nights you didn't sleep because I stayed up watching action movies.

Below, a river smeared with bridges and tiny boats wound through a concrete sprawl peppered with familiar landmarks. Big Ben, the Thames—everywhere was rushing closer as she fell. With deafening roars that filled the sky, more blurs appeared on the horizon. They streaked towards Isabella and her nation's capital.

Get even closer this time. We've got this.

Purple smoke.

Gone.

This time, in the fractured heartbeat within which she appeared, the blur was close enough for her glowing purple arm, the arm that wouldn't be ripped off by the impact, to already be touching what looked like a PROXUS starfighter.

Purple smoke.

Gone.

The frozen vacuum of space punched the life out of Isabella's lungs. This was the same star-pricked darkness where she had appeared during her unsuccessful attempts to bring the Husk to Earth.

The starfighter shot away from her, before being subjected to the sort of sudden deceleration and chaotic course corrections prompted by a pilot flying over London one moment and through space the next.

Isabella didn't hang—or float—around any longer. She was more interested in not asphyxiating. Purple smoke accompanied her to Westminster Bridge, where she collapsed onto the pavement with her skin on fire, her eyes bloodshot, her sweat frozen. Her hair felt cruelly tangled and windswept. Patches of ice still clung to her dress, which was torn to oblivion. There was at least one positive to come out of this—she wouldn't have to wear the dress again.

It took her a few unstable attempts to stand. The last time she had visited this bridge had been on a day trip to London with both her parents, so she must have been young. Paradise Moon had stolen her and gotten her hopelessly lost, but she always remembered this bridge. Its thick concrete sides were where Paradise Moon had clambered up, ready to jump before someone had grabbed her arm and Isabella had woken up.

More blurs and sonic booms thundered over her. She picked one. Purple smoke, a grasping purple hand, and frigid inky darkness followed. She returned to the bridge in an even worse state than before, leaving another pilot beyond Earth's orbit.

After her eighth painful but momentary glimpse of the stars today, London's blue sky lay silent and empty—much unlike the bridge, which was filling up with loud spectators. Before the gathering crowd could film her on their phones any more than they already had, Isabella vanished through purple smoke back to her perch on the Eiffel Tower. She found a pigeon attempting to eat her clutch bag. By the time she had rescued her bag, which took her longer than it had to save London from a PROXUS invasion, she could hear the predictable beats starting to dance inside her bag. Unzipping it, she found her phone and answered the call.

"Mum, it's fine. I'm okay."

"That's good," her mum replied in a strained, panicked tone. "Darling, I thought you should know. A shuttle landed at Cemetery Junction. It's blocking traffic and causing quite a stir. And the people who came out of it have guns, darling."

"Stay inside, mum," Isabella warned. The girl's voice was calm enough to hint that perhaps an invasion from outer space was easier for her to get her head around than tea with the Prime Minister on live TV.

"I am, darling. But they're coming into our house."

Isabella paused for a necessary heartbeat so she could process what her mum had told her, then another to process her mum's chosen hierarchy of information, which she would definitely bitch and moan about later. If there was anyone to bitch and moan about it to.

Purple smoke.

Gone.

Isabella arrived in the narrow hallway of her home as the front door splintered into a cloud of debris. Through the remains of the door emerged the tip of the rifle that had conjured the blast. That was all she needed. Tiny explosions of purple smoke lingered in the doorway and on the street outside as she vanished and appeared, vanished and appeared, amongst the Silver Fists attacking her home. Wherever another burst of plasma began its journey towards her, instead it met a double cloud of purple smoke and the surprised body of another Silver Fist who, moments earlier, had been elsewhere. Through the muddle of red flashes, purple smoke and armoured bodies collapsing onto the tarmac, Isabella vanished in and out, beside and behind, only ever needing the smallest tap on their armour to vanish each Silver Fist into the path of another's plasma fire.

After the firing stopped and only gasping, twitching bodies remained, Isabella collapsed through a cloud of purple smoke into the kitchen—and her mum's embrace.

"They're gone," she said into her mum's cardigan.

Her mum didn't reply, just held her. She was still holding her when Isabella heard her own name being called from upstairs. The voice was as unmistakable as it was unwelcome. Exhausted, she pulled away from her mum—with difficulty—and trudged upstairs to her bedroom. Grabbing the gauntlet Fleur had left for her, she tapped the icon of light it was projecting into the air.

"You came after my mum," she said. Her voice was shaking uncontrollably.

"I am so glad to have got your attention, although honestly it was the gauntlet we were homing in on, not your dear mother." Striker's voice was infuriatingly calm.

"You came after my mum," Isabella repeated.

"And your capital city too, don't forget. Lynch said it's called London, is that right? This was meant as a demonstration of our power, though, not yours. You have rather forced my hand."

"My mum, you son of a bitch."

"Young lady, I suggest you start listening. The ordinance I am about to drop on London will erase the whole city. Erase," he repeated both syllables of the word with cruel and careful emphasis. "Even from where you are in Reading, you should still feel the impact."

Isabella sank onto her bed. Even though she had never heard the word 'ordinance' before, Striker's meaning was inescapable. Her voice was grim, shaky. "You want me."

"Immediately. You understand the alternative?"

"Let me say goodbye."

"Don't take too long, otherwise—"

Isabella cut him off. Dragging the weight of every soul on Earth with her, she slumped downstairs. Her mum was waiting in the living room. From her face, she had heard everything. Amongst the confusion of wet-eyed hugging and a cardigan that smelled only of her mum, their embrace held Isabella together.

"I'm sorry," Isabella tried, after a few false starts. "I love you."

Her mum just held her. She refused to let go.

Well?

Your plan is ridiculous.

Really?

Yeah. I love it. You ready?

In response, Isabella disappeared from her home in a cloud of purple smoke.

CHAPTER THIRTY-EIGHT

Lynch was still swearing bloody murder when the clamps closed around his legs and arms and neck. Faceless Rangers had dragged him from his cell and what felt like halfway across Xarr. They spun on their heels and marched out of the med bay with enough military precision to make Lynch want to vomit. Without sunlight or regular meals in his cell to gauge the passage of time, it was impossible to know how long had passed since his encounter with the Empress. His guess was at least a couple of weeks, but that was speculative at best. He stared up at the sterile white ceiling. Next to the Sau Daran side of his skull, he could hear the clicks of something mechanical being assembled.

"Who the Hell are you and what the Hell are you doing?" Lynch demanded at the ceiling.

"Right now," replied a distracted male voice, "I am preparing an ID Tag."

Lynch didn't understand. He tried a lot of swearing.

More clicks. Something beeped affirmatively. "The Empress doesn't ask for much, does she?" muttered the voice.

"The fu—"

"A replicated ID Tag of the First Duke adapted at great expensive for Sau Daran hardware. Not at all, Empress! That sounds so easy, Empress! The work of a moment, Empress!"

Thin plumes of acerbic smoke drifted over Lynch's face. "Looks like you broke it," he said with a smirk.

"No," came the distracted reply of someone who was concentrating intensely, "that smoke is coming from you. There's no input for the ID Tag in the Sau Daran part of your head, so I am being forced to manufacture one."

"Manufacture?! Manufacture what?!"

"An input. With a laser. I know, I'm not happy about it either. My work is usually much tidier, but this is all so experimental. Ah, there we go." A wizened face leaned over him. The man had wild eyebrows, a crude buzzcut and mismatched artificial eyes that moved independently of each other. His overalls were a ludicrously garish orange that belonged in a prison. "ID Tag coming online… now!" said the strange technician.

Lynch didn't know what he was expecting to happen. He had suspected screaming might be required, but in truth he felt no different. "Are you sure it worked?"

"My work is beyond question. Now, the Empress wants you to destroy all the clones. Striker too, if you can. But she believes that would be unlikely given your lack of training. His clones should be easier. They can't fight back."

"I didn't agree to anything," Lynch snarled.

"Irrelevant. When I induce your coma, the First Duke's ID Tag I have installed in your Sau Daran hardware will believe you are dead. It will transfer your consciousness to one of Striker's clones." He tapped a few projected symbols from his gauntlet. "Don't contemplate betraying the Empress the same way you betrayed everyone else. Your body will still be here with me, remember."

"Betray? Like you know anything about me."

The old man's expression was stony. "Everything I know dies with me. The Empress understands that better than anyone, so she trusts me with a great deal."

Instead of biting back with the vile, sweary response he had been preparing, Lynch opened his mouth and wheezed pathetically. His whole body shuddered as it began to shut down. His breathing snagged halfway out of—his lungs tightened like they were in a—his muscles slackened until they—darkness was the only—heartbeat later, any sense of the—reaching for—gone.

In Lynch's dream, he was cold. Numb fingers were waking, along with every other frozen appendage. His tattered breaths sounded more like ghoulish gasps. He felt heavy. Undiminished, his dream was still there when he opened his eyes to whatever frozen Hell this was.

"I'm the fat man," Lynch realised out loud. This was followed by a torrent of foul language. "I'm the fat man," he repeated, because it was one thing to be told something was possible and another thing entirely to realise you were, indeed, the fat man. Or at least you were inside his meat. Having two human eyes again felt *weird*, too. The glass in front of his face actually looked normal—as much as normal was possible, given he had never woken up in a glass coffin before. He felt naked without his Sau Daran tech's cheat mode to zoom and scan and process everything. Which was ironic, given he was also naked in an incredibly literal sense.

Lynch was still adjusting to the strange sensation of wearing someone else's body when something exploded—metaphorically—inside his brain. The explosion's ignition had been information only Striker could have known, the resulting debris only conclusions Striker could have drawn. Memories were firing as though from machine guns down every neuron in Striker's brain as it adjusted to Lynch's sudden cerebral arrival and the increasing neural re-wiring that was being triggered by every Lynch-like thought. It felt overwhelming. First, Lynch's presence on a brain grown for someone else. Then, worse, the sudden avalanche of Striker's memories landing on Lynch. Too many memories to process were burying the boy. He tried to ignore them, to focus on the pod around him, but scraps of unsorted, unwanted information kept popping into his head. Into Striker's head. Quickly, one certainty grew beyond doubt. Based on Striker's own memories, Lynch had seen every gut-wrenching sliver of evidence to confirm that the First Duke was indeed the worst human who had ever lived.

Lynch pushed aside everything within him that was Striker. "Ah well," said the boy, "when life gives you lemons—break everything." His scowl was loud and nasty.

With caged fury that had been simmering for a lifetime, Lynch hurled open the cloning pod's foggy door so hard that it shattered. With a discordant popping of tubes and wires from the body he was piloting, he staggered around the broken glass and into a small, circular room. It was ringed with identical pods. Wiping away the frost from the nearest pod door revealed another of Striker's faces inside, his soulless expression no different to what Lynch would have expected from a corpse. He opened the pod door and flicked the other Striker's ear, then to be sure he poked the other Striker in a vacant, open eye. No response except for the promise of bruising. He checked the other pods. Ten pods in total, two empty, the other eight filled with

Striker's identical, lifeless meat sacks. A vertical row of clear blue lights gleamed up the side of each pod, except for the pod that had been his and the other pod that was empty. Those lights glowed red.

Everyone has the capacity for violence, but few have the history of violence or inclination towards it to ever truly embrace the monster inside. This was not a problem for Lynch. Thanks to his upbringing, he had completed that bingo card long ago. He glanced around the small chamber. Anything can be a weapon if you really want it to be. Lynch wanted everything to be a weapon. He settled on shards of glass from the smashed pod door and his own bare hands. The glass gnawed at his palms, but pain had been his friend many times over the years and by now such agony merely felt like coming home. He didn't waste any more time. Necks were snapped, throats cut. One by one, the lights on each pod flickered from blue to red.

Lynch surveyed his carnage. He was no doctor, but it was a safe bet none of these clones on *Black Nebula* would ever be serviceable again.

The bloody scene was illuminated in a sudden, radiant burst of light that shot down the centre of the chamber and pinned Lynch in its spotlight. A pair of black-clad Rangers aimed their rifles through the doorway. Crowded behind them in the corridor was a black sea of similarly armoured Rangers, their faces equally anonymous behind their dark helmets, their pistols and rifles eager to fill Lynch with plasma.

Lynch raised his dripping hands, gloved in blood, still holding a thick fragment of glass. "I didn't do it," he replied out of habit.

"Drop it!" shouted the closest Ranger through a hiss of static.

Lynch glanced at the sliver of jagged glass clutched in his bleeding hand. "Do you know who I am?" he asked in his best Striker impersonation. It wasn't that bad—he was certainly wearing the right face and vocal cords for the part.

"Yes," replied the other Ranger in the doorway. "The First Duke says you're the boy from Earth. Your name's Lynch. You're to be detained."

"Alright, you got me," Lynch admitted. "Worth a try though, am I right?"

"Drop the weapon," cut in the first Ranger. "We have orders to take you alive."

Lynch gave them his most infuriating smirk, the one he reserved for only the busiest of busybodies and the pettiest teachers. "Thanks, that's helpful know."

He drove the glass shard into the side of his skull.

Shortly after his suicide, Lynch woke up to find he was being murdered.

His wild eyebrows still sprouting in every direction, the aging technician was leaning over Lynch's restrained body, the silver cylinder of a cutting laser aimed adeptly at the boy's human eye. So far, no laser had burst from the item. The mere fact that Lynch knew a device he had never seen before was a cutting laser felt strange, but it was hard to dwell on this when someone was in the process of killing him.

"That was quick," the technician said with stern disapproval. "Did you even kill any?"

"The clones are dead. And you should be letting me leave, psycho. Empress' orders."

Chuckling, the technician twirled the cutting laser between his fingers like a cowboy spinning a revolver. "You are to be executed immediately upon waking. And the Sau Daran technology removed from your skull for

322

thorough research." He aimed the laser again, this time at Lynch's temple. "Also Empress' orders."

From his vantage point below the technician, he could barely read the personnel number on the chest pocket of his orange tunic. One of Striker's memories recognised it. Lynch had never blurted out anything in his life, but he found he spoke with more haste than he was accustomed to when the cold tip of the cutting laser's metal cylinder pressed against the human side of his forehead. "I know about your secret projects!" Lynch shouted. He was tearing through the overwhelming volume of information he had inherited from Striker's ID Tag after the memories had landed in Striker's brain. He could feel everything still inside him. Somehow, he had taken the memories back with him. "I know all about your experiments, even the ones you kept from the Empress. I know what Striker knew—including where you incinerated the bodies."

"Yet another reason to kill you."

Lynch was grasping inside his head. Striker knew everything about everyone, if only Lynch could find something useful amongst all that information. "That won't help your daughter," he warned, although he was still processing what that meant as he said it.

The technician clicked his tongue in irritation. "My daughter is dead. You don't have the First Duke's memories, otherwise you would know that, dpresh."

Lynch tried to shake his head in response, but the clamp around his neck was too tight even for that. It probably looked like he was doing a random little head dance.

"Are you having a fit?"

"She's not dead," Lynch said. "That's what the Empress wants you to think."

The technician's thumb applied a little pressure to the button on the metal cylinder he was pressing into Lynch's forehead. "Choose your next words carefully."

Lynch did. He shared the exact address where the technician would find his daughter, along with a few precise, impossible to know facts about her to push his credibility.

The technician's face went through a long journey. Finally, dropping the laser on the floor, he stared at Lynch. "What happens next?" he asked.

Lynch had been wondering the same thing, but Striker's memory was full of answers. "Next, I walk out of this room unharmed. I know where I am. When I am safely leaving Xarr's orbit, I'll send you a security code that will let you into the place I told you about. You'll leave there with your daughter."

"And if you're lying?"

"Striker would, but I'm not him."

Nodding in agreement, the technician fumbled open the clamps and helped Lynch sit up. The boy felt the exterior of his Sau Daran headwear but found nothing different. "Where's Striker's ID Tag?"

"Inside. More efficient."

Lynch grinned. "Nice."

"I don't need your validation. Where will you go?"

Stretching out his arms, Lynch cracked his knuckles and tilted his head to either side like he had seen prize boxers do before a fight. "Where will I go with all Striker's secrets, not to mention all his points?" Lynch grinned his cheekiest grin. "I hear there's a rebellion going on. Funnily enough, I've always fancied myself as a bit of a rebel."

CHAPTER THIRTY-NINE

Isabella took a lightning-quick detour on her way to *Black Nebula*, only allowing time for the briefest double flash of purple smoke in Paris as she grabbed what she needed.

Upon arriving on *Black Nebula*'s command bridge, she had less than a moment to glimpse the Silver Fists lurking in a ring around Striker, their plasma rifles and plasma pistols ready to rock. There was no doubt they had been expecting Isabella and Paradise Moon. However, no one had been expecting the Eiffel Tower.

Over one thousand feet of dark iron weighing over ten thousand tonnes punched Striker in the face in much the same way that a freight train at top speed might clean up a bug.

Isabella was only there for a heartbeat, the tip of her purple finger glowing against the base of a black iron pillar. That heartbeat was almost too long. The command bridge and everyone in it disintegrated as the giant construction of wrought iron tried and failed to fit into a space considerably smaller than it was. Isabella never saw what happened next, but she expected to spend every nightmare for the rest of her life imagining it.

She collapsed onto her bed in a burst of purple smoke. Pulling Fleur's gauntlet off the edge of the duvet, she thumbed on its transmitter and set it to every PROXUS channel the device knew. Paradise Moon sent her glowing purple hand to wipe sweat and someone else's blood off her face as she tapped the broadcast symbol hovering above the gauntlet.

"This is the girl you've been chasing across the universe—AND THE GOD YOU'VE BEEN CHASING, MOTHER FU—and I'm speaking to everyone on that battle station. Look out your window." Isabella spat a gob of blood onto the carpet and snatched in a shaking breath. "Whatever you see drifting past is all that's left of First Duke Striker after he went after my mum and my planet. My mum. And my planet. I never wanted to hurt anyone and maybe you didn't either, but, well, yeah. Whatever you decide, it's on you. You want a better life? You want to escape PROXUS? Well, you're a long way from home and you have your own battle station. Go nuts. You won't get a better chance. Or come after me like Striker did and find out what else I can do. But Earth's protected. So back off."

Dog-tired, Isabella let the gauntlet fall. She didn't care where it landed.

They're gonna come back.

Not a chance.

Really?

After that? Really.

As she stumbled downstairs, every step felt alien. Their carpeted creaks and groans were old and familiar to her ears, yet their memory belonged to someone else now. Perhaps this was a stranger's house she had once known. It did not feel like hers any more. She felt as broken as she did reforged. No less one nor the other. Stronger for wounds that could never heal.

Isabella's mum hadn't left the living room. There was no sign she had moved at all. Examining the stillness of her face, Isabella wasn't sure her mum had taken a single breath since she had left. When she noticed Isabella, it was as though a meteor had struck her between the eyes. Ignoring the mess of blood and people splattered over Isabella, short arms reached around the girl's back and drew her in. Isabella's cheek landed on the shoulder of her mum's cardigan, while two pairs of limpetlike hands clung. And clung. And clung.

Subtle flecks of purple blended with the chestnut in Isabella's eyes, but Paradise Moon said nothing.

Acknowledgements

Life is hard. I hope this book has offered a welcome escape. Perhaps a little fun, too. However, this book could not exist without the kindness, patience and cleverness of others.

Thank you to my amazing wife Becca, who supports me in everything. You always believe in me. Throughout this journey you have read the good with the bad, and helped me understand which is which. Not to mention all those accidental double entendres you alerted me to in early drafts. For better or worse, there will be no fingers of daylight poking *anywhere*.

Thank you, Dad, for feedback that helped me set my sails to catch the breeze. Without being able to draw on your wisdom as an author and your support as a father, this book would have been shipwrecked long ago.

Thank you to Robin and Dave, who know this genre so well and, as I drew closer to publication, became star beta readers. Your feedback changed this book. Of course, thanks go to our whole phyxin' gang, without whom the Known Galaxies would have far fewer cusses.

Thank you to my sister Katie, as well as the wonderful Emma and Patrick, for your advice on art, cover design and typesetting. You are artistic geniuses.

Thank you to all the teachers, librarians, teaching assistants, parents and everyone else who champions creative writing. Writing groups like our beloved Writers of Nym, and every teacher who—unlike me—remains in the classroom doing the most important job in the world. Inspiring our children. Thank you to Heather and Kerry, whose feedback on my earlier—thankfully unpublished—writing equipped me to write what you have just read.

And finally, thank you to everyone out there who is brave enough to add their stories to our world, whether by the stroke of a pen, the tap of a keyboard or however else you share your voice.

However you do it, be heard.

For more information about the Paradise Moon duology
and the author Rob Birks, visit:

www.robbirks.com

Printed in Great Britain
by Amazon